AN ACT OF VILLAINY

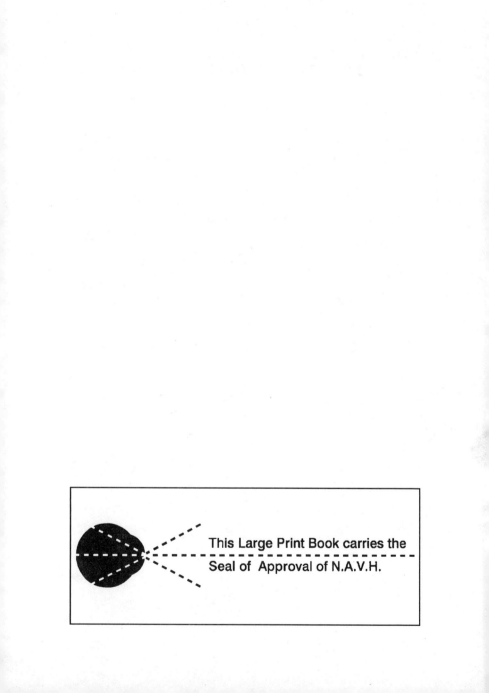

This Large Print Book carries the
Seal of Approval of N.A.V.H.

AN AMORY AMES MYSTERY

An Act of Villainy

Ashley Weaver

THORNDIKE PRESS
A part of Gale, a Cengage Company

Farmington Hills, Mich • San Francisco • New York • Waterville, Maine
Meriden, Conn • Mason, Ohio • Chicago

Copyright © 2018 by Ashley Weaver.
An Amory Ames Mystery.
Thorndike Press, a part of Gale, a Cengage Company.

LIBRARY OF CONGRESS CIP DATA ON FILE.
CATALOGUING IN PUBLICATION FOR THIS BOOK
IS AVAILABLE FROM THE LIBRARY OF CONGRESS

ISBN-13: 978-1-4328-6093-6 (hardcover)

Published in 2019 by arrangement with Macmillan Publishing Group, LLC/St. Martin's Press

Printed in the United States of America
1 2 3 4 5 6 7 23 22 21 20 19

For my Mimi, Minnie Weaver

And in loving memory of
Dan Weaver, Sr.
Clarence Larson
and Ethel Larson

1

London, June 1933

Murder in fiction is not nearly as thrilling as murder in real life.

This wicked thought slipped unbidden into my mind as my husband, Milo, and I exited a West End theatre after a performance of *Death Comes at Midnight,* an original drama sorely lacking originality.

My dearth of enthusiasm was not entirely the fault of the play. Truth be told, I rather suspected the blame should be laid at the feet of my recent endeavors in detection. I had found myself immersed in several mysteries as of late and, in consequence, the play's puzzle had proven less than enthralling.

It hadn't helped matters that Milo had, annoyingly, deduced the culprit and his motives not twenty minutes into the first act, and I had spent the remainder of the performance hoping that he would be proven wrong.

"Perhaps you'll guess the killer correctly next time, darling," he said, deducing my thoughts as easily as he had the solution to the play.

"It was too obvious," I retorted. "I was looking for a cleverer motive."

"Ah, I see," he replied with a smile.

"Mysteries are rarely ever that straightforward, as you well know."

"All the same, it's nice to take part in a mystery where loaded guns aren't being waved about," he answered dryly.

"I suppose," I said, though I still felt attempting to solve a fictional crime was disappointing in comparison to the real thing.

I took Milo's arm and we walked along Shaftesbury Avenue, making our way through the crowds of people coming out of other theatres into the brightly lit streets. It was a lovely evening, clear and cool, and I was glad that we had decided to walk to a restaurant in Covent Garden rather than take a cab. There was something magical about strolling through this part of town late at night, surrounded by other theatre-goers, all of us laughing and talking about the performances we had just seen.

"I say, Milo Ames, is that you?"

We stopped and turned at the sound of the voice behind us.

It was Gerard Holloway, an old friend of Milo's. He came toward us through the crowd, smiling.

"It is you. And Mrs. Ames. How delightful." It did not escape my notice that he had not been certain it would be me on my husband's arm. Milo's reputation had been less than sterling in the past, and I suspected Mr. Holloway had encountered Milo on other occasions when I had not been the woman in his company.

"How are you, Holloway?" Milo asked.

"Never better," he said.

I had always liked Gerard Holloway. He cut a dashing figure. Tall and well built, he had a handsome, friendly face with a thin dark moustache above a mouth that was generally smiling. His pleasant appearance was complemented by his amiable disposition. The youngest of an earl's four sons, he had had the liberty to eschew duty and politics and had devoted his energies and wealth to a more creative milieu. He was a patron of the arts, known to frequent the theatre district, and was often looked to as the last word on the current trends in London theatre.

"Have you been to a play?" he asked.

"Yes, we've just seen *Death Comes at Midnight*," I told him.

"Of course. A mystery. That's rather in your line, isn't it?" he said with a smile. It had not escaped society's notice that Milo and I had been entangled in more than one murder investigation, and we had yet to live down our reputation. "How did you like it?"

"A bit predictable," Milo said.

"I thought the same," Mr. Holloway said. "It's only meant to be light entertainment, of course, so I suppose one shouldn't judge too harshly. But so many plays these days aren't what they used to be. I hope to do something on that score, however. I'm producing a new play of my own, *The Price of Victory*."

"Yes, I heard something about that," Milo said. "Wrote it yourself, didn't you?"

"Yes. The script's given me a devil of a time, but we've smoothed it over." He was warming to the subject now, the spark of enthusiasm gleaming in his dark eyes. "We've got Christopher Landon, quite a rising star, as our lead man. And Balthazar Lebeau in a supporting role."

"Lebeau is still acting, is he?" Milo asked.

"In a manner of speaking. Half the time, I don't know how the man manages to put one foot in front of the other, let alone turn out a decent performance, but his name still holds a certain sway. Besides, we have a bit of a history, and I feel I owe him a chance. Anyway, I think it's going to be a great success. We'll be opening this weekend. I hope you'll come and see it."

"We'd like that very much," I said, though I knew that Milo would probably be annoyed with me later for having agreed to see a play we would be required to praise, whatever its merits. My husband had very little patience for such things, and, even though Mr. Holloway was an old friend, I knew Milo would likely try to get out of attending.

"Good, good," Mr. Holloway said. "We've been working very hard on it. It's rather my pet project. That's why I decided to direct it as well. It's my first time at the helm, so to speak. I'm afraid I'm making a nuisance of myself about every last detail, but so far they haven't kicked me out."

Such a thing was unlikely, given that he had no doubt financed the entire venture. Mr. Holloway was incredibly wealthy, and, in addition to his interest in London's art world, he and his wife were involved in numerous charities throughout the city.

"How is Georgina?" I asked. It had been

11

some time since I had seen Mrs. Holloway, though, over the years, we had formed a warm friendship through mutual social engagements and had worked on several charity committees together.

A strange expression flickered almost imperceptibly across his face, and he hesitated ever so slightly. "She's quite well."

"I'm glad to hear it. It's been a while since I've seen her. I'll have to ring her up."

"Yes, I'm sure she'd like that," he said. "Well, I'm afraid I must be off, but I do hope you'll come to the play."

"Thank you," I told him. "We'll look forward to it."

He hesitated, as though he wanted to say something else. Then he added, "And, Ames, perhaps we might have a drink together soon?"

"Certainly."

"Perhaps at my club? Are you free tomorrow afternoon? Say three o'clock?"

"Yes, I think so," Milo said. "I'll stop by."

"Excellent," he said. "I'll see you then. Good evening, Mrs. Ames."

He tipped his hat then and left us.

"Laid that on a bit thick, didn't you?" Milo said mildly as I took his arm again and we resumed walking.

As I had anticipated, he was less than

pleased that I had agreed to attend an amateur performance. "I couldn't very well refuse his invitation," I pointed out. "It's only one evening; it won't hurt to attend. Besides, you know Gerard Holloway never does things in half measures. I'm sure it will be a good play."

"That's not what I mean," he said.

I was suddenly confused. "Well, what do you mean?"

"Asking about Georgina."

I hadn't the faintest idea what he was getting at. "Why shouldn't I have asked about her?"

"Because Gerard Holloway's new play just happens to star his mistress."

I stopped walking and turned to face him. "What?"

He smiled. "My sweet, innocent darling. You really didn't know?"

"No," I said, genuinely shocked. Perhaps it was dreadfully naïve of me, especially given the less than perfect state my own marriage had once been in, but I still managed to be rather taken aback at the rampant infidelity in our social circle.

"It's been the talk of London. She's the theatre's newest darling, as well as Holloway's. Flora Bell, she calls herself. I'm rather surprised you haven't heard something about it."

I had long ago developed an aversion to the gossip columns. I could find no amusement in the troubles of others.

"It did cross my mind that he didn't mention the female lead in his play," I said. "And I thought he looked a bit strange when I asked about Georgina."

"I expect he thought you were pointedly mentioning her."

"I hope he did," I replied. "Someone ought to remind him of her. Poor Georgina. She must be dreadfully upset."

Of all the couples that I knew, the Holloways were perhaps the last I would have expected to have this sort of trouble. The pair had been a love match. They had married young and had always seemed very much devoted to each other. Their romance had, in fact, been the sort of fairy tale young women dreamed about. They had grown up together and suddenly found one day that they were in love. After an opulent wedding that had been the talk of London, he had whisked her away on a summer-long wedding trip, and that had only been the beginning. From then on, they had traveled to countless exotic locales, doing all manner of adventurous things.

Whenever I had seen them together, I had

admired their relationship. I had often noticed between them the little unspoken hints of affection that truly happy couples shared, the subtle gestures and glances that spoke volumes. It was astounding to me that he had taken a mistress.

I didn't know why, but this news felt like something of a personal blow.

"She needn't worry," Milo said lightly. "These things never last."

I felt a little pang of sadness at this careless comment. Milo would know about such things, of course. But the knowledge that an affair would be short-lived did not make it any easier for the wife in question. Georgina was a strong woman, and I knew it was not likely she would take her husband's infidelity in stride. This could very well be the end of the Holloways' marriage.

"It may not last," I said quietly, "but the consequences of it surely will."

I didn't look at him, but I saw him glance my way out of the corner of his eye. He was aware, I knew, that I was thinking of the impact of past scandals upon our own marriage. We had surmounted our difficulties and the past was not something I liked to dwell on, but I could not help but feel exceedingly sorry for Georgina Holloway.

We let the subject drop as we reached the

restaurant, but I was feeling much less carefree than I had been a few moments before.

I ought to have recognized the feeling then, but I didn't. Couched as it was, in the guise of concern about my friend's connubial disharmony, I am ashamed to say I hadn't an inkling that my unsettled feeling meant we were on the precipice of another mystery.

2

The Holloways' marriage trouble was still on my mind the next morning as I sat down to breakfast. I didn't know why I couldn't seem to forget the matter. They were not, after all, the first couple of our acquaintance whose marriage had gone by the wayside. I had always felt, however, that their relationship was different from most, stronger somehow. Surely it was a shame to throw something so valuable away?

The more I considered it, the more certain I was that Gerard Holloway still loved his wife and was making a terrible mistake. If only he could be made to realize it before it was too late. The trouble with men was that it was very difficult to make them see how stupid they were being.

Milo's paper was folded by his plate, and, as he was still in bed, I picked it up, deciding to peruse the gossip columns over breakfast to see if there was any mention of

Gerard Holloway and Flora Bell. It wasn't just morbid curiosity on my part. I felt the stirrings of the desire to take action.

I was glad that Milo was not awake, for he would know what I was thinking about and tell me not to interfere.

I flipped through the pages until I found what I was looking for. Nestled between wedding announcements and a notice about a charity gala, there was one small item that was clearly related to the matter:

A certain earl's son has continued to be seen in company with a certain actress. The lady in question seems to have captured his heart along with the lead in a new play. It remains to be seen whether her talents will translate to the stage.

I put the paper aside in disgust. Poor Georgina must be heartbroken. In that moment, I made up my mind. I was going to do what I could do to remedy the situation. At the very least, I could offer Georgina support and sympathy.

Now I just had to find a way to go about it. I could not very well show up at her door saying that I had heard about her husband's affair. We weren't on close enough terms for that. There had to be some other way for me to put myself into her company.

In the end, the means for doing so came from a most unexpected source. I glanced back at the paper, and my eyes fell on the notice for the charity gala. This time I noticed the names written there:

The charity gala held by the Honorable Mr. and Mrs. Gerard Holloway will commence following the opening-night performance of Mr. Holloway's new play, *The Price of Victory,* at the Penworth Theatre. The play, which features Miss Flora Bell and Mr. Christopher Landon, is expected to be a great success.

The notice gave the date as the Saturday three days hence and said that all tickets to the gala had long ago been sold, but tickets to the play were still available for the following weeks. Apparently, the opening-night performance was exclusive to gala-goers, the proceeds going to a notable charity. This sort of elaborate philanthropic function was very much in the Holloways' style, and they had had a great deal of success with it in the past.

I wondered why it was that Mr. Holloway hadn't mentioned the gala last night. Milo and I would have gladly contributed to the cause, even without tickets. Perhaps he had not wanted to mention the charity event, as it would only lead to conversation about Georgina. I imagined the whole thing must be very awkward for the Holloways, given the circumstances.

I glanced again at the odious bit of gossip beneath the gala notice. No doubt the snide remark about Mr. Holloway had been purposefully placed there. I felt another twinge of sympathy for Georgina. She would see her charity event through to the end, but I could only imagine how embarrassing this was for her.

My mind began turning, wondering how I could possibly be of some help.

I picked up my cup and had just drained the last of my coffee when there was a knock at the door. I glanced at the clock. It was very early. I wasn't sure who could be calling at this time of day.

A moment later, I heard the door open and the murmur of voices, and then my maid, Winnelda, hurried into the room.

"Your mother's here!" she whispered, her eyes wide. Winnelda served as my lady's maid, but she had never been properly trained for the position and was thus wont to make her emotions and opinions plain. Not that I blamed her in this instance. My mother could no doubt find a way to rattle the king himself. "She went right to the sitting room."

"Thank you," I said. "I'll go and speak with her."

I didn't know what my mother was doing here at this hour. What was more, I didn't know what she was doing in London. She and my father spent the majority of their time in the country, and when they did come to town we did not spend much time together. It was not that there was any animosity between us, but they had always treated me as they treated each other: with polite reserve tempered by the occasional hint of vague affection. Over the years, we had fallen into a comfortably distant relationship that seemed to work well for all concerned.

I walked to the sitting room and found my mother standing before the mirror, checking her lipstick. With the reflection of my face beside hers, I had to admit that we looked a good bit alike. We had the same dark hair, the same gray eyes, and the same mouth. She caught sight of me in the glass then and turned to face me. She was dressed in a black suit accented with rows of pearls and an ermine stole.

"Hello, Mother," I said.

"Hello, dearest," she said, holding out her fur-draped arms. I obediently went to her, and she embraced me, brushing kisses across my cheeks. She smelled, as she always had, of vanilla and rosewater.

The formalities thus observed, she stepped back and ran her eyes over me. "It's been far too long since I've seen you. Capri, Como, and then Paris and not a single letter to your dear mother. You're looking well, perhaps a bit too thin. And you've been in the sun. You'll ruin your complexion that way."

"Can I offer you some breakfast?" I asked.

"Thank you, no. You know I take only tea in the morning. It's much too early for eating."

"Yes, I was rather surprised you called so early."

"I've a busy day scheduled, and I wanted to see you first thing." She moved to a chair near the fireplace and took a seat.

I followed her lead and sat on the sofa. "How is Father?"

"He's much the same as always, I suppose," she said absently, shifting her fur on her shoulders. "But I haven't come for pleasantries. I've come to enlist your aid."

"Oh?"

"Lady Honoria is holding a charity event,

and I told her that I would speak to you about taking part in it."

"What sort of charity event?" I asked warily. I knew Lady Honoria and her lavish charity events, and I wondered what this one might entail.

"It's an auction. A great many items will be listed, and she wants society ladies to model the items to make them more attractive to buyers."

Under different circumstances, it might have been the type of thing that I would have enjoyed. As it was, I felt certain that, with my mother involved, it would prove to be a taxing experience. I would certainly donate to benefit the cause, but I did not care to model items at the auction.

"I don't think I'll have the time," I said. "I'm so busy as of late."

"Nonsense," she said. "It's for a good cause. Surely it's a much more worthwhile use of your time than your recent — and frankly vulgar — hobbies." She waved a hand, and I knew she was dismissing my distasteful forays into the world of detection.

"All the same," I said. "I'm not sure . . ."

"Surely you don't mean to disappoint Lady Honoria."

Inwardly, I sighed. I could feel myself

weakening. While I hated to give in to my mother, it was, after all, for a good cause. Besides, I could not hold it against Lady Honoria that my mother had commandeered her charity event.

"When is it?" I asked resignedly.

"Saturday evening."

I seized suddenly upon an idea as one in danger of drowning seizes upon a life preserver. "I'm afraid we've somewhere else to be on Saturday."

"Some nightclub, no doubt. Surely you can put that off. You will be in rather good company. Lady Margaret Allworth, Mrs. Camden . . ."

"No, I'm afraid I'm going to the Holloways' charity gala," I interrupted. I had no idea, of course, if I could procure tickets, but my mother didn't need to know that.

She looked up suddenly. "Gerard and Georgina Holloway?"

"Yes, there is the premier performance of Mr. Holloway's new play and a party to follow," I said. "I'm sure it will be a very nice event."

"Hmm. I suppose," she said grudgingly. Though I was sure my mother would have liked nothing better than to disparage my plans when they conflicted with hers, the Holloway name held too much sway for her to do so.

"Perhaps next time I may be of assistance to Lady Honoria," I offered.

"I shall count on it." My mother's objective effectively thwarted, she had no further use for me. She rose from her seat and I rose with her.

"Where is your husband?" she asked as she pulled on her gloves. "Still abed? Or has he run off again?" There was no malice in the words. It was simply the delightful way she had of saying things that were probably better left unsaid.

"Good morning, Mrs. Ames," said Milo dryly from the doorway. My maiden name having been, by coincidence, the same as my married name, it was always a bit unnerving to hear my mother referred to as "Mrs. Ames" by my husband.

She turned to him, unabashed. "Oh, you are here. Well, what a nice surprise."

"I might say the same thing," he said, moving to her side and brushing a kiss across her cheek.

Her eyes swept over him. He had not yet dressed and was wearing a black dressing gown over his nightclothes.

"You seem to be handsomer every time I see you." The way she said it left doubt as to whether it was a compliment, and her next words confirmed this impression. "Rather flies in the face of the idea that blameless living keeps one young."

"It's love that keeps one young," he replied, unflustered. "So, with Amory at my side, I shall probably never age."

"Hmm," she said, her favorite means of expressing nonverbal disapproval.

I had always been somewhat amused by the relationship between Milo and my mother. I had been engaged to another man when I had met Milo, but my mother had not balked at the idea of my marrying Milo instead. It was not that she was a romantic woman, not by any means. Indeed, I had never seen much more than an average regard between her and my father, and any of my adolescent infatuations with boys she deemed unsuitable had been met with stern reminders that I was to marry well. Frankly, I would have expected the potential scandal of a broken engagement to outweigh my long-term happiness on her scale of importance, but Milo had managed to charm her quite easily, his good looks and winning manner supplemented by extensive wealth and excellent connections.

He might have gone on charming her, despite his numerous transgressions, had he been a bit more discreet. But indiscretion was the one thing my mother could not abide, and I suspected it would take many years of very good behavior before she would be willing to accept that his reformation was legitimate.

Milo, for his part, had given up trying to impress her long ago. He was not one to waste effort when it didn't benefit him, and, now that he had won me, there was very little reason for him to care whether my mother liked him or not.

It all made things very interesting for me when they were in a room together.

My mother turned back to me. "I'll come to see you again before I leave town if I find the time."

"Very well, Mother."

"I'll show myself out. So nice to have seen you, dear," she said as she walked toward the door.

"And you. Send my regards to Father."

She went out without further comment and, hearing the front door close behind her, I sat down on the sofa with a heavy sigh.

"Well. She remains as charming as ever," Milo observed.

I smiled wryly. "You might have stayed in the bedroom and avoided her."

"I heard her voice and thought I should

rally to your defense," he replied. "What did she want?"

"She wants me to take part in a charity event."

"Don't tell me you've accepted?"

"No, I said I was too busy." I debated confessing my developing plans to Milo. It was sometimes better to let him know when everything was accomplished than to try to win his approval ahead of time.

"Well, thank heavens for that," he said. "One thing I can say for your mother: there's nothing like a visit from her to clear one's head early in the morning."

"She's had the opposite effect on me," I said, rubbing my temple. "I've now got a roaring headache."

"I think some coffee would serve us both well." He turned his head ever so slightly toward the door. "Winnelda."

She came instantly into the room. No doubt she had been hovering just outside, probably trying to be certain that my mother had gone.

"Yes, sir?"

"Bring us some coffee, will you?"

"Yes, sir."

She went out again, and Milo came to sit across from me.

"What are your plans today?" I asked.

"I've got to see Ludlow about a few business matters. I'll probably eat lunch out. And old Felix Hill is selling a horse I might want to have a look at. Do you have anything scheduled today?"

"Nothing in particular," I said absently. His plans would give me plenty of time to implement my own.

Winnelda brought in a tray with the coffee things, and I poured a cup for Milo.

"You're not forgetting drinks with Gerard Holloway?" I asked, stirring milk and sugar into the coffee.

"No," he said, taking the cup. "I suppose I'll go round to his club this afternoon and see him."

"He seemed very eager to speak with you," I said. "What do you suppose he wants to talk to you about?"

"I haven't the faintest idea," he said, bringing his cup to his lips. "Perhaps he's looking for investors in his play or some such thing, though he ought to know that I have no interest in the theatre."

"I wonder if you might have the opportunity to talk to him about his marriage," I said casually.

Milo looked up from his coffee. "Amory . . ." He somehow managed to convey both wariness and a warning in the

29

simple utterance of my name, and I knew that I had been correct in my assumption that he would not endorse my plan to help the Holloways mend their broken relationship.

"Oh, I don't mean anything invasive, of course, but you might find a way to remind him what a lovely woman Georgina is."

"No, Amory."

"You know how happy they have always been together," I said. "It seems a shame that he should throw it all away for an actress."

"That may well be, darling, but it's really none of our concern, and I have no intention of expressing any opinions on the matter."

"Oh, I'm sure he'll broach the subject," I said. "Gentlemen like to brag about their conquests."

"Do they?" he replied.

"Don't they?" I challenged.

"I'm afraid I don't remember," he said. "It has been far too long since I made any conquests."

"Hmm," I said skeptically.

He set his cup down in the saucer. "I hesitate to point this out, darling, but you're starting to sound like your mother."

He was quite lucky he escaped the sitting
room unscathed.

3

As soon as Milo had gone, I rang up Georgina Holloway. I telephoned on the pretext of discussing the charity gala, but I also wondered if she might need someone to talk to. Georgina Holloway had a great many friends, but I knew many of the women in our circle would enjoy nothing more than feigning sympathy only to relate all the sordid details to others when the opportunity arose. If Georgina needed a confidante who could keep secrets, I was more than happy to oblige.

"It's good to hear from you, Amory. It's been a long time."

She sounded glad enough to speak with me, though it is difficult to read a person's feelings on the telephone. Emotions, it seemed, did not travel well across the wires.

"I'm afraid I have rather an ulterior motive for phoning you," I said. "I've just seen the notice about your charity gala, and I was wondering if, perchance, you still have any tickets available."

It seemed she hesitated ever so slightly. "Well, yes, I believe we do, in fact. The Langstons purchased a box but got called away to Brussels. You could have their box, if you like."

"That would be perfect," I said. "Where may I collect the tickets?"

Again, there was a hesitation before she spoke, almost as though she was trying to decide something. "Why don't you come for tea on Friday?" she said at last. "We could chat a bit, and I could give you the tickets then."

"That would be lovely." I knew she had a very busy social schedule, and I thought she must indeed be in need of a sympathetic ear if she had invited me at such short notice, especially the afternoon before the gala.

We rang off then, and a feeling of satisfaction stole over me. My plans were falling into place.

Milo did not come home before dinner, nor did he telephone. It seemed he and Gerard Holloway must be getting on famously.

I had learned over the years that it was never any good waiting around for him, so I went out for dinner alone, returning home to find our flat still empty.

I had given Winnelda the night off and Milo's valet Parks was away for the week visiting family after our extended travels, so I had only Emile, our pet monkey, for company.

Milo had acquired the mischievous little thing in some sort of reckless wager while we were in Paris, and we had been unable to bring ourselves to part with him.

We hoped, at some point, to send him to Thornecrest, our country home, to live a life of ease, but for now he lived with us at the flat, where he spent the better part of every day following Winnelda from room to room and tipping things over. Thus far we had lost two vases, a clock face, and a porcelain bird.

Tonight, however, he seemed to be content to sit with me as I read. I fed him bits of fruit, which he nibbled quietly as I flipped the pages, and he further occupied himself by cracking open some nuts which I purchased for just such a purpose.

"At least I know I shall always have you to keep me company when your papa neglects to come home," I told him in French. Though I felt ridiculous explaining it to people, Emile did not speak English. At least not yet. Winnelda was making strides in teaching him our native tongue, a task she had devoted herself to with great zeal.

He tittered something at me, which I felt sure was a concurrence, and then we went back to our mutual pursuits until ten o'clock. This was Emile's bedtime, and he went readily to his cage to sleep.

I decided to retire for the evening as well and had just reached the door to our bedroom when I heard Milo's key in the lock.

I stopped, hand on the doorframe, and waited for him to come in.

"Did it ever occur to you that you might ring me up if you don't plan on coming home at the appointed time?" I asked when he entered.

"I didn't know there was an appointed time," he said lightly. "Anyway, you won't be cross when you hear what Holloway wanted to talk to me about."

It was very typical of him to dismiss my concerns out of hand, but I pressed onward. "I should still like to know if you don't plan on coming home for dinner. For all I know, you might very well be dead in the street."

"Oh, hardly in the street, darling. When my end comes, it's much more likely to be in a gambling club or at the racetrack."

I could tell that he did not mean to take

my objections seriously, so I let the matter drop for the time being. We had come a long way in our marriage, but that didn't mean that we had quite reached the goal. One step at a time.

I turned and went into the bedroom without comment. He followed me, loosening his necktie. "Did you have a nice day, darling?"

"Oh, yes," I said as I took off my silk robe, tossing it across the back of a chair, and moved to the bed. "It was very pleasant. Emile is excellent company."

"Well, you're fortunate," he said, ignoring my sarcasm. "That's more than might be said of Gerard Holloway. He was in a morose mood, and, in consequence, the night was less than amusing."

I knew from long experience that Milo liked to pretend as though nights spent drinking and gambling were a great inconvenience, and I had no pity for him.

I pulled back the bedding and slid beneath it, leaning back against the pillows that lined the tufted black velvet headboard. "Did you spend the entire evening with Gerard Holloway?"

"Yes, we had drinks at the club this afternoon and then went to dinner. It took Holloway a great deal of beating about the bush and an even greater deal of brandy before he was ready to tell me why he really wanted to see me. It's rather a delicate matter."

"What sort of delicate matter?"

"I think you can guess."

I looked up at him, an alarming thought occurring to me. "Don't tell me he means to do something drastic? He's not going to abandon Georgina?"

"Oh, as far as that goes, I wouldn't think so. We didn't talk much about Georgina. It had to do with Flora Bell."

I suddenly wasn't sure that I cared for Milo keeping company with Gerard Holloway. As much as I had always liked the man in the past, I couldn't help but feel that he was treating his lovely wife very shabbily.

"Oh, I see," I said absently, suddenly focused on smoothing out the wrinkles in the bedspread. I was beginning to lose interest in whatever plight might be befalling Milo's wayward friend. Truth be told, the scandal of infidelity was a sore topic with me, and I was not sure I wanted to know the details.

Milo took no notice of my sudden lack of enthusiasm for the topic and went on talking as he undressed.

"Holloway's concerned. Apparently, someone has been writing rather nasty letters to Flora Bell."

I looked up. "What sort of letters?"

"Threats."

"Threats to harm her?"

"It seems so. He showed me one of them. It was vague, but clear enough. 'Your time is coming. You'll be sorry.' That sort of thing."

"Sorry for what?" Despite myself, I was growing interested.

"That's just it. The letters don't say. If they did, I expect it would be easier to narrow down the sender."

"And Miss Bell doesn't know to what they refer?"

"If she does, she hasn't told Holloway about it. I find it a bit difficult to believe she doesn't have at least an inkling of who might want to do her harm. Then again, she may have made several enemies on her road to success."

"Gerard Holloway has no idea who might be sending them?"

"Apparently not. I put it to him, delicately, of course, that it was possible his wife had decided to try to get Flora Bell out of the way."

"Georgina wouldn't do something like that," I said immediately.

"That's what Holloway said," Milo replied. "He defended her staunchly, in fact."

"How gallant of him," I said, unable to keep the acidic edge from my tone.

Milo glanced at me, but didn't respond to my comment. "I know Georgina Holloway is a fine woman, but I maintain that one never knows what a desperate person is capable of."

"Oh, I agree that desperation can lead to questionable decisions," I said. "Even uncharacteristic actions. But I don't think anonymous letters are the way in which Georgina would act. If she wanted to chase the girl off, there are other ways to do it."

"Perhaps," he conceded.

"How many letters have there been?"

"Three so far. The first one came the week they began rehearsals, but Miss Bell apparently kept it to herself. Holloway was with her when she received the second letter and was forced to confide in him. The third came only a few days ago. It's been weighing on his mind, and he said when he saw us in the street he remembered we had had some experience solving mysteries as of late and decided to take me into his confidence."

"Surely there are potential suspects?" I asked.

"There are, in fact. Miss Bell has a brother

who's something of a disreputable chap. He's always coming to her for money, gambling it away, that sort of thing. They recently quarreled when she refused to indulge him any further."

"I don't see how an anonymous threat would change her mind on that score."

Milo shrugged. "Maybe she knows he's behind the letters but hasn't told Holloway."

I considered this. "Yes, that's possible. Perhaps she doesn't want him to know that her brother would threaten her. Maybe that's why she was reluctant to tell him about the letters to begin with."

"There has also been some trouble on the set of the play, I understand. There have been difficulties with Flora Bell's under-study, and some of the actors have been known to be temperamental."

"A full cast of possible culprits," I said, beginning to turn the matter over in my mind.

"So it seems. Holloway's worried sick about it, though he tried at first to seem offhanded about his concern. Despite his love for the theatre, the fellow's not much of an actor."

"It would be interesting to talk to Flora Bell, to see how she truly feels about the letters," I said. "I mean, if they are really puzzling her or if she seems to know from whom they might be coming."

"Well, you're going to have your chance," Milo said. "Holloway said he would like us to come to the theatre and see the dress rehearsal tomorrow night. He said he would introduce us to some of the actors. I believe that, after some of our recent experiences, he feels we may be able to offer some insight into the situation."

I realized suddenly what Milo was telling me. We had once again been called upon to assist in a mystery. I felt that familiar sensation of excitement that came with the prospect of another puzzle before us.

He went into the bathroom to wash and dress for bed, and I sat thinking of ways we might discover the identity of the mysterious letter writer. It seemed the best place to start would be to determine how the letters had arrived.

"Have they been posted to her?" I called, when he had turned off the water.

"No," he said, coming out of the bathroom. "They were slipped under her dressing room door at the theatre."

"That seems to narrow it down," I said.

"Yes, somewhat. Of course, people are always coming and going. There are the stagehands and those working on building the set. It would be fairly easy for any of them to have done it. Or even for a stranger to have slipped in unnoticed."

"It seems to rule out Georgina," I said. "I don't imagine she would care to be any-where near Gerard Holloway and Flora Bell."

"Unless she came to the theatre or paid someone else to deliver the letters."

He did have a point.

I pondered this information. Was it possible that the letter writer was serious? Could Flora Bell really be in danger?

"I see from the gleam in your eyes at the potential mystery I've laid at your feet that I am forgiven my late evening," Milo said, walking to the bed.

"I'm surprised you've told me about it," I said. "Normally, you'd try to keep me from finding out."

He leaned to drop a kiss on my lips. "You'd only find out anyway."

I couldn't help but smile. He was right about that.

"Besides," he said, going around to his side of the bed and sliding in beside me, "this seems a minor matter. After all, if someone meant to do Flora Bell harm, I doubt they would warn her about it before-hand. I don't suppose there will be much danger involved."

Milo's reasoning made sense, and I couldn't help but agree with him. Unfortunately, we were very wrong.

4

I found myself very much looking forward to the dress rehearsal. For one thing, it was going to be interesting to be the first audience to see the play. Gerard Holloway might be perceived as only a dabbler by the serious theatre set, but I knew he was the type of man who threw himself into ventures wholeheartedly and I expected the play would be very well done.

Of course, more than that, I was anxious to meet Flora Bell and to learn more about the mysterious letters she had been receiving. Now that mystery was in my blood, I was finding it harder and harder to resist its pull. It was a rather unsettling addiction.

Milo glanced at me as Markham, our driver, drove us toward the theatre.

"I hope you won't be disappointed if there's no sinister undertone to the evening. It may be nothing more than a harmless prank."

"Of course I won't be disappointed if nothing's wrong," I said. "I may heartily disapprove of Flora Bell — and Gerard Holloway — but that doesn't mean I wish her ill."

"I don't think it's serious between them. It's an infatuation on Holloway's part, nothing more," Milo said, as though that made everything all right. I felt that little twinge of sadness, but I pushed it away. This was not a discussion I wished to have in front of Markham.

"I'm also interested to see the play," I said. "I didn't know Mr. Holloway was a writer."

"Yes, well, you know he likes to throw himself into all sorts of projects. I believe he tried his hand at acting and wasn't much of a success. I suppose playwriting and directing appeal to him more."

The Penworth Theatre was a lovely old building that had seen better days. The paint was faded and the red velvet seats were worn, but there was an air of quiet dignity about the place, as though it knew its own worth and was unashamed of its somewhat shabby appearance. In fact, I suspected that was exactly the reason Gerard Holloway had not had the building renovated.

We had walked in through the open front doors and into the auditorium without seeing anyone, but a moment later Gerard Holloway came out onto the stage and spotted us.

"Oh, good. You're here," he said in what seemed to be an artificially jovial tone as he came down the little flight of steps off to one side of the stage.

"Thank you for having us, Mr. Holloway," I said when he reached us.

He smiled, a bit tightly, I thought, and I wondered suddenly if the invitation had been extended more to Milo than to the pair of us. "I do hope you like the play. We've worked very hard on it."

"Gerry! Gerry, where are you?" The voice came from somewhere backstage, rising as the speaker came nearer. "Gerry?"

"Yes, Flora, I'm here," Mr. Holloway called. His voice sounded slightly strained, and his posture seemed tense, as though he was bracing himself for something unpleasant.

There were footsteps on the stage. Then she stepped into the light, and I got my first glimpse of Miss Flora Bell.

She was beautiful, I would admit that much. A halo of golden curls surrounded a cherubic face that managed to convey both sweetness and sensuality. With her wide blue eyes and pink cheeks and full lips, she would not have been out of place in a Botticelli painting.

"Oh, hello," she said when she saw us. She came across the stage and down the steps, in graceful, measured movements. She wore a pale blue satin gown in the high-waisted Regency style, which clung to her figure and swirled about her feet as she moved toward us. She was certainly aware of how to make an entrance.

I glanced at Milo to see what sort of impression she might be making on him, but, though he was watching her as I was, it was impossible to tell anything from his features. It was always difficult to tell what went on behind those blue eyes of his, but, in this instance, I could guess. No doubt he thought her stunning.

She came to Gerard Holloway and clasped his arm, pressing against his side. "These are your friends, I assume? Aren't you going to introduce me?"

"Yes, of course," he said stiffly. He didn't seem at all comfortable to have her on his arm. I assumed it was because I, a close friend of Georgina's, was present. If he felt uneasy, I could only think that he deserved it.

"Mr. and Mrs. Ames, allow me to introduce Miss Flora Bell. Flora, these are my

47

old friends Milo and Amory Ames."

She smiled up at us. More specifically, she smiled at Milo. I had not been able to tell what he thought of her, but it was very apparent what she thought of him. Her blue eyes glittered with interest as they scanned his face. Not that I could blame her for that; his dark good looks and vivid blue eyes had the same effect on most women.

"How do you do?" she said. To her credit, she pulled her eyes from Milo and gave me a smile as well. "It's so nice to meet some friends of Gerry's. We've been rehearsing so often, I feel as though I'm beginning to lose touch with the real world."

Though I didn't want to admit it, I could see why men might find her difficult to resist. She had a charm that was not typical, an airy warmth that apparently encompassed everyone with whom she came in contact. That didn't excuse Gerard Holloway's behavior, of course, but it made it a bit easier to understand.

"Speaking of the rehearsal, we'd better get the show started," Gerard Holloway said, disentangling her from his arm in a movement that was not entirely subtle.

She looked at us with a conspiratorial smile. "Always the show. Well, I do hope you enjoy it, Mr. and Mrs. Ames. Perhaps we can speak again afterward. Or go to dinner? Gerry, might we all go to dinner?"

"We'll discuss it later," Gerard Holloway said. There was the faintest tinge of impatience in his tone now, and even Flora Bell seemed to realize that she shouldn't press the topic further.

With one last smile in our direction, she turned and walked back up the stairs onto the stage and disappeared from sight.

"Sit anywhere you like," Mr. Holloway said quickly, as though he was avoiding having to say anything about Miss Bell.

"Thank you," I said, equally glad to avoid the topic. "I'm very much looking forward to seeing the play."

He smiled at me, a bit of relief evident on his features. Milo was right; Gerard Holloway was no actor. It was painfully obvious that he was embarrassed about his liaison with Flora Bell and was trying to keep from making it evident. Well, he had no one to blame but himself.

He left us, and Milo and I moved to seats in the center of the theatre, a few rows from the front. It seemed like it would give us the best view of the stage.

It was a new experience for me, to have an entire theatre to myself. It was going to be an interesting way to watch the performance.

I was especially intrigued now that I had been introduced to Flora Bell. I wondered if that pleasant energy she had presented would translate well to the stage.

"What did you think of Miss Bell?" I asked Milo in a low voice as we settled into our seats.

"She's a pretty girl, if you like that sort of thing," he replied without any particular enthusiasm.

"Blond-haired, blue-eyed beauties, you mean?" I said dryly. "You don't like that sort of thing, I suppose." He could not convince me for a moment that he had not been impressed by her. Even I had had a favorable impression, despite my determination to dislike her.

He slid his arm across the back of my seat and leaned close, his breath whispering down my neck. "You know perfectly well what I like."

The lights dimmed just then, and I turned my attention to the stage, though I was suddenly very aware of the warmth of Milo beside me.

The red velvet curtains parted, revealing an elaborately decorated drawing room. Though the theatre was not new, Gerard

Holloway had clearly spared no expense on the sets.

Flora Bell stood alone on the stage, her blue evening gown gleaming in the footlights.

" 'There's a ball tonight, but there is no celebration in my heart,' " she said.

The play was set during the Napoleonic Wars. Flora Bell played Victoire, a young woman whose lover must choose between his love for her and his loyalty to France.

I was not exactly sure what I had been expecting of Flora Bell. Perhaps, given the circumstances of her sudden rise to fame, I had thought that she would be nothing more than a beautiful girl who had been in the right place at the right time. It was a surprise to me, then, to discover that she was a superb actress.

When she first walked out onto the stage, I could think of nothing but her relationship with Mr. Holloway and the mysterious letters. Only a few moments into the performance, however, I ceased to remember that she was anyone other than the character she was portraying. Every word, every expression, every subtle gesture, served to convey the essence of Victoire, a woman who struggles to deal with her personal heartache as well as the defeat of her nation's armies.

There was something mesmerizing about Flora Bell when she was onstage. It wasn't just the bright lights shining on her fair skin and golden hair, nor was it the warm, clear tone of her voice that carried her words out across the auditorium. It was some unnamable quality, a talent that surpassed mere words or gestures.

"She's wonderful," I leaned to whisper to Milo.

He nodded.

Though Flora Bell's character was the undisputed focus of the play, she was not the only one who gave a noteworthy performance. The lover, Armand, an officer in Napoleon's army, was played by Christopher Landon. Mr. Landon was very handsome and there was an easiness to his performance, as though he was so comfortable with his dashing and heroic character that it was no great effort to portray him.

The best of the supporting actors was Balthazar Lebeau, who played Durant, a wicked nobleman, also vying for Victoire's hand. I remembered Mr. Lebeau's name from when I was a girl, as he had once been a matinee idol and acclaimed Shakespearean actor. I hadn't heard much of him in the past several years, but I could see why he had enthralled audiences.

His deep, rich tones were mesmerizing, his every move calculated to enhance his speech. Whether it was due to natural talent or years of experience, he was clearly a master of his craft, and I found myself wishing that he had more time on the stage.

The play, though framed in the somewhat melodramatic context of a young woman's tragic wartime romance, served to illustrate the struggle between love and loyalty, the need for self-preservation, and the desire to follow one's heart no matter what the odds. In the end, Victoire found that happiness is an ending we are often denied. Armand killed in battle, her prospects vanishing before her as her country faces defeat, she was forced to consider the unthinkable: that she must ally herself with Durant.

As the play drew to a close, she stood alone on the stage. Instead of the blue dress, she now wore one of scarlet that emphasized her pale skin and flaxen curls. Stepping forward, she was bathed in light, Victoire's mingled grief and strength, the agony of conflict, etched into every line of her beautiful face.

" 'Life holds light and darkness, and sometimes one must step into the shadows to see which will prevail.' "

The curtain fell and I blinked, suddenly

remembering where we were. So entranced had I been by the story and the actors' power to tell it that I felt vaguely as though I had just awoken abruptly from a dream. I was struck by the fact that Victoire had not made her choice. It was left to the viewer to decide what she would do, an interesting concept.

"What do you think?" Milo leaned in to ask me.

"She's brilliant," I said, my eyes still on the stage.

"Yes," he agreed. "It certainly wasn't what I expected."

It was not what I had expected either, and I found that Miss Bell's talent was somehow more disturbing to me than if she had been a mediocre actress.

The curtain rose, but the actors did not come to take their bows. Instead, Mr. Holloway stepped out on the stage. I had almost forgotten that we were at a dress rehearsal and not an actual performance.

"Well, what did you think?" he asked. Something in the way he asked it made me think our answers were important to him.

"It was excellent," I said sincerely. As much as I had wanted to dislike Flora Bell and the play out of loyalty to Georgina, I couldn't deny that it was good and that

Miss Bell's performance had been something special. "I think you're going to have a great success."

He smiled. "I'm glad to hear you say so. There are always a few things that seem to go wrong at a dress rehearsal, but I thought tonight went well. Come backstage, will you? I'll introduce you to the others."

We rose from our seats and went down the aisle to the front of the theatre, where we took the steps up onto the stage. From there we followed him backstage and through a tangle of twisted ropes, props, and stagehands, until we found ourselves in a long, dim corridor. There were several doors along the walls, and I saw that all of them were unmarked, except for one that had a star on it and the name "Flora Bell" written in dark letters.

"Most of the actors have gone to change," Mr. Holloway said. "The uniforms are uncomfortable. But they should be out fairly soon."

As if on cue, the door nearest us opened and Christopher Landon, the male lead in the play, came out into the corridor. He was tall and handsome, with dark blond hair and an appealingly angular face. Dark eyes came up and saw us standing there, and it seemed as though impatience flickered across his expression before he suppressed it.

"This is Christopher Landon," Mr. Holloway said. There was something in his tone that I didn't quite know how to interpret. It wasn't dislike, exactly, but there was a certain wariness there, as though the two of them were not on the best of terms. "Landon, allow me to introduce you to my friends, Mr. and Mrs. Ames."

Judging from Mr. Landon's expression, he didn't seem any keener on Mr. Holloway than Mr. Holloway did on him. Nor did he seem particularly interested in meeting us.

"How do you do?" he said without enthusiasm.

"I very much enjoyed the play, Mr. Landon," I told him.

"Thank you."

"I was very particularly struck by the ending. I can't really believe that Victoire would have accepted Durant."

Mr. Holloway smiled. "That is for you to decide. But, alas, sometimes the villain wins, Mrs. Ames."

Flora Bell's door opened then and she came out into the corridor dressed in an evening gown of aubergine satin.

"I thought I heard your voice, Mrs. Ames. I hurried to get ready so I didn't miss you. I'm sure I must look a fright."

She was perfectly aware that she looked magnificent, but somehow even this insincerity was charming.

"You were wonderful, Miss Bell," I said.

"Oh, do you really think so?" she said, clasping her hands together in apparent delight at my compliment. "I'm so glad. I did so want to do Gerry's play justice."

"I'm sorry to rush off," Christopher Landon said abruptly, "but I've somewhere to be. Good evening."

I happened to be looking at Flora Bell as he said this, and a strange expression crossed her face. Almost as soon as it was there, it was gone, and I wondered if I had imagined it. I didn't quite know what to make of it, and I tucked the impression away to think about later.

I had noticed that Miss Bell and Mr. Landon possessed an exceptional chemistry in their climactic farewell scene together. I had watched, spellbound, as Victoire and Armand had said their final good-byes, and now I wondered if there was a reason they were able to convey longing so convincingly.

"Gerard, aren't you going to introduce me to this beautiful creature?" said a deep, rich voice behind us. I recognized it at once as that of the man who had played the supporting role of Durant, the diabolical nobleman who would stop at nothing to win Victoire's hand.

We turned to see him approach from the dressing room at the end of the hallway. He was a tall, broad-shouldered gentleman, a bit on the heavy side, with flashing dark eyes in a handsome, ruddy face, and thick black hair going gray at the temples.

Though there was a group of us standing there, he came directly to me and he took my hand and bent low over it. "Balthazar Lebeau, at your service."

"How do you, Mr. Lebeau," I said, a bit awed to be speaking to so famous a gentleman. "It's a pleasure to meet you. I've long heard of your talents and was happy to witness them tonight."

He straightened but didn't release my hand. Instead, his grip on it tightened, and he stepped closer. "I thought the brightest days of my life were behind me, but you have given me reason to hope."

"Steady on, old boy," Mr. Holloway said with a laugh. "You mustn't allow him to alarm you, Mrs. Ames. Lebeau has rather a reputation, but he's harmless enough."

Mr. Lebeau flashed a wolfish smile. "I'm not altogether harmless," he said.

I laughed, extracting my hand from his grip. "Then I shall certainly be on my guard, Mr. Lebeau."

"No need to worry. I'm nothing like Durant."

"And this is Mr. Ames," Gerard Holloway said somewhat pointedly.

Balthazar Lebeau turned to Milo with a bow. "I am pleased to meet you, sir. I congratulate you on your excellent taste."

"Thank you," Milo said with a hint of amusement.

Mr. Lebeau turned his eyes to Miss Bell.

"There's just one thing I wanted to speak with you about, my dear. When you're saying that final line as Victoire, perhaps you could do it with just a bit more ambiguity in your tone."

"I didn't think there was anything wrong with the way I said it," she replied sweetly. "Victoire despises Durant. I don't believe for a moment she would choose to marry him."

Mr. Lebeau smiled indulgently, but there was irritation in his eyes. "That's not for you to decide. There should also be the possibility of acceptance in her words. Trust me, my dear. I have been doing this for much longer than you have."

"Yes, I know," she replied. "Perhaps we aren't doing things the way you're used to any longer."

Mr. Holloway seemed to sense, as I did, that things were potentially headed in the direction of an outright argument, and he stepped in. "We'll discuss this later, shall we?"

Mr. Lebeau looked as though he wanted to say something more, but instead inclined his head. "I wish you all a good evening."

With that, he turned and left. I glanced at Flora Bell and saw the unfiltered annoyance in her expression before it was cleared away. She obviously did not care for his criticism of her performance. Then she turned her attention back to us, the aura of sweetness once again suffusing her face.

"Gerry and I would love for you to come to dinner with us, Mr. and Mrs. Ames," she said brightly. "Wouldn't we, Gerry?"

Gerard Holloway looked extremely uncomfortable at the suggestion, but he managed to smile gamely. "I would love to, but I'm afraid I have a business matter that's come up. Another night, perhaps?"

"Yes, that would be nice," I said. Inwardly, I heaved a sigh of relief. I had not relished the prospect of being seen in public with Gerard Holloway and Flora Bell.

Flora Bell, however, was clearly displeased at Mr. Holloway's excuse. Her eyes narrowed ever so slightly and her posture stiffened. I wondered if she realized Holloway was embarrassed of their relationship, at least when it came to exhibiting it in my presence.

It seemed that, if he had asked us here to discuss the threatening letters, he had changed his mind. At least for the time being.

5

"Well, what did you make of the evening?" Milo asked me when we were back in our car, riding toward home.

"I'm not sure what to make of it," I said absently. I felt unsettled about the entire affair. Though I had enjoyed the play, the underlying atmosphere at the Penworth Theatre had been filled with tension. None of the principal actors much cared for one another; that much had been evident.

That wasn't the only thing that concerned me, however. I was thinking of how disheartening it had been to watch the interactions between Gerard Holloway and Flora Bell, for, despite Mr. Holloway's evident discomfort, he clearly had strong feelings for her. I had hoped to find Flora Bell a woman of good looks and little talent. Instead, she had been possessed of a rare gift, just the sort of thing that was sure to keep Mr. Holloway enraptured. I sighed heavily.

"What's wrong?" Milo asked.

I debated on whether to reveal what was on my mind and decided to tell him the truth. It was, after all, terribly difficult to hide anything from him. "I'm concerned. Mr. Holloway is clearly besotted with Flora Bell. It's worse than I thought."

"A passing fancy, nothing more."

"I'm not so certain."

"Georgina Holloway is a woman of substance. Holloway is sure to realize that eventually."

"Eventually might be too late," I said. Marriages had crumbled under lesser strains.

Milo didn't reply to this. I could only assume that he had wisely decided to steer clear of the topic.

"Did you see anyone amongst that illustrious group who you think might be sending the notes?" he asked.

I considered. We hadn't learned much, after all, about the players in this particular drama, and I was uncertain who might be the best fit for the role of villain.

"Mr. Holloway didn't seem eager to discuss the matter this evening."

"No, I suppose he thought we'd got a good look at the potential culprits and could discuss it later. There is also an ambitious understudy who has yet to make her appearance."

So far as we knew, it could be any of them or none of them. There was also the possibility that things were simpler than they seemed.

"I wonder if she might have written the letters herself," I mused.

"That's rather cynical of you, darling."

"Perhaps. It would be a good way to secure Gerard Holloway's attentions for the duration of the play."

"She seems to have done a fine enough job of securing them already," Milo pointed out.

"I did have the impression there was a great deal of tension in theatre," I said. "There are clearly jealousies and rivalries at work there. But it is possible that she is working on Mr. Holloway's sympathies. She isn't my first suspect, but I wouldn't rule her out."

"Who is your first suspect?" he asked.

I considered. "It's plain that Miss Bell and Mr. Lebeau don't like each other," I said.

"No," Milo replied. "Though he seemed to like you immensely."

"He was very charming."

Milo gave a dry laugh. "That fellow's played the aging lothario for so long he's

forgotten how to behave as anything else. I expect you'd do well to steer clear of him."

"I know how to manage a lothario," I said. "I've had six years of practice, after all."

This barb gained me only a mild grunt as he lit his cigarette.

"It doesn't seem outside the realm of possibility that Mr. Lebeau might be behind the notes," I went on. "After all, he's a dramatic sort of person, and there is a certain melodrama to the notes. Perhaps he has only sent them to upset her, as a sort of malicious prank."

"Yes, it's possible. Holloway told me Lebeau wanted the lead and Flora Bell refused to have him as her leading man. No doubt he bears her a grudge."

"That would account for the tension between them. The role of Durant is not nearly as good as Christopher Landon's role."

"There's something unspoken going on between Christopher Landon and Flora Bell," Milo observed as he leaned bac' against the seat.

"You noticed that, too, did you?" I aske "She looked strange when he said he } an appointment this evening. I wonder she assumed it was a woman and had a of jealousy."

"He was very careful not to look at her. It's the action of a man who doesn't want to make his feelings known. I've seen the same expression countless times on the face of a gentleman with a very bad hand of cards."

"You mean you think he cares for her but can't match the prestige of Gerard Holloway."

"Something like that," Milo said. "Holloway may make her career for her. If I had to guess, I'd say that's what's keeping her attention. Holloway's a decent fellow, but he isn't exactly the type of man women go mad for."

Not women like Flora Bell, anyway. She was young and beautiful and could have any man she wanted. Gerard Holloway was gallant and handsome, but I did not imagine he was the sort of man who would make a young woman's heart race.

Then again, I could be wrong. In his younger days Gerard Holloway had been quite the adventurer. It could be that Flora Bell still saw the streak of thrilling recklessness in him. Perhaps he was looking for someone who could bring it out again.

"It all comes back to the character of Miss Flora Bell," I said. "What aspect of her life has caused someone to write these notes to

her? Her role in the play? Her role as Mr. Holloway's mistress? Or perhaps some other role of which we are unaware."

"She plays the part of the ingénue well enough," Milo said, "but I'd wager she's not as innocent as she seems."

I gave a dry laugh. "I think that may be an understatement."

"You don't like her," he observed.

"I don't know her," I replied. "However, she certainly hasn't given me any reason to view her sympathetically, breaking up the marriage of my good friend."

"The marriage isn't broken up," Milo said.

"If not, this affair has done the sort of damage that's very difficult to repair."

"I'm sure they'll sort it out. Whatever this thing is with Flora Bell, Holloway still cares about Georgina."

"And you think that makes everything all right, do you?"

He sighed. "All I'm saying is that the Holloway marriage is none of our concern."

I lapsed into silence. The cavalier way Milo referenced the relationship between Gerard Holloway and Flora Bell was beginning to grate. Perhaps he could accept it casually, but I could not.

What was more, I knew Georgina Holloway was not the type of woman who would accept it for long. Whatever Milo said, I felt that I had a duty to my friend.

Now that I knew what we were dealing with, I was looking forward to tea with Georgina tomorrow.

The following afternoon found me at the Holloways' Belgravia residence, their house all white pillars, gleaming windows, and tidy hedges.

I was shown into the sitting room, decorated in shades of blue and gray, and Georgina Holloway came in a moment later to greet me. She looked much the same as when I had last seen her, perhaps a bit thinner. Her expression was pleasant, as always, but there was a shadow in her blue eyes that seemed accentuated by the colors of the room.

"How are you, Georgina?" I asked.

"Very well, Amory," she replied. "How have you been? You look well."

We settled into our seats and talked for a few moments about the weather, my recent trip abroad with Milo, and the London Economic Conference that had just commenced.

At last we came around to discussing the charity gala.

"I'm so surprised I didn't hear of it before

now," I said. "But we haven't been back from Paris for very long."

"Well, I'm glad you will be able to attend. I think it will be a lovely event." There was something unsaid in the words, and I knew she was avoiding mention of *The Price of Victory*. It seemed I would have to be the one to broach the subject.

I moved forward carefully. "We encountered your husband in the West End Tuesday evening, and he invited us to see the dress rehearsal of the play."

"Did he?" she asked, refilling her teacup with perfect poise.

"Yes, we went last night."

"What did you think of it?" she asked, her eyes still on the teapot as she set it back on the table.

"It was very good," I said honestly.

We both knew that we were skimming the surface of a topic, speaking carefully in the polite way women had of tiptoeing around the matter on our minds. Luckily, Georgina decided to dispense with the prevaricating.

"You've heard, I suppose, about Gerard and Flora Bell," she said, stirring a lump of sugar into her tea.

Now that she had brought it up, I saw no need to dissemble. "I've heard rumors, yes," I said.

A hint of a humorless smile touched her lips as she at last looked up at me. "I'm sure almost everyone's heard of it by now. What did you make of her?"

I hesitated as I considered how best to answer the question.

"I'd like your honest opinion," she said.

With any other woman, I might have felt extremely uncomfortable having this conversation. However, Georgina Holloway was not like most women. She was honest and direct, and she expected the same from other people.

"She's a talented actress," I said.

"And young and beautiful," Georgina pressed.

"Yes," I agreed. "But youth and beauty are such fleeing qualities."

She gave a soft laugh. "If Gerard only agreed with you, my troubles would be over."

I didn't point out to Georgina that she was also a beautiful woman. She was perhaps five years older than I and ten years older than Flora Bell, but she could easily have passed for much younger. Her complexion was flawless, smooth and unlined, and her honey-blond hair was styled in the latest fashion, which, in combination with her impeccable taste in clothes, made her appear chic and youthful.

Of course, all of that would matter very little to someone whose husband was seeking the companionship of a younger woman. Flora Bell's allure would likely run its course, but that wouldn't erase the hurt.

"I'd tell you it won't last, that people will forget, but I know that's poor consolation," I said.

She looked up, her blue eyes troubled. "You're right, of course. These things do pass in time. At least, the public interest in them. Today's gossip is tomorrow's old news. That's not what concerns me. I'm thinking of my marriage."

I nodded. "I'm sorry, Georgina," I said. I meant it. I knew what it was like to open a gossip magazine and see my husband's picture there.

"I suppose he still loves me, in his way, but it's more than a matter of love, isn't it?" she said. "Loving someone who doesn't truly love you isn't enough. At least, it isn't for me. Oh, I know women who have done it. Women who have turned a blind eye to their husband's —"

She stopped suddenly, and I realized that she was worried that I might think she meant me. It was true, in a way. For years, I had ignored most of what was printed about

Milo. I knew that much of it was exaggeration and even outright lies, but that hadn't meant that there was no truth to any of it or that it hadn't hurt me deeply to see the careless way he threw away his reputation, and mine with it.

"I'm sorry," she said, acknowledging what she clearly viewed as a faux pas, when another woman would have attempted to move quickly past the subject.

"There's no need to apologize," I assured her. "It's true that Milo and I had more than our share of difficulties."

"You seem very happy now," she said.

"Yes, very happy," I said. "We've managed to sort out our differences."

She looked up at me, her gaze suddenly intent. "How did you do it?"

I felt the weight of the question, as though her actions might be guided by my next words.

"There came a moment of crisis," I answered at last. "When I decided that things must be addressed, one way or the other."

It had been one of the hardest things I had ever done, but it had been necessary. Luckily, the turning point had set us in a positive direction.

"And that was the end of your troubles?" she asked.

"It was, at least, the beginning of the end," I said with a smile.

"I'm glad," she said. "I've always thought you and Milo were meant for each other."

"Thank you," I said. Our relationship was in a better state than it had ever been, even at the beginning. The shallow foundation of infatuation and desire on which we had built our marriage had, thankfully, evolved into something deeper. I felt, more now than ever before, that our future together looked very bright.

"So, you see," I told her. "There is hope."

"Yes," she answered. "I suppose only time will tell. Thank heaven the children are too young to be affected by this, at least in theory."

"I do hope it will all work out for the best, Georgina," I said sincerely.

She smiled, and this one was less forced than the last. "Thank you. But you haven't come here to discuss my husband's foibles, so let us talk of other things."

I had, in fact, come to discuss just that, but it was clear from the pained look in her eyes that it was not a topic on which she wished to dwell.

We spoke of lighter things then, and, when I left, tickets in my handbag, it was with something of a heavy heart. I had tried to be encouraging, but I could tell that she viewed the situation as very bleak indeed. What was worse, I was not sure I disagreed with her. Even if Gerard Holloway were to give up Flora Bell, the damage had already been done.

Georgina seemed almost resigned to the situation, as though she were waiting for things to play out fully before she made any decisions. But perhaps that was only on the surface. Was it possible that she was sending the threatening notes to Flora Bell? Given what I knew of Georgina's personality and her attitude today, I didn't think so. But one could never be sure.

I arrived back at the flat to find Milo waiting for me.

"There you are, darling," he said, coming out of the sitting room as I closed the front door behind me. "I've been wondering when you might return home."

I had not told Milo of my errand, knowing he would, in all likelihood, disapprove of my visiting Georgina. It was all well and good for him to involve us in Gerard Holloway's affairs as far as the mysterious letters went, but he wouldn't like my wading too deeply into the Holloways' matrimonial struggles.

"I had some things to attend to," I said,

vaguely surprised that he had been waiting. "What is it?"

"Holloway wants us to come back to the theatre."

"Now?" I asked, surprised.

He nodded, and though his expression didn't change, there was a glimmer of interest in his blue eyes. "I'm afraid there's been another threatening letter."

6

Milo drove us to the theatre in his blue Talbot. Pulling the car up to a curb I was fairly certain was not meant for parking, he alighted and came round to open my door. We walked toward the theatre, but instead of going in the front door as we had the night before, Milo led the way to the stage entrance at the end of the narrow, cobblestoned alley between the theatre and the building next door. The brick walls rose high on either side, casting the alleyway into shadow, even in the brightness of late afternoon.

"Holloway said he would hear if we knocked," Milo explained, rapping on the somewhat battered red door.

A moment later, it opened slightly and Gerard Holloway eyed us through the space before stepping back and pulling the door open. I preceded Milo into the theatre, and Mr. Holloway quickly closed the door behind us and locked it.

I looked around. We were at the end of the passageway that led to the dressing rooms. The lights were on, but it was still dim, and all was quiet.

I turned back to Mr. Holloway, who had yet to speak. It was then I noticed he held a pistol at his side. It looked strange in his hand, perhaps because it was so unexpected.

"What do you mean to do with that?" Milo asked mildly.

"I wanted to have it on hand."

"Is it as bad as all that?" Milo gave every appearance of perfect ease, but I noticed he had shifted ever so slightly, so as to put himself between me and the gun. It was not the first time he had shielded me in such a way, and I hoped this instance would be much less traumatic than the last.

"I didn't want to go into details over the telephone, but I'm afraid things may be worse than we assumed," Mr. Holloway said.

"Gerry?" Flora Bell's voice came from farther down the hall. "Have Mr. and Mrs. Ames arrived?"

"Yes, Flora. We're coming," he called back.

He turned back to us, his face taut.

"She's in her dressing room," he told us. "Come this way, will you?"

We followed him down the corridor and into Miss Bell's dressing room. She was sitting in a velvet chair in the corner, and any doubts I had had about her involvement concerning the letters were erased with one look at her face. She was as pale as death, her blue eyes wide. Her hands were in her lap, clutching a handkerchief, her knuckles white.

"Hello," she said as we came in; her uncertain expression reminded me of a child. I was half tempted to embrace her.

"It's going to be all right, my dear," Mr. Holloway said as he mercifully put the gun away in one of the dressing table drawers. He reached for a single piece of paper that lay atop the table and turned toward us. "Here it is."

He held it out to Milo, who ran his eyes across the page before he handed it to me.

It was written in block letters, so as to obscure the handwriting, in dark ink that had bled out onto the inferior-quality paper.

Let your opening performance be your best. It will be your last.

Though I had come prepared to read an unpleasant note, I felt a jolt at the words. This was no harmless prank. Someone was very clearly threatening to do harm to Flora Bell.

"When did you find the note?" Milo questioned Miss Bell.

"I came to the theatre to go over a few things."

"Alone?" I asked. As I said it, it occurred to me that it was more likely that she had come to the theatre to meet Gerard Holloway. What better place for them to be alone together, after all?

If this was the case, however, she didn't intend to admit it. "I like being here alone," she said. "It helps me really think about the character, about the movements I want to make on the stage. After every performance, I like to go out on the stage alone and consider how things might be done better. Well, today when I got here, the note was pushed under the stage door. It had my name written on it."

"If it was pushed under the stage door from the alleyway, anyone might have done it," I said.

"But who would want to?" Holloway demanded. "I want to know who was here and who is behind this. This cannot go on. I will not allow it." His face was very red, and his voice had grown unsteady with heightened emotion. He seemed to realize it, for he drew in a deep breath, his jaw tightening as he worked to suppress his feelings.

"I think you ought to ring the police," Milo said.

"Oh, no," Flora said quickly. "I don't want the police. Someone only wants to make me uneasy before my performance, and I shan't give them the satisfaction."

"I don't care what their motive is," Mr. Holloway said, his voice still loud and unsteady. "I intend to find out who is responsible. I'm going to ring the police now."

"No," she said sharply. "We agreed, Gerry."

I looked at her, surprised at the determination in her voice. What reason could she have for objecting so strongly? If I felt my life was in danger, nothing could induce me to keep from contacting the authorities.

She seemed to sense that her reaction was being observed, for her expression softened and she smiled. "Word is sure to get out," she said, "and I couldn't bear it if that happened, not before the play. I don't want anything to ruin it. Gerry has worked so hard. That's why I agreed when he suggested we speak to you. He was certain you could get to the bottom of things."

I felt the sudden weight of the responsibility Mr. Holloway and Miss Bell had laid at our feet. After all, Milo and I might be good at solving mysteries, but I felt we would be sadly inadequate protection against physical harm.

A possible solution occurred to me. "I know a policeman," I said. "A Scotland Yard inspector. He's very efficient and clever, and I'm sure that he would be discreet."

Milo cast a glance in my direction, but made no comment. Though he and Detective Inspector Jones had not always been on the best of terms, I knew Milo had fairly judged the inspector as an excellent policeman and a good man to have on one's side in time of trouble.

Flora shook her head, her blond curls bobbing. "It's very kind of you to suggest it, but I don't think that will be necessary, thank you." There was a note of finality in her tone that told me it would be no good to press the matter.

She poured a drink with perfectly steady hands and gave it to Gerard Holloway, who was looking up at her as a child might look at a trusted adult for reassurance. I was struck by his demeanor, by the way he apparently relied on her. I once again felt a sinking feeling about the depth of their feelings for each other. This was no passing fancy. Emotions ran deep, at least as far as Mr. Holloway was concerned.

"Would you care for a drink, Mr. or Mrs. Ames?" she asked in a cheerful voice.

We declined, but I felt the tension in the room begin to dissipate as if by the sheer force of her will. Despite her calm demeanor and easy dismissal of the facts, however, I found my initial discomfort had begun to develop into a sick feeling in the pit of my stomach. Someone meant to harm Flora Bell, but she seemed determined not to acknowledge the severity of the situation.

"Hello," a voice called suddenly, and I saw Flora flinch. I wondered if it was with surprise or at the sound of that particular voice. "Flora? Mr. Holloway, are you here?"

I watched Flora Bell and Mr. Holloway exchange a glance as the voice echoed along the hallway. Then Mr. Holloway rose to his feet and went to the door, looking out into the corridor.

"We're here, Dahlia," he called.

I heard quick, light footsteps approaching, and a moment later a woman stood in the doorway. She was tall and slim, with bobbed red hair and large brown eyes.

"I thought I might find you here, I . . ." Her voice trailed off as she caught sight of Milo, and I recognized that instant look of

82

predatory interest I had seen in the eyes of so many women over the years.

"I didn't realize that you had company. Are you going to introduce me to your guests, Mr. Holloway?" she asked with a smile.

"Oh. Oh, yes, these are my friends, Mr. and Mrs. Ames," he said distractedly. "Mr. and Mrs. Ames, Miss Dahlia Dearborn."

If she had heard that there was a "Mrs." included in this introduction, she gave no sign of it. Her eyes were still on Milo. "How do you do?"

Milo gave her the barest of nods. "Good afternoon." He was very aware of the effect he had on women, but it seemed that he was not in the mood to be charming.

"What are you doing here, Dahlia?" Mr. Holloway asked.

"What a greeting," she laughed. "As though I am quite unwelcomed."

I noticed that neither Mr. Holloway nor Miss Bell made any effort to deny this.

"How are you feeling, Flora?" she asked, turning to Miss Bell. "No sign of ill health, I hope."

Flora, despite the masterful control she exerted over her pretty features, seemed to pale a little at this remark, and I saw Gerard Holloway's posture stiffen. Miss Dearborn, however, didn't seem to notice the effect her words had had.

She turned back to Milo. "I'm Flora's understudy. Of course, there's little chance I'll ever see the stage, but one never knows, does one?"

We all looked at her, the possible implications of her words sinking in. Surely she would not be so brazen as to reference such a thing if she were the letter writer. Then again, it might all be part of the game she was playing.

"What's the matter?" she asked. "You all look like you've seen a ghost."

It was Flora Bell who roused herself first. She gave a careless laugh. "I'm afraid we were all being rather gloomy," she said. "It's nothing. But what brings you here, Dahlia?"

"I left my coat," she replied. "It's the only fur I've got, and I want to wear it for my date tonight. I have plans with a reasonably amusing gentleman. Unless anything better happens to come along." I'm sure I was not mistaken that her eyes flickered momentarily to Milo as she said this. I never ceased to be amazed at the number of women who made their availability known to Milo, whether or not I was present.

No one said anything to this and she sighed heavily. "Well, it seems there's no fun to be had here, so I shall go. I'll see you all at the performance. I hope you manage to be a bit more cheerful then."

When she was gone, Gerard Holloway turned to us, his face tight. "I think you can see why she might be a good suspect."

"Oh, Gerry, don't," Flora Bell said. "Dahlia isn't clever enough for something like this."

"It doesn't take a great deal of cleverness to write nasty letters."

"Perhaps not, but I don't think . . ." She stopped, glancing in our direction. "In any event, I'm sure these letters are nothing of consequence. You shouldn't have bothered Mr. and Mrs. Ames. Think no more of it. Just come to the performance and enjoy yourselves." She gave us a dazzling smile then, and I realized that we had been dismissed.

Despite my misgivings, it was clear that Flora Bell did not want to discuss the matter any further, and a few moments later Milo and I made our exit.

"What do you think of all of this?" I asked as we walked through the shadowy alleyway and back into the sunlit street.

"I think she's in danger and either doesn't know it or doesn't want anyone else to,"

Milo said, opening the door of his car for me.

"Then what are we going to do?"

He shrugged. "There's nothing that can be done, really. They don't want the police called. I suppose the best we can do is watch the performance and hope for the best."

"Then why do you suppose Mr. Holloway called us here?" I asked. "Surely he knew that we would recommend the police."

"He called us here because he's practically frantic with worry. You saw it as well as I did."

He went around to the driver's side and got in as my thoughts shifted to the other person we had met today.

"Flora Bell and Miss Dearborn don't like each other," I said as he settled into his seat.

"No, though they both tried very valiantly to pretend that they do. Miss Bell is a much better actress, so she was the more successful of the two."

"I thought the same," I replied. "Then again, there is bound to be jealousy on Miss Dearborn's part. Miss Bell has everything that she wishes for: a good role and a handsome benefactor. She may have more motive than the others to have written the letters. Maybe she left the letter, waited awhile, and then came back to see if it had had its

86

desired effect."

"It's possible," he said.

"Miss Dearborn is rather lovely, don't you think?" I asked, wondering if he had noticed the way she had been appraising him.

He glanced over at me with a smile as the car roared away from the curb. "I didn't notice. I was too busy looking at you, the most beautiful woman in the room."

7

The next day seemed interminable as I waited to attend the play and gala. While I knew society had been looking forward to it with great anticipation, I was merely anxious for the evening to be over. I could not bring myself to view this as just another social event. I felt somehow that it was much more than that. There was a sense of foreboding that I could not seem to shake.

"You seem tense," Milo observed as we at last made our way to the theatre that night.

"I am," I replied. I felt certain that something bad was going to happen, but I also felt powerless to stop it. But perhaps there was nothing to worry about. Perhaps the letters had only been a cruel joke, a ruse contrived by a jealous person to ensure that Flora Bell did not give her best performance. I certainly hoped that was the case.

The streets were packed with cars when we arrived. A crowd of people was moving toward the theatre, and there were photographers taking pictures of the new arrivals as though it were a film premiere, the bright flares of the flashbulbs nearly lost in the glow of the theatre lights. Never let it be said that Gerard Holloway missed an opportunity for spectacle.

As we stepped from our car and into the fray, I was glad that I had chosen to wear the gown of black silk and chiffon that I had purchased recently in Paris. I had known that Georgina Holloway and the other women involved in the event would be dressed in the height of fashion, and I had not intended to do any less. Diamonds and a silver fur added to my ensemble. I did not often wear black, and I thought that, in combination with Milo's black evening clothes, we made a striking pair.

We moved with the crowd, and I greeted several acquaintances as we made our way into the lobby of the theatre and presented our tickets. Some of these people, I was sure, had scarcely ever set foot in a theatre before, and I suspected they were more interested in the drama that might play out between Gerard and Georgina Holloway than the one that would happen onstage. But whatever their motivations for coming, it was clear that the Holloways' charity was going to benefit greatly from this evening's entertainment.

As I always did when I entered a theatre, I felt the little thrill of excitement that accompanied the viewing of a live performance. The cinema was enjoyable, but, in my opinion, it didn't have the same depth of feeling as did flesh-and-blood people baring their emotions before you on a stage. There was nothing quite like it in all the world.

We made our way through the throng, the air thick with cigarette smoke and expensive perfume. Voices mingled in the pleasant hum of scores of conversations overlapping one another. I caught a few phrases as Milo and I threaded our way through the crowd.

"They say she is quite talented."

"You know what they are saying about her and Holloway."

"I don't see how Georgina stands for it."

It seemed the theatregoers were well attuned to what was happening in the Holloway household.

We went up the scarlet-carpeted stairs to the first floor and an usher pointed us in the direction of our box. Before we could reach it, however, we spotted Mr. Holloway coming from the other end of the corridor, the one at the opposite side of the staircase we had just come up.

"Good evening," he said cheerfully to us as he approached. "You look stunning, Mrs. Ames, as always."

"Thank you."

He looked dashing, as usual, in his evening clothes, but something was off. Though there was a pleasant expression on his face, his eyes were uneasy. Clearly, he was still concerned about the threats against Flora Bell. Perhaps he was also worried about how his play would be received and how the evening would go with his wife and mistress under the same roof. All things considered, I couldn't blame him for his apprehension.

A passing couple stopped to speak to Mr. Holloway just then, and when they had gone there was another woman who came to tell him how much she was looking forward to the performance. He thanked them graciously, but once or twice I saw his eyes flicker in our direction with suppressed impatience.

"I came up the back staircase to avoid the crowds," he told us when we were once again alone, "but it doesn't seem to be working. I want to talk to you for a moment, but I'm afraid we won't get any privacy here. Come backstage, will you? You can have a bit of an inside look at what happens before a performance." He smiled, but it was strained.

We followed him down the corridor, the murmured voices of the lobby growing distant, and through a door that led to a narrow staircase. We descended and went through another door and found ourselves backstage. People were moving about quickly, anticipation in the air. Everyone had been working very hard for this moment, and I could feel the excitement as the actors and stagehands prepared for the product of their months of effort to come to fruition.

It was not excitement emanating from Mr. Holloway, however.

"Is something wrong?" Milo asked, apparently having noticed the same feeling of tension that I had.

"I don't know," Mr. Holloway said. He looked very uncomfortable suddenly, as if he would rather the conversation had never begun. "I . . . ah, I was going to ask if you'd seen Georgina."

There was a moment of silence as this question settled between us. I was unsure, really, what he meant. Was he wondering if I had spoken to her recently?

"I haven't seen her tonight," I said coolly.

"I . . . ah, I'm afraid I haven't seen her

either. I only wondered if she was here . . ."

Silence fell again as his words trailed off. I wasn't sure what he expected from us. It seemed rather strange that he had brought us backstage just to ask about his wife's whereabouts.

His next words revealed that this was not entirely the reason. "I wonder if I might have a word with you, Ames," he said. "It's about something rather urgent. You don't mind, Mrs. Ames?"

I did, in fact. I very much disliked being shooed away from important conversations. But I supposed there was nothing to do about it. In any event, I would make Milo tell me later what Gerard Holloway had to tell him.

"If you'd like to wish Flora good luck, I'm sure she'd be happy to see you," Mr. Holloway said, nodding in the direction of the corridor that led to the dressing rooms.

"I'd hate to intrude before the performance," I said.

"Nonsense. She likes company. Especially . . . given recent events." I had the distinct impression that he was trying to make me believe he wanted me to go and make sure she was safe. Though I was fairly certain this was a ploy to get me out of the way, it wouldn't hurt for me to keep her company until he had finished with Milo.

I went down the corridor, full now of people hurrying to and fro, doing whatever last-minute things needed to be done before a performance. I stopped before Miss Bell's dressing room door and was just prepared to tap on the door when I heard the sound of voices.

It seemed that Flora already had a visitor.

"Come now, be reasonable," the male voice was saying.

"You're the one who's being unreasonable," Flora Bell replied. "You can't expect me to help you. Not again. Especially after what you did."

"I'm hard up. I need more money."

"I don't want to talk about this again, Freddy," she said. "I've told you already that I'm not in a position to give you anything more. You already owe me more than you'll ever be able to repay. I have my own expenses. I can't keep supporting your . . . unsavory habits."

He laughed harshly. "You didn't mind my 'unsavory habits' when they kept us from starving or from being separated and sent to live with people who cared nothing for us."

"Your luck seems to have changed since then," she said softly. "I appreciate what you did to keep us going after Mum died, but times are different now."

So it was her brother. I remembered now that Milo had mentioned she had a sibling who had been involved in some distasteful business dealings. It had not occurred to me that the two speakers might be related, and then I realized why. Flora Bell's accent was much more refined. It seemed she had worked to shed that particular remnant of her past on the way to the stage.

"Yes, times are different now," he said. "You have money enough for both of us."

"I'm telling you, Freddy. I don't have any money to give you."

"Don't give me that, Flo," he said. "You've got Holloway wound around your little finger, and he's rich as Croesus. Don't tell me you don't have any money at your disposal."

"I don't ask Gerard for money," she said. "It isn't like that. I'm going to make a name for myself. I don't want to owe anyone. Do you hear me? Not anyone!"

"If you're so keen on making a name for yourself, why did you drop that actor for Holloway?" My ears perked up at this.

"Freddy." It was difficult to tell what emotions were encased in that single word, but she clearly felt strongly about his mention

of an actor. It seemed we might not be wrong about her attachment to Mr. Landon.

"Holloway gives you things, doesn't he? Jewelry, furs? I could sell them."

"No," she said, her voice suddenly hard. "I've told you that I'm not going to give you anything more, and I mean it."

"They'll hurt me if you don't, these people I owe money to."

"You should have thought of that before you got into debt."

"You'll be sorry if something happens," he said. Was it a threat? It was difficult to tell.

"Nothing's going to happen," she replied.

"You're my sister. You ought to help me," he said pleadingly, and I tried hard to determine if the distress in his voice was real. Whether or not it was, Flora Bell did not appear moved by his plight.

"We're done talking about this," she said. "You're welcome to come and see me, Freddy, but don't ask me for money again."

I had thought to quietly retreat, but the door to the dressing room was suddenly flung open and there was no time for me to turn away.

It was Flora who had opened the door, and she was still facing her brother. It was not until she saw his gaze light on me that she turned.

Something sharp crossed her eyes before she smoothed it away and a lovely pink flush came to her cheeks, as though she was merely embarrassed and not angry to see that I had overheard the conversation. She really was a marvelous actress.

"Oh. Hello, Mrs. Ames," she said.

"Hello, Miss Bell. Mr. Holloway suggested that I come and wish you luck for the performance."

"That was very kind of Gerry," she replied. "And of you."

She was being terribly polite, but there was a certain stiffness in her manner. She disliked that I had overheard that conversation with her brother.

The gentleman in question stepped out into the hallway. The resemblance was immediately apparent. He was tall and lanky, with a sort of languorous ease to his movements. His hands were shoved in the pockets of his brown suit, and he moved with a restrained energy. Judging from what Flora had said about his taking care of her when their mother died, I assumed he was older than she, but he looked just as young. He had the same fair, curly hair and the same blue eyes as his sister, but there was something hard about his eyes. His gaze swept over me in an unconcerned way.

"Mrs. Ames, this is my brother, Frederick Bell."

"How do you do," I said.

"Hello," he said.

"Mrs. Ames and her husband are old friends of Gerry's. They've taken an interest in our little play." There was something not quite friendly in her tone. I wondered if she resented our sudden interference in her life. I suspected that she wished Gerard Holloway had never told us about the threatening letters, though, from what she had said yesterday, our involvement had been the price she had paid for keeping the police out of the matter.

"It's a wonderful play, made all the better by your sister's performance," I said, hoping to ease the atmosphere a bit.

"Yes, my dear little sister's a marvel, isn't she?" he asked, his tone heavy with sarcasm.

"I'm sorry you've got to rush off, Freddy," Flora said pointedly. "I hope you'll come and see me soon."

"Yes, I'm sure you do," he replied. "Break a leg, sister dear."

With a careless nod in my direction, he walked past me and ambled out of the theatre.

Flora turned back to me. "My brother never stays for my performances. It's a little superstition of mine."

"I see," I said.

She looked as though she was about to say something else, but seemed to think better of it. She turned back into her dressing room. "Come and talk with me while I finish my makeup, will you?"

I followed her into the room. "You're sure I'm not disturbing you?"

"Oh, not at all. I'm rather used to people coming in and out of my dressing room. There's no privacy in the theatre. But close the door, will you?"

I did as she asked and then took a seat on the chair in the corner.

"I've never asked you how you know Gerry," she said. She smiled at me in the mirror, the disarming, youthful smile that made me feel as if we were young girls sharing confidences.

I briefly wondered if I should tell her the truth, then decided there was no reason why I shouldn't. "I'm actually a friend of his wife's."

If I had expected the flush of embarrassment to cross her face, I was to be disappointed. She didn't seem at all uncomfortable at the mention of Georgina. "I have heard Mrs. Holloway is a charming woman," she said. "Gerry speaks very highly of her."

I found myself at a loss as to how to respond to this, which was, perhaps, her aim.

"I hope to be able to meet her tonight," she went on. "I want to congratulate her on the success of the charity gala."

She spoke in a perfectly natural tone, despite the rather shocking way she referred to congratulating her lover's wife. I rather hoped that Gerard Holloway was smart enough to prevent such a meeting. I couldn't imagine that it would end well. Surely Miss Bell realized that?

She picked up a tube of lipstick and applied it to her lips, rubbing them together to achieve the desired effect. "What do you think of this color?" she asked.

"It's very nice."

She studied it, turning her head from side to side. "I'm not sure. It's rather dark. I'm not sure if it's becoming. I imagine it would look lovely on you with your coloring."

"I think it suits you," I replied. In truth, I supposed there were few things that would not suit Miss Bell.

She turned suddenly in her chair to look at me. "Don't you think Kit is handsome?" she asked.

"Kit?"

"Christopher Landon."

"Yes," I agreed carefully, unsure why she had switched the topic so suddenly to her leading man. I realized there was something very searching in her gaze, despite the flippant way she spoke.

"All the ladies are very fond of him, which can be a nuisance. But I'm glad he's so good-looking. I don't think the play would have worked as well without someone very handsome in the role. I like to look well with my leading men."

I remembered how Milo had mentioned that she hadn't wanted to star opposite Balthazar Lebeau. Though he was handsome, I suspected he was too old for Miss Bell's taste.

"Yes, I suppose that helps," I said vaguely. I decided I might as well press the topic a bit further. "He doesn't seem an exceptionally pleasant person."

For the space of an instant, it seemed that her expression slipped, but she recovered quickly. "Oh, Kit's a lamb, really. One just has to learn to understand him. I'm beginning to realize that people aren't always what they seem to be."

I wanted to press her for more details on their relationship, but I couldn't bring myself to do it.

She stood then, dropping the robe she was wearing, leaving it on the floor, as she walked to the closet and took out an evening dress of shiny white satin.

"Do you like this one?" she asked. "I think I'm going to wear it to the gala."

"Yes, it's lovely."

"I do hope I'll get to visit with you after the performance," she said. "I'd like to get to know you better. I always like to know the right sort of people, you know."

I wasn't exactly sure what to make of her. There was a guileless quality about her, as though she didn't know the impact of what she was saying. She blithely said the most startling things and then moved on from them as if they were of no importance.

There were moments, however, when her eyes became sharp and there was a flash of what might even have been cruelty in them. It was as if, for just a moment, her mask slipped.

It might, of course, have been my imagination, but I didn't think so. There was more to her than the charming, careless girl.

I thought that Milo would have had much better luck with her if left alone for a while. He had a knack for drawing women out.

There was suddenly a loud rap on the

door. "Ten minutes to curtain, Miss Bell," someone called.

Flora looked up and smiled at me in the mirror. "Almost showtime."

I rose. "I'll leave you to finish then. Good luck, Miss Bell."

"Oh, no, you mustn't say that," she said with a smile. "It's unlucky."

8

There was no sign of Milo or Mr. Holloway backstage, and I was nearly knocked over twice by rushing stagehands as they went about making final preparations, so I retraced our path back up the narrow staircase to the corridor where we had first encountered Mr. Holloway. The din of voices had subsided now, as nearly everyone had made their way to their seats.

I passed through the red velvet curtain into our box, but Milo was not there either. I decided to take my seat and wait for him. There was no use roaming around looking for him.

Our seats had an excellent view of the stage. It was a different vantage point from the one where we had previously watched the play, and I was eager to watch the story unfold again.

I only wished that I could be certain that nothing bad was going to happen onstage tonight. I felt misgivings about not having contacted Inspector Jones. Despite Flora Bell's protests, I would have felt much better knowing that the inspector was in the audience.

A moment later, Milo slipped into the seat beside me.

"What did Mr. Holloway want?" I asked.

"He wanted my advice," he said in a low voice.

"What sort of advice?"

"Thing are . . . tense between him and Georgina."

"Did he expect anything less?" I asked.

"No, but he's also worried about Miss Bell. He says she hasn't seemed herself tonight. He thinks there may be some strain between her and the other actors. He said he feels like she's keeping something from him."

"As we suspected, there was — or is — something between her and Christopher Landon," I said. "The way she spoke about him all but confirmed it."

"The plot thickens," Milo said.

The lights dimmed then, and I felt a sense of nervous anticipation that had nothing to do with the performance I was about to see. My interactions with Mr. Holloway and Miss Bell had not left me feeling any more relieved. In fact, the sense that something bad was going to happen only seemed to get stronger.

Milo must have noticed the tension in my posture or on my face, for he glanced at me, then reached over to lay a reassuring hand on my leg, leaning in to murmur, "Holloway's instructed the stagehands to keep a close eye on Miss Bell throughout the performance. It's going to be all right."

I nodded. I certainly hoped he was right.

The curtains parted and, as Flora Bell stepped onto the stage, I could feel the shift in the audience. They were ready to see what Gerard Holloway's mistress had to offer. There were, I knew, a great many people here who were friends of Georgina's, and I suspected they would not have been displeased to see Flora Bell fail.

If Miss Bell sensed the mood of the audience, however, she gave no sign of it. She began to speak her lines, and I could almost feel her drawing the onlookers in with every word, every subtle gesture. They had been prepared to scoff at Gerard Holloway's mistress, the unknown actress to whom he had given a choice role, but it was becoming clear to them that she was much more than that. She had been wonderful during the dress rehearsal, but tonight she was magnificent.

By the time the first scene was over, she had the audience in the palm of her hand.

As the play went on, I found myself relaxing into my seat as some of my tension faded away. As it had done at the dress rehearsal, the combination of the gripping plot and the wonderful performances pulled me into the world of the story, and I began to forget that there was possible danger at hand. I began to forget that Flora Bell was anyone other than Victoire, the character she played.

As each scene moved past without incident, I began to think that nothing was going to happen, after all. Perhaps the perpetrator had been discouraged by the watchful stagehands. Or, more likely, it had been an overreaction on my part to take the notes so seriously. They had been a malicious prank, but likely nothing more.

I determined to let down my guard and enjoy the rest of the evening.

During the intermission, the tone of the talk regarding Miss Bell had changed.

"She's an excellent actress," I heard someone say as Milo and I roamed the hallways, mingling with the other audience members. "I ought to have known Holloway wouldn't put just anyone into his plays.

Always the best for Holloway, I've always said."

"I must admit, the girl has talent," another opined. "It's not just looks like I'd suspected."

Whatever they felt about Miss Bell's relationship with Mr. Holloway, it seemed that her talent was no longer in question.

The second act was even better. It seemed Flora Bell was feeding upon the audience's approval, absorbing their energy and enthusiasm and channeling it into her performance.

As she spoke her last line I noticed that, despite her disagreement with Mr. Lebeau about the interpretation of the words, there was a new uncertainty in her tone as she spoke them: " 'Life holds darkness and light, and sometimes one must step into the shadows to see which will prevail.' "

The curtain fell, and there was a moment of silence before applause burst forth from the audience. It was not the tepid appreciation of polite spectators, but the thunderous approval of those who marveled at what they had just seen, the true admiration of viewers who had relished an excellent performance.

The curtain rose again and, as Flora Bell came to take her bows, I could see the look of triumph in her eyes. She had won them over, and she knew it. The entertainment notices tomorrow would be full of praise. Flora Bell had just seen the beginning of an excellent career.

I let out a breath, feeling a sense of relief as the curtain fell for the final time and people began to leave their seats. Nothing had happened. I didn't know why, but the tone of the note had left me believing something would occur during the performance. Now that everything had gone off smoothly, I felt as though a weight had been lifted. "It appears that it was only a taunt," I told Milo.

"Yes, I suppose so," he said, his thoughtful gaze still on the stage.

The performance concluded, it was time to move on to the gala. I still had not spotted Georgina Holloway, but I didn't think it unusual that she might have stayed away from the performance. I was glad, for I thought it would be difficult for her, on top of everything else, to see her rival's success.

I hoped the gala would prove uneventful. If Mr. Holloway was smart enough to keep the two women away from each other, we might be able to pass the evening without incident.

■ ■ ■ ■

The gala was held in the building directly beside the Penworth Theatre, the one that made up the other side of the alley along the stage door. It had apparently once been a restaurant, and Mr. Holloway had purchased it along with the theatre with just such an event as this evening in mind.

I knew Georgina's charity events were often lauded as the city's most elegant, and the gala did not disappoint. I stepped into the room and found that it was everything that I had imagined it might be and more. Tables were clothed in white linen with glittering crystal and silver. Towering candelabras held long, flickering candles and each table was bedecked with an exquisite arrangement of flowers. Gold chandeliers, clearly not native to the building, shone brightly overhead, throwing a warm light over everything they touched.

"Georgina has outdone herself," I said to Milo.

"Did you expect anything less?" he replied.

I certainly hadn't. Georgina Holloway was the sort of hostess every society woman hoped to emulate. Her parties were legendary. And, given the current situation, she had more reason than ever to put on a good show.

We moved further into the room with a crowd of other guests. An orchestra was playing soft music, and already the room was filled with the clinking of champagne glasses and the laughter of the crowd, everyone in good spirits after enjoying an excellent performance.

Georgina stood near one of the long tables overflowing with food. I was certain now that she had not been at the performance, for I would have noticed her gown in a crowd. It was a bright shade of not-quite-red, like an orange sunburst against the cool, muted tones of the room. The dress was stunning, a masterpiece of fashion, and something more. It seemed to tell the world that no matter what had happened between her and her husband, no matter how magnificent her rival's performance had been, Georgina Holloway was not going to shrink from the spotlight.

"Amory, I'm so glad to see you," she said, reaching out to take my hands in her soft, cool ones as we arrived at her side. "You look stunning as always. Hello, Milo."

"Good evening, Georgina," he replied.

"It's you who looks stunning, Georgina,"

I said. "Your dress is magnificent."

"Thank you. I thought something in an unusual shade would be appropriate for a dramatic event." She did not elaborate on exactly what sort of drama she had anticipated, but there was plenty to be had if one was looking for it.

"You've arranged things beautifully," I told her, looking admiringly around the room. "The gala is sure to be a great success."

"Thank you. I hope so." I noticed that she did not ask about the play. Perhaps she had already heard the glowing reviews of Miss Bell's performance.

Other guests came up to speak with her then, and so we began to move away.

She reached out and caught my arm, however, leaning toward me, her voice lowered. "Find me before you leave, will you, Amory? There's something I want to talk to you about."

I nodded, wondering what it was that she wanted to discuss.

Milo and I found our place at a table and sat to enjoy the festivities. Everyone seemed to be in excellent spirits, and I thought again how successful an event this had proven to be. Not only were the guests having a wonderful time, but the recipients of the event's proceeds were going to benefit handsomely. It was unlikely any charity function would be able to surpass it, either in pleasure or monetary success, for years to come.

A short while later, the actors and actresses made their way into the room and were greeted with great applause and enthusiastic cheers.

Flora Bell led the way, resplendent in her white satin evening gown. She held Gerard Holloway's arm, her head held high. She was very aware that all eyes were on her as she entered the room, and she seemed just as comfortable with this attention as she had been on the stage.

Someone handed her a bouquet of flowers, which she held in her free hand, and I realized suddenly that her dress almost resembled a wedding gown. I could not help but wonder if that had been the impression she was trying to make, if she had designs upon Gerard Holloway that went beyond a love affair.

It crossed my mind that the two women in Mr. Holloway's life had dressed for the opposite of their roles: Georgina in the color of fire and desire and Flora Bell in innocent white.

I glanced to where Georgina had been

standing a moment before, but she was no longer there. I wondered if she had realized what was coming and had wished to avoid being scrutinized as Miss Bell made her appearance. There was so much potential for things to go wrong.

I hoped the gala would manage to remain a pleasant affair. If only I had known.

I watched the cast of characters throughout the evening and found that many of them were still performing, in one way or another.

Gerard Holloway was trying valiantly to play the carefree host, but I could tell that he was tense. More than once I saw him remove his handkerchief from his pocket and dab his brow. To his credit, he had managed to avoid Flora Bell for much of the evening. She had been surrounded by congratulatory admirers throughout the night, so it had not been difficult.

He and Georgina seemed to be avoiding each other as well. The size of the crowd made it possible without attracting too much attention to the fact, but I had noticed them glance in the other's direction more than once. I wished that something could make them realize that they still cared for each other. I was half tempted to bring them together and give them a good talking-to, but one couldn't berate one's friends into a happy marriage, so it seemed I must leave them to work things out for themselves.

It was just near midnight when Gerard Holloway stood, motioning to the orchestra, who quit playing in a remarkably graceful fading out of notes.

"I'd just like to say a few words," Mr. Holloway said. "I want to thank everyone who worked so hard to bring this production to life, and all of you who have joined us tonight to benefit this cause. Clearly, it has been a great success."

The room broke into appreciative applause. When it had died down, Mr. Holloway picked up his glass of champagne. "I would also like to propose a toast. To the talented cast of *The Price of Victory.* You have surpassed what I imagined as I put these words on paper, and I cannot thank you enough. Especially our rising star." He lifted his glass. "To Flora Bell and the best cast in London."

Glasses lifted across the room, though I could feel an undertone of speculation as the partygoers drank their toast.

I looked in the direction in which Mr. Holloway had lifted his glass. Flora Bell stood there, and I was surprised to see she did not look as triumphant as I might have imagined. In fact, she looked almost distracted as she smiled and nodded at those congratulating her.

My gaze then went to the flash of fire-colored fabric on the other side of the room, and I looked at Georgina. She, too, was talking to people around her. She looked very composed, as though the toast had had no impact upon her.

I caught sight of Dahlia Dearborn then. I had noticed her earlier, coming in with the other actors, though she had had no part in tonight's performance. She wore a gown of copper-colored satin that looked lovely with her coloring, but the effect was marred by the expression of scorn on her pretty face that she was either unable or unwilling to hide. I noticed the glass in her hand was still full. Apparently, she had not joined in the toast.

The music resumed then and couples returned to the dance floor. I lost sight of Georgina and Mr. Holloway as the crowds began to move again.

The room had grown rather hot, and I drank a glass of cold punch and chatted idly with those at our table. Though the party showed no signs of slowing, I was beginning to feel that I had had enough excitement for one evening.

Milo, it seemed, shared the sentiment.

"Have you had enough, darling?" he leaned in to ask me a few moments later.

I smiled at his phrasing. Milo enjoyed a party as much as anyone, but a charity gala was not quite in line with the sort of events he normally found amusing.

"Yes . . . Oh, but I need to speak to Georgina first," I said, remembering her words. In truth, they had never been far from my mind. I had looked more than once for an opportunity to speak with her, but she was forever disappearing into the crowd.

I glanced to where I had seen her standing, but there was no sign of her. Nor did she appear to be anywhere else in the room. I realized that Gerard Holloway, too, seemed to be missing. I wondered if the couple had slipped away to have a private conversation. I felt a little glimmer of hope.

Then something occurred to me. Another quick glance around the room confirmed that Flora Bell was not present either. I felt a sinking feeling in my stomach. Had they all gone off someplace to have a scene? I sincerely hoped not.

"Have you seen Georgina?" I asked Milo. "Or Mr. Holloway or Miss Bell?"

"Not recently, no."

"I do hope everything's all right," I said.

"I'm sure it is, darling," he said. "You're just on edge because of the letters."

"That may be, but I still need to find Georgina," I said.

"I'll wander around a bit and send her your way if I see her," Milo said. I knew what the result of his restless wandering would be: liquor and friendly conversations with the prettiest women in the room. I had no great objections, however, as long as he wandered back to me at the end of the evening.

We parted ways then, and I began my search for Georgina. Thinking she might have stepped out to bid some of her guests adieu, I went out into the building's foyer.

There was no sign of Georgina, but there was a familiar figure near the cloakroom. The Holloways having thought of everything, the furs and hats had been transferred from the theatre. It seemed Balthazar Lebeau was preparing to make his exit, for he was talking to the hat check girl, leaning toward her, a smile on his face as he spoke to her in a low voice.

His efforts were apparently not in vain, for the pretty girl was laughing at something he said, her cheeks flushed.

I hated to interrupt, but I felt that it might be my only chance to speak with him.

"Mr. Lebeau," I called.

He turned at the sound of his name, a smile coming instantly to his lips. I had the sensation that the smile had less to do with how he felt about me than the habit of presenting his customary persona to the world. He draped a black cape across his broad shoulders with a flourish and moved toward me.

"Mrs. Ames," he said pleasantly, taking my hand and bowing over it. "How lovely you look this evening."

"Thank you. Are you leaving the gala so soon?"

"Unfortunately, yes. I have an appointment for drinks with a noted producer. There may be another play in my future, a better one than this."

I thought it odd that he had made such an appointment on the night of the gala, but I didn't know how such things worked. Perhaps the producer had limited time to spare.

"I won't keep you, then," I said. "I just wanted to tell you how much I enjoyed your performance tonight. You were wonderful."

"Thank you, my dear," he said, his tone tinged with the faintest trace of regret. "It is not, by any means, the greatest of my roles, but I do hope that I can bring a bit of light to a darkened stage, breathe a bit of life into lifeless lines."

"You don't like the play?" I asked. I didn't know how much he would want to confide in me, but it didn't hurt to try.

"It's not the fault of the play," he said, which was not exactly a direct answer. "It's just that my talents exceed the part I have been given."

One could not accuse him of false modesty. One could not, in fact, accuse him of any modesty at all.

"I think it's a very crucial role," I said, though I knew he had coveted Christopher Landon's part. "After all, there is a certain amount of importance that hinges upon your character. It is only through his treacherous actions that we see the nobility of Armand and the strength of Victoire."

It was the wrong thing to say. He drew himself up. "I have performed for kings, Mrs. Ames. I was not meant to be a member of the supporting cast."

I had heard rumors about Balthazar Lebeau, about his unruliness, his penchant for drink, his personal scandals. All things considered, I thought it generous of Gerard Holloway to ask him to be in the play.

That was not to say, of course, that Balthazar Lebeau was not talented. He was.

What I had said had not been empty flattery. There was an elegant ease he had on the stage, a naturalness that was curiously at odds with the affected persona he presented face-to-face. It was almost as though the stage was his real life and everything else was the act.

"I have very much admired your illustrious career," I said sincerely. "But I suppose there is always room for new talent. Flora Bell and Mr. Landon were wonderful; perhaps they will follow in your footsteps and become the next stars of British theatre."

The words had a curious effect. His expression went blank, as though his features could no longer support the amiable mask he had been wearing. His eyes, which thus far had always seemed to exude a lazy amicability, were suddenly sharp and hard.

"A star of the British theatre?"

He stepped closer, and I fought the urge to step back. It wasn't that it was a threatening gesture. It was just that something in his posture and expression were so different from the Balthazar Lebeau I had met that it was like being advanced upon by a stranger.

"The lesser talents of the world will come and go," he said in a rough voice that had lost all the luster of oration. "But true artists will stand immortal."

Then, instantly, the mask was back on, and he smiled. "Goodnight, Mrs. Ames."

"Good night, Mr. Lebeau," I murmured.

It was not until he turned and walked away, his evening cape fluttering behind him, that I realized I had been holding my breath.

9

Still unable to locate Georgina, I wandered back into the ballroom and immediately encountered Christopher Landon. He seemed well into his cups, for his eyes were bright, his handsome face flushed.

"Good evening, Mr. Landon," I said.

"Good evening," he replied.

"Allow me to congratulate you on an excellent performance. I enjoyed the play immensely."

"Thank you," he said.

"I wonder if you've seen Miss Bell?" I asked casually. "I have been wanting to congratulate her too."

"I haven't seen her since after the performance," he said. "We all came in together and then she disappeared. Perhaps you might ask Holloway where she went." There was a certain bitterness in his tone that he made no effort to hide.

"I don't seem to be able to find him either."

An expression of contempt crossed his features. "Then they've probably sneaked off together. It seems just the sort of vulgar thing Holloway might do."

It did not, in fact, seem at all like something the Gerard Holloway I knew might do, but it was so difficult to tell as of late what sort of behavior he might have adopted.

"I assume he's trying to woo her back after that row they had," Mr. Landon went on.

"A row?" I asked. It seemed he was inclined to gossip, and I certainly had no objection.

"Yes, they were shouting quite loudly at each other just minutes after the play ended."

"I wonder what they might have had to quarrel about," I said innocently.

He smiled, his eyes hard. "I don't know, but Gerard threatened to wring her neck, and there was something smashed in her dressing room before she came out."

I was surprised at this newest bit of information. I wondered what it was that had come between Mr. Holloway and Miss Bell. Certainly, nothing about the performance had seemed amiss. Perhaps it was to do with Georgina.

"There are some empty rooms along that corridor if you want to go and look for them," he said, as though remembering my original objective. He nodded in the direction of a door at the side of the room. I had seen people slipping in and out of it all evening, mostly waiters and the like, and had assumed that it led toward the kitchen facilities. That part of the building had no doubt housed the cooking, preparation, and storage areas when the building had been a restaurant.

"I suppose Mrs. Holloway might be there as well," I mused aloud, knowing Georgina had been known to oversee every aspect of her events. Her attention to detail was well known and she had never been one to shy away from wading into the minutiae.

He shrugged. "She might be."

Without another word, he wandered away. If the empty glass in his hand and the thirsty gleam in his eye were any indication, he had gone in search of additional refreshment.

I glanced over at the doorway to which he had pointed. There was no guarantee, of course, that I would find the Holloways or Miss Bell beyond it, but it wouldn't hurt to look.

Just then I caught a flash of orange and saw that Georgina was in the doorway. I waved to her and she lifted a hand in response.

I made my way across the room toward her, skirting the dance floor. The musicians had apparently indulged in drink as well, for they were playing at an almost frantic pace and the dancers were doing their best to keep up. When I looked back at the door, Georgina was no longer there. Something must have called her away.

Once through the door, I found myself in a hallway that seemed to run the length of the building along the side closest to the theatre. I saw several members of the kitchen staff moving about at one end and assumed it must be the kitchen. I went there, dodging waiters with heavy-laden trays and a woman carrying a gigantic flower arrangement.

"Can I help you, madam?" a harried-looking young woman in an apron asked.

"I'm looking for Mrs. Holloway."

"She's not here," she said, wiping the back of her arm across her flushed face. "She left a moment ago."

"Thank you."

I knew Georgina had not gone back out into the ballroom, so I moved down the hallway in the other direction. I had not gone far when I heard the sound of voices coming from one of the rooms. As reluctant as I was to eavesdrop, I couldn't help but hear what was being said.

"I don't care. I've had enough, Gerard. Or shall I call you 'Gerry'?" It was Georgina Holloway, her voice brimming with anger.

"Georgina, darling, do try to be reasonable."

"Don't say that to me again!" she said. "I am being perfectly reasonable. It's you who are making a fool of yourself."

I stilled. It was as I had suspected. Georgina and Mr. Holloway were having a confrontation. I knew that I should leave to give them their privacy, but I couldn't resist waiting just a moment to see if Miss Bell's voice joined the conversation.

"I saw the way you were running around after her, as though you were a lost puppy," Georgina said coolly, her voice full of disdain.

"I did no such thing," he replied tightly.

"If you love her, then you might as well make a clean break of it," she said.

"I . . . Georgina, let's not do this now."

"I thought you loved me," she said, her voice calm yet full of heartbreak. "I thought we would go on being happy forever. And then all it took was this girl to . . ."

"Georgina, you must stop this now," he said, his voice rising slightly. "This is neither the time nor the place . . ."

I felt that it was time that I stopped listening, and slowly eased away from the door and back down the hallway, out into the ballroom. I was saddened by what I had heard. It seemed to me that there was very little hope of a reconciliation now.

I went back to the ballroom and found that Milo had been drawn into conversation with a young woman in a plunging evening gown of lavender satin. Not wishing to spoil his fun, I took a canapé from a passing tray and nibbled on it as I made my way around the room. A moment later, a gentleman asked me to dance and I accepted. If I was going to wait for Georgina to emerge, I might as well dance while doing it. Mercifully, the musicians seemed to have worn off some of their earlier energy and were playing at a more subdued pace.

As I danced, I looked across the room and was surprised to see Freddy Bell standing near the doorway. I thought he had left the theatre, but I supposed he had come back for the party.

He was standing alone, his brown suit in

striking contrast to the evening dress the other gentlemen wore.

When the song concluded, I thanked my partner and moved toward Flora's brother.

"Good evening, Mr. Bell," I said when I reached him.

He had been lost in thought and seemed surprised when I addressed him.

"Good evening. Mrs. . . . Ames, isn't it?"

"Yes. Your sister said she doesn't like you to stay for her performances, but I want to tell you that she was wonderful."

"She always is," he said, and, despite their disagreement earlier in the evening, there was a sincerity in his words. "I . . . I wonder if you've seen her anywhere about?"

"No, not recently," I said. "In fact, I was hoping to find her and tell her how marvelous she was."

"She's probably off with Holloway," he said darkly, echoing Mr. Landon's sentiments.

"You don't care for Mr. Holloway then," I said lightly.

"He's a rotter," he said succinctly.

"Oh," I said vaguely, hoping he would elaborate.

"It's hard, of course, to make women understand that sort of thing."

I was about to give him my opinion on

this when I spotted Mr. Holloway coming out of the corridor. Georgina was not with him. I had wanted to speak with her, and I somehow felt that she might need a friend even more now that she had had it out with her husband.

"If you'll excuse me, Mr. Bell," I said.

"Certainly," he said. "I'm on my way out. I've had enough for one evening."

I left him and made my way to Mr. Holloway's side.

"Ah, Mrs. Ames," he said, smiling, though his expression was strained and his eyes unnaturally bright, as though he was suppressing some strong emotion. "Are you enjoying the party?"

"Yes," I said. "Though perhaps not quite as much as Milo."

Mr. Holloway's gaze followed mine to where Milo sat at a table with three women, all of them apparently having a marvelous time.

The strained smile remained fixed on his face. "Well, Ames has always known how to enjoy himself."

"Yes. I was hoping, however, to congratulate Georgina on tonight's success. Would you happen to know where she is?"

I asked the question innocently enough, but he became flustered. "I . . . I crossed paths with her a short while ago," he said. "I'm not sure where she is now, however."

He glanced around the room, though it was perfectly apparent that Georgina was not there.

"Maybe she went out to take some air," I suggested. I had been engrossed in my dance and then in conversation with Mr. Bell, so it was possible that Georgina had slipped past me.

"Yes, maybe she did. Or she might have gone to the theatre," he added almost absently.

"The theatre?"

I thought that strange, considering she had made it a point to avoid the place all evening. Mr. Holloway seemed to have guessed what I was thinking, for he sighed, a look of resignation crossing his features.

He leaned toward me ever so slightly, lowering his voice, though I didn't think he would be overheard among the din of conversation and the lively music the orchestra was playing. "We had a bit of a row, I'm afraid."

"Oh," I said, feigning ignorance. "I'm sorry."

He shrugged. "I'm afraid this whole thing wasn't a very good idea. I . . . I've made rather a mess of things."

I didn't disagree with him.

"Georgina was . . . well, crying, and wanted to freshen up her makeup, but I don't think she wanted to use the powder room here, you understand."

I certainly did. It wouldn't do at all for the hostess of this elaborate gala to be seen crying in the powder room while rumors flew about her husband and his protégée.

"She has a key to the theatre and knows it will be private there."

"Perhaps I should go and look for her," I said.

"Would you?" he asked quickly, relief crossing his features. "I'd like to go myself, but I don't think she cares to see me at the moment."

"Of course," I said. "I'd be happy to go. What's the best way to access the theatre?"

"It will all be locked up now, but you can take my key." He reached into his pocket and fished out a brass key. "It fits the lock in the front door."

"Thank you," I said, taking it from him.

"Thank you, Mrs. Ames. I . . ." He hesitated, as though there was something he wanted to say but didn't know how to put into words. At last he sighed. "I appreciate your looking after her. I'll let Ames know where you've gone."

"Very well." I somehow doubted, however, that Milo would even notice my absence.

"I . . ." He hesitated again, and I noticed his eyes moving around the room. "I don't suppose you know where Miss Bell is?"

"No, I'm afraid not," I said coolly.

"I suppose she's gone off to speak with that brother of hers," he said irritably. "I saw him hanging about after the performance."

I glanced to where I had been speaking with Freddy Bell, but he had disappeared.

"If you see her outside, will you let her know that I've been looking for her?"

I nodded and turned away, quite cross with him that he should have brought her up.

I could tell from the way he had spoken about Georgina that he still cared about her, but he was too enamored with the charms of Miss Bell to realize it. If he had any sense he would find his wife, make amends, and forget all about the young actress.

I did not see Miss Bell outside. I saw no one, in fact. It seemed that all the party-goers were still enjoying the gala. I walked the few steps to the theatre, and inserted the key into the lock.

The door opened and I stepped into the

lobby, closing it behind me. It was strange how different it was in the building now from how it had been only hours before. All was still and quiet. I felt the faintest hint of uneasiness, though I couldn't say why. Perhaps it was just the contrast to the loud liveliness of the party I had just left. I half wished I had told Milo to accompany me, but if I did find Georgina it would probably be best that we spoke alone. After all, Mr. Holloway had said she had been crying, and I suspected she would still be upset.

It was very dark inside the building, for all the lights had been extinguished, save for one that glowed dimly from inside the auditorium. The ghost light, I had heard it called, a single light that always illuminated the stage.

I remembered that the powder room was to my right as I entered, and I went that way in the darkness.

"Georgina?" I called, pushing open the door. It was dark inside. Then perhaps she had gone to one of the dressing rooms. What better place to fix her makeup, after all?

I crossed the lobby and went into the auditorium. The quickest way to the dressing rooms, I recalled, was to go up onstage and into the corridor beyond. I moved along the main aisle in the dim light, my footsteps muted by the thick carpeting.

I was not ordinarily afraid of the dark, but there was something uncomfortable about the shadowy stillness of the building. It felt empty, and I somehow doubted that Georgina was here. I almost turned around before deciding I might as well see it through.

"Hello? Georgina?" I called, hoping she would hear me and make her presence known. "Are you here?"

I thought that I detected a faint movement, but when I stilled to listen there was silence. Perhaps it was only my imagination.

I reached the stage and walked up the little flight of steps.

Again, I thought I heard a soft movement. I turned around and looked out at the rows of seats. The theater was dark and quiet. It was eerie being in an empty room that was designed to be filled with people. The silence, here in a place of words and music and applause, felt unnatural. I do not consider myself at all superstitious, but I felt as if I were not alone.

I turned to make my way to the dressing room and started.

Flora Bell was standing there in the shadows near one of the curtains that framed the stage.

"Oh! You gave me a start," I said.

No wonder I had felt as though I was not alone. The actress stood perhaps ten feet from me. At least, I assumed it was she. Her back was to me, but she had on the white satin gown she had worn to the gala. It briefly crossed my mind that it was strange she had not made her presence known or turned at the sound of my voice. But her head was bowed, and I thought perhaps she was crying and didn't want me to see, for it seemed as though she shifted ever so slightly, almost indiscernibly.

"Excuse me," I said. "I didn't mean to disturb you, Miss Bell."

She didn't respond, and I stepped closer. I saw then that she was not standing near the curtain, but leaning against it, her face buried in its scarlet folds.

"Miss Bell, are you all right?"

She still didn't answer, didn't even lift her head.

I could tell something must be very wrong. I glanced over my shoulder, wondering if Georgina Holloway was somewhere about. Perhaps they had had a row over Mr. Holloway.

"Miss Bell, is there anything I can do?" I asked, reaching her and putting my hand on her shoulder.

She swayed and then turned to face me, and I stumbled back with a gasp of horror.

She was dead, her beautiful face an ugly shade of purple, the gold curtain rope wrapped tightly around her neck.

10

I had, over the past year, encountered more than my fair share of dead bodies. Indeed, I had encountered more than any woman of my situation might reasonably be expected to encounter in a lifetime. And yet I found myself just as shaken this time as I had been the first.

There was no coherent thought in my head at that moment, just the urge to flee. I rushed from the stage, nearly tripping down the stairs, and ran down the aisle, my breath caught in my throat, my stomach clenched in fear and revulsion.

Bursting through the front doors of the theatre and onto the pavement, I stumbled and had to right myself. One hand against the building, I closed my eyes and forced myself to breathe deeply of the cool evening air. My thoughts cleared ever so slightly, though my hands were shaking.

I didn't know how I was going to go back

to the gala without making a scene, for one look at my face would likely be enough to alert everyone in the place that something was terribly wrong. The silly idea that I hated to ruin Georgina's party flittered across my mind before I reminded myself that the gala was now the least of our worries.

Drawing in a steadying breath, I moved toward the building where the gala was still being held. I could hear the music and laughter from here and they were jarring sounds against the backdrop of what had just happened. I had nearly reached the door when I caught sight of Milo walking toward me and gave a little sigh of relief.

"What's the matter?" Milo asked as soon as he saw me.

"It's . . . it's Flora Bell," I said. "She's dead. On the stage. She . . ." I broke off, unable to put into words at the moment what I had seen.

"Stay here. I'll be right back," he said.

"But . . ."

"Stay here."

He moved past me and disappeared into the theatre while I waited outside, drawing in great lungfuls of the cool evening air. I liked to think of myself as a capable woman in a crisis, but something about this situation had been so shocking that I could not seem to make myself focus. I tried to draw some sort of conclusion about what had happened, but I was still shaking and the only words that would come to my head repeated themselves over and over again: *Poor Flora Bell. Poor Flora Bell.*

A few minutes later Milo came out, his expression grim.

"I found a telephone inside and rang the police," he said.

"Do you think we should go and find Mr. Holloway?" I asked, my stomach knotting tighter at the thought. What would he do when he found out Flora Bell was dead?

"We'll let the police do that."

"Oh, Milo, this is terrible."

He pulled me to him and embraced me, one hand rubbing my back soothingly. "I know, darling."

We stood like that for just a moment, my head pressed against his chest. It was reassuring to know that, whatever this evening had in store, I would not have to go through it alone. I was immeasurably glad that I could take refuge in his arms.

A few people took their leave from the party, and I supposed they thought us just another amorous couple seeking a moment of privacy in the darkness outside a crowded event.

I could only imagine the tumult this news was going to cause at the gala. But perhaps the police would be discreet. It would be better that way, I thought. To keep things quiet for as long as possible.

Milo and I stood for what seemed a long time out on the now-quiet street. I could still hear the music drifting from the building next door, and I was glad that no one had yet raised the alarm. It would be better, too, I thought, for the suspects to remain where they were.

"I'd say it was a pleasure to see you again," said a familiar voice. "But under the circumstances I don't think it would be appropriate."

I looked up to see Detective Inspector Jones walking toward me as if from out of the shadows.

He stopped before us.

"Mr. and Mrs. Ames. I shouldn't be surprised, and yet I find myself somewhat startled to see you here," he said.

"Hello, Inspector," I said with a sigh.

"You've stumbled upon another body, I hear," he said.

"Inspector, might we dispense with the pleasantries until Amory's had a chance to collect herself," Milo said, his tone just short of polite. "It's been rather a shock."

Inspector Jones looked at Milo with his calm, steady gaze. "I can appreciate that, Mr. Ames, but I'm sure you can appreciate that time is often of the essence in these cases."

"It's all right, Milo," I said, my hand on his arm. "I'm all right."

"I need to go inside for a few moments," Inspector Jones said. "Perhaps you can wait for me somewhere?"

I nodded. As long as I didn't have to go inside the theatre. I imagined she was still there, hanging limply from that curtain rope, the gold tassel suspended against her chest like some ghastly lavaliere, that grotesque expression frozen on her face. My stomach turned.

"Do you want to go back inside?" Milo asked, and I knew he meant the building next door. However, I couldn't imagine going back into the gala, either. I couldn't pretend that everything was all right. I was sure my face must be white.

"No," I said. "Let's stay out here."

"All right."

Inspector Jones nodded at us and went into the theatre, followed by several uniformed policemen, and a man in a suit who

I assumed must be a doctor.

I leaned into Milo again, relishing his warmth, as I was suddenly very cold. I was glad for his arm around me, for the support, both physical and emotional.

Though I tried not to think about what I had just witnessed, in the back of my mind, I could feel the wheels beginning to turn as questions began to form. Who had had access to the theatre? Who had been away from the gala?

"I couldn't vouch for anyone's whereabouts tonight," Milo said, echoing my thoughts. "Everyone was moving around so much."

I nodded. "Perhaps if they can determine how long she's been . . ." I stopped, that sick feeling coming again. It was almost unbelievable that she was actually dead. That lovely, vibrant, talented woman who had electrified the audience with her performance only hours before was gone forever.

A few moments later, one of the policemen stepped outside. "Inspector Jones would like you to come in," he said.

"You don't have to if you don't want to," Milo told me.

"It's all right," I said, mustering up my resolve. If we were to find Flora Bell's killer, I was going to have to face the facts.

We went through the front doors and the policeman closed them firmly behind us. The theatre was no longer dark. In fact, it seemed as though every light in the place had been thrown on, every corner of it illuminated.

Though I didn't want to, I couldn't help myself: I glanced up at the stage. Mercifully, Miss Bell's body had been removed. Inspector Jones stood in the spot where she had died, examining the curtain rope that had been tied around her neck.

"Have a seat, Mr. and Mrs. Ames," he called as we came in. "I'll be with you in a moment."

Milo and I moved into a row of seats in the back of the theatre and sat down, Milo's hand taking mine. I hadn't realized how weak my legs were until I felt the rush of relief at being able to sit.

I watched Inspector Jones as he moved around the stage, occasionally stopping to jot things in his familiar and ever-present notebook. I wondered idly if he had a stock of them somewhere, just waiting to be filled with notes about murders. Did he keep them when he was done or toss them away once the case had been solved?

Despite everything that had happened tonight, I was intrigued by his processes.

There was something in the calm and methodical way he moved around the scene of the crime that soothed me.

After a few more moments, he came down from the stage and joined us where we sat.

A thought occurred to me suddenly. "What a lucky coincidence it was you who was sent to us," I said.

"It wasn't a coincidence," he said. "Mr. Ames asked for me specifically."

I glanced at Milo, a bit surprised. I knew that he and Inspector Jones did not have the warmest relationship. Then again, as Milo surely realized, Inspector Jones had always been exceedingly efficient and fair-minded. I realized how exceptionally relieved I was that he was here.

"I know this has been upsetting, Mrs. Ames," he went on, "but I'm afraid I'm going to have to ask you a few questions."

I nodded. I had been prepared for this. It was, after all, not the first time I had been in such a situation. Again I thought how glad I was that Inspector Jones would be the one to do the interview. It would have been trying and wearisome to relate this story to a stone-faced stranger barking brusque queries in my direction.

"Why don't we start at the beginning," he said. "How was it that you happened to be here tonight?"

"Gerard Holloway is an old friend," Milo said. "We purchased a box for the performance, as the event was to benefit a charity. The gala next door was held afterward."

"And so, to use Mrs. Ames's term, it's just coincidence that you happened to be here," Inspector Jones pressed. I might have known that he would suspect there was more to it than that. Of course, I had to admit that it might be conceived as strange that Milo and I ended up at the scene of so many murders.

"It isn't exactly a coincidence that we were here either," I admitted.

He waited.

"Tell him about the letters," I told Milo.

"Letters?" Inspector Jones inquired expectantly.

"Yes, it seems that Flora Bell had been receiving some threatening letters," Milo said. He related the details as they had unfolded. As he spoke, I contemplated the significance of those letters. They had seemed like idle threats, something meant to frighten. I had had no idea that they would lead to something like this. I realized now that, even in my uneasiness, I had not really thought that Miss Bell's life was in danger. How stupid it was to have underestimated the menace in those anonymous missives.

"Did Mr. Holloway notify the police?" Inspector Jones asked when Milo had finished.

"I don't believe so," Milo said. "Miss Bell was opposed to the idea."

I couldn't help but wonder if things might have ended differently if we had.

"I wanted to notify you," I said, looking up at Inspector Jones. "I suggested to her that I might ring you up and tell you about it, but she wouldn't let me."

As I spoke the words, I realized that I felt guilty that I had been convinced not to contact him. If I had, perhaps none of this would have happened.

Inspector Jones seemed to realize what I was thinking, for when he spoke, his voice had taken on a gentle note that I had seldom heard there. "It was her decision, Mrs. Ames. If she didn't want you to contact the police, you had little choice but to respect her wishes."

"But if I had told you . . ."

"I might have come to the play," he said. "But then I would have been in the gala with the rest of you. Apparently, she slipped away from the party and very few people seemed to have noticed."

"Except for the killer," I said.

147

"Did Mr. Holloway or Miss Bell say who they thought might be behind the letters?"

"No, they didn't know. Although, there seem to be several people that might have had motive to send them."

"That's very interesting. We'll come back to that," he said. "In the meantime, do you know where these notes are now?"

"I think Holloway must have them," Milo said.

He nodded. "I'll ask him. Now, Mrs. Ames, if you'll relate to me how it was that you came to discover the body."

I drew in a slow breath, dreading reliving it all, but knowing that I must.

"Georgina — Mrs. Holloway — had told me earlier in the evening that she wished to speak with me before I left, but when it came time to leave, I couldn't find her. It was Mr. Holloway who mentioned that she might be in the theatre."

"Then Mr. Holloway was the one who suggested you come here."

"Yes."

He made no comment, but jotted something down.

"And how did you get into the theatre?" he asked.

"Through the front entrance. Mr. Holloway gave me his key," I said.

"Did you see anyone?"

"No. Everything was very quiet when I came in, but I supposed Georgina might still be there somewhere."

"Then what?"

"It was very dark, and I didn't know how to turn on the lights, so I made my way toward the stage. There was a little light, and I was trying to reach the corridor where the dressing rooms are located."

"You thought it advisable to venture into the dark auditorium alone?" he asked.

"It didn't cross my mind that anything like this would have happened," I replied, a bit defensively. After all, I had certainly not thought that Miss Bell would be murdered. I had been so unsuspecting. It seemed almost ridiculous now that I had ventured into the dark building and onto the stage without a thought. In all likelihood, the killer might still have been in the building, perhaps even watching me. I shuddered, and Milo squeezed my hand.

"What made you come out onto the stage?" Inspector Jones asked.

"It's the quickest way back to the dressing rooms. I thought Mrs. Holloway might be there, freshening up her makeup."

"And did you see or hear anything unusual?"

I frowned, considering. That was an excellent question. I thought back. My mind had been all in a jumble, but now the vaguest memory was beginning to surface. "I think I heard something," I said. "The smallest bit of movement."

Inspector Jones watched me, waiting.

I realized, with sudden horror, that it might have been the sound of Flora Bell's body swaying on its rope. But no. It had been more than that.

"Now that I think about it," I said at last, "I think perhaps there was someone else here. I thought, just now, that it might have been Miss Bell . . . but it couldn't have been. She . . . appeared to have been dead for some time when I found her."

"I know it might be difficult, but would you come up onto the stage and show me how it was that you came across her?"

I nodded, my throat tight.

We all rose and walked to the front of the theatre, taking the little set of steps up to the stage. Milo's hand never left my arm.

"I came up here," I said, pointing to the way I had gone up to the stage. "I didn't see her right away. And when I did, at first I thought . . . that she was just standing on the stage. It took me a moment to realize . . ."

He jotted down a note, then looked up, his brown eyes on my face. "When you first saw the body, did you have any sort of impression as to how it might have happened?"

"An accident or some such thing, do you mean?" I replied. I shook my head slowly. "There was no way it could have been. The cord was . . . knotted tightly. It was done deliberately."

He nodded. I wondered if it had been a test of my observational powers. If so, it seemed that I had passed it.

"You saw nothing else?" he asked.

I shook my head. "After I realized what had happened, I hurried out."

"And you saw no one nearby?"

"No. The first person I encountered was Milo."

"What were you doing outside, Mr. Ames?" he asked.

"Holloway told me that Amory had gone in search of his wife, so I came to look for her."

"I see. And did either of you notice when Miss Bell left the gala?"

I thought back. I hadn't been paying particular attention to her whereabouts.

"No," I said. "I . . . don't know. I didn't notice."

151

"Nor did I," Milo said.

Inspector Jones nodded. "Well, thank you. I know this was unpleasant, Mrs. Ames, but you've been most helpful. We'll see to the others now. It's likely to be a long night, but I don't think you need stay any longer."

"Has . . . has someone told Mr. Holloway?" I asked.

"Yes." Something in the way he said the single word let me know that Mr. Holloway had not taken the news well.

"Is someone with him?" I asked.

"There's an officer with him," Inspector Jones said. "I'm going to have a word with him next. Since you found her, I thought I would talk to you first. Besides, we do have a bit of a history, don't we?" He offered me the barest hint of a smile, and I felt a sense of relief, almost comfort, as though I had laid a heavy burden in his hands.

He turned to Milo. "Perhaps you'd better take her home now, Mr. Ames."

I did not miss the shared look between Milo and the inspector, and I felt a glimmer of irritation. I did not want to be coddled. Discovering the body had given me a start, yes, but I was not going to faint or fall into hysterics, and I did not need to be treated as though I might.

"I'm all right," I said firmly, though, to

152

my annoyance, my voice wobbled ever so slightly when I said it, undermining the words.

"Certainly you are. You're a very strong woman," Inspector Jones said. "But I think you've told me all I need to know for tonight. Why don't you let Mr. Ames take you home and we can discuss this more at a later time."

I nodded. I wanted to protest, to tell him that we could discuss it all he liked now, but the truth was that I felt horrible, the surge of shock and fear having abandoned me to a trembling I couldn't seem to overcome. I would be glad to go home, though I knew I would not be able to stop thinking about what I had seen tonight.

The words came to me again. Poor Flora Bell.

I felt tired and very shaken when I returned home. Milo told Winnelda to make tea and then took the tray from her in the doorway to our bedroom, preventing her from asking questions. I knew she must be concerned, but she had witnessed, in her short time in my service, enough of the aftermath of violent tragedy to know that Milo would be able to take things well in hand.

Milo poured my cup of tea, stirred in

sugar, and brought the saucer to where I sat on the edge of the bed. I had changed from my evening gown into a comfortable nightdress of gray silk, but I hadn't been able to bring myself to lie down. I knew I would not yet be able to rest.

I took the teacup, glad to see that the residual shaking had subsided and my hands were steady.

Milo sat next to me, his eyes searching my face. "Are you all right, darling?" he asked.

"Yes," I said softly. "It was just so awful."

"You've rather rotten luck when it comes to this sort of thing," he said.

"I suppose it's my own fault for pursuing matters of this nature, but I did so want to help. I thought that we would be able to do some good. She needed help and . . ." I stopped rubbing a hand across my face, the weight of guilt suddenly very heavy. "I feel so terrible."

"It's not your fault, darling. We couldn't have known that something like this would happen."

"But if we had taken the letters seriously . . ."

"We did. It was Miss Bell who didn't," he said. "There's nothing that we could have done. And there's no changing it now that it's happened. The only thing to do is move forward."

I nodded miserably, taking a sip of the scalding tea.

"People will say it was Gerard Holloway," I said suddenly. "They apparently quarreled after the performance. Mr. Landon told me about it, said that everyone heard them."

"A quarrel isn't conclusive proof of anything."

"No, but . . ." I gasped, suddenly remembering Mr. Landon's words. "He said that Mr. Holloway threatened to wring Miss Bell's neck." I felt a surge of queasiness at how close that description was to the way she had died.

"It's not an unusual phrase," Milo said.

"But when one considers how she was killed . . ."

"What were they quarreling about?"

"Mr. Landon didn't know. Even if it was something trivial, I suppose it will be looked upon as a motive. I'm concerned for Mr. Holloway."

"For that matter, he might have done it," Milo said.

I looked up, surprised. "You don't really believe that?"

He shrugged. "If I've learned anything this past year, it's that it's very difficult to tell who might be a killer."

That was very true. One just never knew. I found it difficult to believe, however, that Gerard Holloway might have killed the woman with whom he seemed so enamored. Then again, a great many murders had been committed in the heat of passion.

A second thought occurred to me. The police might also believe it was Georgina. There was a good deal of talk about the rift Flora Bell had caused in the Holloways' marriage. Though it seemed that strangulation was a brutal way to kill someone, it would not have been difficult for a woman to accomplish, I supposed. One would have only had to wrap the cord around tightly and then hang on.

I shuddered.

"Why don't you try to sleep, darling. You'll feel better if you get some rest."

"I doubt I'll be able to," I said, but I set aside the cup and saucer on the bedside table and rose to turn down the blankets. Milo went around to his side and we got into bed.

"There's something I think we should discuss," Milo said, when we were settled.

I turned my head on the pillow to look at him as he turned to me, his dark head propped up on his hand.

"What is it?"

"I know how that brain of yours works," he said. "I know you're already running through the list of suspects and trying to determine a way in which we might catch the killer."

"Of course," I said. "I feel as though we have an obligation to Flora Bell."

"That's debatable, but I know you feel strongly about it, and I'm not going to ask you to keep out of this."

I was surprised. I had expected protests from Milo, not this easy acceptance.

"I know you won't let it drop anyway, no matter what I say," he said. "But if we are going to look into this matter, we'll do it together. I won't have you putting yourself in danger."

I nodded. "I'd much rather do it together anyway." We had always been better as a team.

"I don't want you to do anything foolish," he went on, "and I insist upon your telling me everything that you learn."

"Then I shall expect the same of you," I said.

"Very well."

"I feel as though we should shake hands," I said with a laugh.

"I've a better idea," he said, leaning forward to kiss me gently on the lips.

We settled into bed then, though I knew I would have a hard time sleeping. At least one difficulty had been cleared up. I had suspected Milo would try to keep me out of this, as he always did when we were faced with a mystery. It was a relief that he had agreed that we should look into it. But I realized my way was not completely clear.

Milo was only the first obstacle. Detective Inspector Jones was the next.

11

As it turned out, I would not have long to wait for Detective Inspector Jones to call.

I was feeling somewhat better when I rose the next morning. The haziness of shock had worn away, and I was ready to face the day. I felt a sense of renewed purpose this morning. We had not been able to keep Flora Bell from being harmed, but we could bring her killer to justice.

I found Milo in the sitting room, drinking coffee and reading the newspaper. He had already risen and dressed by the time I awakened, an unusual turn of events, as I was normally a much earlier riser than he was.

He looked up as I came into the room. "Good morning, darling," he said, setting the paper aside. "How do you feel this morning?"

"Much better," I said. At any rate, I felt much more composed than I had last night.

His eyes searched my face, as if to be sure I was telling the truth. Apparently, he was satisfied with what he saw. "I'm glad to hear it."

"Anything of interest?" I asked, nodding toward the paper.

"The usual headlines: 'Charity Gala Ends in Murder,' 'West End Killer At Large,' that sort of thing," he said. "There's a lot of rumor and speculation. The accounts of anonymous members of the audience, sly rumors voiced by 'a person in a position to know.' You can imagine what a boon a thing like this is to the newspaper industry."

I grimaced. I certainly could. No doubt all of London was poring over every sordid detail this morning.

"Have you spoken to Mr. Holloway?" I asked.

"Not yet," he said. "I thought I would go over and see him later today."

"I hope he's all right."

"I'm sure he'll bear up."

I looked at him, caught by something in his tone. "You don't sound as though you pity him."

"Holloway is not the type of man who wants pity," he replied. "In any event, pity doesn't do any good."

He was right, of course, but I still felt

sorry for Gerard Holloway. I hadn't approved of his relationship with Flora Bell, but I could sympathize with his loss all the same.

My thoughts turned to Georgina. She had been through so much scandal as of late, and now this. I wondered what she was thinking about it all. I would need to go and see her, though I hated to intrude at such a difficult time. I didn't want her to think I was trying to pry into her private affairs, though I supposed, in a sense, that's exactly what I was doing.

Another thought occurred to me then. "What's going to happen to the play?" I asked.

"I don't know," Milo replied. "Holloway's invested a lot of money in it, so they may keep it going once things are settled. They've got an understudy waiting in the wings, after all."

Our eyes met, his words taking on a new significance in light of the murder. It was a thin motive, perhaps, but a motive nonetheless.

"Excuse me, sir, madam," Winnelda said, coming into the sitting room.

"Yes, what is it?" Milo asked.

"That policeman is here," she said with the faintest hint of disdain. Winnelda did

161

not approve of my association with Detective Inspector Jones, no doubt because she secretly suspected he would, at any moment, try to take me off to prison for unknown crimes. Winnelda was very protective of me, which I thought quite sweet of her.

"Show him in, please," I said.

"Yes, madam."

A moment later, Inspector Jones came into the room. He wore a dark gray suit and, though I was sure he had had a very late night, he looked completely rested and composed. I thought how his outward appearance was always as tidy as his thoughts seemed to be.

"I'm sorry to disturb you so early," he said. "But I thought it best that we spoke again soon, while your memories of the event are still fresh."

"I'm afraid my memories of last night are not going to fade anytime soon," I said. I had had several unpleasant dreams, the details of which had, thankfully, faded away upon waking, but what I had witnessed last night seemed imprinted upon my brain.

"All the same, I'd like to ask you a few more questions." He paused almost imperceptibly. "And there is something else I'd like to discuss with you."

If his goal had been to pique my curiosity, he had succeeded.

"Please, have a seat," I said.

"Thank you." Though the chair closest to Milo was open, he moved to take one that sat near the fireplace. Always strategic in his movements, he had chosen a seat that would allow him to observe both Milo and me at the same time.

"Will you take some coffee?" I asked. I expected him to decline, for, though we had developed a mutually respectful relationship, he usually maintained an air of formality when he came to call that did not allow for social pleasantries. To my surprise, however, he accepted.

"That would be very nice. Thank you."

I nodded at Winnelda, who still stood in the doorway, and she went to fetch the coffee.

"You came to call more quickly than I thought you might," I said, turning back to Inspector Jones. "I imagine things were quite hectic after we left last night."

"Yes," he said. "We've discovered the window of time in which the murder was committed. Miss Bell was apparently seen by several people around midnight, so she died sometime between then and your discovery of the body, at around one o'clock."

I nodded. "Mr. Holloway gave a speech at midnight, and I noticed her then. But I don't know when she might have slipped out."

"Very few people seem to have noticed," he said. "You'd be surprised how little attention people pay to their surroundings."

This was disappointing. I had been sure that someone must have noticed her leave the gala. After all, she had been the star of the evening. I realized what he had not added, however, was that it had been quite late and there had been a good deal of drinking and revelry, a combination which was not known for sharpening perception.

"You mentioned wanting to discuss something?" I asked.

"Yes, but before we get into that, I wanted to ask you who you think might have killed Miss Bell."

I had not expected so straightforward a question. Did he already have someone in mind and was hoping for a confirmation?

"I don't imagine idle speculation will be of much help to you, Inspector," I said carefully. I had learned always to be on my guard with Inspector Jones. One never knew exactly what he was playing at. It was, I supposed, what made him such an excellent policeman.

I glanced at Milo, but his expression was unreadable.

"The fact remains that you are likely to know the killer," said Inspector Jones.

I wondered just how he had surmised this. It then occurred to me that he had already winnowed down the suspects.

"You've ascertained, then, that it wasn't a stranger," I said. "Could it have been one of the guests at the gala, someone unconnected with the play?"

"It seems unlikely," he said. "Only a few people had a key to the theatre, and, if the killer did not possess a key, he must have gone into the theatre with Miss Bell. So far as I've learned, no one at the gala but those involved in the play knew her personally."

That did seem to narrow the field.

"Why don't you tell me who you think it might have been and what you know about each of them?" Inspector Jones said, as usual asking for answers before giving any.

I hesitated. I did not want to cast aspersions upon anyone without proof, least of all my friends. "I'm really not sure . . ."

"Come now, Mrs. Ames. You don't expect me to believe that."

He was right; I didn't. If there was any man as difficult to deceive as Milo, it was

Detective Inspector Jones. He had a deceptively mild way of looking at one as he took in everything that was being said. Then somehow his brain parsed through it, and he knew with uncanny certainty what was truth and what was not. It was an extremely useful skill for a policeman to have, but it was not altogether comfortable to be on the receiving end of one of his searching gazes.

I sighed. I might as well tell him what I knew and be done with it. "There is Mr. Holloway, of course," I said.

"In addition to his involvement in the charity event, he also wrote and directed the play, I understand?"

I nodded. "He has a reputation for being very much involved in all aspects of the projects he takes on."

" 'All aspects' having taken on an additional meaning in this case," he said, and I realized that he was hinting at the relationship between Mr. Holloway and Flora Bell.

"So it seems," I replied. "He and Miss Bell were . . . quite close."

"They were having an affair," he said. I wondered who had revealed this to him. It hadn't exactly been a secret, so I imagined anyone might have mentioned it.

I nodded my confirmation, though I knew he didn't need it.

"Did they seem to be on good terms last night?"

"I . . . I'm not sure." I glanced at Milo. I did not want to implicate Mr. Holloway on the basis of hearsay.

Milo, however, seemed to have no such qualms. "Apparently, Holloway was overheard telling Miss Bell he'd like to wring her neck shortly after the performance," he said.

I was relieved that he was the one to have revealed this. After all, if Mr. Holloway was innocent, I hated to cause him any more grief than he was already feeling at the moment. Milo, however, had never been one to worry about people's feelings.

If Inspector Jones found this news surprising or alarming he gave no sign of it.

"And are love affairs of this sort usual behavior for Mr. Holloway?" he asked. I could never quite get used to the way he asked such probing questions with perfect ease. This conversation was not one I was entirely comfortable having, but I supposed there was no getting around it.

"I don't know Mr. Holloway well enough to say," I replied, glancing again toward Milo. "Perhaps my husband might better answer that question."

"Holloway and I are friendly, but he has

167

never been one to share confidences. I should have thought it unlikely, but one can never tell. However, I don't know of any other women in his past."

"Then this is an unusual occurrence."

"Before all this happened, I should have thought it impossible," I said.

"What do you mean?" Inspector Jones asked.

"I wouldn't have thought that Mr. Holloway would be . . . swept away by a woman like Flora Bell. By any woman, for that matter. He has always seemed to be very much in love with his wife."

"Ah, yes. Tell me about Mrs. Holloway."

"Georgina and I have known each other a long time," I said. "We're not exceptionally close, but I consider her a friend."

"Did she know about Mr. Holloway's relationship with Miss Bell, do you think?"

"Yes."

He looked up from his notebook, and I realized that I had spoken with absolute assurance. Now he was waiting for me to tell him how I knew this.

"I had tea with her a few days ago, and she discussed the matter with me."

I saw Milo shoot me a look, and I remembered that I had not told him about my visit to the Holloways' home.

"What did she say about it?" Inspector Jones asked.

I realized that, just as I had feared, Georgina Holloway might find herself the chief suspect. The woman scorned was, after all, the classic culprit.

"She wasn't happy, of course."

"Naturally," he replied.

I drew in a breath and told him the rest. "I heard her and Mr. Holloway arguing perhaps thirty minutes before I discovered the body. Georgina resented the fact that Flora Bell had ruined her marriage."

"And what did he say?"

"He said the gala wasn't the place to discuss it. But please know, Inspector, I don't believe Georgina Holloway would resort to murder."

"You know as well as I do, Mrs. Ames, that unlikely people have killed before this."

"It isn't just that," I protested. "I don't think Georgina is capable of murder, but if she was, I don't think that . . . strangulation would be the way she would do it. It's so ghastly."

"But it was shortly after this disagreement between Mr. and Mrs. Holloway that you went to look for Mrs. Holloway in the theatre?"

"Yes," I said. "Mr. Holloway came from

169

the corridor along the ballroom and said that Georgina had gone away crying."

"What time was this?"

"Shortly before I discovered the body. Perhaps a quarter or ten minutes to one. There was a space of several minutes after I overheard their conversation before Mr. Holloway reappeared."

"Could either of them have slipped out between Mr. Holloway's speech and the argument between him and his wife?"

I thought back. "It's possible, I suppose. If they did, however, I didn't notice it."

"Was there time enough between the argument you overheard and his reappearance for him to have gone to the theatre?"

"It would have been a small window of time, but not impossible. It would depend, I suppose, on how long the argument had continued." We had reached a nice rhythm in our questions and answers now, and I thought again what a skillful interrogator Inspector Jones was. His next question, however, gave me pause.

"But Mrs. Holloway would have had a bit more time after the argument, as you saw no sign of her, and Mr. Holloway said she was missing."

"Yes," I admitted, realizing what he was getting at.

"He told you she might have gone to the theatre, and you thought you heard movement in the auditorium, correct?"

"Yes," I said uneasily. It seemed Georgina looked guiltier by the moment.

He made no reply to this, but jotted something down in his notebook.

"Did you speak with Mrs. Holloway?" I asked, certain that if he had he would see that she was not capable of a crime like this.

"I did," he replied.

"What did you make of her?"

He looked up at me, his expression blank. "I'm not really at liberty to discuss that, Mrs. Ames."

"Oh, but you can tell me, unofficially, of course, what you make of her," I said with a smile. "Not what she had to say about the matter, but your impressions of her."

I wanted very much for Georgina's innocence to be quickly proven. I could not believe that she had taken part in this horrible crime, and it was going to be an added trial waiting to see if he would suspect her.

"She seems a very elegant woman," Inspector Jones said, effectively telling me nothing.

"Did she give an account of her whereabouts at the time?" I pressed.

"She said she had a conversation with her

171

husband and then went to the powder room in the floor above the ballroom to freshen up her makeup before coming back to the gala. She was still there when my men arrived and began asking questions. She was most cooperative."

"As I said," I told him, "I don't think she's at all the type of person to strangle someone."

"What type of person is the sort to strangle someone?" Milo asked dryly.

"That's just the thing," I said. "I don't know who might have done it. It was such a . . . brutal thing. I wouldn't have imagined that any of the people close to her would be capable of such violence."

"Crimes of passion are often more violent than one might expect," Inspector Jones said.

Crimes of passion. Was this a hint of some sort?

"You mean someone might have done it without planning to," I said.

"It's possible," he said. "Flora Bell and the killer may have met there, to be alone, to talk, for any number of reasons. Something went wrong and the killer acted in a fit of rage."

"You think she had arranged a meeting with someone," I asked.

"I presume so," Inspector Jones replied. "What other reason would she have for going to a darkened theatre alone in the middle of a party in her honor?"

Another thought occurred to me. "Did they . . . did they say if the killing seemed to have been done by a man?" I asked, just as Winnelda brought in the tray of coffee.

Inspector Jones looked at me for a moment with that perceptive gaze of his, and I had to force myself to keep from shifting in my seat. He was one of very few people who could make me feel like I was an unruly student being scrutinized by a stern headmistress.

"The doctor has said that the crime could have been committed by a man or a woman," he said. "One had only to get the curtain rope around her neck, perhaps when she was facing away, and pull it tightly."

Winnelda set the tray down with a rattle.

"But she would have struggled," I said.

He nodded. "She did. Her fingernails were broken in the fight, but once the rope was around her neck, it would have been difficult to remove it. The killer had only to keep a grip until she lost oxygen."

"It's horrible," I said.

"Yes," he agreed. "Not at all a pleasant way to die, though she would have lost consciousness before the end."

"Will that be all, madam?" Winnelda asked, her face white.

"Yes. Thank you, Winnelda," I said, picking up the pot to pour. She hurried from the room. Poor girl. I sometimes forgot that such talk might be distressing to her.

"How do you take your coffee, Inspector?" I asked.

"Black. Thank you."

I poured his coffee and handed him the cup and saucer.

"Milo?" I asked.

"No, thank you. I've had enough for one morning."

I poured myself a cup of the steaming liquid, stirring in a bit of sugar and milk. Winnelda was not what one might call a culinary master, but her pots of tea and coffee were above reproach. What more could one ask for, really?

"If it was possible for it to be a woman, it might also have been Dahlia Dearborn, Miss Bell's understudy," I said, remembering Milo's earlier comment. "She'll be next in line for the role. Not a very good motive, but people have killed for less."

Inspector Jones nodded. "Did you speak to her at the gala?"

"No, but I did notice how angry she

looked when Mr. Holloway gave a toast to Flora Bell. She looked very much as though she wished the glasses had been raised in her direction."

"Duly noted. Who else do you see as having a possible motive?" Inspector Jones asked.

"Her brother was there," I said. "Frederick Bell. They'd been arguing about money earlier in the evening. I heard them." I related the gist of the conversation to Inspector Jones.

"And his whereabouts, too, are unaccounted for?"

"So far as I know. I think he meant to leave when we finished speaking, so he might have gone to the theatre. But I doubt very much he would kill his sister," I said. "They seem exceptionally close."

"I shall bear that in mind," he said. "Anyone else?"

"Mr. Landon, the lead actor in the play," I said. "He and Miss Bell were involved before she took up with Mr. Holloway. I don't think he had quite forgiven her for it."

"I'll look into it," he said. "Did you happen to notice Mr. Landon's location during the time in question?"

I thought back. "I spoke to him once. It

was after Mr. Holloway's speech."

"That was when he told you he had overheard Mr. Holloway and Miss Bell arguing."

"Yes."

"And did you see him again after that?"

I tried to recall if I had seen him there before I went to the theatre, but it was difficult to remember. There had been hundreds of people at the gala, and my focus had been on locating Georgina. "I'm afraid I don't remember," I said at last.

"What about you, Mr. Ames?"

Milo shook his head. "I wasn't paying much attention."

I fought the urge to be annoyed that drinking and women had kept him from being observant. Then again, we had both let down our guard at the gala. We had never truly believed that something like this might happen.

"I never saw them together," I said. "But he might have arranged to meet with her later in the evening. Did he have a key to the theatre?"

"He did. It seems Mr. Holloway gave each of the principal performers a key when the play began. It was rather a relaxed atmosphere, and he wanted them to be able to come and go as they pleased."

"Then Mr. Lebeau had one as well."

He looked up. "Ah. Balthazar Lebeau."

"Do you know him?"

"My wife is rather fond of him," he said. "She's been to see four or five of his plays and follows his movements quite closely in the society columns."

I smiled. "You should bring her to meet him."

"We'll ascertain first that he is not a killer," Inspector Jones replied. "He was not there when I arrived."

"No," I said. "He was preparing to leave before I made my way to the theatre, said he had an appointment with a producer, but he could have conceivably killed her and then disappeared into the night."

"And do you suppose he might have any reason to have wanted Miss Bell dead?"

I considered the question. I didn't like to cast unwarranted suspicions upon anyone, but there was the matter of the way he had spoken about her.

"He didn't like her," I said. "He . . . disapproved of her, I think."

"In what way?"

"I complimented Flora Bell's and Christopher Landon's performances, and it made him angry. He seemed to think that they were parvenus in the theatre world, that their fame would be fleeting."

"It sounds not unlike the opinion of the mysterious letter writer," Inspector Jones observed.

"It could be construed that way, I suppose. I don't know, of course, that he meant any harm. Illustrious actors are sure to have strong opinions about the newer generation."

"Perhaps." He did not sound entirely convinced.

"You think her death is connected to the letters Miss Bell was receiving," I said, now that he had brought them up.

"I'm afraid, at present, there's no way to say for certain. If not, the timing is certainly strange. But coincidences are not unheard of, so we shall see. In either case, I certainly intend to get to the bottom of those letters."

I felt again that sense of calming comfort that came with knowing Inspector Jones was on the case. I was half tempted to leave it in his capable hands, but I also knew that I had access to information that he did not.

"There's one more thing," he said. "Something about the scene does not sit right with me."

"What do you mean?" I encouraged him, surprised that he seemed inclined to share something more.

"If someone wanted to kill Flora Bell, they might have done it anywhere. They might have killed her on the street outside or at her boardinghouse. Why did they choose to do it on this night and in this place?"

I considered it. "It's the same with the notes," I said at last. "Why warn her at all?"

He nodded. "The nature of the scene is, if you'll forgive me, rather *theatrical.*"

I knew exactly what he meant. It had not fully occurred to me, at least not at the moment, but in the back of my mind I had been struck with the possible symbolism of the action.

"You think it was meant to send a message or some such thing?"

"Perhaps. Or perhaps someone is enjoying the sense of the dramatic," Inspector Jones said.

Unfortunately, given who the suspects were, that didn't narrow the list much at all.

He rose from his seat then. "I think I've taken up enough of your time for one morning."

"I want to do everything in my power to help," I said.

"I appreciate that, Mrs. Ames. Which brings me to what I wanted to discuss."

"Oh?" I was suddenly wary. I did hope he

179

was not going to forbid me to involve myself.

"I know from past experience that it's hard to dissuade you from doing things when you've made up your mind to do them, so I may as well take advantage of your . . . persistence. As you're already involved, I'm sure nothing will stop you from seeing this thing through."

Well, this was a pleasant surprise.

"That's the same thing Milo said," I told him, not knowing whether to be amused or a bit insulted by this assessment of my character.

"Yes, well, I think Mr. Ames and I have both learned that it's better to work with you than against you," Inspector Jones said.

It was, I realized, probably the closest Detective Inspector Jones had ever come to making a joke with me, and I was oddly touched.

"I'm sure you'll find a way to be in contact with those involved in the matter. I only ask that you be careful and that you let me know if you learn anything."

"Of course, Inspector."

"Very good." He gave Milo a look that I interpreted as strict instructions to keep me out of trouble, but I was too busy contemplating the task ahead to be much annoyed.

I felt certain that, with my social ties to those involved and Inspector Jones's official connections, we would catch the killer in no time. And, I told myself, unwilling to give up this particular fight, with any luck we could reunite Gerard and Georgina Holloway in the process.

12

Milo and I parted ways shortly after Inspector Jones left, Milo to locate Mr. Holloway and me to try to see Georgina. If I were a betting woman, I felt that Milo's odds were much better than mine. He had access to Mr. Holloway's club, which was no doubt where he was staying. Georgina, on the other hand, was likely at home and not accepting guests.

It was, I realized, a bit rude of me to call on her so soon after something of this nature had occurred, but it wasn't only morbid curiosity that was drawing me there, or even the possibility of gathering information. I was genuinely concerned about my friend. I knew that things had not been easy for her with half the city talking about her husband's affair. I could only imagine what it must be like now, with a sordid murder having taken place at her own charity event.

I chose a double-breasted, belted suit of

black over a white silk blouse and a black close-fitting hat bedecked with a small bow and a netted veil for my visit. It was both stylish and slightly somber, which I thought fitting.

Winnelda confirmed this impression as I prepared to leave.

"You look ever so elegant, madam," she said, her blond head bobbing approvingly as she handed me my gloves. "Lovely enough to be going to a funeral."

With that dubious compliment to buoy me, I was on my way.

I approached the Holloways' home with something like trepidation. I was not one who was normally uncomfortable making social calls, even in cases of family tragedy. After all, I had paid my share of condolence visits throughout the years. No, my unease stemmed from more than the potential awkwardness of discussing the murder of Flora Bell. There was something different about this.

At last I forced myself to recognize what it was. I was nervous about what Georgina's reaction might be, that I might perceive some sign that she had had something to do with the murder. I told myself it was a ridiculous fear, but I couldn't quite push it away. She had, after all, more of a motive than anyone else.

As Markham, our driver, pulled the car up to the Holloways' home, I realized I was not the only one who had come to visit Georgina Holloway. There were several reporters standing outside the gate, cameras in hand. I had not really considered the fact that they might wait outside the house for Mr. Holloway or Georgina to appear, but it seemed that was exactly what they were doing.

"Do you want me to stop, madam?" Markham asked. "It seems as though there's a crowd."

I briefly considered telling him to drive on. I could pay Georgina a visit another day. Then I thought of her alone in the house, trying to sort out everything that had just happened, and I realized that I needed to see her.

"No, I'll go in," I said, adjusting the veil of my hat across the upper half of my face as a precaution.

"Very good, madam."

He parked the car and came around to let me out, doing his best to block me from the view of the gathered press.

"Excuse me, miss!" one reporter called. "Who are you? Do you know anything about the murder?"

I, of course, knew better than to answer any questions. I did not want my name to appear in tomorrow's gossip columns alongside misleading statements on my opinions on the matter. I was already a bit afraid I might be recognized, despite the veil, and some connection would be drawn between my appearance and the other murder cases in which I had been involved.

Luckily, Markham walked me to the front door without incident, and I was very much relieved not to be turned away. Instead, I was shown to the quiet sitting room.

"Mrs. Holloway will be with you shortly, madam," the maid said.

"Thank you."

I had been in this room before, though it had been some time. I had always found it a charming place, for it was scattered with artifacts of the Holloways' adventures. Photographs lined the mantel. There was one of the two of them standing before a lion they had shot in Africa. Its skin lay before the fireplace, teeth bared in its final roar, the mighty beast now a rug.

Another photograph showed them standing on the peak of a mountain. I remembered that climb well, for it had been the talk of London. They had climbed together, pressing forward to the top after half of the party had died in an avalanche. It had nearly proved fatal for them as well. Mr. Holloway had dug Georgina out of the snow, no doubt saving her life. And yet they had continued upward.

Despite the hardship of what they had endured, they had reached the summit. The photograph was evidence of the bond they shared: their arms were around each other, eyes aglow with the triumph of what they had accomplished and what they had survived to get there.

It made me sad to see that joyous confidence on their faces. They had been through so much together. How on earth could Gerard Holloway throw it all away?

I was still looking at the photographs, at the happiness on their expressions, when Georgina came into the room. I had been so lost in thought that I didn't hear her enter at first, and it was only as she moved closer that I realized that she was there.

"Those were good times," she said.

I turned to her. "There may be good times again," I answered softly, hoping that it was true.

"Perhaps."

I felt the stir of uneasiness as I looked at her, and it took me a moment to realize why. I was not sure what I had expected, but I was a bit disconcerted to see that she looked practically radiant.

Despite the solemnity of her words, her face was completely devoid of the tightness that had been there when I had come for tea. Her expression was untroubled, her eyes no longer clouded with the worry she had been trying to suppress. I was not sure what to make of this dramatic change of countenance.

"Will you sit down, Amory?" she asked me, nodding toward one of the chairs arranged near the fireplace. I sat and she took the seat opposite.

"Can I offer you some tea?"

"Thank you, no. I don't intend to stay long. I just wanted to look in on you. How are you, Georgina?" I asked carefully. I knew she would not want me to tiptoe around the subject, but I couldn't very well ask her how she felt that her husband's mistress had been murdered.

"I'm fine," she replied, her crystal blue eyes meeting mine. "Why shouldn't I be?"

I paused. If she was going to be purposefully evasive, I would have to get to the point.

"It was a terrible thing that happened to Flora Bell last night," I said.

"Yes, I suppose it was," she replied. I was

almost startled by the complete lack of emotion in her voice.

"I'm sure it was quite a shock," I pressed.

"I'm not sorry she's dead, if that's what you mean," she said. Her eyes held mine defiantly for just a moment before she looked away. "That's a cruel thing to say. I don't mean it. Of course, I'm sorry that she's dead. No woman should have to go through such a thing. But I'm not heartbroken about it, if that makes sense."

"I understand what you mean," I said carefully. I supposed one could not exactly fault her for being glad that her rival had been removed. However, this did nothing to relieve that nagging worry that she might be involved. It was, perhaps, a traitorous thought to have about an old friend, but, if I had learned anything in the previous investigations in which I had been involved, it was that a great many people were capable of murder when pushed too far.

On the other hand, just because Gerard Holloway had been having an affair didn't mean that Georgina had killed his mistress. After all, there had been rumors about Milo and numerous women, and I had never once thought of killing them — or him. Well, perhaps that was not *entirely* true. But I had never thought seriously of it. And I felt that Georgina and I were very similar in terms of temperament.

She would have tolerated it for as long as she could, and then she would have forced Mr. Holloway to make a decision. She would not, I was sure, have begged him to stay. She had too much dignity for that. If she thought, in the end, that he wanted to be with Flora Bell, then she would have gone on her way, her head held high.

Even if she was inclined to murder, I simply could not envision her going to a theatre and strangling her rival to death. It was too vulgar. Georgina Holloway was calm and dispassionate. As a murderess, I thought she would use poison or something equally refined. If refined was a term that might be applied to murder.

"Is there any idea who might have done it?" she asked, bringing my attention back to the matter at hand. She asked the question as though she was asking about the weather.

"I'm afraid I don't know," I said.

She looked up at me with a smile. "I know how you have a tendency to get involved in these sorts of things, Amory. I thought you might know a little bit more about it than the papers seemed ready to divulge."

There was something in the way she said

it that put me slightly on my guard, as though she was trying to determine what I might know for reasons of her own. Was that why she admitted me into the house when she had no doubt refused other visitors?

"I'm afraid I really don't know anything," I told her truthfully. "It was so dreadful, I can hardly believe it really happened."

"I don't know much about it at all either," she admitted. "The policeman I spoke to was cool and unforthcoming." This description of Detective Inspector Jones was startlingly accurate.

"Do you have any suspicion who might have done it?" I asked.

Was it my imagination, or did a flicker of something cross her eyes? "No," she said. "I'm afraid I couldn't say. As I'm sure you can imagine, I've made it a point to stay away from the theatre."

"Yes," I said. "Then you don't know any of the cast very well."

"No," she said. "I know Balthazar Lebeau and Christopher Landon slightly. We had dinner with them when the play was first getting started. I . . . I helped Gerard make decisions on some of the casting."

"I see." I wondered if she had helped to cast Flora Bell and had lived to regret it.

I remembered something Mr. Holloway

had said the night he had first told us about his play. "Your husband mentioned that he felt he owed Mr. Lebeau a chance. What did he mean?"

"Oh, that," Georgina said with a wave of her hand. "I think a few years back, when Gerard first considered acting, he was given a role that Mr. Lebeau wanted. Mr. Lebeau's career began a decline shortly afterward, and Gerard thought it would be nice to give him a role in *The Price of Victory*. Of course, he's very talented. I'm sure he played his part well."

"He did," I confirmed. "And what do you know about Mr. Landon?"

She shrugged. "Not much. He seems a very interesting young man, a bit moody, perhaps. But you know how actors can be. I always had the impression he didn't much care for Gerard. I could be wrong, of course."

It seemed, then, that she was not aware that the young man had been a rival for Miss Bell's affections.

"I don't imagine either of them would kill Flora Bell," she said. "But I suppose we never really know what a person is capable of."

I looked up at her, wondering if she was thinking of anyone in particular.

"I suppose the police will suspect Gerard," she said suddenly. "But he'd have no reason to kill her, not a lover's quarrel or any such thing. You see, he was about to break things off with her."

I found this information a bit surprising. From all I had seen, Gerard Holloway had been very much attached to Miss Bell.

"I had a talk with Gerard," she said. "Last night at the gala."

"Oh?" I asked. I was no actress and hoped it would not be apparent that I already knew this.

"Yes. I took your advice. I told him that he needed to make a decision."

That had not been advice, per se. I had only told her what had happened in my own relationship. I was certainly not an expert on matrimonial harmony, as my somewhat troubled history with Milo could attest.

"Well, I hope it went well," I said, not knowing what else to say.

"It did," she said. "He told me he was going to give her up."

I had not heard their entire conversation. Perhaps it had ended differently than it had begun. What I had heard, however, had not led me to believe that Mr. Holloway was planning to break things off with Flora Bell. If anything, I had had the impression that things were coming to a head in the Holloway marriage.

There was a discrepancy here, and it made me a bit uneasy.

I wondered if he had said it simply to appease her. Worse still, I wondered if he had meant it, and, when he went to break things off with Miss Bell, things had gone badly.

"I see," I said, not wanting to pursue this particular line of thought at present. "Well, perhaps Mr. Holloway has an idea who might have wanted to kill her."

"Perhaps. I'm sure he has his own opinions. He will, no doubt, be of more assistance to the police than I could be."

"You haven't talked to him about it?" I asked. It was, admittedly, none of my business, but I was very curious to know if she and her husband had discussed the matter.

"I didn't see him last night, and he hasn't been home," she said without looking up.

I wasn't exactly surprised. After all, Gerard Holloway was not likely to seek comfort in the arms of his wife for the death of his mistress. All things considered, it was rather a rotten mess.

"I'm sorry, Georgina," I said.

"It's probably for the best at present," she said calmly. "After all, Gerard is still suffering from . . . shock. I don't imagine that he'll be eager to discuss the incident — or the state of our marriage — anytime soon. He'll be back eventually."

I supposed he would. There was an uneasiness between them now, but tragedy often brought people together in unexpected ways. I had experienced the same thing with Milo. The first murder investigation in which we had been involved had, against all odds, brought us closer together. When it came to a crisis, people often sought comfort in the arms of the familiar.

Some little part of me couldn't help but wonder traitorously if that might have been Georgina's intention all along.

I went home to await Milo's return and spent a good deal of time reading the newspaper articles written about the gala. As Milo had said, there was a great deal of lurid speculation. There were also a few genuinely moving pieces about Flora Bell, a rising star who had been so tragically extinguished.

It was late in the afternoon when Milo finally came in. Emile, who had grown quite bored with me, leapt into his arms to greet him and chittered excitedly.

"Hello, Emile," Milo said. "Hello, darling."

"Hello," I replied, setting aside the newspaper I was reading.

"I had a devil of a time tracking down Holloway," he said, carrying Emile to the sofa. "He wasn't at his club or any of the other places I thought he might have gone."

"Where did you find him?"

"He found me, in fact. I left word at his club, and shortly after I returned home he rung me up. Said he'd been wandering the streets, thinking."

"Wandering the streets?" I repeated.

"He said he feels that people are looking at him everywhere he goes; he needed fresh air and time alone."

I frowned. It didn't sound as though he was holding up at all well. What sort of power had Flora Bell had over him? What was it about a beautiful woman that made men lose their heads?

"How did Flora Bell do it?" I mused aloud.

Milo looked up from where he was feeding nuts to Emile, who sat quietly by his side on the sofa.

"Do what?"

"Both Gerard Holloway and Christopher Landon were mad about her. What was it that made her so appealing?"

"I don't see why you're asking me."

"Come, Milo, don't be so modest," I

195

replied dryly. "When one has a question, one consults the experts. And women are definitely your field of expertise."

His eyes narrowed. "I feel very much like I have walked into some sort of trap."

"I simply want to know what it was that made Gerard Holloway fall for her so quickly. She was beautiful, yes, but it must have been more than that. He knew her for a few months at most; he's been married to Georgina for ten years."

Milo shrugged. "Some men like women who rely on them and make them feel wise and important, who will do what they ask. Wide-eyed adoration can be very effective on the right audience. Not that that sort of thing has ever appealed to me."

"Oh, doesn't it?" I asked sweetly.

"I should think it obvious," he replied. "If I wanted a pliant and adoring woman, I certainly wouldn't have married you."

I threw a little pillow at him, which sent Emile jumping to the back of the sofa, where he chattered irritably at me.

"I do apologize, Emile," I said. "If only your papa wouldn't talk such nonsense."

"Whatever it was, Holloway's taken her death hard. He says he doesn't think he'll be able to rest until the killer is brought to justice."

"I . . . I hope it wasn't Georgina," I said suddenly.

Milo looked up at me. "What do you mean?"

"I don't know," I said. "I just feel uneasy after speaking with her. She didn't seem at all upset that Flora Bell is dead."

"Did you expect her to be?" he asked. "As you've pointed out, darling, the woman stood in her way of happiness. She doesn't have to have killed her to be happy that she's dead."

"It's just so cold," I said. "I would have thought she would be horrified by a murder at the theatre, but, though she tried to appear sympathetic, I didn't get the feeling that she was."

"That doesn't mean she did it. You know Georgina Holloway has always been aloof and self-possessed. She may be more upset than she appears."

"Yes," I said slowly. "But there was something more, some impression I had that she was trying to get information out of me. She was asking questions, very casually, but I could feel that the answers meant something to her."

"Perhaps she thinks Holloway did it."

I considered this. It was possible. She might suspect her husband of the crime and was alert to see what others knew.

"Would she shield him, do you think?" I asked. "Despite everything?"

"What would you do if I killed someone?" Milo asked, effectively distracting me from my train of thought.

"I beg your pardon?"

"If you thought I had killed someone, would you shield me or turn me over to the police?"

"Milo," I protested, "my head is already hurting."

"Come, darling," he said with a smile. "Humor me."

I considered the question for a moment, though I found this exercise fruitless and in poor taste. My instinct would be to protect Milo, but I also had a very strong sense of duty and justice.

"I suppose it would depend on who you had killed and why," I said at last.

"Not very loyal of you," he said.

"Well, one can't have one's husband going around killing people," I replied. "What about you? Would you shield me?"

"Certainly," he replied without hesitation.

"Just like that? You wouldn't have to weigh the circumstances?"

"Definitely not." I could hear the smile in his voice. "I know you wouldn't kill anyone without a very good reason."

"You're quite ridiculous, Milo."

"Well, anyway, you haven't let me tell you the most interesting thing. Holloway's made a request."

This caught my attention. "Yes, what is it?"

"He says he's worried about the play."

"What about the play?" I asked.

"It's scheduled to run for some time, and a great many expenses have been tied up in the production. Most of the actors have made investments as well."

"But a murder is rather an extenuating circumstance," I said.

"Which is why Holloway wants to hold a meeting with the cast to discuss things," Milo said. "He feels that he owes it to the players to let them decide if they wish to continue."

It was like Gerard Holloway to think of the well-being of the others, despite his own tragedy. One might think him mercenary for wanting to continue the play if it wasn't a well-known fact that his family was incredibly wealthy. Despite the financial troubles that had beset the globe, the Holloways had no financial woes.

I wondered why Milo should find this the most interesting piece of news, and then an idea struck me. "Are we to attend?"

"Better," Milo said. "Holloway had an idea that we host the meeting."

"That we host it?" I repeated, surprised.

"He said the police haven't yet finished with the theatre, and he can't exactly hold it at his house. He's currently avoiding Georgina like the plague."

"But he could have chosen any restaurant in London," I pointed out. "Or any number of other places."

"Yes, but I've told you he's trying to avoid publicity. Besides, his real motive is to continue to find the letter writer, and I think he's rather hoping that we'll be able to help him. He thinks that whoever wrote the note is the killer, and he wants us to have a look at some of the suspects."

I considered this. It seemed a bit unusual that he should have asked to hold the theatrical meeting in our flat, but I was certainly not going to complain about this excellent opportunity.

"When does he want to do it?" I asked.

"I suggested tomorrow night."

I couldn't help but smile. "You've already agreed to it."

The more I thought about it, the better I liked the idea. It would be good to get several of the suspects in one room, to observe their reactions to the things that were being said.

"You don't mind?" Milo asked when my silence stretched out.

I looked up, pulled from the schemes I was already making in my mind. "Of course not," I said. "It's almost too perfect."

He smiled. "I thought you might say that."

13

Winnelda and I spent that evening and the rest of the next day making preparations for the arrival of our guests. Mr. Holloway had suggested we call the meeting late the following evening. It would be a small affair with just coffee and after-dinner drinks. In addition to the group of suspects, several minor players had been invited as well. I assumed this would help to hide the fact that we were looking into the motives of the group of people who had had access to the Penworth Theatre.

"Now, remember the plan," I told Milo as we went into the sitting room to wait for our guests to arrive. "You're to pay special attention to Dahlia Dearborn. Make her believe that you find her fascinating."

I had no doubt that Miss Dearborn would be more than willing to talk to Milo, and he excelled at gleaning information in a round-about way. For my part, I was going to see what I could get out of Balthazar Lebeau and Christopher Landon. Both gentlemen were still high on my list of suspects.

Milo sighed as he poured himself a drink. "It's going to be a dull evening. I haven't the least interest in Dahlia Dearborn."

"I'm glad to hear it," I replied. "But do try to be nice to her."

"Being nice is not in my nature."

"Perhaps not, but you're very good at pretending," I said. "Besides, it's not as though an hour or two of conversation with a pretty young woman is a chore."

"Things are never as amusing when one has been assigned to do them," he remarked over his glass.

I shot him a look and turned to survey myself in the mirror. I had had my dark hair freshly waved and I wore a good deal more makeup than was my usual habit, dark red lipstick to match the crimson evening gown I had chosen. It was, perhaps, a bit of a dramatic choice for such a meeting, but, after all, our guests were dramatic people and likely would all be coming from dinner parties elsewhere.

I glanced once more around the sitting room. The furniture had been arranged, a cheerful fire was glowing in the grate, and the sideboard was well stocked with drinks.

We had only to await our guests.

Dahlia Dearborn was the first to arrive. She let her mink coat slide off her shoulders, and, when Winnelda nearly failed to catch it, she turned to her and snapped, "Be careful with that. It's very expensive."

I saw Winnelda's nose wrinkle in annoyance as Miss Dearborn turned back to me, and I had to stifle a smile. Winnelda had not yet mastered the fine art of hiding her opinions.

The dress Miss Dearborn wore beneath the coat was gold lamé, and I no longer felt overdressed.

"Mrs. Ames," she said, smiling brightly and reaching out a hand aglow with artificial diamonds to take mine. "It was so kind of you to invite me."

"I'm so glad you've come." As I heard myself say the words in a convincingly sincere tone I thought that perhaps I was a much better actress than I had given myself credit for being.

Though she was trying to be subtle, I noticed the way her gaze kept moving to the door behind me. As I had hoped, it appeared that she was looking for Milo. I waited for the question, and I did not have to wait long.

"Will your husband be joining us as well?"

she asked in a passably casual tone.

"Oh, yes," I replied. "He's in the sitting room. Come this way, won't you?"

We made our entrance, and I saw the gleam in her eyes as she caught sight of Milo, who looked handsome and mysterious, his elegant figure backlit by the glow from the fireplace. Though I had concocted this plan myself, I gritted my teeth a little. I did not relish the idea of setting that woman loose on my husband. I could only hope the ends would justify the means.

He came to my side to greet her, and it was only the work of a moment for him to lead her off to fetch a drink.

The next to arrive was Balthazar Lebeau. He had decided to forgo his cape for the evening, but was still dashingly attired in evening dress.

"Good evening, Mrs. Ames," he said, taking my hand. "I was very glad when I heard that our paths would cross again."

"I'm glad you could come."

He smiled, and I recognized it as the smile of a man who had had a great deal of success with women.

I had seen photographs of Balthazar Lebeau in his younger days, and there was no denying that he had been extremely handsome. Even now he was very attractive. He reminded me of an aging pirate, the swagger and bravado built up by a lifetime of licentious behavior. Though the years of hard living seemed to have taken their toll, as evidenced by the lines on his face and a certain weariness in his pale blue eyes, he was still appealing, his rugged air nicely balanced by an elegant manner.

"I hope we may get to know each other a bit better this evening." Perhaps it wasn't only his looks that reminded me of a pirate. It was the way he looked one over with that somewhat plundering gaze.

"Yes, that would be nice," I said vaguely, hoping not to give him too much encouragement.

Fortunately, a small group arrived just then, and as I greeted them, Mr. Lebeau made his way to join Milo and Miss Dearborn.

Christopher Landon was among the latest arrivals, and I tried to take stock of his mood. There was an air of forced nonchalance in his manner, and he met my searching gaze with an almost aggressive smile, as though he was trying to prove to the world that he had not been affected by Flora Bell's death. It made me think that he was almost certainly suffering deeply.

It was Mr. Holloway who arrived last. I

had heard Winnelda open the door and thought that perhaps I should greet him privately. As I walked into the foyer, I was hit with the very strong odor of alcohol. When Mr. Holloway looked up, his face was pale and drawn, his eyes revealing the depth of his pain, though he had certainly tried to numb it. I had to fight the urge to embrace him.

"Good evening, Mrs. Ames," he said somberly.

"Good evening, Mr. Holloway. I'm very sorry about Miss Bell," I said, reaching out to squeeze his forearm.

"Thank you." It seemed to me that he steeled his expression, as though trying to keep his emotions in check. "And thank you for hosting this rather unconventional meeting. I know it was irregular of me to ask you, but I . . . I couldn't have them at home. And the police are still at the theatre . . ." His jaw clenched as he struggled to contain a strong emotion, and I reached out quickly to pat his arm again.

"Yes, I understand," I said. "Milo and I are only too happy to help."

"Thank you."

"Would you like to come into the sitting room? I believe everyone is here."

I led him into the room, and the group's

conversation faltered slightly at our entrance. It seemed everyone was unsure of how to react, and there was a moment of awkward near-silence as Gerard Holloway stood frozen at my side, perspiration beginning to gleam on his forehead.

I looked at Milo, and he took the situation quickly in hand. "Come sit down and have a drink, Holloway," he said easily, stepping forward to hand Holloway a drink he had already prepared him. "The evening is young. There is time for discussing business later."

Led by Milo's example, the others began to converse again and I breathed a sigh of relief. Winnelda brought in a tray of coffee, which most everyone eschewed in favor of stronger drinks, and the room settled into a low hum of conversation.

Now that everyone had been plied with alcohol, it seemed like a good time to begin asking questions. I moved toward Balthazar Lebeau first.

I was not, as a general rule, in favor of using what one might term "feminine wiles." Aside from the insulting assumption that women had no better tactics at their disposal than to simper and blink their lashes, I was not comfortable feigning what might be construed as romantic interest in men who were not my husband. I had not mastered Milo's ease with casual flirtation.

Nevertheless, I could tell that Balthazar Lebeau would be susceptible to flattery and the attentions of a younger woman. He had made his interest in me clear, and I could not help but feel that it could be used to my advantage.

One does what one must.

And so I went to where he was standing, drink in hand, examining the portrait of me that hung on the wall. It had been done by a rather famous artist, and Milo had insisted on hanging it in the sitting room, though I thought it a bit gauche to have myself on display.

"It's a very good likeness," he said when I reached his side. "By Gareth Winters, I see."

"Yes, he painted it for me earlier this year."

"It's lovely. Of course, a painting could not quite match your beauty in the flesh."

"You're too kind," I said, nodding at the nearly empty glass in his hand. "May I get you another drink?"

"Thank you, no," he said, surprising me. I had not thought Balthazar Lebeau would be the kind of gentleman to refuse a drink. "I see you're not drinking, Mrs. Ames."

"Oh, no," I said. "I think a hostess should always keep a clear head."

His eyes sparkled with amusement. "I should think a clear head is the last thing a person might want, especially given recent events."

"It has been a rather shocking few days," I admitted, glad he had introduced the topic. "I almost can't believe Flora Bell is dead."

"Yes, a dreadful tragedy," he replied. "She was a fine actress. Her death is a great loss." There was an artificiality to his tone, as though he were speaking lines. I had the sensation that Balthazar Lebeau lived his life as though it were a role he was playing. Or was that merely the impression he wished to give? I couldn't help but feel that there was some other emotion he was hiding beneath the airy affectation.

"Who do you think might have done it?" I asked. I had hoped to throw him off guard with the question, but it appeared to have had the opposite effect. His eyes flashed sharply for a moment, and he paused before he answered.

"I don't know," he said at last. "Who do you think might have done it?"

"Oh, I haven't the faintest idea," I replied, hoping that I seemed like nothing more than a society lady eager to gossip. "It's just so dreadful. I can't imagine who would be capable of such a thing."

"Ah, yes. It's an intriguing question. Which of us is 'a goodly apple rotten at the heart.'"

"Do you think it's one of us?" I asked.

"I don't suppose a stranger would have any reason to kill Miss Bell," he said, swirling the dregs of the drink in his glass. "In fact, I should say only someone who knew Miss Bell intimately would be inclined to kill her in such a manner."

I wasn't sure what he was hinting at, but I had the distinct impression he was toying with me. I would have to try harder.

I leaned closer, my voice lowered. "You . . . you don't suppose that Mr. Holloway might have done it?"

He smiled. "My dear, I'm afraid I cannot tell you what evil might lurk in anyone's heart, even the Honorable Mr. Holloway's."

"Oh, surely there's nothing evil about Mr. Holloway," I said with an incredulous little laugh. I was being coy now, hoping to encourage him to make some sort of revealing statement.

If he knew anything about Gerard Holloway, however, it appeared he was disinclined to tell me. "He seems, by all appearances, to be a very upstanding gentleman. Of course, appearances can be deceiving."

I suddenly had the distinct impression that

211

Mr. Lebeau was hiding an adamant dislike for Mr. Holloway.

"In what way?"

He shrugged. "I merely point out that someone has committed a murder and is hiding a blacker heart than their appearance might suggest."

"What about Mr. Landon?" I asked with a conspiratorial smile, as though we were now playing some sort of enjoyable game. "I heard he was also fond of Miss Bell."

He looked at me speculatively, but did not ask where I heard such a thing. "Kit Landon is fond of a great many women, Mrs. Ames."

"I suppose a handsome and successful actor might consider that part and parcel of his life," I said lightly.

If Mr. Lebeau noticed that this light jab might also be aimed at himself, he didn't show it. His eyes were on Mr. Landon, who sat talking to one of the supporting actors. "Kit Landon is the sort of man who gets one role and feels as though he is entitled to fame, as though those of us who have spent years of blood, sweat, and tears should be cast aside to make room for a generation of talentless usurpers. He doesn't have what it takes to last in this business."

I remembered what he had said to me at the gala, the words about lesser artists coming and going and true talent standing immortal. It seemed now that they had been directed more at Christopher Landon than at Flora Bell. He clearly resented the younger actor's rising success.

"If he did have feelings for Flora Bell, I don't suppose he liked it that she took up with Mr. Holloway."

"I suppose not," he replied. "The best way to hurt a man is to win over the woman he loves."

This line of inquiry was leading nowhere, so I decided to change course.

"What about Miss Bell's brother? Did you know him well?"

His gaze came back to me.

"I didn't know her brother at all," he replied.

"Oh. I was under the impression that he came to the theatre frequently."

"If he did, our paths never crossed. Miss Bell and I did not spend much time together offstage."

There was something different in his manner now, something more guarded. I wondered if he realized that there was more than mere curiosity behind my questions. Perhaps I needed to do a better job of posing my queries in the guise of simple inquisitiveness.

"I suppose you think I'm a dreadful gossip," I said with a smile. "It's just that it's all so terrible. I suppose one can't help but speculate about it. I hope I'm not boring you."

"Not at all. I find you very amusing, Mrs. Ames." I had the feeling this statement was disingenuous, but I pretended not to notice.

"Now you're flattering me, Mr. Lebeau," I teased.

"Who shall we talk about next?" The question came with a rakish smile.

"Miss Dearborn, perhaps?" I said, my eyes turning to where she and Milo sat comfortably ensconced on the sofa. Despite Milo's protests, he seemed to be having a perfectly good time entertaining her.

Mr. Lebeau's gaze followed mine, the slightest hint of a contemptuous smile turning up the corner of his mouth.

"Do you suppose she might have wanted the role badly enough to eliminate her rival?" I asked, hoping to spur him on.

"You would be surprised what some women would do to achieve their aims," he said.

"Men, too, have been known to go to great lengths to get what they want," I couldn't resist retorting.

His gaze came back to me, and he smiled.

"Touché, Mrs. Ames. Perhaps there is a bit of the mercenary in all of us."

"But you think Miss Dearborn more mercenary than most."

"My dear, I don't care to offend your ears with what I truly think. Suffice it to say, she is not the sort of woman with whom I would care to associate."

I wondered. Mr. Lebeau did have, after all, a reputation for being rather undiscriminating in his tastes. From what I had heard, he had moved through relationships with various women at a dizzying rate in his younger days. It was possible age had mellowed his vices, but somehow I didn't think so.

"I see."

"I don't mean to be indelicate," he said, though I was sure he cared very little whether he was or not. "But she's the sort of woman who gives of herself freely . . . but only if there's something to be given in return. She'll do anything to work her way up in the world. She tried very hard to turn Holloway's head, but I'm afraid she was no match for the charms of Miss Flora Bell."

I looked up at him. "Miss Dearborn tried to seduce Mr. Holloway?"

"Yes, attempted seduction is precisely what it was. Surprised him one evening in his office at the theatre, divested of all attire, shall we say."

"Oh . . . I see," I said again, a bit scandalized by this revelation. It was certainly a shocking way to behave, if she had done it. But I knew perfectly well how quickly rumors spread, and just because the story existed didn't mean it was true.

"How do you know this happened?" I asked.

"Everyone knew about it," he replied. "It became something of a joke among us."

"What about Miss Bell?" I asked. "Did she know?"

"I suppose she did," he replied, "though I don't recall her ever saying anything about it. Holloway had made her very secure in her charms." There was something less than complimentary in his tone, and I wondered if it was directed at Mr. Holloway or Flora Bell.

"Where did Mrs. Holloway fit into all of this?" I asked. "Did you ever see her at the theatre? Did Mr. Holloway ever talk about her?"

"This is the most charming interrogation in which I have ever taken part," he said with a smile.

I returned his smile, doing my best to look abashed. "If I am honest, I have a bit of a personal investment in the matter. Georgina Holloway is a very dear friend of mine, and I have found this whole situation to be very distressing."

"You needn't fret, my dear," he said. "I suppose it will end well enough for your friend now. She'll get her husband back, after all. Their family will be mended, and that's a happy ending, isn't it?"

"I'm not entirely certain of that," I said. "Mr. Holloway has made rather a mess of things."

"He doesn't seem to have appreciated her the way he ought to have." He glanced over to where Milo was still engaged in conversation with Miss Dearborn. "Few men, in fact, appreciate their wives to the extent they deserve."

I followed his gaze and didn't have to feign annoyance. I had told Milo to try to get information from her, not to try to get her in his lap before the evening was out.

Mr. Lebeau smiled. "Husbands are a rotten lot, on the whole. That's why it's sometimes best to forget one has one for a while."

So that was his tactic, was it? I could not fault his methods, for they were sound. I was sure they had been successful with a number of neglected society wives.

"I think Georgina would have a hard time

forgetting Mr. Holloway," I said, purposefully misconstruing his words.

"As to that, I couldn't say," he said. "We never saw much of Mrs. Holloway at the theatre. We knew, of course, that she was involved in the charity gala. The entire thing was all her idea, I believe. I suppose she didn't realize that this would happen with Holloway and Flora, but 'the course of true love never did run smooth' and all that. One never knows when Cupid's arrow may hit."

"No, I suppose not," I replied. "Though I can't help but feel one might be less inclined to be shot if one keeps oneself out of the line of fire."

He laughed heartily. "You're right, of course. Holloway ought to have known better than to take up with a child like that."

"How did you feel about Flora Bell?" I asked suddenly. I didn't know if he would be offended at the question, but we seemed to have developed something of a camaraderie, and I didn't think it would do any harm to try to understand. To my surprise, some unnamed emotion, almost like sadness, flashed momentarily in his blue eyes before he blinked it away. He drained the rest of his drink.

I thought for a moment that he wasn't going to answer or that he would make some offhanded remark, and then he surprised me with a straightforward reply. "She had talent, a rare gift."

"Yes," I agreed. "She was remarkable."

"Oh, I grew annoyed with her a time or two when she didn't want to take my advice. But that's because I am just a bitter old man."

"Oh, come, Mr. Lebeau," I said lightly. "You are neither old nor bitter."

His eyes met mine, an unreadable expression in them. "Few of us are really what we seem, Mrs. Ames. We all have our little secrets." His mouth tipped up at the corner. "Of course, that doesn't mean that we would kill for them."

"No," I said slowly. "I suppose not."

"Alas, it seems my glass is empty. You'll excuse me while I refill it?"

"Of course."

As he walked away, I could not shake the feeling that I had just been treated to a Balthazar Lebeau command performance.

14

As I looked toward Mr. Landon, my next target, I noticed Mr. Holloway draining his glass. He had been close to being drunk when he arrived, and I thought we had better get to the meeting portion of the night before he was too inebriated. I glanced toward Milo, hoping to make eye contact with him and steer him toward Mr. Holloway, but he appeared to be too deeply entrenched in his own role to have noticed.

He and Miss Dearborn still sat on the sofa, Milo with his arm draped casually along the back of it, a drink in his other hand. Miss Dearborn sat close beside him in her revealing dress of gold lamé, her body angled toward him to give him the best view of her décolletage. They appeared to be engaged in a very friendly conversation.

Milo said something, and she laughed, throwing her head back to reveal her long, white neck. I stepped a bit closer, though I didn't want to interrupt anything. I was very curious to hear what they had to say to each other and decided to pass behind the sofa on my way to speak to Mr. Landon.

"Have you ever thought of a career on the stage, Mr. Ames?" she asked, her eyes moving over him in that assessing way women had of attempting to determine what his level of interest in them might be.

"I'm afraid not," he said.

"A pity. You'd make quite an impact, I think." She smiled, revealing very white teeth. "The theatre could use more handsome leading men."

"You're too kind," Milo replied. "But I'm afraid I haven't the discipline for that sort of thing."

She was leaning closer, her hand resting on the sofa between them. The barest shift would have that hand on his leg. I waited.

"Oh, it's not as disciplined as one might think. In fact, I like to think we're rather free and open-minded. Of course, there are other skills required." This was said in a husky, suggestive tone that begged for him to ask for details. As men are wont to do, Milo took the bait.

"What skills might those be?" he asked.

"First of all, one need be a very good liar," she said, looking up at him through her lashes. "I don't imagine you are skilled at anything so wicked."

"On the contrary," I couldn't resist interjecting as I passed the sofa, "Milo excels at a great many wicked things."

He looked up at me over his shoulder with a smile and she subtly shifted away ever so slightly. Enough to lessen the suggestion of impropriety but not enough to signal full retreat.

She needn't have worried. I had no intention of separating her from Milo, at least not at present. Instead, I moved to where Mr. Holloway was moving somewhat unsteadily toward the sidebar, effectively cutting him off from another drink.

"Are you ready to speak to everyone now?" I asked softly.

"Perhaps in a moment," he said. "I think . . . Perhaps if I have one more drink."

"Certainly," I said, taking the glass from his hand. "Why don't you go and sit, and I'll bring you something."

He nodded, moving back to the seat he had vacated. His eyes had taken on a glassy look, and I was becoming concerned about his condition. I knew he was mourning, but the hangover he would have tomorrow would certainly not make him feel any better.

On the whole, he seemed to be taking this harder than I might have thought. I had assumed — hoped, rather — that his relationship with Miss Bell had been mostly of a physical nature. It appeared, however, that his feelings had run deeper than that.

Or, I wondered, could there be some other reason behind his decline, something like guilt? Was it possible he had killed Flora Bell during the heat of the moment and was now regretting it?

I moved to the sidebar, preparing to concoct a cocktail with very little alcohol content. As luck would have it, Christopher Landon had come up to refill his glass.

"How are you, Mr. Landon?" I asked.

"I'm fine."

"Can I fix something for you?"

"Another whisky, perhaps. I can pour it."

"Very well. Please help yourself." I lingered, waiting to fix Mr. Holloway's drink. "It's dreadful what happened."

"Yes," he agreed, reaching for the crystal decanter.

"I'm sure it has been difficult for you," I pressed.

His hand stilled on the stopper, and he looked up at me. "Why do you say that?"

"Oh, I thought you and Miss Bell might have been . . . close."

His gaze searched mine, as though trying to determine exactly what I knew.

It seemed he realized that I knew about their past, for he suddenly shrugged, his expression taking on a look of indifference, and he pulled the stopper from the bottle.

"I suppose you heard that we had a bit of a romance before she took up with Holloway?" He poured his drink and then looked up, his expression a mask of amusement. "Well, it didn't mean anything. I know you're not of the theatre, Mrs. Ames, but there is not much that goes on here that is done in the name of love. Oh, there is passion, but it seldom lasts. That bright star burns itself out as easily as the rest."

It was a pretty speech, but I could not quite believe that it was sincere. Something in his manner told me that he felt the death of Miss Bell much more deeply than he let on.

"And who do you suppose might have killed her?" I asked.

Something hard and dark flashed in his eyes. "I don't know," he said.

I asked my next question for the sole purpose of seeing what his reaction might be. "Did you know that Miss Bell had been receiving threatening letters?"

I was certain that a flicker of surprise

crossed his features before he quickly smoothed it away.

"No. I didn't know," he said.

"The last one she received said her opening-night performance would be her last."

"I never heard about any letters," he said with an almost disinterested casualness. "Flora and I weren't on the closest of terms anymore, so she would hardly have confided in me."

"Who do you suppose might have written them?" I asked.

"I haven't the faintest idea."

He was being purposefully evasive.

"If you had to guess," I pressed him. "Surely you must have some idea who might have wanted to frighten Miss Bell."

"It might have been any number of people," he said. "But the most obvious suspect is Miss Dearborn." He said this without any particular emotion, without even looking in Dahlia Dearborn's direction, and I had the impression he was trying to fob me off with the first thing that came to mind.

"Why do you say that?"

"She resented Flora because Flora was everything she was not. And, anyway, Dahlia's got a mean streak."

"What do you mean?" I asked.

"You ask a great many questions, Mrs. Ames," he said suddenly. "I'm not entirely sure what your motive in all of this is."

"I suppose I'm merely curious."

"Curiosity is not always an attractive quality," he said coldly. "Now, if you'll excuse me."

He walked away from me then, and for some reason I felt oddly ill at ease. I had not imagined that look in his eyes. It had been a look of pure hatred. At whom had it been directed?

I fixed a gin and tonic — mostly tonic — and brought it to Mr. Holloway. He took a long drink, and, if he noticed the ratio was a bit off, he did not comment. Instead, he drew in a deep breath and rose to his feet.

"I want to thank you all for coming," he said, and, as if he had been on a stage, a hush fell over the room. "I . . . I know that Flora's death has been a great shock to all of us, and . . . an inestimable loss to the theatre world."

I glanced around the room, trying to gauge the reactions of those present.

"I've been struggling with what we should do," he went on. "About whether or not we should continue with the play."

I glanced toward Milo, and saw he was no longer the focus of Miss Dearborn's attention. Instead, she was looking at Mr. Holloway, and I was surprised by the intensity of her expression. Then I realized it had likely never occurred to her that the role might not be hers. No doubt she felt that her career hung in the balance. If she was allowed to continue in Flora Bell's role, she might very well make a name for herself.

I looked at Mr. Lebeau. He, too, was watching Mr. Holloway, but his expression was almost one of amusement, perhaps even contempt.

I glanced at Mr. Landon, but he was looking down at his drink, his features expressionless.

"I had planned to speak with each of you," Mr. Holloway went on, "to see what your feelings were on the matter. But after much thought, I think it would be in everyone's best interest if we go ahead with it, in Miss Bell's honor."

Miss Dearborn's relief was practically palpable, and she struggled to keep a smile from her lips.

"I know that it will be difficult to carry on . . ." Mr. Holloway stopped a moment, licked his lips, and then continued. "To carry on . . . on the very stage where Miss Bell met her tragic end, but I believe the best way to mourn her death is to honor her life and the things that she cared so much about."

There was a moment of silence that was broken by Balthazar Lebeau. "Bravo!" he said, raising his glass. "To Flora Bell."

Though I had the impression Mr. Lebeau's toast had been proposed more to put an end to Mr. Holloway's speech than out of any depth of feeling, the others followed suit with apparent sincerity. "To Flora Bell" came the chorus of voices.

His announcement concluded, Mr. Holloway seemed to slump ever so slightly, and he drained the rest of his tonic water.

The company went back to their drinks, but there was the sensation that the meeting had come to an end. It wasn't long before everyone began to take their leave.

Mr. Lebeau was the first to make a move to leave.

"Going so soon, Mr. Lebeau?" I asked as he reached the door.

"Yes, I have another engagement, I'm afraid."

"A pity. I hope to see you again."

Balthazar Lebeau took my hand before he left. "I have no doubt our paths will cross again, Mrs. Ames," he said.

Christopher Landon left with a barely civil "good evening," and Milo personally escorted Dahlia Dearborn to the door, which I'm fairly certain was the only way to be rid of her.

Finally, only Mr. Holloway was left. He had remained in his seat, empty glass in hand, and as the door closed behind the last guest, he looked up.

"Oh," he said, rising to his feet. "I'm sorry . . . I'll just be going."

"You needn't leave yet if you'd like some company," I said. I knew he would not be going home to Georgina, and I was concerned he might get himself into some sort of trouble.

"No, no. I won't bother you any longer," he said.

I looked at Milo, silently urging him to say something. "Where are you staying, Holloway?" he asked.

"At my club."

"You're going there straightaway?" Milo asked.

"Yes."

We all walked to the foyer, and Mr. Holloway stopped at the door. "I want to thank you both for . . . for helping me with this. Do you . . . do you think that you might be able to come by the theatre? Not tomorrow. It's . . . it's the funeral. But in a day or two."

"Yes, we'll be there," I assured him.

"When I think that someone did this to her, I . . . We've got to find out who did it. We've got to."

"We will," I promised. I only hoped it was a promise I could keep.

"Well, that was as tedious as I imagined it would be," Milo said, coming into our bedroom after returning from accompanying Mr. Holloway downstairs to a cab.

"Really?" I asked, rising from my dressing table where I had been removing my makeup and jewelry. "You seemed to me to be having a marvelous time."

"Don't tell me you're jealous of Miss Dearborn," he said as he pulled loose his necktie.

"I'm not jealous of anyone," I retorted, turning my back to him as I began to unfasten my dress. "It's just that I daresay there's nothing more annoying to a woman of good sense than a man who falls for the overt ploys of a . . ." I stopped, unable to think of a fitting description of Miss Dearborn.

He laughed, coming up behind me to finish the unfastening. "If you think I am in danger of falling for the wiles of Dahlia Dearborn, you do me a disservice."

" 'Have you ever considered the stage, Mr.

Ames?' " I mimicked in a low, sultry voice, turning in his arms and pressing myself against him.

"It's a pity you never considered the stage, Amory," he said, his arms tightening around me. "You'd have taken London by storm."

It was my turn to laugh as I pushed away from his embrace. "I will not be flattered into forgiving you for your disgusting display with Miss Dearborn."

"It was your idea, after all," he protested as I moved away to finish undressing. "You told me to make her like me and to try to get some information from her."

"Well, it's quite clear you succeeded admirably on the first count," I said. "Did you have any luck with getting information out of her?"

I slid into a becoming blue satin nightdress and moved back to my seat at the dressing table to put my jewelry away in the velvet-lined jewelry box.

"I'm not entirely sure," he said. "She has a great many opinions about her follow actors, but it's all the sort of thing one might expect. Mr. Landon makes a habit of seducing and abandoning women. Mr. Lebeau doesn't respond well to criticism. However, there was one thing that I thought you might find interesting. She seemed to be enjoying Holloway's misery."

I turned to look at him. "What do you mean?"

"More than once I saw her look in his direction with a definite kind of satisfaction. And when I mentioned that he wasn't looking well, she replied that it was his own fault that he was suffering."

"She said that?" He had my attention now. I turned on the stool to face him.

"She did. I asked her what she meant and she said that he ought to have known better than to make a fool of himself chasing after Miss Bell."

It was a callous thing to have said, if not entirely surprising. After all, she had been rebuffed by Mr. Holloway in favor of Miss Bell.

"Mr. Landon says she has a mean streak," I said. "And Mr. Lebeau told me that she tried unsuccessfully to seduce Mr. Holloway."

"That might account for it," Milo said. "From the little hints she gave me, I gathered that Holloway had shown some interest in her before Miss Bell came along."

I frowned. "Surely not. I can't believe Mr. Holloway would be enamored of every young actress that came his way."

"It's likely Miss Dearborn was exaggerating," he said. "Whatever the reason, she held him in very definite disdain. That is, until he began his little speech and she realized that she had not quite secured the role after all."

"I noticed that, too," I said. "She looked almost shocked, as though the possibility had not occurred to her."

"All the same, I somehow doubt that she would plan to kill someone by strangulation."

"She might not have planned it," I pointed out. "She might have followed Miss Bell to the theatre to have it out with her and then, when a nasty argument had ensued, she might have lost herself in a rage."

"It's possible. I don't deny that anger and ambition can be a lethal combination."

I was not entirely satisfied with this theory, however. While it would be convenient to lay the murder at Miss Dearborn's door, there were still several other avenues to be explored.

"What did you make of Mr. Holloway tonight?" I asked.

"Well, I've never known him to take to drink."

"He's taken her death harder than I thought he might," I said. "His grief seems genuine. I'm rather afraid he was in love with her."

"It could be guilt, of course," Milo said. "Perhaps he killed her and is having a difficult time hiding it."

"I had the same thought," I admitted. "Do you really think that he might have done it?"

"I don't know, but I certainly wouldn't rule him out."

He said this with perfect ease, as though the idea that one of his old friends might be a murderer was of little concern to him. Of course, I could not be entirely surprised that Milo made no concessions for Mr. Holloway; Milo was perhaps the least sentimental person I had ever met. Quite a feat when my mother was included in this grouping.

"Well," I said. "I suppose something good came of your evening in Miss Dearborn's clutches."

"And what about you and that old lecher?" he asked.

I feigned surprise. "Do you refer to Mr. Balthazar Lebeau?"

"I saw the way he was leering at you. Don't suppose you're the only one to notice when their spouse is being advanced upon."

I laughed. "I don't quite know what to make of him. I feel that he's always playing the role of the consummate performer, but there's a shrewd gentleman underneath it all. He made some very valid points."

"Such as?"

"Oh, for one thing, he thinks husbands are quite useless as a whole," I said airily as I rose from my seat.

"Does he indeed?" Milo asked, moving toward me, a recognizable gleam in his blue eyes.

"Yes," I went on, suppressing a smile. "He says that it's sometimes better to forget one has one for a while."

"I hate to contradict the illustrious Mr. Lebeau," Milo said, pulling me hard against him. "But I intend to be unforgettable."

He leaned over to kiss me then, and I forgot all about the Holloways for the remainder of the evening.

15

The next day was the day of Miss Bell's funeral. I knew there was going to be very little I could accomplish as far as the suspects were concerned, as most, if not all of them, would be attending the service.

Nevertheless, there had to be some way to gain more information about those involved. After all, everyone in the group was fairly well known, and rumors and speculation abounded.

I decided to start close to home.

"Winnelda," I said as she poured my coffee. "What do you know about Flora Bell?"

As usual, she brightened at the possibility of sharing gossip. "Oh, I've heard ever so many things," she said. "I know that she was a wonderful actress. People often talked about her beauty, but it was her talent that really shone through. She was going to be the next Sarah Bernhardt, someone said."

"What else?" I asked.

"Well, there were rumors that she had a . . . gentleman friend who was . . . well, not exactly unattached. I suppose that would be your friend, Mr. Holloway," she said, confirming my suspicions that, despite her flighty air, Winnelda was very much aware of what was going on around her.

"Have you heard anything about her brother?"

Winnelda thought about this for a moment, no doubt searching the corners of her mind for any small bit of information she might have heard. "I believe they were orphaned," she said at last. "Poor, too, I think. With no one in the world to lean on. But she was going to make something of herself. And she would have become a great actress if only she hadn't been murdered so cruelly." She sighed. "It's a very hard world we live in, isn't it, madam?"

"It is indeed," I replied. "What about the others? Balthazar Lebeau and Christopher Landon, for example?"

"Oh, I'm afraid Mr. Lebeau was a bit before my time, madam. I've heard my mum speak of him, of course. She said he was a fine actor, did Shakespeare and the like. And of course, he had something of a reputation, if you know what I mean."

"I'm afraid I do," I answered.

"I don't know much about Mr. Landon," she went on. "I've seen his name a time or two in the society columns, I think. He's very handsome, isn't he?"

"Yes."

"But there's something sad about him. A kind of haunted look, I would say."

This caught my interest. Winnelda could be very perceptive on occasion. "What do you mean?"

"Oh, I don't know, madam. He just strikes me as a gentleman with some secret sorrow."

Winnelda read a great deal of sensational fiction, and I wondered if it had somehow tainted her impression of Mr. Landon. He did, after all, look the part of a tragic hero.

"Now that I think on it, I believe he was in my scrapbooks," she mused.

"Scrapbooks?"

"Yes, I used to cut clippings when I was young. I made special pages for some of my favorites or people I thought might prove interesting later on. The scrapbooks are still in my old room at home. I seem to recall Mr. Landon, though I don't remember why."

"You're going to see your mother soon, aren't you?" I asked, remembering that she had mentioned going on her night off.

238

"Yes, madam. I'll bring them back, shall I?"

"That would be marvelous, Winnelda. And one more thing," I said, saving what was sure to be the most amusing reaction for last. "And what did you make of Miss Dearborn?"

"Which was she?" Winnelda asked.

"The one in the fur."

"Oh, that one," she said with a roll of her eyes. " 'Don't drop that. It's very expensive.' " Really, her talent for mimicry was uncanny.

She seemed to realize suddenly that it was probably not the done thing to mock my guests. "That is, I don't think . . . she was . . . well, she's not a very nice lady, is she?" she asked, coming back around to her indignation.

"I don't know her very well," I said neutrally, not wanting to set a bad example.

"Well, I didn't drop her old fur. And, anyway, it wasn't half as nice as any of your furs, so I don't know what she was going on about."

With this parting sally, Winnelda went off to the kitchen and I sipped my coffee, trying to see if we were any closer to finding the killer than we had been yesterday.

What had we learned the previous eve-

239

ning? I wasn't really sure. For one thing, not all of the suspects had been assembled. I still needed to find a way to speak to Freddy Bell. And I needed to learn more about each of the players in this little drama, preferably from an outside source who might be familiar with them. Luckily, I knew just the person.

I was pleased that Mrs. Roland had agreed to see me on such short notice. Then again, we had something of a mutually beneficial relationship. Yvonne Roland was a society widow who secretly sold stories to the gossip columns, so I was often able to provide her with some interesting tidbits of news, not the least of which involved my own marriage. In return, she often gave me insight into the suspects I wanted to learn more about.

I was shown to an elaborate sitting room and she swept in almost immediately behind me, making a dramatic entrance as she was wont to do. Today she was dressed in flowing gold silk trousers with a matching blouse, over which she wore a long, embroidered waistcoat of bright green bedecked with all manner of jungle life. A turban with a glittering jewel at its center rested atop her henna waves.

"Mrs. Ames, I'm so glad you've come," she said, brushing kisses across both of my cheeks, enveloping me in the scent of patchouli and orange blossom. "It's been far too long since I've seen you. You've been abroad, haven't you?"

I might have known she'd be familiar with my itinerary. "Yes," I said. "Italy and France. We had a lovely time."

"No mysteries to solve?" she asked, her shrewd gaze on me.

Since I didn't care to discuss the details of what had happened in Paris, I simply smiled and said, "It was a pleasure trip, Mrs. Roland. I did not go looking for mysteries."

I wasn't sure if she believed me or not, or what her contacts abroad might have whispered in her ear about what had gone on during our holiday, but she didn't press the matter for the time being.

"Do have a seat, dear," she said, waving me toward a red silk chair. "We'll have tea and a nice chat."

I took a seat and a maid brought in the tea things, setting them on the little ebony table between us. As Mrs. Roland poured, I took in our surroundings.

The room in which we sat was not the same room in which we had taken tea the last time I had come to visit Mrs. Roland. This room seemed to have been decorated with objects from the Far East. There were silk tapestries on the walls, a great deal of delicate pottery, and a bamboo tree in a pot in the corner. A painted dragon with an angry expression wound his way along the mantel, and a stone soldier, nearly as tall as me, stood in one corner, his face looking out with contempt upon the proceedings.

"My second husband was quite fond of the Orient," she said, noticing that I was looking around the room with interest. "When he died, poor thing, I tossed out most of the stuff, but there were a few good things and so I put them all here. I sit here occasionally, on days when I'm in the mood for the exotic."

I looked at the embroidered tiger preparing to eat a monkey on her waistcoat and could see that today had been one of those days.

"It's a lovely room," I said.

"Yes, well, wives must often accommodate their husbands' excesses, mustn't they? And how is your husband, dear?" she asked, making this segue into my personal life without so much as an extra breath.

"He's quite well," I replied.

Her sharp gaze met mine over her teacup.

242

"Been behaving himself, has he?"

"Marvelously, in fact," I replied.

She looked a bit disappointed, and I could not entirely blame her. The gossip columns had lost a great deal of fodder when Milo had begun to toe the line.

"I've come today because I was at the gala when Flora Bell was murdered," I said.

A spark of interest flickered in her eyes, though she tried to hide it. She clicked her tongue. "It's a shame. Of course, I suppose it will be something of a relief to Georgina now that her competition has been removed."

"You've heard about Miss Bell and Mr. Holloway?" I asked, though I had come here on the assumption that she had. If there was something that someone wanted to keep hidden, the odds were that Yvonne Roland would know about it.

"Hasn't everyone?" she replied. "It's none of my business, but I've always had a soft spot in my heart for the Holloways. They always seemed so very much in love."

"Yes," I replied. "I thought the same thing."

"Of course, not everyone approved of the sort of life they led, traipsing about from here to there doing one reckless thing after another. I've never been much of an adventure seeker myself, though I suppose it's obvious from this room that I've married them often enough," she said with a wave of her hand and a tinkling laugh. "But the Holloways settled down once they had children, and that's the important thing."

I thought again how it seemed that steadiness had brought about the end to their relationship. When there had been no more thrills, Mr. Holloway had sought them elsewhere. It was a disconcerting thought.

"Now that the other woman is dead, poor dear, perhaps they will be able to make things right between them. Marriages can be mended. You know that well enough."

She certainly wasn't very subtle in her hints, but I wasn't going to take the bait. I hadn't come here to talk about my marriage. It had been going very well as of late, and I didn't intend to let some slip of the tongue be misconstrued into a society column story. I liked Mrs. Roland very much, but I didn't at all trust her. I imagined that a friendship with her must be very like having a dangerous exotic animal for a pet. One is perfectly fond of them, but knows not to let one's guard down.

"What do you know about Flora Bell?" I asked, shifting the conversation away from more personal topics.

"Not much," she replied, clearly disappointed to be required to give such an answer. "I know that she came from a poor family of somewhat dubious origin and that she tried very hard to hide it. Gossip has it that their mother died young and no one knew what became of the father. She had to make her own way in the world from a young age."

I nodded. That fit with the conversation I had overheard between her and her brother, and also what Winnelda had told me this morning.

"I am not what you might call a patron of the theatre. Oh, I enjoy a good play well enough. My last husband and I used to attend the theatre very often. He liked the most dreadfully boring tragedies. I prefer a comedy myself. Though, I'd rather attend a musicale any day. I don't often let it be known, but I was something of a singer in my younger days. Of course, I don't sing much now. But I do still enjoy the piano. Do you play, Mrs. Ames?"

"Yes," I said. "I very much enjoy music. Do you know anything about Miss Bell's brother?" I had learned that, when in conversation with Mrs. Roland, it was necessary to stay the course. One could get too easily led astray by her conversational derailments.

"He's something of a ruffian, I believe," she said, drawn back into the matter at hand. "I've heard he went to sea for a short time and came back after some trouble. Of course, no one takes much interest in that sort of thing. If it were Flora Bell's lover, perhaps, people would be inclined to be a bit more interested. It being her brother, no one pays it much mind."

"What about Christopher Landon?"

"Ah, yes," she said, sitting back in her seat as she prepared to recite the facts. "Christopher Landon comes from a good family. Not too good, mind you, but good enough to be displeased that their son decided to become an actor. His older brother died in the war, and I suppose they hoped he would carry on the family name in a more noble manner."

"He's making a very good name for himself," I said.

"Yes, they say he's quite talented. Handsome, too. That sort of thing goes a long way in the theatre. There was some trouble with a young woman in his younger days, I believe, though the details escape me."

"Oh?" I pressed. This was something I hadn't heard.

"A broken engagement, if I recall. Of

246

course, he was quite young then and I don't think she was the sort of girl of whom the family approved. It's all been forgotten now. Those little scandals never stay around for long."

"He and Flora Bell would have made an attractive pair," I said casually, hoping this would spur her on to further comment.

"Yes," she said reflectively. "I suppose they would, now that you mention it. Of course, one can never tell what might make people fall in love. I wouldn't have said a pretty young thing like that should have gone wild for Gerard Holloway, but one never can tell. Of course, I don't suppose his family name and money hurt."

It was a cynical observation, but I was inclined to agree with her. Under normal circumstances, I didn't think that a woman like Flora Bell would have chosen a gentleman like Gerard Holloway. Then again, I had seen more than my share of unconventional pairings over the years. Such a thing was rather common in the world in which I lived.

"I don't suppose you know Dahlia Dearborn?" I asked. She was the least prominent of the suspects, and I was surprised when a flash of recognition showed on Mrs. Roland's face.

She frowned. "Dahlia Dearborn. I've heard the name somewhere. But where?" Her eyes moved upward as if searching for answers on the ceiling.

"Ah!" she said suddenly, snapping her fingers loudly. "I have it! She's a relation of someone in government, though, at the moment, I can't recall who. Dearborn, of course, is not the family name. Harris! That was it. There was, I believe, some difficulty with her when she was young, an unruly sort of girl. And perhaps some trouble while she was at school? I shall have to think on it." I didn't know if information on Miss Dearborn's school antics would be of use, but one could never be sure.

"And what about Balthazar Lebeau?" I had saved him for last because I suspected his name would bring forth a wellspring of gossip.

To my surprise, Mrs. Roland flushed. "Balthazar Lebeau," she murmured, almost to herself. "I haven't thought of him in years."

"You know him?" I asked.

"Oh, we had a bit of a romance at one time," she said.

It was only by the strongest of efforts that I was able to keep my mouth from gaping at this surprising news. I knew Mr. Lebeau was rumored to have been quite successful where ladies were concerned, but I would not have thought Mrs. Roland his type. Then again, she had worked her way fairly swiftly through three husbands, so there was no doubt she had a certain sort of appeal.

"I didn't realize," I said. Yvonne Roland and Balthazar Lebeau were two of the more outlandish persons I had yet to meet, and I could only imagine what they must have been like in combination. Just the thought was exhausting.

"Oh, it was long ago. Between my first and second husband, I believe. He was always a rascal, and I knew, of course, that it wasn't going to last. But one does love a rascal when one is young."

Now that she was telling the story, she seemed to be enjoying herself. Her eyes were sparkling and her cheeks still held a pleasant pinkness. "He was always a handsome devil. Good-looking in a way that makes sensible ladies lose their heads. Like your husband, dear." I could not argue with this assessment.

"Why did you break it off?" I asked. I was not generally comfortable prying into people's personal affairs, but Mrs. Roland had no such qualms and I didn't see why I should when talking to her.

"Oh, he ran off with another woman. That's the way things go. In any event, I met my second husband and was very happy with him until his untimely demise. Besides, Balty and I would never have suited."

"Why not?"

"For one thing, he was too fond of drink. I like a drink myself, but there is such a thing as excess, and Balthazar surpassed it. For another thing, he could be very difficult to manage when he didn't get his way, apt to lose his temper at times."

This caught my attention. I would not have taken Mr. Lebeau for a man of high temper. In fact, he had been remarkably self-possessed in the situations I had observed him in thus far; sober, too.

"Well, if he was violent, I'm glad you were rid of him," I said, hoping to draw her out.

"Oh, he never did me harm," she said. "I'd like to see the day when I would allow a man to do such a thing."

I would pity any man who tried it. She had, after all, seen three husbands buried.

"No, I believe his problem was that he really felt things very deeply but made an effort to hide it — always came across as though he was speaking lines — and sometimes his emotions would no longer be suppressed."

It was the same impression I had had, as though sometimes he was playing a character, delivering lines. I wondered why it was that he should feel the need to hide behind this artful posturing.

Mrs. Roland continued, giving her answer to my unspoken question. "He hadn't had an easy life, you see. His parents were eccentric, and he lost a sister he cared about; she disappeared or some such thing. He was moody and restless at times. I always felt that there was some part of him that was searching for something that might never be found." She looked up, seemingly eager to brush aside the nostalgic tone her words had taken on. "But, of course, that was all a long time ago."

"I wonder who it was that did harm to Miss Bell," I said, moving toward the reason I had really come.

She looked at me searchingly. "Trying to catch another killer, Mrs. Ames?"

There was no sense in denying it, as Mrs. Roland wasn't likely to believe any protests on my part.

"I just want to do everything I can to help the Holloways," I said. "And, of course, if I can contribute to bringing Flora Bell's killer to justice, I'll be only too glad to do so."

"In this case, I would suggest looking hard at their faces."

This was not the sort of advice I had been expecting. "Their faces?" I repeated.

She nodded sagely. "I've known actors in my day, Mrs. Ames, and there's something I've noticed about them. The more involved they become in their roles, the more drastic the change is when reality slips through. You just keep an eye on all of them. Sooner or later, every mask slips."

16

The following morning, I had my first opportunity to put Mrs. Roland's theory to the test.

I sat alone at the breakfast table, Milo still abed, and looked at the paper. As I had suspected, the society columns had devoted a great deal of space to discussing Flora Bell's funeral the previous day, complete with a photograph taken as the mourners left the church.

I looked closely at the photograph, hoping Mrs. Roland's words about a mask slipping might prove true at such a solemn event.

I had never been to an actress's funeral, but the photograph looked as though it was a perfect representation of what one might expect from the attendees. They all stood on the steps of the church, dressed in black, a striking collection of characters. There was Dahlia Dearborn in a tailored black suit, pressing a handkerchief to the corner of her eye beneath the black tulle veil on her hat, her profile turned, just so, to the camera. Her grief, I was certain, was not genuine, but that did not mean she was a killer.

Christopher Landon was there as well, his handsome face taut and expressionless. He was a difficult man to read, though there was something tense in his posture that seemed to speak of some emotion he was trying to quell. Sorrow, perhaps, or something else?

I was surprised to see that Balthazar Lebeau was also in attendance. I had thought, somewhat cynically, that, though he was the sort of man who enjoyed the fanfare of a public event, he would not be tempted to attend the funeral of someone he had not liked for mere secondhand attention. There was a certain sadness in his expression, but I couldn't help but wonder if it was feigned.

Of those involved in the theatrical production, only Mr. Holloway looked as though he was truly grief-stricken, though he appeared to be doing his best to hide it. He stood at the center of the group, his head slightly bowed, as if he had not noticed the cameras. Despite his obvious efforts to control his expression, his face was grim and tight, and there was that same defeated slump to his shoulders that had been present at the meeting at our flat.

I skimmed the article and found that there were several snide references to his relationship with Miss Bell, and I could not help but feel terrible for poor Georgina. I didn't think she was the type to read society columns, and I was fairly certain she would be making an effort to avoid them now. Sometimes it was better not to know.

I looked again at the photograph, willing something to jump out at me. The only problem with attempting to read people's emotions was that guilt was so easily masked as something else: sorrow, regret, pain. My gaze went last to Frederick Bell, Flora's brother, who stood at one side of the group. He looked like an outsider, almost as though he did not quite belong with them, though his claim to mourning Flora was stronger than any of theirs. His attention was not on the group, but on something in the distance. He looked as though he was lost in thought, and I wondered if he was remembering the good times he and Flora had had. I hoped the memories would comfort him.

I wondered if Inspector Jones had accounted for Freddy's whereabouts the night of the performance. After all, I had heard him quarrelling with Miss Bell shortly before she took the stage. It was possible he had come back and their argument had turned violent.

I folded the newspaper with renewed purpose. Though the photograph of the mourners had not proven to be revealing, it had made me realize the direction we must look next.

We needed to find a way to speak to Frederick Bell.

If I thought my afternoon was going to be free to consider the various aspects of the case, I was due for an unpleasant surprise.

Milo had gone out, promising to see what he could do to locate Frederick Bell, and I was just sitting down at my writing desk to make some notes when there was a buzz at the door. I had a feeling of foreboding that proved prescient as Winnelda came into the room a moment later.

"Your mother's here again," she whispered.

I closed my eyes and let out a breath. I had thought that she was returning to the country, and I could guess why it was that she had made this unexpected return.

"So you've gotten yourself involved in another murder, have you?" she asked as she swept into the room without waiting for Winnelda to return and show her in.

"Will you make us some tea, Winnelda?" I asked.

"Yes, madam," she said, glad to make a hasty retreat.

"Sit down, won't you, Mother?" I said, leading her to the arrangement of chairs near the fire.

She sat with an attitude of protest. "I'm quite upset, Amory."

"I'm sorry to hear that," I said with all the sincerity I could muster.

"Your father and I were visiting the Fairleys in Norfolk when we heard the dreadful news," she said accusingly.

"News certainly travels quickly," I said.

She frowned at me. "The entire city is talking of nothing else. I saw the photograph of you visiting Georgina Holloway in three separate society columns, as though that flimsy veil would disguise your appearance."

So I had been recognized after all. I made a mental note to invest in headwear that would truly allow me to travel incognita.

"I would have come back sooner," she went on, "but I didn't like to call any more attention to the matter. Here you are involved in this sordid affair when you might have engaged yourself in Lady Honoria's charity without the hint of scandal."

"I certainly didn't know there was going

to be a murder at the Holloways' gala," I pointed out reasonably.

"I do wish you would consider your father and me," she went on, as though I hadn't spoken. "It is dreadful to have people mention your escapades to us. We're quite vexed by it."

I highly doubted my father was at all vexed by any of it. He was a person exceptionally unmoved by the tides of life. He seldom expressed strong opinions on anything, a result of both his taciturn nature and the fact that he had learned in thirty years of marriage that acquiescence was easier than conflict. If my parents had disagreements, I could not recall them ever having been openly discussed.

"I shouldn't think it would make much difference to you, Mother," I answered coolly. "After all, we don't see each other often. You can't be expected to be held responsible for my actions."

"Nevertheless," she said.

I waited for more, but it appeared she thought the "nevertheless" sufficient.

We sat for a moment, looking at each other. I wished Winnelda would hurry with the tea.

Then it occurred to me that if my mother was going to make a nuisance of herself,

perhaps there was a way that she could be of use.

"Have you heard of Flora Bell's involvement with Gerard Holloway?" I asked.

She looked at me as though I had said something very silly indeed. "Dear, just because your father and I spend a good deal of time in the country does not mean that I am not aware of what is going on here in London."

That was just what I had been counting on.

"Who do you think might have killed her?" I asked.

"I haven't the faintest idea," she said, adjusting her furs with great disdain.

"Surely you must be curious. As you said, this murder is the talk of London."

"I am not acquainted with any actresses and could not venture to guess who would want to kill them."

I fought down my irritation. She was being purposefully obtuse, as she knew how much it annoyed me.

"You know I don't approve of these things, Amory," she said, her voice taking on a tone of weariness. "It distressed me greatly to see your name linked to such vulgarities."

"Milo and I have been friends with the Holloways for years," I said. "We don't

259

mean to abandon him in difficult times."

"Friendship is one thing. Ruining one's reputation is quite another."

"It's not a question of reputation, Mother. Don't you agree the killer should be brought to justice?"

"Of course," she said archly. "But I believe the city employs policemen for such things."

I considered telling her that I was working with the police, but decided against it. I couldn't be sure of her reaction, and I didn't know if we had any smelling salts on the premises.

Thankfully, Winnelda arrived with the tea things then, giving me sufficient time to formulate my next plan of attack.

"What do you think about Georgina Holloway?" I asked as I poured the tea.

"She's a lovely person," my mother said. "She comes from a very good family, as you know. I'm sure all of this has been a great blow to her."

"I always thought she and Gerard Holloway seemed very happy together," I said, handing my mother a cup and saucer.

"One can never tell what happens behind closed doors. You of all people ought to know that what seems to be an ideal marriage can quickly go sour."

Despite this barb, I supposed she was

right. I had judged the relationship between Gerard and Georgina Holloway based on their interactions in public. Though I believed a certain amount of information could be gleaned from such exchanges, it was still difficult to say how two people really felt about each other without observing them privately. I was certain, however, that I had not misjudged their affection for each other.

"Do you think that she might have killed Flora Bell?" I asked.

I said it, at least in part, out of spite to shock my mother, and I was surprised by her response.

"It isn't impossible, I suppose."

"You think she might have strangled Flora Bell with the curtain rope?" I pressed.

She made an expression of distaste, letting me know how repulsive she found the question, but she answered it nonetheless. "I don't say that she did it, but there is a streak of determination in that family. I never approved of those reckless things she did, traipsing about scaling mountains and wrestling lions and any number of things. She was always strong-willed. If she thought the girl was going to take her husband away, she might have decided to put a stop to it."

My mother, for all her bluster, was a keen

observer of human nature, and I wondered if it was possible she was seeing something that I was not. After all, I was friends with Georgina Holloway. I didn't want to believe that she might have done something like this. Sometimes outside observations were more accurate than those of close acquaintances.

Of course, I still found it difficult to believe that Georgina would have killed Flora Bell over her affair with Gerard Holloway. It was much more likely that she would have ended the marriage than killed her rival. What was more, she was always so cool and poised. A rage killing was not in her nature. An intrepid spirit did not a murderess make, mountain climbing and lion wrestling notwithstanding.

"There are other suspects, naturally," I said. "The male lead in the play, Christopher Landon; Miss Bell's understudy, Dahlia Dearborn; and Balthazar Lebeau."

My mother — against her will, I suspected — looked vaguely intrigued. "Balthazar Lebeau, you say?"

"Yes," I said, feeling that perhaps I had stumbled upon my trump card. "I've spoken with him several times. He's a very charming gentleman."

She was impressed, though she tried not

to show it.

"I saw his Hamlet once," she said. "He was magnificent." My mother was not given to effusive praise, so I knew that I had struck a chord with her.

"He's in the play," I said.

"I'm sure such a man would not have anything to do with something as sordid as murder," she pronounced. Never mind that Balthazar Lebeau had been involved in one sordid scandal after another over the years.

"One never can tell, I suppose," I said vaguely.

"But what is he doing in a supporting role? And in something written by Gerard Holloway?" she asked. "Mr. Holloway is a charming enough gentleman, but he's certainly no Shakespeare."

"I suppose the role will bring him a good deal of attention now. I imagine people will be lining up to see it, all things considered."

She looked at me, aghast. "You don't mean to say the play is going on?"

"Yes," I said warily.

She seemed to consider this for a moment, and then she said exactly what I feared she might.

"Well, I suppose I shall have to come and see it for myself." She set her cup and saucer down then and rose quickly to her feet. "Procure some tickets for me, will you, Amory? I'll call again soon to collect them."

She left the room before I had a chance to respond, and I heard the front door close behind her.

Winnelda poked her head into the room a moment later. "Is everything all right, madam?" she asked.

"Yes, thank you. But will you bring me another pot of tea, Winnelda?" I asked. "Very strong. And some aspirin."

I hadn't heard from Milo by dinner and as the hours crept past I began to suspect that he had indeed located Frederick Bell at his gambling club. No doubt he had decided the best course of action would be to blend into his surroundings. It wouldn't be the first time he had been distracted by such a thing.

At last I went to sleep, and was awakened some time later as he slid into bed beside me.

"What time is it?" I asked sleepily.

"I don't know," he replied, moving closer. "Nearly dawn, I should think. I didn't mean to wake you."

"Did you have any luck?" I asked, having decided that chiding him again for neglecting to telephone me would be of no use.

"In more ways than one," he said, his arm encircling my waist to draw me against him. "Would you like to hear about it? Or shall I wait until morning?"

"You certainly aren't going to wake me up and then make me wait," I said.

He laughed. "Well, first of all, I won quite a bit of money." This was no great surprise. Milo was notoriously lucky. It seemed he was always managing to win money in the course of his investigative pursuits. I sometimes wondered how much of a night spent away from home was spent collecting information and how much was spent playing roulette.

"Secondly, I learned some very interesting things about Freddy Bell."

"Such as?" I asked. I was feeling less sleepy by the second.

"Well, it seems the young man is in quite a lot of trouble," he said. "He owes a significant amount of money to people to whom it is not wise to owe money."

"Then he did really need the money he was asking Flora for."

"Undoubtedly. And not only that, it seems that he will get all of Flora Bell's money now that she's dead. She's managed to put a tidy sum aside."

"How on earth did you manage to learn

that?" I asked.

"I shouldn't reveal my methods, but remind me never to have a drunk for a solicitor. Makes me glad old Ludlow is such a crashing bore."

I didn't know how it was that Milo had managed to contact Freddy Bell's solicitor, but I was not going to complain about his uncanny knack for locating people and prying information from them.

He didn't give me time to compliment him on his success before he moved on to the next bit of news.

"I saw Holloway this evening too."

"Oh? How is he?"

"Not well, I'm afraid. He said he doesn't think he'll be able to go to the theatre tomorrow. He's asked that we look in on things for him."

I found this surprising. After all, Mr. Holloway had overseen every aspect of the play until now. Surely he didn't mean to just abandon it? Had his feelings for Flora Bell really run that deep? Or was he just not ready to return to the scene of a murder — perhaps one he had committed?

"That will be a good opportunity to talk to the suspects," I said. "There are some things I've been wanting to ask some of them. I do wish I could speak to Freddy

Bell, though. Did you talk to him personally?"

"No, I didn't get the chance. He came in only briefly, perhaps to make assurances that he would be able to pay off his debts, and then left before I could speak with him."

It was as I suspected then. Milo had accomplished his aims early and spent the rest of the evening gambling. I had to admit, however, that the information he had collected had earned him a night of amusement.

"Then we may have lost our chance. Perhaps he won't be back to the gambling club with so much debt hanging over him," I mused.

Milo gave a derisive laugh. "I don't think you need worry about that. He'll be back. Gambling gets in one's blood, just like an addiction. Some people can't resist its pull."

"People such as yourself?" I asked casually.

"I can resist it," Milo said. "But I see no reason to give up a diverting pastime that is also lucrative."

He did have a point, I supposed. So far as I knew, Milo's gambling had never been a financial detriment to us.

Besides, I somehow doubted Milo could ever really care enough for anything to be addicted to it. He did everything with a casual interest that spoke of amusement but never deep enthusiasm. The things that might be vices in other men — gambling, drinking, carousing — he did with enjoyment, while still managing to give the impression that should any of them cease to exist tomorrow it would be of little matter to him. The only exception to this rule was his horses, which he genuinely cared about. And possibly me, though I could never be entirely certain.

"That isn't all," Milo said. "It seems Freddy Bell was no great admirer of Holloway. He claimed Holloway was using his sister ill."

"I don't believe he intended to marry her or any such thing, if that's what Freddy Bell meant," I mused. "But nor did I have the impression that Flora Bell was deeply in love with Mr. Holloway."

"I would hazard to guess that love has nothing to do with her relationship with Holloway. If anything, I'd have said he was the one being used. But I suppose he knew what he was getting into."

"Do you think so?" I asked softly, as Milo once again spoke casually of Mr. Holloway's affair.

"Perhaps he found a change of pace amusing. Georgina Holloway is very reserved and serious, after all."

"Yes," I said, thinking how similar I was to Georgina Holloway.

"Well, I don't suppose it much matters now," Milo said.

I didn't answer, but Milo didn't seem to notice. He pressed closer beneath the blankets and was soon asleep.

I stared up at the shadowed ceiling until the sun came up.

17

When we went to the theatre the following morning, I was not sure what to expect. The world of the stage was entirely outside my milieu. I had never harbored any secret desire to be an actress. The scope of my theatrical experience was a play in which I had participated as a girl when one of my school friends had been quite keen to be a playwright. She had written what seemed to our group of fifteen-year-old girls to be a stirring melodrama. The experience had, however, cured me of any desire to tread the boards.

It seemed that the old adage "the show must go on" was accurate, however, for the rehearsal was already in progress.

Dahlia Dearborn was on the stage, preparing to give one of Victoire's longer speeches.

Milo and I slipped quietly into seats in the back.

I had wondered what Dahlia Dearborn

would be like in the role. She had beauty and ambition, but that was not at all the same thing as talent. Granted, actresses before her had succeeded on the strength of this combination alone, but I was not sure the same would happen for Miss Dearborn, at least not in this play. The performance Flora Bell had given would be nearly impossible to rival.

Miss Dearborn wore the same dress that Flora Bell had worn. The exact same dress, I thought, for it was a bit too long for her. Likely they hadn't had the chance to alter it in time for tonight's performance. One does not expect, after all, that the understudy will ever need a wardrobe.

" 'What is more important, victory or honor?' " She spoke the line in a flat, breathless voice, and I knew at once that the performance was not going to be a success.

It was not that she was bad. It was just that she was nothing compared to Flora Bell. I knew, of course, that future audience members who had never seen Miss Bell perform would not compare them. However, I couldn't help but feel that for them, too, Dahlia Dearborn would be a disappointment.

"She isn't very good," Milo said in a low voice.

"No," I replied. "Surely she must realize that she'll never be a celebrated actress."

"Darling, you know as well as I do that few people see the limitations of their own talents." This was true. I had known a great many people who had overestimated their abilities.

We were quiet then, watching the remainder of the play from the back of the theatre. This was the third time I had seen it, but I had to admit that it still drew my interest. Even with Dahlia Dearborn's unsteady performance, the story line was strong.

The scene where the heroine, Victoire, bids her lover, Armand, farewell as he prepares to ride into the battle for the last time was especially touching. I remembered how well Flora Bell and Christopher Landon had expressed the emotions of that moment. Dahlia Dearborn and Mr. Landon exhibited no chemistry whatsoever. Granted, this was only a rehearsal, but there was something awkward and stilted about their interactions that did not bode well for the performance.

Despite the lack of feeling between them, however, the words were still touching. After my conversation with Milo last night, I felt the little twinge of sadness knowing that Holloway had written this play, this stirring defense of the power of love, with Georgina by his side. Had either of them had any inkling of what trouble the play would bring to their lives?

The curtain closed and, from behind it, I heard Dahlia Dearborn's exuberant laugh. "I think it went well, don't you?" she loudly asked someone who either did not answer or whose voice lacked enough enthusiasm to carry.

So Dahlia Dearborn would have her moment to be a star. She stood behind that curtain, on the stage where Flora Bell had died, and awaited her time in the limelight. The question was, had she been desperate enough for her time upon the stage to kill for it?

Somehow I found it difficult to imagine. After all, there were any number of ambitious actresses in London who were anxious for good roles. Most of them did not have to resort to violence to achieve their aims. Dahlia Dearborn was, after all, very attractive. Even without great talent, she could easily have insinuated herself into the good graces of a man willing to finance her success. It was a cynical thought, but not altogether unfair. It was much the same as

Flora Bell had done, after all. But Flora Bell had been talented. That was the difference.

"Perhaps you should go and speak to Miss Dearborn," Milo suggested, surprising me.

"I should have thought you'd want to speak with her," I teased.

"You may have more luck getting information out of her than I did," he said.

I suspected what he really meant was that she would not be able to concentrate on the matter at hand in his presence, but I didn't press the issue.

"What are you going to do?" I asked as I prepared to go toward the dressing rooms.

"Wander about a bit," he said, then disappeared before I could quiz him further about his intentions.

As it was the quickest route to the dressing rooms, I walked down the aisle toward the stage. Despite the fact that the theatre was brightly lit and that I could hear the voices of those backstage, I felt a little queasy as I retraced my path from the night of the murder. I went up onto the stage and past the curtain where I had found Flora Bell hanging. I noticed that the gold curtain rope had been replaced. It was almost as though nothing had ever happened there.

Stepping backstage, I moved along the corridor. Aside from a few stagehands, who paid me little attention, I saw no one.

I reached the corridor where the dressing rooms were and hesitated. Would Dahlia Dearborn have taken over Flora Bell's dressing room? My instincts told me yes.

I moved to the door and knocked.

"Yes? Come in," she called.

"Hello, Miss Dearborn," I said as I opened the door and stepped inside. The room was mostly unchanged from when I had visited last, though I noticed that there was a box on the floor beside the little settee that seemed to contain some of Flora Bell's personal effects. It was sad how quickly all reminders of her had been cast aside.

"Hello, Mrs. Ames," Miss Dearborn said. "Please excuse the untidiness. I've been moving my things in here."

"It's a lovely room," I said, for lack of something better to say.

"Yes. And this dressing table is much larger than the one in my old dressing room. Except for one of the drawers is locked, and I haven't found the key."

This piqued my interest. Had Flora put something of importance inside the drawer?

"Oh?" I asked. "Which one?"

"This one," she said, tugging ineffectively on the bottom drawer on the left.

"Is it stuck?"

"No, locked. I suppose Flora kept some of her secret things in it."

"Secret things?" I repeated.

"Oh, she was always receiving letters and the like," she said, her eyes now on her reflection as she smoothed out her hair. "I saw her reading one once and then putting it there. It was from an admirer, I suppose."

I wondered if the letter she'd seen could have been one of the threatening notes Flora had received. So far as I knew, Gerard Holloway was now in possession of those letters. So why was the drawer still locked? Might there be something else hidden there?

"I suppose Mr. Holloway has the key," I suggested.

"It isn't likely. I think she didn't want Mr. Holloway to see them," she added slyly before changing the subject. "Did you only just arrive, Mrs. Ames?"

I realized that any more questions on the topic would likely draw suspicion, so reluctantly I let the matter drop.

"No, I've been here for perhaps half an hour. I saw some of the performance. You've done a wonderful job of taking over the part." This, at least, was not a lie, for she had seemed very much at ease assuming the role Flora Bell's death had left vacant.

"Thank you. I believe I have brought

something a bit different to the role than Flora did. I don't like to think of myself as replacing her, just as carrying on her legacy." She said this in a somewhat artificial tone, as though she were practicing the lines to recite to the press should the opportunity ever arise.

I decided perhaps this would give me an avenue of conversation that might make her warm to me. "Have you always wanted to be an actress, Miss Dearborn?" I asked.

"Oh, yes," she said. "I saw Lilian Braithwaite perform when I was very young, and, from that moment on, I never wanted to do anything else." Suddenly her eyes were alight and there was more animation in her face than I had yet seen there, even on the stage. I realized how powerful that dream had been and how much this moment had meant to her.

She seemed eager to talk now, warmed by my interest in her career, and waved me to the chair where Flora Bell had sat the day Milo and I had first come to the theatre.

"Did you grow up around the theatre?" I asked.

"Heavens, no," she said. "I grew up in a rather conventional family. I don't tell many people this, but Dahlia Dearborn isn't my real name."

I fought very hard to repress a smile at the way she treated this rather obvious piece of information as a confidence. "Really?" I asked.

"It was Mary Harris. Not a very suitable name for the stage."

"Dahlia Dearborn is certainly memorable," I said.

"My mother's favorite flowers were dahlias, and I thought 'Dearborn' sounded very nice with it. Besides, I didn't want to use 'Harris.' All the Harrises are in government, and I thought the name might leave a bad taste."

"Yes, I see." I remembered that Mrs. Roland had mentioned that Miss Dearborn came from an influential family.

I thought of what else Mrs. Roland had told me, that there had been some sort of trouble in Miss Dearborn's past.

"I'm sure you performed in a great many plays at school."

Was it my imagination, or did her pleasant expression falter for just a moment?

"Oh, not so very many," she said airily. "My parents liked me to concentrate on other things, and, anyway, they mostly did dull plays at school, stories for children. It was after school that I really began to develop my talent. My father has always

278

thought theatre was a waste of time, so I am hoping that this role will convince him otherwise."

It seemed that, like Mr. Landon's family, they had not been thrilled with her entrance into the theatre world.

"How did you come to meet Mr. Holloway?"

"It was rather a lucky thing," she said. "I had been wanting to be in a play, and I heard that he was looking for someone to star in *The Price of Victory.* I knew it was a wonderful opportunity. His name is well known in the theatre world, and the charity gala was sure to bring a lot of influential people to see it."

This assessment had been an astute one, for I had indeed seen many prominent individuals at the gala. It was possible that Miss Dearborn was shrewder than I had taken her to be.

"I wanted the lead role, of course, and I almost had it. Mr. Holloway was very interested in me. We were getting on well. He had me read some of the part and we became fast friends. I told him all about how I had longed to be an actress and my struggles with my family, and I was sure he was sympathetic and intended to offer me the part. But then a few days later, he said that he was very sorry but he had decided to cast Flora Bell instead."

She had meant to relate this in a careless way, but I saw the bitterness in her eyes as she spoke.

"That must have been very disappointing," I said sympathetically.

"It was more than just talent that got her the role," she said.

"You mean he was . . . attracted to her," I suggested.

She smiled, but her eyes were hard. "You might say that. She told me later that he seemed instantly drawn to her. She said they talked the whole night when they first met." She gave me a skeptical look that suggested talking had not been all they had done.

"I see."

"She said she felt as though she had known him for years. He convinced her that she should take part in his play. I don't think she really wanted to at first. It's not the sort of play she had hoped to be in. She had dreams of being a serious actress. Shakespeare and things like that. But she did all right in the part."

She had done more than all right. I had no doubts that, had Flora Bell lived, her performance in *The Price of Victory* would have led her to great things in the theatrical world. Her death was a great shame in more ways than one.

"Who do you suppose killed her?" I asked.

I meant to throw her off guard with the questions, but Dahlia Dearborn was not the sort of woman who was easily flustered. "Oh, I don't know," she said with a shrug. "I think perhaps it was some maniac who followed her into the theatre. Perhaps someone saw her performance and was so overcome that they decided they had to have her and, when she resisted, they killed her."

It was, perhaps, the sort of melodrama that would work well in a radio play or an inexpensive theatre production, but it wasn't very plausible from a more realistic standpoint. After all, I didn't think Flora Bell could have been easily surprised on that stage. It seemed certain that she had been standing there with someone that she knew before the curtain rope had been suddenly forced around her neck.

"But suppose it was someone she knew," I pressed. "Who do you think it might have been?"

She seemed to consider this for a moment. "I think it might have been Kit," she said at last. She said it without any sign of malice, and I was very curious as to why she had picked him out as the most likely suspect.

"Why do you think so?" I asked.

She had definitely warmed to me. I almost felt as though we were becoming friends. Or perhaps it was just that she was enjoying giving her opinion on the matter. Whatever the reason, she leaned toward me, her eyes suddenly bright. I recognized the look of a woman who had a bit of juicy gossip to share.

"I oughtn't say anything," she said. "But I suppose it will be all right to tell you. I think it might have been Kit because I heard him talking to Flora one day. They were having a bit of an argument. He said, 'I know you love me, Flora. You're wrong about all of this. One day you'll see.'" She recited the words carefully, as though they had made a strong impression on her.

"Wrong about what?" I asked. "Her relationship with Mr. Holloway?"

"I don't know. Someone went by just then and I didn't hear her reply," she said, not the least bit embarrassed by the implication she had been eavesdropping. "But then he said something that caught my attention. He said it in a low voice, so it was difficult to hear, but I'm certain he said something about how her behavior would be the death of her."

"Did he indeed?" I asked.

She nodded. "I didn't think much of it at the time. But ever since the murder happened, I have begun to wonder. Kit is the sort of man who doesn't like being rejected. He hasn't much experience with it, after all. Anyone he's ever set his eyes on has fallen sway to his charms. So when Flora Bell turned to Mr. Holloway, I think it was a bit of a blow to his pride."

I had suspected as much myself, but I was a bit surprised at this bit of insight from Miss Dearborn. I wouldn't have thought her to be a particularly observant sort of woman, but it seemed that I had misjudged her. One could never tell, I supposed.

I did have one question, however. "If she had felt an attraction to Mr. Holloway from the start, how was it that she came to be involved with Mr. Landon?"

She shrugged. "I suppose Mr. Holloway fought his attraction for a while, being married and all. When we first started the play, his wife came around fairly often. I think Flora might have taken up with Mr. Landon in part to make him jealous. I suppose it worked."

"Yes, I suppose so."

"Of course, I don't suppose that means Kit killed her," she said.

"Not necessarily," I agreed.

"But he had a reason, all the same."

"It seemed to me that Mr. Lebeau was not particularly fond of her," I ventured, hoping to draw her out.

She smiled, and it seemed that this smile was a bit malicious. "I think he had a fancy for her, too. Everyone seemed to be drawn to Flora, though I'm not sure why."

"And you think she rebuffed Mr. Lebeau's advances."

"I couldn't say for sure," she said. "I didn't ever see anything telling between them. But I saw him watching her often enough when she wasn't looking. His eyes would follow her around the stage, and more than once I saw him look at her with a certain sort of longing."

I wondered. Was it possible he had been infatuated with the young, pretty actress and she had looked on him as nothing more than an aging player well past his prime?

Of course, I reminded myself, it might well be that the killer was neither Christopher Landon nor Balthazar Lebeau.

It was all well and good to say that these gentlemen had had their pride wounded by a woman who had ended up murdered. But, after all, many gentlemen were rebuffed by women and did not resort to killing them. I would not do either of these men the disservice of assuming they had been so desperate for the attentions of Flora Bell that they had decided to murder her when she had rejected them. Mr. Landon and Mr. Lebeau had apparently had great romantic success, and I did not think that one failure would be enough to drive either of them to such a drastic action.

However, the fact that they had both had difficulties with her did mean it was possible that some sort of violent confrontation had occurred. A strangulation with a curtain rope did not speak of premeditation, and it still seemed to me that whoever had killed Miss Bell had done so under the influence of some sudden uncontrollable emotion.

But where, then, did the threatening letters fit into all of this? I realized I had never questioned Miss Dearborn about them, though she had given me an excellent opportunity.

"You mentioned that you saw Miss Bell receiving a letter," I said. "Did you know someone was sending her threats before she was killed?"

The effect of my words was startling. Miss Dearborn turned quite pale before giving a casual shake of her head that was not at all convincing. "No, I didn't know. In fact, I'm not even sure it was a letter I saw her receive. It might have been anything, a bill, perhaps."

She turned to her dressing table and shifted a few things around before turning back to me.

"I still think it was a maniac that killed her," she said with a sudden, almost aggressive assurance. "After all, a decent person just doesn't do something like that. And one likes to believe that one's friends are decent."

One did like to believe it. But that didn't make it true.

I left Miss Dearborn's dressing room just in time to see Mr. Lebeau leaving his.

"Hello, Mr. Lebeau," I called.

He looked up sharply, but the surprise that flickered momentarily in his eyes was soon smoothed over by his usual expression of indolent amusement.

"Mrs. Ames. How lovely to see you again."

"Mr. Holloway asked us to come by the theatre and say that he was sorry he couldn't be here today and that he hoped the rehearsal would go on without him."

"Yes, I believe he telephoned. But I suppose he sent representatives to make sure everything was in order."

"Everything seems to be going well," I said. "It seems Miss Dearborn has stepped quite readily into the role."

His mouth tipped up at the corner. "Yes, well. I suppose desperate times call for desperate measures."

"You've elected to stay on with the play?" I asked.

"For now. I have a few other things lined up that I may move on to, if things work out right."

I remembered the meeting he had mentioned with a producer the night of the play. Had Inspector Jones looked into that? If Mr. Lebeau had been with the man at the time of Flora Bell's death, he could be eliminated as a suspect.

"I see. Well, I'm certain your public would enjoy seeing you in another play when your time with *The Price of Victory* has run its course."

"I hope so," he said vaguely.

For all his easy charm, there was something distant about Mr. Lebeau today. I could not quite put my finger on what it was. I decided that perhaps I should change topics.

"I've recently discovered that we have a mutual acquaintance."

"Oh?"

"Yes, Yvonne Roland."

I was not sure what reaction I had been expecting, but I found myself vaguely surprised by the wide grin that spread across his face, clearing away the clouded expression that had been there a moment before. "Yvonne . . . Roland now, is she? There have been so many husbands that it's difficult to keep track."

"Yes, I suppose that's true," I replied with a laugh. Somehow the mention of Mrs. Roland had broken through the barrier that had existed between us, and now he seemed much more at ease. "She speaks fondly of you, though I understand you broke her heart," I said with a smile.

"Hardly that," he replied. "She married quickly enough after we parted. She was never one for sentiment."

"No," I agreed. "She doesn't seem as though she would be."

"I wouldn't mind seeing old Yvonne again," he said, the expression on his face speaking of pleasant recollections.

"It's always nice when a person from the past evokes pleasant memories rather than unpleasant ones," I said. I had been speaking from personal experience, but I realized as I spoke the words that they could be construed as having another meaning.

He looked at me searchingly, something flickering in his eyes for only an instant before it was gone.

"I was engaged to be married to someone else before my husband," I explained. "I saw him again not too long ago, and it was nice to part again on more pleasant terms."

"Ah, yes," he said, and I was certain he had thought I was hinting at something else.

"But I suppose not everyone has had such an experience," I said, meeting his penetrating gaze with one of my own. "Sometimes partings can be painful."

"Yes," he answered. "Mr. Landon can tell you about such things, I'm sure."

"Oh?" I asked. I was very curious what he might have to say, after what Miss Dearborn had told me.

"I don't mean to cast aspersions," he said, though clearly he did.

"Everyone has their secrets."

"Do you think so?" I asked.

He gave a short laugh. "Do you suppose any of us here are spotless? No, I'd wager there are enough skeletons in this theatre alone to fill Highgate Cemetery."

"But you meant something specific about Mr. Landon?" I asked.

He looked at me, that canny look coming back into his dark eyes. "I meant that Flora

Bell is not the first woman of Kit Landon's acquaintance who has ended up dead."

18

With his characteristic flair for the dramatic, Mr. Lebeau had swept away at this pronouncement, leaving me to wonder just what he had meant by it. Mrs. Roland had mentioned an unfortunate event in Mr. Landon's past. If it had indeed been the tragic death of a woman with whom he was involved, I was surprised that Yvonne Roland had not remembered all the sordid details. Then again, perhaps it was the sort of thing that would have been covered up at the time. I was going to have to see if I could discover the particulars.

I had yet to see any sign of Milo and went back out onto the stage. I stopped, a bit startled to see Christopher Landon sitting on the edge, his feet dangling into the orchestra pit, a bottle in his hand. I had not realized he was still here.

Under normal circumstances, I would have tiptoed quietly away. I was not one to intrude upon people's privacy, and something in his posture, plus the presence of a bottle — sans glass — at this hour of the day, indicated that he was indulging in a moment of private emotion. Considering all that had occurred, however, I thought perhaps it would be best for me to speak to him while his guard was down.

"Mr. Landon?" I said softly, walking out onto the stage.

He didn't turn. "Good morning, Mrs. Ames."

"I'm sorry if I'm intruding," I said.

"You are, but an intrusion is welcome at the moment," he said. "Come and sit with me, will you?"

His words were not slurred; he had too much mastery over his voice for that. But there was a hazy quality to his tone that led me to believe that the contents of the bottle had begun to take effect.

My suspicions were confirmed as I reached him.

He held up the bottle. It was nearly empty, and the lingering smell of what had already been consumed wafted up from his person. "Would you care for a drink?" he asked.

"Thank you, no," I said. I lowered myself onto the stage floor beside him, my feet dangling into the pit like his. It occurred to me that this was something of a vulnerable position if he was a murderer, but we were not really alone in the theatre, after all. I had just left Dahlia Dearborn and Balthazar Lebeau near their dressing rooms. And Milo was somewhere about.

For a moment we sat in silence.

"I don't know what I'm still doing here," he said at last.

"Some of the others are still here as well," I said.

"That's not what I mean," he replied. "I don't know why I'm still here, still doing this wretched play."

"Perhaps you're doing it to honor Miss Bell's memory."

"Do you think it's possible to hate someone and love them at the same time?" he asked, staring out at the empty seats.

"I . . . I think so," I said. In the lowest depths of our marital difficulties, I had hated Milo a great deal even as I loved him desperately, and I could relate to the sentiment.

"There have been other women in other plays, but she did something to me. If I believed in curses and such rot, I'd say I was bewitched. As soon as I saw her, I knew that I wanted to have her. She was all that I could think about."

"Love strikes unexpectedly at times," I said.

He raked a hand through his hair. "I began to think ridiculous things. That we could go on performing together, make a name for ourselves as a couple of the stage. I began to think that we might even get married . . ."

He stopped, opened the bottle, and took a long drink from it. I said nothing, having learned from experience that one could often be most useful to a person in need of a confidante by saying nothing at all.

After a moment, he continued. "And then Holloway came along and swept her off her feet. I couldn't compete, not with all he could offer her. She couldn't see that he didn't really care for her."

"You don't believe he loved her?" I asked.

"No, Holloway didn't love her," Mr. Landon said scornfully. "In fact, they were always arguing over one thing or another, like that blazing row that night after the play, where they said all those things to each other. I suppose Holloway regrets that now." There was something a bit smug in his tone, as though he would be glad to know that Gerard Holloway was suffering. This bit of vindictiveness was not what had caught my attention, however.

"What did they say to each other?" I asked. The first time I had questioned him about it, he had claimed not to know what it was about. But he had not been drinking then. Perhaps now he would be more forthcoming.

"I had wanted to congratulate Flora, to tell her what a wonderful job she had done. I hadn't yet had the chance to speak to her."

It struck me that he would have had plenty of time to congratulate her on her performance after the play had ended. They had taken their bows together and would presumably have gone down the long corridor to their dressing rooms at roughly the same time. Of course, it was always possible in the rush and post-performance euphoria that they had not spoken. He might very well be telling the truth, but it was strange that he had been seeking her out.

"I had seen her a few moments before, going offstage," he said. "I walked that way to have a word with her when I heard their voices."

"You're sure it was Mr. Holloway?" I asked.

He snorted derisively. "I know his voice well enough. I've been listening to him drone on about one thing or another for months."

"What was the argument about?" I asked.

He looked at me speculatively, as though suddenly realizing that I had been asking questions. It had certainly taken him long enough. "What's your stake in all of this, Mrs. Ames?" he asked. His tone had lost some of its hard edge, and I felt that he was genuinely curious about my involvement.

What was my stake in this? It was a good question. Though I had told myself that I was doing it to help my friend Georgina and to assist Detective Inspector Jones in whatever way I could, a part of me knew that it was more than that.

I was invested in this situation because I wanted to help find a way for Gerard and Georgina Holloway to be together again. They had loved each other so desperately once. It seemed impossible that that love no longer existed.

I realized that he was still waiting for an answer, so I gave him a somewhat embarrassed smile. "I'm afraid this isn't the first such case in which I've been involved," I told him. "It's silly of me, perhaps, but I find I enjoy trying to work out the puzzle."

He watched me for a long moment, as though trying to determine what I was concealing behind that answer. He was an astute gentleman, and I was not at all sure that my society-lady façade would be satisfactory to him. Apparently, it was, however, for he answered at last.

"I didn't hear the beginning of it. They were both already in high dudgeon by the time I was within earshot. Holloway was haranguing her about something to do with her performance."

"Her performance?" I frowned.

"Yes, one of the scenes between Victoire and Durant. 'What was that with Lebeau?' he asked her."

"What did he mean?" I asked.

He shrugged. "Probably a bit of staging gone wrong. Holloway is mad about his staging. He likes everything just so. And he was overstrung about the whole evening. Wanted it to go off well."

"And what did she say?"

"Flora could hold her own when need be. She replied that she had had the right to make her own decisions, that Holloway was not her lord and master." He laughed. "That riled him, I'm sure. If there's one thing Holloway enjoys, it's being lord and master. That's when he said the bit about wringing her neck."

"I see," I said thoughtfully. There had been no sign of tension between them when they had come to the gala, so perhaps they had smoothed things over. Or perhaps they were just very good at acting.

"Did you hear anything more?" I asked.

He shook his head. "No, I didn't want to hear anything else. I was very much afraid I was going to hit Holloway if I heard any more. I didn't like the way he spoke to her. But it was none of my business, not anymore."

It was curious. I wondered why it was that Mr. Holloway should have been angry with Flora Bell. The performance had been a huge success, and I had noticed nothing amiss in her interactions with Balthazar Lebeau onstage. The audience had risen to their feet and had showered her with praise from the first moment that she stepped into the ballroom. Why then had he been dissatisfied?

It seemed to me more likely that he was piqued over the trouble with Georgina, as he had mentioned to Milo before the performance. His strained relationship and the stresses of opening night had no doubt put him in a temper, and he had taken it out on Flora Bell.

Of course, there was also the possibility that it might be a lie.

Christopher Landon looked to all the world like a carefree playboy of the theatre, yet he had clearly felt strongly about Flora Bell. Was it possible that he had killed her and was trying to shift blame onto Mr. Holloway, saying he and Flora had quarreled?

Then again, it might just be the alcohol, making him morose and speculative.

As if to prove my point, he took another long drink from the bottle and mumbled, "It's my curse, to be in love with a dead woman."

"I'm sorry, Mr. Landon," I said softly. "I know words are inadequate in cases like these, but I do hope you'll find happiness again."

He didn't answer, staring out into the darkened auditorium.

There was nothing else to say, so I thought it best to take my leave. I started to rise, and just as I did, my foot slipped off the edge of the stage and I nearly lost my balance. He reached out and caught my arm, keeping me from a nasty tumble.

"Be careful, Mrs. Ames," he said with a smile. "We should very much hate for another tragedy to happen on this stage."

I retreated from the stage and made my way out into the foyer, where Milo was waiting for me.

He looked up as I walked toward him.

"Oh, there you are, darling," he asked. "Ready to go home?"

"Yes," I said. "But where did you get off to?"

"I walked around the theatre a bit, getting the lay of the land, so to speak."

"Did you learn anything of interest?" I asked.

"Only that it would have been a fairly easy thing for the killer to slip out unnoticed, if he was indeed still in the theatre when you discovered Miss Bell's body. There are several exits, including the stage door, which is directly across from a door to the building where the gala was being held."

"Then the killer might have gone across the alley and back to the gala without being observed by anyone on the street."

"Yes. What about you? Did you learn anything from Dahlia Dearborn?"

"Perhaps," I said. "We'll discuss it later. Is there anything else we need to do for Mr. Holloway?"

"I don't think so. They seem to have everything well in hand."

We returned to our car, and, as we rode home, I related the information I had gotten from Miss Dearborn and Mr. Lebeau regarding Mr. Landon. "I know it's not definite proof of anything," I said, "but if both of them suspect him, there might be something to it. However, when I spoke to Mr. Landon, I had a different impression. He doesn't seem as though he wanted to kill her. In fact, I'm certain he was still in love with her."

"Men have killed women they've professed to love before," Milo pointed out.

It was not exactly a happy thought.

We pulled up in front of our flat, but Milo didn't get out of the car. "I'm going out," he said. "I'm going to look into Mr. Bell's whereabouts a bit more. I'm not sure when I shall be home."

"I want to speak to Mr. Bell," I said. "So if you decide to talk to him, ring me up."

"It may be late."

"I'll be waiting," I said firmly.

I watched as the car pulled away and wondered if he had learned something that he was keeping from me, as he had been known to do in the past. I hoped not.

Even if he was really looking for Frederick Bell, I somehow doubted he would ring me up to let me know. That would remain to be seen.

I walked into the flat and was greeted by Winnelda, who almost seemed to have been waiting for me near the door. "That policeman is here again," she said in an urgent whisper.

"Inspector Jones?" I asked, taking off my hat and gloves. "Has he been here long?"

"No, madam. I told him I didn't know when to expect you back, but he said that he would wait a few minutes to see if you arrived."

"I'll go and see him now. Thank you, Winnelda."

I went into the sitting room and found Inspector Jones looking at the portrait of me Balthazar Lebeau had been studying the night of our little party.

"It's an excellent likeness, Mrs. Ames," he said, turning as I entered. "He's captured that look of determination in your eyes."

As the portrait had been painted during another murder investigation, I felt that perhaps Inspector Jones's appraisal was accurate.

"Thank you. I'm glad you've come by, Inspector Jones," I said. "Would you care for some tea?"

"Thank you, no. I was just in the neighborhood and thought I would drop in. Do you have a few moments to compare notes?"

"Certainly," I replied, excited at the prospect that he might be willing to give information as well as receive it.

I ought to have known better.

We settled into our seats and Inspector Jones regarded me expectantly. "Why don't you begin?"

I was forced to acknowledge that, though I was certain Inspector Jones liked me and had come to value my opinion when it came to certain things, we were not equal partners in this venture. Not that I expected the police to share all their evidence with me. But having worked together on previous cases, I did feel as though I was entitled to a bit more than a common civilian.

"I'm not entirely sure what I've learned," I admitted. "Nothing definitive, that's certain."

"Even little pieces of information might prove useful when viewed as a whole."

I considered all I had discovered and decided to begin with what was potentially the most telling piece of gossip.

"Did you know about Christopher Landon's past?" I asked him. A part of me hoped not. I enjoyed being able to present him with information he had not yet uncovered on his own.

"About the girl who threw herself off of the bridge?" he asked, spoiling my surprise. Apparently, he knew more than I did.

I was trying to decide whether to feign knowledge of the details or ask him outright when he seemed to deduce that I did not know the particulars and went on.

"It probably has nothing to do with any of this," he said. "Although, one never knows for certain. He was involved with a girl, Helen Whitney. They were engaged to be married at one point, but, when things had run their course, he broke it off with her. They found her in the Thames. Apparently, she had thrown herself off a bridge, but, given the circumstances, one wonders."

"Yes," I replied. "It's a bit strange that two women he was reportedly involved with died violent deaths."

"Of course, it sometimes happens," Inspector Jones replied noncommittally. "Young people these days can be volatile."

"But what do you think?" I pressed. "Are the two deaths connected?"

"I have not found anything to suggest so," he said. "For one thing, the first woman left a note. She was distraught that their relationship had ended. This business with Miss Bell seemed to be the other way around. It was he who was upset that she no longer returned his affections."

"Speaking of notes, have you any more information on who was sending those threatening letters?"

"I'm afraid not. Mr. Holloway gave us the

letters in his possession, but an analysis of them has proven inconclusive. The handwriting had been disguised and both the paper and ink are of an inferior quality, easily purchased at any corner shop in London."

I sighed. "Then we are no closer to finding the killer."

He smiled. "You mustn't let this business trouble you too much, Mrs. Ames. After all, it's my job to lose sleep over the matter."

I returned his smile. "That may well be, Inspector, but I can't help but feel that I should have done something to stop it happening in the first place."

"You couldn't have done anything."

"I still feel that if I had telephoned you when she received those letters, or if I had paid closer attention to her whereabouts on that night . . ." My voice trailed off. I had not really realized until now how deeply I felt the weight of Flora Bell's death. I had known that the woman was being threatened, had believed the threats to be a danger, and yet I had not been able to prevent her murder.

"You offered to telephone the police and she refused," he said. "Miss Bell was a woman very capable of making her own decisions. The notes were addressed to her, and if she did not want the police contacted then there was not much you could do about it."

He was right, to a certain extent. Flora Bell had been adamant that she didn't want the police involved.

I suddenly began to wonder why she had been so insistent. Did she know more about the matter than she claimed? Did it have something to do with the locked drawer of her dressing table?

"What are you thinking about?" Inspector Jones asked quietly.

I looked up. I wondered if I should say something about the drawer. Surely the police would have opened it if they thought it important. I decided instead to mention the other matter on my mind.

"She was strongly against the presence of the police, and I am beginning to wonder if she might have been trying to protect someone."

"Her brother, perhaps?" he said, reaching the same conclusion I had.

"That would make the most sense," I replied. "Perhaps she suspected that he was sending the letters to frighten her and didn't believe that he would do her harm."

"An interesting conjecture," Inspector Jones said. "I look forward to having a word with the young man."

I looked up, surprised. "You haven't spoken with him yet?"

"No. I'm afraid Mr. Bell has proven . . . elusive."

So Freddy Bell had been dodging the police. That did not seem to be a point in his favor. Of course, he had just lost his sister, his only living relative so far as I knew. It could not be an easy thing to reconcile himself to.

I wondered if I should tell Inspector Jones that Milo had located him at his gambling club and was currently trying to learn more about his whereabouts, but I decided against it. If I could speak to Freddy Bell tonight, I was sure he would reveal more to me than if he was questioned by the police.

"Have you any other leads?" I asked Inspector Jones, hoping my change of subject was not too abrupt.

"There's one more thing," he said. "You mentioned Balthazar Lebeau told you he had a meeting with a producer that night of the gala."

"Yes," I said. I should have known Inspector Jones would not miss this angle. "He said he was leaving the gala to meet with him."

"When I asked for the name of this gentleman, Mr. Lebeau was unable to provide any other information. Said he had received a telegram arranging the meeting but he had thrown it out."

"But surely someone must have seen him with the gentleman?"

Inspector Jones shook his head. "According to Mr. Lebeau, the gentleman did not keep the meeting."

Strange. It was possible, of course, that it was a legitimate story and the producer in question had been detained. However, I wondered if there was something more to this story than met the eye.

"It's very odd," I mused.

"That's what I thought."

"Have you any theories?" I asked.

"A few," he replied, his expression growing, in that inevitable way, slightly more guarded when faced with a question, "but nothing much more to share at the moment. As I said, I was just in the neighborhood and thought I would drop by."

"Then this might almost be considered a social call," I said with a smile. "You haven't taken your notebook out yet. I'll take that as a good sign."

He smiled back. "Am I as officious as all that?"

"I don't know whether you realize it,

Inspector, but you're very intimidating."

"I shouldn't have thought anything could intimidate you, Mrs. Ames," he said.

"I shall take that as a compliment. You might tell Mr. Ames, too. He seems to think my lack of timidity a weakness rather than a strength."

"I think Mr. Ames is well aware of your strengths and is learning to appreciate them," he said. "You'll pardon me for saying so, but I've always thought that you and Mr. Ames made better allies than enemies." Inspector Jones had been witness to several of the problems in my marriage, and I had always felt that he was someone who sympathized.

"Things are . . . much improved, thank you," I said.

"I'm glad to hear it."

"And how are your wife and daughters?" I asked.

I had never met the inspector's family, but it had been, somehow, intriguing to me to find that he had one. Our interactions had always been professional, not social, so it always seemed a bit foreign that he engaged in normal family pursuits. I somehow had a difficult time picturing him sitting with his family playing cards and listening to the wireless. What kind of music did policemen prefer?

"They're very well, thank you," he said. As usual, he volunteered no more information than was necessary, no doubt a habit of his profession that had extended itself to his personal life.

"Well, I suppose I shan't keep you any longer," he said, rising from his seat. "Thank you for taking the time to talk with me, though I arrived unannounced."

"We should be happy to entertain you any time," I said sincerely.

He left and I thought how glad I was that we were on such friendly terms. Of course, he was not going to be happy if he learned we had been keeping Freddy Bell's whereabouts from him.

But one problem at a time.

Inspector Jones had not been gone for ten minutes when the telephone rang. It was Mrs. Roland.

"I don't have much time to talk, dear," she said without preamble. "It's nearly time for my fencing lesson. However, I've just remembered something that might be of use to you. It's about that Harris girl."

"Dahlia Dearborn?" I asked, suddenly alert.

"Yes. I've remembered what the trouble was. There was a fencing instructor involved; that's what called it to mind. I was just preparing for my lesson when it all came rushing back. There was an instructor at Miss Harris's school. He was young, and, one assumes, French. Miss Harris, or Dearborn, developed a schoolgirl's crush on him, but it was one of the other girls who was his star pupil. Apparently, Miss Harris grew resentful and wrote, shall we say, inappropriate letters to the instructor, signing the other girl's name."

"She wrote letters, did she?" I said, my pulse picking up the pace.

"It caused a great scandal, and the other girl was very nearly sent home, but it all came out at last and Miss Harris was reprimanded severely. Of course, her family was influential and the whole thing was smoothed over rather quickly. You know how such things go."

"Yes, I suppose so," I said, my mind spinning.

"Well, I must dash. My instructor is rather charming himself." She gave a deep laugh. "Good-bye, Mrs. Ames."

She rang off, and I set the telephone down, lost in thought. So Miss Dearborn had once employed letter-writing as a strategy. I remembered how she had paled when I had mentioned the threatening letters during our conversation in her dressing room. Had it been fear that she was found out? Her school days were long behind her and she had a different name now, so perhaps she had thought there would never be anything to connect her to that tactic. It hadn't worked for her before, but I couldn't help but wonder if she had decided to give it another try.

19

Milo, predictably, was not home for dinner. After I had eaten, I went into the sitting room, where Emile kept me company. I tried to keep from glancing expectantly at the telephone, with limited success.

It was close to midnight, and I was just about to go to bed, when the telephone rang.

I hurried to answer it, and was both surprised and glad to find that it was Milo.

"Darling, I know it's late but I'm with Freddy Bell. I'm afraid he's losing rather a lot of money, so I don't expect they'll let him continue his gambling for long. If you want to talk to him, you'd better hurry."

"Where are you?" I asked.

Milo gave me the name and address of the gambling club, and I scribbled it on a little notebook near the telephone.

"Don't let him leave," I said, reaching for

my handbag and gloves. "I'm on my way."

I took a cab to the address Milo had given me, as he had taken the car earlier in the day.

Alighting from the vehicle, I found myself on a well-lit street, a great deal of people in evening dress milling about. Apparently, this was a fashionable nightspot, though I had certainly never been here before and the condition of the neighborhood was nothing to speak of.

I glanced again at the slip of paper in my hand. The address in question corresponded to a nondescript building at the corner of the street. It seemed it was the sort of gambling club that did not like to advertise itself. Before I could move toward it, however, a gentleman approached me. He was dressed in a somewhat shabby tweed suit with a cap pulled down low over his eyes, and I had the distinct impression I had seen someone in an identical ensemble in an American gangster film.

"Mrs. Ames, is it?" he asked in a low voice.

"Yes," I admitted cautiously.

"Your husband says to tell you that he's in the café across the street." He nodded in the direction of a poorly maintained building on the corner that I would not have taken for a café at first glance.

How very like Milo to send an underworld character to fetch me so that he could remain comfortably settled in the café. I did hope this meant that he had managed to keep hold of Freddy Bell.

I thanked the man and tipped him before walking across the street and into the café. The interior was only marginally more cheerful than the exterior had been. The lighting was poor and the worn tables sat atop a scuffed tile floor. This did not seem to adversely affect business, however, for there were a great many people inside. The air was thick with cigarette smoke, and a radio somewhere behind the counter was playing a mournful jazz tune.

"You want a table, miss?" a waitress with a dirty apron and untidy hair asked me.

"No . . . I'm meeting someone," I said, looking around the room for Milo. I spotted him sitting at a table in the corner with Freddy Bell. "There they are. Thank you."

Milo looked up as I moved toward the table and started to rise, but I put a hand on his shoulder.

"Don't get up, gentlemen," I said as I slid into a seat beside him. "I don't want to interrupt."

Freddy Bell didn't seem to have heard me.

He sat with an empty plate and a cup of coffee on the table before him. I had wondered how Milo had managed to lure him here, but it seemed that a meal might have been incentive enough. I suddenly doubted Freddy Bell had been getting enough to eat since his sister died.

"Hello, Mr. Bell," I said softly. "We met at the theatre and again at the gala."

He looked up at me, a bit of a startled expression on his face. He looked different from when I had seen him last, and I realized the youthful confidence had been replaced by a look of sadness.

"Yes, I remember," he said at last.

"I'm very sorry about the loss of your sister."

"Thank you." There was something very restrained about his responses, as though he was trying very hard to keep his emotions in check. I remembered how he had looked in the photograph at the funeral, a bit bewildered by this sudden shifting of his world on its axis.

"Would you care for something to eat, miss?" the waitress asked suddenly, having followed me to the table.

"No, thank you. Perhaps just a cup of tea."

"Very well, miss."

She went off to fetch it, and I turned back

to Freddy Bell.

He had picked up his spoon and was list-lessly stirring his coffee.

"I know Flora was very special to you."

He nodded.

"Tell me, what was she like?" I asked.

He looked up at me as though I had asked a silly question. "You met her," he said.

"Yes," I replied. "But I'm sure a meeting with her as an actress did not represent who she really was."

He seemed to consider this for a moment, and then he spoke. "She was a good sister. Oh, we quarreled more than our share, but I always knew that she meant to do right by me."

"I could tell she cared a great deal for you."

It was as though, with these words, I had broken through some sort of barrier. He seemed to forget that Milo was there, and leaned toward me, his eyes filled with tears. "It was just the two of us. She was the last of my family. Now that she's dead, I don't know what I'll do."

"I'm sorry," I said.

" 'Chin up, Freddy,' that's what she would have said. No matter how bad things go, she'd always tell me, 'Chin up. Things'll work out all right in the end.' I expect she'd tell me that now if she could."

"I'm sure she would," I said sincerely.

"I've had a bit of hard luck lately, too. Flora had some money put by, and I could certainly use it. But that old witch of a landlady won't let me into her room. She doesn't like men, it seems. Wouldn't let me in the house, even though I was Flora's own brother."

"Well, I'm sure the police will be able to retrieve things for you," I said.

"I still can't believe she's gone," he whispered, and the brokenness in his tone brought tears to my eyes. " 'Family's important, don't you think?' she said to me not long ago. 'Blood matters more than anything else in the end.' Now the last of my blood is gone."

"I know it's been a dreadful shock. It was all so unexpected."

"She should never have got involved with this play. Never should have taken up with Mr. Holloway. Our mum always tried to discourage her, always said the theatre would lead to a bad end for Flora. I expect she was right."

I searched for something comforting to say, but Freddy Bell charged ahead without waiting for platitudes.

"It was Landon's fault," he said bitterly.

I glanced at Milo before turning my attention back to Freddy Bell. "Why do you say that?" I asked.

"He broke her heart, and she turned to Holloway."

Now I was confused. "I'm not sure I understand."

"She was involved with Landon before Holloway," he said, as though that explained it all.

"Yes, I know," I replied. "But I was given to understand that it was she who broke it off."

He shook his head. "I came into her dressing room one day after she had gone to see him and found her crying. When I asked her what was wrong she said, 'I never should have fallen in love with an actor. They're too good at pretending.'"

"Did you ask her what she meant?" I asked.

He shook his head. "I tried to comfort her as best I could. But I think it was why she took up with Holloway like she did. She said, 'One can't go on living in the past; it isn't healthy.' Of course, I don't think she really believed that. She wanted to get back at Landon, all right."

This story certainly didn't fit with Mr. Landon's account. I wondered now if he,

too, had been putting on a performance onstage this afternoon.

" 'It's just like in the play,' " Freddy Bell
said.

"I beg your pardon?"

"That's what Flora said to me the night
she died."

"What do you mean?" I pressed.

"She said, 'Everything's gone wrong. It's
just like in the play.' "

The Price of Victory was a story of love lost.
Did she mean her affair with Mr. Landon?
Or perhaps she had sensed that Holloway
was trying to break things off, as Georgina
had said.

"Do you think things were going poorly
between her and Holloway?" Milo asked.

"I don't know. Flora wasn't much of one
for confiding in people. She always kept a
stiff upper lip. She wanted to protect me
from things, I think, but I should have
protected her. I . . . If I had only known
that something was really wrong."

"Then you didn't know about the letters?"
I asked.

He looked up, and I was certain that, for
just an instant, fear crossed his features.
"No," he said. "What sort of letters?"

"Letters telling her that she should leave
the play."

"She didn't tell me anything about that," he said. "But I suppose if the police find the writer, they'll find the killer."

"The police are trying to get information from everyone who was at the gala; they haven't been able to reach you," I said.

It was the wrong thing to say.

He rose from his seat suddenly, the chair wobbling, its legs clattering against the tiles. "I've taken up too much of your time. Thank you for the dinner, Mr. Ames. And thank you for taking the time to talk with me."

"I was glad to, Mr. Bell," I said, though it felt strange to call him Mr. Bell at this moment, for he seemed suddenly very young.

He walked away, and I felt a little stab of pity for him, along with the uncomfortable sensation that he was hiding something.

We went to bed when we arrived home, but I couldn't sleep. My mind kept turning over the murder, and I found that the more I thought about it the more disturbing everything was. I couldn't seem to make sense of any of it.

"What are you thinking about?" Milo asked into the darkness.

"How did you know I was awake?" I asked.

"You breathe differently when you're asleep," he said. "Besides, I can feel how rigid you are, like a marble statue but with exceptionally soft skin. What's the matter?"

I sighed. "I've been thinking about this murder."

"I know that," he said. "There's little chance you'd be thinking of anything else. I mean what aspect of it is troubling you?"

"For one thing, I'm sorry for Freddy Bell," I said.

"Freddy Bell can take care of himself," Milo said.

"I know he seems hardened in some ways, but he's still very young. Flora's death is bound to affect him greatly. I do hope he'll be all right."

"I'd wager that was just the sort of impression he hoped to make on you," Milo said. "He seemed to be doing well enough when I bribed him to come and speak to us."

So it had been more than the promise of a meal that had brought him to the café. Well, I could not fault Milo's methods when they had been so successful. Besides, I was glad he had helped Freddy Bell, though what the boy really needed was someone to look after him.

"He's hiding something," I said. "When I mentioned the letters, his manner changed."

"Yes, I noticed that," Milo said. "He seems to know more about the matter than he let on."

"And I don't know what to make of what he said about Christopher Landon. Surely Flora Bell wasn't in love with him? He spoke to me only this afternoon about how difficult it was to lose Flora, about how Holloway had stolen her away. It completely contradicts what Freddy Bell told us tonight."

"Then one of them is lying," Milo said.

"Yes, but which? And why?" If Christopher Landon had indeed been the one to break things off with Flora Bell, it seemed a better argument against his having killed her than if she had broken it off with him. Why, then, wouldn't he have said so? But what would Freddy Bell have to gain by lying?

"Come, darling, don't think about it anymore tonight," Milo said, as though it was as easy for me to brush things aside as it was for him. "Try to get some sleep."

He pulled me against him, and, though I was sure I was not going to be able to rest, something about the warmth of him and the soothing, steady sound of his breathing relaxed me, and I soon drifted off.

I was roused from a very heavy sleep

sometime later by a loud pounding sound. I sat up, disoriented, wondering what the noise was. It took me a moment to realize that it was an insistent knock at the front door. It was pitch black in the room, so I could not see the clock, but I knew that it was very late and I could think of no reason why someone would be pounding upon our door at that time of night.

It briefly crossed my mind to worry about Winnelda opening the door, but I remembered that she was away visiting her mother.

I switched on the lamp and then reached over and shook Milo. He slept very soundly, and it took several vigorous shakes before he opened his eyes.

"What's the matter?" he asked.

"There's someone pounding at the door." Another loud knock sounded then.

"Who do you suppose it is?" I asked.

"There's only one way to find out," Milo replied. He rose unhurriedly and pulled on his black dressing gown over his nightclothes as he walked toward the bedroom door.

"Wait here," he said. Then he went out of the bedroom.

20

I got out of bed, pulling on the lavender satin robe that matched my nightdress, and stood in the bedroom doorway, listening to see who it was.

I could just make out the voice of Gerard Holloway, though he sounded strange, different somehow. Then Milo said something in a voice too low for me to hear, and all was quiet.

I stepped out of the bedroom in time to see Milo coming out of the sitting room.

"It's Holloway," he said.

"What is he doing here at this hour?" I asked.

"He's very drunk."

"Oh, I see." The fact that he was drunk, however, did not really answer my question. I didn't know why it was that he would come to us in the middle of the night. Of course, intoxication often gave one strange ideas.

"I'll make some coffee," I said, turning toward the kitchen.

Milo caught my arm. "Perhaps it would be best if you went back to bed," he said. "I can handle Holloway."

"Nonsense," I replied. "I certainly won't be able to go back to sleep now."

Milo looked as though he was prepared to argue with me but then thought better of it. He went back into the sitting room and I went to the kitchen.

As I went about brewing a very strong pot of coffee, I considered the reasons why Mr. Holloway might have come here. Had he had another row with Georgina? Had he even been home? Or perhaps he had, in his drunken state, somehow remembered something important. Occasionally, the sound of his poorly modulated tone drifted into the kitchen, but I could not make out what he was saying.

When the coffee was finished, I carried the little tray with the pot, cups, sugar, and milk, as well as the last-minute addition of a tin of biscuits, into the sitting room. Gerard Holloway was sitting on a chair before the fire, his head in his hands.

I glanced at Milo, who gave me a look that I interpreted as one of suppressed irritation.

Gerard Holloway looked up, and I was

startled at his appearance. He looked ghastly. His face was gray, his eyes red, and there was an expression of such absolute misery on his features that I couldn't help but feel a bit alarmed.

He attempted to rise when he saw me, though it seemed a difficult thing for him to manage. He swayed on his feet, and I was very much afraid he was going to topple to the floor. He reached out, however, and caught the mantel.

"I'm sorry to come here at this hour, Mrs. Ames," he said, his words slurred. "I know it is very ill-mannered of me."

"It's quite all right, Mr. Holloway," I said. "Please sit down."

"I'll take that tray from you, darling," Milo said, coming to my side.

I knew perfectly well what he was doing. He was trying to gently hint that I might leave him alone with Holloway. I pretended as though I didn't understand.

"Thank you," I said, handing him the tray and going to sit on the chair across from Mr. Holloway.

I could feel Milo's gaze on the back of my neck, but I didn't turn around. I knew he wanted to spare me Mr. Holloway's drunkenness, but if he thought that I was going to be excluded from this conversation, whatever it was, he was sadly mistaken.

Milo set the tray down on the little table near Mr. Holloway's chair and poured coffee into one of the cups.

"Why don't you drink this, Holloway," he said.

I didn't know how Mr. Holloway was going to manage a cup and saucer in his condition, but Milo seemed to have thought of this before I did, and handed him the cup without the saucer. Mr. Holloway clasped it in his unsteady hand. I knew the cup was probably hot, but he didn't seem to notice. It was almost as though he forgot it the second he took it, for he did not try to take a drink.

"Is there anything we can do for you, Mr. Holloway?" I asked gently.

He shook his head, his hand and the cup moving with it, sloshing a bit of coffee over the side. He didn't even blink as it dripped down his hand and onto his trousers. "I don't think anyone can really be of help now," he said.

"I know things seem bleak," I said gently. "But with time . . ."

He looked up at me and then said, his voice very faint, "What am I going to do now?"

I didn't know how to respond. I hadn't

liked his relationship with Flora Bell, but his pain was almost palpable.

"I'm sorry," I said softly.

He seemed to collect himself then. He drew in a deep breath through his nose, and when he spoke again his voice was steadier. "I know that Flora didn't feel the same way about me as I did about her."

I was not sure what he meant by this, so I waited for him to continue.

"Oh, I think she was fond of me. But she was young and beautiful, and I'm . . . well . . ." He waved a hand, sloshing more coffee. "But I cared for her, and I thought . . . I don't know . . . She was fond of older gentlemen, after all, and I . . . I didn't think it was only the money . . ."

He was rambling now, not making sense.

"I think perhaps you'll feel better if you sleep," I said, getting up and going to take the coffee cup from his hand.

"Milo, have you a handkerchief?"

He found one in the pocket of his dressing gown, and I took it. I dabbed the coffee away from Mr. Holloway's hand, though he didn't pay me any mind. Even his clothes smelled of alcohol.

"Would you like to go lie down?" I asked him.

He shook his head. "I couldn't bear to

sleep. I haven't been able to since . . . since it happened."

I thought of Georgina. I wondered if she was concerned about Mr. Holloway's whereabouts. I remembered, however, that she had told me he had not been home since the murder, so I doubted that his absence tonight would be cause for more alarm than usual. In any event, calling her at this time of night would likely only upset her.

"Do you want me to take you home?" Milo asked.

"No!" he said quickly. "I can't see Georgina now. She . . . that is . . ." He was struggling very hard to conceal something, but alcohol is good for nothing if not for bringing the truth to light.

"What is it, Mr. Holloway?" I pressed.

"She . . . I . . ." He rubbed his hand across his face, swallowed as though trying to force down the words.

I waited.

"I'm afraid she killed Flora," he said in a rush.

I stilled, my eyes rising to meet Milo's.

"Why would you think that?" Milo asked with a casualness I would not have been able to muster.

"I . . . I don't know. It's just that she was

so angry when we quarreled, and then I couldn't find her afterward. She . . . I thought she had gone to the theatre. I . . . had the feeling she was going to speak with Flora, to have it out. But she wouldn't have done it. Would she?"

He looked up at me so pleadingly that I didn't have the heart to argue with him.

"I don't think so," I said gently, though I was less sure now than ever.

"I . . . she's such a good woman. I don't think she could have done it . . ."

"Perhaps you might lie down for a few moments," I said, arranging pillows on the sofa. "I think you'll feel better."

"You're very kind, Mrs. Ames," he said as he reclined against the cushions. "I've been a fool, but I do love Georgina, you know."

"Yes, I know."

His head dropped onto the pillow and, despite his claims of insomnia, he was almost instantly asleep. When it appeared that he was not going to stir, Milo and I went quietly back to our bedroom.

"This is dreadful," I said, turning to Milo as he closed the door behind us. I was keeping myself from wringing my hands only by the strongest efforts.

"He oughtn't to have come here in that state," Milo said. "I don't know what he was thinking."

"He's thinking his wife may be a killer and he doesn't know who else to turn to," I replied, annoyed at Milo's callousness.

"Just because Holloway worries Georgina did it doesn't mean she did."

"I know, but he thinks her capable of it."

"He's soused, darling. You can't take anything he's saying seriously."

"But he's clearly been worrying about this since it happened," I said. It all made sense now. Why he had looked so strained and anxious, why he had taken to drink. It hadn't been because he was madly in love with Flora Bell. He was worried that his wife was a murderess.

Somehow, this was not a relief.

"I still don't believe Georgina did it," I said. "But this will only be a further wedge between them. If things don't work out . . . he's already so distraught."

"He'll pull himself together," Milo said unconcernedly, sitting on the edge of the bed and lighting a cigarette. "A few weeks more and he'll feel much less strongly about everything than he does now. People have survived much worse, after all."

I stared at him. "I don't know how you do it," I said.

He looked up. "How I do what?"

"How you take everything in stride, remain indifferent to the bad things happening around you."

One dark brow rose. "What else am I to do?"

It was very annoying when he presented me with a simple question that defied an answer.

"I don't know," I said with a sigh.

"Unpleasant things happen, darling. Most times, there's nothing I or anyone else can do to change them. What good is it to worry about them?"

It was an eminently practical approach to life, but so difficult to implement. That was a part of Milo's nature, however. He went through life with the sort of ease that was impossible for most people, myself included.

That was not to say, of course, that his own life had been untouched by trouble. His mother had died when he was born, and he and his father had never been on good terms. Though Milo had good looks, money, and a great deal of charm, for most of his life he had not had anyone upon whom he could rely. Sometimes I thought that was what had developed that maddening combination of cynical outlook and ironclad composure.

"Unpleasant things happen, yes," I said.

"But that doesn't mean we can't do something to make them better when we can."

He blew out a stream of smoke. "I have a feeling you view this as one of those instances?"

I came and sat down on the bed beside him. "I feel that everything would be better if Gerard and Georgina Holloway realize what they mean to each other."

"What if one of them is the killer?" Milo asked, leaning to tap the ashes from his cigarette into the Bakelite ashtray on the bedside table.

I realized that I had not really considered this. Oh, I had put both of the Holloways on my list of suspects, but when confronted with the possibility now, I had to admit that I viewed this case as coming to a happy conclusion for them.

"It will be even more heartbreaking," I said at last. "But I feel we should at least try to reunite them."

"Darling, their marriage is none of our business," Milo said.

"They're our friends."

"Yes, but how would you like any of our friends meddling in our marriage?" he asked.

I paused. I had not really considered it from that perspective. There had been friends, during our marital difficulties, who had made careful suggestions and asked in soft voices if there was anything they could do. I had appreciated the sentiment, but not necessarily the action. Their concern had made things worse somehow, made my troubles feel more exposed. I realized that Gerard and Georgina would likely feel the same way.

Perhaps Milo was right. Perhaps there was nothing to be done but let their relationship run its course. I just so hated to see something that had once been so promising go by the wayside.

I rose to my feet, unable to keep still, and walked to my dressing table, idly toying with the bottles and boxes on its lacquered top.

"It just doesn't make sense," I said with a sigh.

"What doesn't?"

"The relationship between Mr. Holloway and Flora Bell."

"I'm afraid it makes perfect sense. Men often look at young women as the antidote to advancing age."

"I don't care," I said. "If he and Georgina truly care about each other, and I'm quite sure they do, he should have known better than to pursue Miss Bell." I looked up at Milo in the mirror. "What makes people do such things, put everything they hold dear at risk for the sake of something so fleeting?"

Milo shrugged. "Sometimes the forbidden holds a great appeal."

It was not the sort of answer I wanted to hear.

"But he ought to have been more discreet," Milo went on. "He and Flora Bell had a perfectly good reason to be seen together, but he made no attempt to hide the fact that it was more than a professional relationship. He was careless, which always makes things worse."

I felt that little twist in my stomach as Milo spoke with apparent authority on the best way to cloak one's infidelity in the guise of something more respectable.

"Do you suppose discretion compensates for unfaithfulness?" I asked, turning to face him, the edge in my tone giving voice to the emotions I had been attempting to suppress.

He looked up at me, as though he had realized that we were no longer talking only about the Holloways.

"Of course not," he said easily. "If he was a smart man he would never have gotten involved with Miss Bell to begin with."

It was the right thing to say, but somehow it did nothing to appease me. The growing resentment I had felt at Milo's casual acceptance of Gerard Holloway's affair with Flora Bell had grown so strong that I realized my teeth were clenched.

His next words did not improve matters. "In any event, I'm tired of talking about the Holloways' marriage. Even if it falls apart, it isn't the end of the world."

"It's the end of their world," I said. "The world they've built together all these years, crumbling into nothing."

"Now you're being melodramatic," he said, rising from the bed to grind out his cigarette. "Trust me: they'll both get on with their lives."

"Do you realize," I said, trying very hard to keep my voice steady, "that flippant way you speak of marriage sometimes makes it seem as though you view it as little more than a temporary convenience."

He turned to look at me. "You know that isn't how I think of it."

"Do I?" I replied. "Sometimes I'm not at all sure."

He gave a little laugh. "You're imagining things and distraught over nothing. You need to get some sleep."

I felt another surge of indignation.

"If you can't acknowledge what I'm saying," I said coldly, "at least do me the courtesy of not speaking to me as though I were a child."

He seemed to realize I was serious then, for the glimmer of amusement that had been in his eyes a moment ago faded, and then there was nothing on his features. I hated that look, the expressionless mask that fell across his face when he was confronted with my emotions. It was as though he had shut me out completely.

We looked at each other. There had been other moments like this in our marriage, moments when I felt that we might be at an impasse. I didn't see how this situation might be resolved, for we would never view things the same way.

"We are not the Holloways, Amory," he said at last.

And there it was. He had cut to the heart of the problem. Somehow this sharp insight into my insecurities only made me wonder if he, too, had been contemplating the way even the strongest marriages could disintegrate with time.

"No," I replied. "Their marriage was better than ours, and look where it is now."

His eyes met mine, and the only thing I could read in them was a flicker of impatience. "What do you want me to say?"

His asking that question only made it

worse. There were so many things I wanted him to say, but I didn't want to have to ask for them.

I realized suddenly that I hadn't the heart for this fight. I couldn't make him understand, and I was too tired to try.

I sighed wearily. "Nothing, Milo," I said, walking to the bed and pulling back the covers. "I don't want you to say anything."

21

I awoke before Milo and slipped quietly from the bed. I was glad he was still sleeping, for I was not ready to continue our conversation from last night.

I knew he hadn't meant to hurt me, and I had to acknowledge that some of my anger had its origins in the comparisons I was drawing in my own mind. Gerard and Georgina Holloway's relationship had been strengthened by adventure, even danger, and I couldn't help but feel that the same might be said of Milo and me. It was a murder mystery that had set our marriage back on course, and I wondered if, as it had done for Gerard Holloway, the adventure would eventually cease to be enough for Milo. Some part of me realized that it was unfair, even irrational, to reflect the problems in the Holloways' marriage onto my own, but that didn't stop the disquieting thoughts.

I ventured out into the sitting room to check on Mr. Holloway and was surprised to see him sitting up on the sofa. Once again, he tried to rise when he saw me, but I hurried to him, placing a gently restraining hand on his arm. "Don't get up, Mr. Holloway," I said.

"I . . . I don't know . . . how did I get here?" he asked.

"You took a cab, I believe," I replied. Thank heavens for that. He might have done any amount of damage if he had tried to drive in his condition.

"I don't remember any of that," he said.

I was not at all surprised, but there was no need to comment upon the state he had been in.

"It's all right," I told him. "No harm done."

"Was I . . . a terrible nuisance? I can be awfully verbose when I've had too much to drink."

I realized suddenly that he probably wondered what he had said and done while he was here. I was sure he had not meant to reveal his suspicions about Georgina in his inebriation.

Should I mention it? I decided against it for the time being. There was no need to bring it up without proof.

"You didn't say much before you fell asleep," I told him truthfully.

"I'm dreadfully sorry about this," he said. I could tell that he was very embarrassed. Not only that, he looked quite ill. I had thought he looked gray when he had come to us last night, but this morning his face was positively white.

"There's no need to be sorry," I said. "We'll make you feel better before you leave. You need to eat something."

He shook his head, wincing as he did so. "I couldn't possibly."

"Perhaps just some tea and toast?" I suggested.

He looked as though he was about to shake his head again but then thought better of it. I imagined his head must be very painful this morning, considering the state he had been in last night.

"I'll be right back," I said, before he had the chance to refuse. He looked wretched, and I wanted to do what I could to help before sending him on his way.

I made some tea, not too strong, and some toast and brought it back into the sitting room.

He was sitting in the exact same position in which I had left him, his gaze fixed on the empty fireplace.

"How do you take your tea?" I asked.

"It doesn't matter," he said.

I poured in a bit of milk and sugar and handed the saucer to him. He hesitated for just a moment and then reached out to take it. I was glad to see his hands were steadier this morning.

"Thank you," he said.

"Drink at least a bit of it for me, won't you?" I asked.

He dutifully brought the cup to his lips and took a sip. Despite his initial reluctance, it seemed the taste was palatable enough, and he took another sip.

A bit of the color returned to his face, and I was glad of it.

"Now perhaps a bit of toast?" I asked. "I think it will make you feel better."

"I don't deserve to feel better," he said.

I was not quite sure how to respond to this. What was it that he was blaming himself for?

"You must keep up your strength, Mr. Holloway," I said.

I held out the plate of toast and he took a piece, bringing it to his lips.

I sat across from him, my hands in my lap. "Do you want to talk about anything?" I asked. "I don't want to pry, but if you need someone to listen . . ."

"I . . . I don't know. I shouldn't be here. I've imposed upon you, taken advantage of your kindness, and I'm deeply embarrassed. I suppose I just didn't know where else to go."

"You can't go home?" I suggested softly.

He looked up at me, the misery on his face increasing, if possible. "I . . . I haven't spoken with Georgina."

"Don't you think you ought to?" Despite my recent admission to myself that their marriage was none of my concern, I couldn't help but feel that things would be so much better between them if they would only talk to each other.

"Perhaps," he said, seemingly unwilling to discuss the matter at present. "But not just yet." Was he worried that if he spoke with her he might be able to read some sort of guilt written on her face?

"I'm sure she will be ready to talk when you are," I said, though I was afraid that Georgina would only wait for so long.

He took another sip of tea. "I . . . I'm afraid things may get worse."

"What do you mean?"

"I . . . well, I wrote Flora some rather . . . indiscreet letters. If she kept them, they may come out." He let out a sigh. "I'm afraid I've ruined everything."

I was inclined to agree. However, now was not the time to let him know what a fool he had been. He was already miserable enough.

"I don't think anyone would give your letters to the press or any such thing."

He gave me a skeptical smile. "You'd be surprised how bitter some people can be."

He had a point. The letters were a concern. I would very much hate for Georgina to suffer any more embarrassment than she already had.

"I wonder if I might ask you a favor, Mrs. Ames. Do you think you could go to Flora's boardinghouse and retrieve them?"

I hesitated. I wasn't too keen on the idea of retrieving the mementos of his illicit relationship, but I also didn't want the letters to fall into the wrong hands. Besides, it had occurred to me that the landlady might have some useful information about Flora Bell. Perhaps I could help Mr. Holloway and Inspector Jones at the same time.

"Yes," I told him. "I can go this morning, if you like."

Flora Bell's boardinghouse was a tidy building in Shepherd's Bush. I was not sure what I had been expecting Flora Bell's residence to look like, but this quiet, modest house was not quite in keeping with her glamorous image. Of course, she had been a rising star. No doubt the penthouses would have come later, had she been given the opportunity to succeed.

I had left Mr. Holloway to drink his tea, and hoped that Milo would be able to convince him to return home. He couldn't very well continue wandering the streets. Sooner or later, he and Georgina would have to talk.

As I rang the bell at Flora's boardinghouse, I wondered if Inspector Jones had visited her residence. I assumed that he would have done so if he thought anything of importance could be learned in that way, but I couldn't help but feel that I, as a sympathetic ear, might be able to get more information from the landlady than a brusque policeman would.

A maid showed me into a cluttered yet spotless parlor, still bearing the furniture and dark acanthus-patterned wallpaper popular in Victorian décor, and a moment later the lady of the house made her appearance. She looked just as one might expect a landlady to look, dressed in prim, dark clothes with a pleasant face that held sharp, searching eyes.

"I'm Mrs. Potter," she said.

"Good morning, Mrs. Potter. I'm Amory

Ames . . . a friend of Flora Bell," I said. It was, perhaps, not entirely true. But I did feel as though searching for her killer made me her friend. I was certainly her ally.

"Were you at the play that night?" she asked.

"Yes," I said, hiding my surprise at the question. Clearly, she was the curious sort. I hesitated, wavering between my natural discretion and revelation for the sake of building camaraderie. Finally, I decided that she would likely be more inclined to share information with me if I first shared it with her. "In fact, it was I who found her body."

The flash of interest in her blue eyes told me I had judged correctly.

"The poor dear," she said with a soft cluck of sympathy. "Such a dreadful thing. I suppose it was rather gruesome."

The way she looked at me could only be described as hopeful. Clearly, she wanted details. I knew, however, that Inspector Jones was not likely to approve of my going about telling people what I had seen.

"It was rather a shock," I said. "I'm afraid I don't much like to think about it." This, at least, was entirely true.

She seemed to accept this, for she nodded. "Yes, I imagine it was dreadful for you."

Her next words confirmed that I had won

her over. "Might I offer you some tea?"

"That would be lovely. Thank you."

She rang for the maid, and in the space of a few minutes we were sipping steaming tea from lovely blue and white chinoiserie china. I was relieved that she seemed to be warming to me considerably.

"Did Flora live here long?" I asked, accepting a ginger biscuit.

"No, only for a few months," she said. "I gather the last place she lived was less respectable, but she had come into some money and could afford more appropriate lodgings."

"Yes, I see." No doubt she had received an advance from Mr. Holloway. I was glad, at least, that he hadn't set her up in a private residence somewhere. It seemed he had been mindful of her reputation, at least to some extent. Or perhaps it was Flora who had insisted on the semblance of propriety.

"Flora was a lovely woman," I said, hoping that Mrs. Potter would elaborate more on the character of Flora Bell. After all, I had only seen the persona she had carefully cultivated. What had she been in her daily life?

"She was a quiet girl," Mrs. Potter said. "Not what one might expect of people from the theatre. When I first heard that she was on the stage, I was concerned. I keep a respectable establishment, you understand."

"Of course," I replied.

"But I consider myself an excellent judge of character, and I felt that she would be all right."

"And she was, wasn't she?" I said it as though I knew it for a fact, but I was really hoping that she would confirm or deny it.

"Yes," she said. "She was rarely here. Spent her time at the theatre preparing for a play or some such thing. And even before that, she was always out at the Empire and the Palladium, filling her head with nonsense. But when she was home, she was always quiet and well-mannered, just the same. Of course, I didn't hold with that gentleman who came to see her."

I looked at her. "What gentleman?"

"She had a gentleman friend that would come by some nights and see her in the parlor. I don't allow men in the rooms, of course."

"Her brother, perhaps," I said.

She shook her head, a frown crossing her expression. "I didn't approve of Mr. Bell, and Miss Bell knew it. They didn't often meet here. He came here a few days ago, trying to get into her room, and I sent him off at once."

This was not entirely enlightening. I couldn't imagine there were many respectable landladies who would approve of Frederick Bell.

"I know well enough what he wanted," she went on. "He was after her money. He'd stolen some from her room before, she told me. Came when neither of us were home and rifled through her drawers. After that, I insisted she keep her room locked."

"I see." So Freddy Bell had not been above stealing. That did not, of course, make him a killer, but it did prove he was willing to go to extremes to get what he wanted.

"Who was the other gentleman?" I asked casually.

If she thought it odd that I continued to pepper her with questions, she gave no sign of it. Instead, she seemed to grow friendlier the more questions I asked. I wished all my interrogations would go so smoothly.

She took a sip of her tea before leaning forward conspiratorially. "That's just it. I don't know. He was very mysterious."

"Was he tall and handsome, with a dark moustache?" I asked, thinking of Gerard Holloway.

"I couldn't really say. You see, he came disguised." She said this as though it were the most natural thing in the world.

"Disguised?" I repeated.

She nodded. "Yes, he usually wore his hat pulled low and a muffler across his face. I thought it was rather strange, but as long as they stayed here in the parlor, it didn't much matter to me who he was. I was a bit curious, of course, but I knew she was an actress. They know all types of strange people."

"Yes, I suppose you're right," I said, my mind in a whirl. I wondered who it was that would have come to see Flora Bell in disguise. It seemed most likely that it would have been Gerard Holloway, but somehow I could not picture him coming in disguise to sit in Mrs. Potter's parlor. If he wanted to see Flora, they might meet at the theatre or any number of places.

"I'm fairly certain that he had no moustache," she said after some reflection, confirming my suspicion that it had not been Mr. Holloway. "Once the muffler slipped and I got a bit of a look at his face, in profile. He was a handsome gentleman."

The next best guess was Christopher Landon. He and Miss Bell had had some sort of a relationship. Perhaps he had come to see her to try to convince her to abandon Holloway's affections for his.

"I don't suppose you might have over-heard any of their conversation?" I asked casually.

She looked up at me sharply. "I'm not the sort of landlady who goes about putting her ear to the keyholes."

"Oh, no, certainly not," I said quickly, in an attempt to soothe her. "I only meant that you might have heard something when passing the room. You see, if she had a gentleman friend, I would like to get in touch with him."

This seemed to appease her, for she took a sip of tea and appeared to think. "I do think it might have been a special friend, so to speak. I heard him say something that caught my ear. He said, 'Love doesn't end with time, and not all bonds can be easily broken.' I thought it a pretty turn of phrase."

"Yes," I agreed absently. So it seemed it must have been Christopher Landon, after all. Though I wanted to press her further, something told me it would be best not to pursue this line of questioning, at least for the time being.

We finished our tea, chatting about mundane things, and then I got around to the purpose of my visit. "I was wondering . . . would it be possible for me to step into her room? There were some letters there that I would like to retrieve. For sentimental reasons, you understand." I did not mention, of course, that I had not been the one to write them.

"Certainly. Come this way."

She led me out into the foyer and up a set of polished wooden stairs, her hand sliding along the gleaming bannister. The walls, papered in a dark green, held dozens of photographs of different individuals, some of them dating back to the last century. Light from the leaded stained-glass windows at the top of the stairs cast colorful, dappled light across the carpet on the landing, and I felt sad thinking that Flora Bell would never grace this cheerful spot again.

Mrs. Potter led me down the hallway past three doors and stopped before the fourth. "This was her room," she said, pulling a large ring of keys from her pocket. With barely a glance, she located the correct key and slipped it into the lock.

"The police were here, going through her things, but I made sure they put everything back as it was," she told me, disapproval plain in her tone. "I don't hold with policemen sticking their noses into every part of a woman's life, just because she's died."

As I suspected, she was not likely to have revealed everything she knew to Inspector

Jones and his colleagues. That meant, perhaps, that I would be able to discover something that they had not.

She pushed open the door for me to enter, and I stepped inside. It felt almost intrusive, stepping into the dead woman's room. I felt another pang of sadness to think that she had left it one morning with no idea that she would never return.

The white lace curtains were open, letting in the morning light. I glanced around. There was a bed, neatly made with a floral-patterned blanket. A table with a lamp sat beside it. There was a wardrobe and a chest of drawers, but the most noticeable piece of furniture in the room was a dressing table with a large mirror and satin stool.

"She brought that thing here," Mrs. Potter said, following my gaze. "I suppose, if no one claims it, my next lodger will be glad to have it. It's the sort of thing young ladies these days enjoy."

"Yes," I answered absently. Now that I was here, I wished I hadn't come. It felt wrong, somehow, to invade this quiet room. Of course, it would be emptied soon enough, just as her dressing room at the theatre had been, another young girl living here with no knowledge or thought of the former tenant.

I walked to the dressing table and opened

one of the drawers. There was an assortment of makeup and costume jewelry inside. I closed it and opened another. This one held a pile of papers, but closer inspection showed that they were playbills from performances Flora Bell had either taken part in or attended. There was also a copy of the script for *The Price of Victory,* bound with a blue hardcover binding. I took it out and set it atop the dressing table, thinking that perhaps Gerard Holloway would want to keep it.

A search through the rest of the drawers yielded nothing. If the letters had been here, they weren't now.

"You can't find them?" Mrs. Potter asked.

"No, perhaps she threw them away," I said. I was about to turn away when my eye caught something on top of the dressing table. Lying between the perfume bottles was a small key.

I reached out and picked it up. I thought at first that it belonged to the dressing table, though none of the drawers had been locked, but when I glanced again I saw that there were no locks on these drawers. The key belonged to something else. I thought at once of the locked drawer in Flora Bell's dressing room.

"She may have kept the letters at the

theatre," Mrs. Potter said contemplatively. "She told me, after her brother took her money, that she had more valuables kept at the theatre. 'No one thinks of looking in a dressing room, Mrs. Potter,' she said with a laugh. She had a lovely laugh."

Mrs. Potter was busy examining the photographs pasted to the edges of Flora Bell's mirror and hadn't noticed when I picked up the key. I slipped it into my pocket.

"She was a lovely girl," Mrs. Potter said. "She wore too much makeup, of course. But that's how actresses are. But she really was lovely. Such a shame."

I looked closer at the photographs. There were several of Flora in various costumes, each of them lovely. There was one of her and Freddy Bell, her arm around his neck, both of them smiling, the resemblance striking as they stood with their faces close together. Despite their disagreements, I knew that a special bond had been severed.

I spotted a photograph of Flora and Mr. Holloway. Their pose was very circumspect. They stood, not quite touching, but there was something about both of their expressions that spoke of intimacy. If I could not find the letters, at least I could return the photograph to Mr. Holloway.

I reached out to take it, and a piece of

paper that had been held in place behind it fluttered to the dressing table.

"Oh! That's the man who came to see her," the landlady said.

I looked up from the photograph, surprised by her words. She nodded to the paper that had fallen onto the desk, and I looked down. It was a playbill, and on it was a photograph of Balthazar Lebeau.

22

A few moments later, I followed Mrs. Potter back down the stairs, lost in thought. Why had Mr. Lebeau visited Flora Bell's boardinghouse? What had he meant by his talk of unending love and unbroken bonds that Mrs. Potter had overheard? As far as I had seen, Flora Bell had shown no interest in him, romantically or otherwise. What, then, was their relationship?

I would have to speak with Mr. Lebeau again. I glanced at my wristwatch. The morning rehearsal with Miss Dearborn would be almost finished. I was not under the illusion that I would be able to question Mr. Lebeau directly on the matter. But perhaps if I hinted at things in a roundabout way, he would let something slip.

I needed to visit the theatre in any case, for I needed to see if the key fit in the dressing table lock. I had the feeling there was something in that drawer that would prove enlightening.

Even as the idea came to me, I hesitated. There was a killer at large, and I didn't want to put myself in harm's way. It wasn't likely that anything would happen during their rehearsals, of course. But I knew I ought to take precautions.

I bid Mrs. Potter a fond farewell, and then walked down the street to the nearest telephone booth. Though I was still irritated with Milo, I phoned the flat.

It was Winnelda who answered, though I hadn't expected her home yet.

"When did you get back, Winnelda?"

"Just a little while ago, madam. My little sisters make me very tired, and I decided to return early."

"Well, I hope your visit was pleasant."

"It was very nice."

"I'm glad to hear it. Let me speak to Mr. Ames, will you?"

"He's gone out, madam." I ought to have expected as much. Milo never sat still for long.

"Oh, I see. Is Mr. Holloway still there?"

"No, madam. No one is here but me."

I weighed the options. I knew Milo wouldn't like me going to the theatre alone, but I also felt that I shouldn't miss the opportunity to speak to Mr. Lebeau.

"All right," I said, settling on something of a compromise. "If Mr. Ames comes back, will you tell him I've gone to the theatre?"

"Yes, I'll tell him."

I rang off and had Markham drive me to the Penworth Theatre directly.

As I walked inside the building, I heard the sound of voices coming from the stage. Perhaps they weren't finished with their rehearsal. I listened. No, it was a single person, and it took me only a moment to recognize the speaker. There was no mistaking that voice. It was Balthazar Lebeau.

I stepped into the auditorium. It was dark in the back of the theatre, and he didn't see me. He was standing on the stage, his gaze trained out on the empty seats. It was clear that he was reciting lines, and it was only a moment before I recognized them from *The Price of Victory,* though there was something about the words that struck me as strange.

" 'I don't ask for glory,' " he said, his voice reverberating across the theatre. " 'I ask only for the chance to love and be loved. This battle will test me; it may even end me. But nothing — not even death — can end my love for you.' "

I felt almost as though I were intruding, but something about his performance was so arresting that I couldn't seem to help

360

myself; I stepped closer.

The movement caught his attention, however, for he stopped suddenly. The change was startling. The expression he had worn, the noble regality of another age, faded and he was suddenly a simple actor standing on the stage.

"Ah, Mrs. Ames," he said. "Good morning."

"Good morning," I replied. "I'm sorry to disturb you."

"You could not possibly disturb me with your delightful presence." He said the words automatically, with that well-worn charm that came so easily to him.

"I thought the rehearsals would be over by now."

"Oh, the rehearsal is done. In fact, I think I may be the only one here."

"Oh?" I asked, wondering if it was a good idea to remain here alone with him. Then again, Milo knew where I was. And Markham was still outside.

"Yes, I was just going over a few things. What brings you here, Mrs. Ames?"

"I . . . I just thought I would come by and see how things are going. I do have a question for you, however."

"Ask me anything you like," he said. "My life is an open book."

I opened my mouth to ask about his visits to Miss Bell, but something stopped me.

"Did you always want to be an actor?" I asked.

His brows rose ever so slightly, as though this had not been the question he was expecting.

"I come from a long line of actors, troubadours, and fools," he said. "I expect if you were to research the history of English jesters, you'd find a Lebeau or two among them. My parents were actors, and my sister and I grew up on the stage. I've been performing almost since birth. I never considered any other profession, for I knew the theatre was in my blood. It's a strange phrase, isn't it? 'In my blood.' As though our blood, that crimson liquid running through our veins, somehow has the power to make us one thing or another."

I wasn't sure where this was leading, but I stood silently, listening to him talk. There was something mesmerizing about his voice.

"It has been an interesting career. I know people who have despised it, but I wouldn't have traded it for anything. Indeed, I have sacrificed a great deal for it. When one gets older, one begins to contemplate the things that really matter. But I'm sorry," he said, stopping suddenly. "I'm afraid I'm boring you."

He knew that he was not, but still there was something sincere in the casual way he dismissed his past, as though it was he himself who didn't want the story to go on.

"I find it fascinating," I replied sincerely. "To have heard about someone one's whole life and then to finally have the chance to meet him is quite a thrill for me."

He smiled. "You should have seen me in my prime."

"Oh, I don't believe you could possibly have been any more talented," I said. "Even just now — that scene you were rehearsing — I was captivated. It was from *The Price of Victory,* wasn't it?"

"You'll think me foolish if I tell you," he said with a smile, though it was perfectly obvious he was not at all abashed. He was the type of man who never felt foolish. I recognized this trait, for Milo was the same way: so supremely confident in everything he did that the opinions of others bounced like flimsy arrows off an impenetrable shield of self-assurance.

"I doubt that very much," I said.

He leaned forward and lowered his voice conspiratorially. "I'm rehearsing the lines for Armand. Landon's hinted that he won't remain much longer, and I intend for Holloway to see that I'm right for the role."

"Oh?" I asked. That was why the lines had sounded strange. I had been used to Christopher Landon speaking them.

"I'm a bit older than the average leading man, perhaps. But I feel that I can play it."

"I'm sure you could," I replied. I remembered something then and added casually, "I understand Mr. Holloway once took a part that you were eager to get. Perhaps now you'll be the lead of his play. It's strange, isn't it, how things work?"

"Did he? I don't remember. Would you like to help me with this?"

"How?" I asked, a bit surprised at the request.

"You can read the lines for Victoire."

"Oh," I said. "I don't know." I had not been expecting this, and somehow I felt a bit uncertain. I had not been raised to be retiring or insecure in my own abilities. Indeed, if life with my mother had taught me anything, it was how to convey confidence in the face of conflict. However, this was something different. With a man of his talent and reputation, I felt suddenly self-conscious.

He seemed to sense this, for he gave me a smile, a genuine one, it seemed, lacking in his normal practiced affability. "I'm sure you'll be wonderful."

He walked offstage and picked up a script from a table, riffling through it until he found the page he wanted. "Ah, here we are."

He walked to me, holding out the script.

I took it a bit reluctantly.

"I know you've seen the play and this set is adequate," he said, sweeping a hand to encompass the stage with its excellent reproduction furniture and tasteful bric-a-brac. "But now let me really set the scene so you can feel the mood. Picture us in a luxuriously appointed drawing room in France early in the last century. Europe is in turmoil. The Napoleonic Wars are raging, the casualties increasing day by day." His rich, deep voice rolled over me, and I found myself caught up in his words, picturing things just as he had described them.

"I am an officer in the emperor's army, in a jacket of blue with epaulets and brass buttons, sword at my side. You wear a high-waisted gown of ivory silk, your hair braided with lace, a knot of pearls at your throat." As he spoke the words, his fingers reached out to brush across my collarbone.

"For months you have worried, feared for the safety of your lover, each morning dawning with the knowledge that it could be the day he dies in a field caked with mud and blood. And now I have come back to you before the penultimate battle. To say good-bye — perhaps for the last time."

It was a very dramatic recitation and I felt as though I ought to be amused at his intensity. But somehow I wasn't. Somehow, he had managed, with his theatrical gravitas, to instill in me the significance of the scene we were about to play. I didn't know how he had done it, but the atmosphere had changed. I felt suddenly as though I were Victoire.

I could feel the sadness, feel the heavy dread in the chest of a woman who might never see her lover again. I had been a child during the Great War, but quite old enough to remember a great many young men who had gone off to battle, never to return. I did not have to try too hard to imagine what it was like.

"Are you ready?" he asked, pulling my thoughts back to the present.

I hesitated momentarily then looked down at the papers in my hand. He nodded at me encouragingly and I lifted them up and, clearing my throat, began to read.

" 'You've come back to me,' " I said. " 'And yet I don't know if I can bear it.' "

When he spoke there was understanding and tenderness in his voice. " 'I didn't want to bring you pain, but I had to see you one more time.' "

" 'I can't say good-bye to you again,' " I said.

He stepped closer. " 'I don't want you to say good-bye, my darling. In a moment, I will turn and walk from this room and I won't look back. But I will be taking you with me. The sound of your voice, the scent of your skin, your silken curls.' " His hand moved as he spoke, caressing my throat, my cheek, and then my hair. " 'Every part of you will be a part of me.' "

He took me into his arms, crushing the script between us, and I could no longer read my lines. Mr. Lebeau took no notice of this.

" 'I want to remember you this way,' " he said in a low voice, his blue eyes boring into mine. " 'I want to remember your beauty and your strength and the fire in your eyes.' "

He lowered his mouth toward mine and I was suddenly recalled to where I was. I put my hand against his chest and stopped him, giving a mild laugh as the luxurious drawing room evaporated before my eyes and I was once again on the shadowy stage. "I think we'd better stop there," I said, surprised that I sounded a bit breathless.

He looked down at me, his arms still around me. There was a look in his eyes I found it difficult to interpret. "You did very well, Mrs. Ames."

"I . . . thank you," I said, unaccountably flustered.

He looked down at me a moment longer, and then he released me, stepping back.

"I'm afraid I've been taking up too much of your time," he said. "I'll just be going now. Thank you for your assistance."

"I enjoyed it," I said. I realized I still clutched the script in my hand. I held it out to him. "Where shall I put this?"

"Keep it if you like," he said with a smile. "Perhaps you may help me with my lines again."

"All right," I said, rolling up the script and slipping it into my handbag. I wavered for just a moment before continuing. "Although, I have another copy of the script. One I found at Miss Bell's boardinghouse."

"Oh?" There was not a flicker of emotion on his face, and I knew at once that he must be hiding something.

"Yes," I said, plunging ahead. "I spoke with the landlady. It seemed she recognized you."

He gave a little laugh. "I ought to have known. Landladies are a cunning lot. Yes, I stopped by once or twice to help Flora with some matters on the script."

It was such a preposterous lie that he couldn't have expected me to believe it, but I had the distinct impression that he didn't care whether I believed it or not.

"Thank you again for your help, Mrs. Ames. I hope we may do another scene together someday."

He left then, and I did nothing but watch him go. I could have pressed him further, perhaps I should have, but I didn't want to push him too far. After all, I didn't know what he was capable of.

Despite that, however, I felt a new appreciation for his talent, having shared the stage with him for just a few moments. I had been given a taste of that legendary magnetism that had made decades of women swoon, and, though I thought myself quite immune to that sort of charm, I had been drawn to it just the same.

Not only that, I had seen the depths of his personality. The swaggering thespian that he had become was just another role he played. There was clearly much more beneath that mask of bluster and bravado. He was a complex, intelligent man, and I wondered if he might possibly be a killer.

I had failed in one aspect of my mission, but I remembered the key in my pocket. At least I could try to accomplish the other.

Going backstage, I moved along the corridor toward the dressing rooms. Though Mr. Lebeau had said he thought everyone else was gone, I wondered if Dahlia Dearborn might still be in her dressing room. If so, I would have to think of some sort of excuse to rummage through her dressing table drawer.

Luckily, when I reached the door and knocked, there was no answer. I knocked again. "Miss Dearborn? Are you there?"

I was greeted with silence, so, with a glance down the hallway, I put my hand on the knob and tried it. The door was open.

With one last glance down the corridor, I slipped inside. I turned on the light and then moved toward the dressing table. Dahlia Dearborn's things were strewn across it now, every hint of Flora Bell's occupation erased.

I took the key from my pocket and leaned down toward the drawer. Inserting the key into the lock, I turned it and felt the tiny click as it released. So it was the right key! It seemed I had beaten the police to this particular clue.

I began to pull the drawer open when I felt rather than heard movement at my side. I started to look up, but it was too late.

I felt a tremendous pain at the side of my head, and everything went black.

23

"Amory. Amory, look at me." I heard his voice as if from very far away. It was as if I were trying to awaken from a dream. Or perhaps a nightmare. Then I felt Milo's hand on my face, and I opened my eyes. His face was a blur. My head ached fiercely.

"I . . . I . . ." I tried to speak, but it came out as more of a moan.

"It's all right. Don't try to talk."

He was leaning close, and I struggled to clear my vision. I focused on his eyes, on the blueness of them. I felt my head begin to swim, and my lids fluttered closed.

"Open your eyes, darling," Milo said gently. "You need to stay awake."

Someone had hit me. That much I knew. I had heard or felt someone nearby and was about to turn when I was struck on the head. This crossed my mind in the space of a moment, but none of the words would seem to form on my lips.

"My head hurts," I said. It was all I could manage.

"Yes, I know," he said, "but you must try to stay awake."

"I'm . . . so dizzy."

He took my hand in his, squeezing it gently.

"The doctor's on his way, but we must try to keep you conscious."

He was speaking in a perfectly calm voice, but I was surprised to detect an undertone of concern. Normally it was impossible to tell what he was thinking. Perhaps I was more gravely injured than I thought.

"Am I bleeding?" I asked.

"Not anymore. There's a little cut, it seems, but it's not bad. You'll have a lovely bruise, though."

"I feel wretched."

"I know, darling."

"How is she? Conscious?" I looked up and, even in the haziness of my thoughts, I was surprised to see that it was Freddy Bell.

"Yes, she's waking up," Milo said. "Any sign of the doctor?"

"Not yet."

I shifted slightly and Milo turned back to me. "Don't try to get up."

"There's no danger of that," I said. I was balancing very precariously on the precipice of unconsciousness, and I felt as though the slightest of movements would send me over the edge.

"Can I get you anything, Mrs. Ames?" Mr. Bell asked, looking down at me.

"No, thank you." I felt quite conspicuous lying on the floor, but someone had put a cushion from the little settee under my head. The floor beneath me felt cool and it was welcoming, for I was strangely hot. Milo was still holding my hand. It was very sweet of him to remain at my side.

My head throbbed mercilessly. Whoever had hit me had got me right on the temple, just as I was preparing to turn around.

Who might have done it? More to the point, why? I didn't think I had done anything that was worthy of being bashed over the head. Then again, my thoughts were somewhat fuzzy at the moment.

I suddenly remembered the drawer. I had been about to open it when I was hit. I needed to know if anything was in it.

"I think I can get up now," I said.

"No, you will not," Milo replied. "Not until the doctor arrives."

I wanted to argue with him, but I felt too tired. I had never felt anything like the blow that someone had dealt me. My ears still practically rang with it. I hoped that my skull wasn't fractured or some such thing. The way I felt, I wouldn't be surprised if it had been split in two. I supposed the very fact that I was lucid enough to be concerned about it was a good sign.

"I'll go and look again for the doctor," Mr. Bell said.

He left, and I suddenly realized this would likely be the only time Milo and I were alone in the room before the doctor arrived.

"The dressing table drawer . . ."

"Don't talk," Milo told me. "Just rest until he gets here."

"The bottom drawer on the left," I said. "Is it open?"

Milo glanced in that direction. "Yes."

Had I pulled it open before I was struck? I couldn't remember.

"Go and see if there's anything in it," I said.

"Amory . . ."

"Go and look, Milo."

With a sigh, he released my hand and rose to walk to the dressing table. I turned my head ever so slightly to watch his progress from the corner of my eye.

He looked down into the drawer, then over at me. "It's empty," he said.

"Well, what have we here?" A voice sounded in the doorway; the doctor, I assumed. I didn't dare turn my head again to look.

"Good afternoon, Doctor," Milo said pleasantly. "Inspector Jones." So someone had called the police as well as the doctor. I was glad.

"What's happened?" the doctor asked, coming over to me.

"I'm afraid someone's bashed Mrs. Ames in the head," Milo said.

I hadn't told him as much, but apparently it was obvious.

The doctor knelt beside me and gently took my head in his hands, his fingers moving across my face. I winced as they brushed my temple.

"It's bled a bit," he said, "but not badly. You're going to have a nasty bump, and the bruising's already begun. Now, follow my finger with your eyes, if you please."

He gave my head a thorough going-over and peered into my eyes, asking me a series of questions that were designed, I assumed, to ascertain that my brain was still intact.

At last, it appeared I had passed the test. He sat back. "You'll survive, Mrs. Ames," he said. "Though you'll need to take things easy for a few days."

"May I get up?" I asked. I felt rather ridiculous lying there on the floor with all these people hovering over me.

"I think that would be all right," the doctor said. "But move slowly."

He and Milo helped me to a sitting position. My head swam for just a moment, darkness dancing at the periphery of my vision, but then it cleared and I felt that I could focus.

That was when Inspector Jones stepped forward. "I'm not going to trouble you long, Mrs. Ames. I just want you to tell me very briefly what happened."

"Someone hit me," I said. "I was going to open the dressing table drawer when I saw a shadow out of the corner of my eye. Before I could turn around, something hit me on the side of the head. Very hard."

"No doubt with this," Milo said, nodding toward something on the floor. "It's a little statue, one of the stage props, no doubt."

"It's a part of the drawing room set," I said. "I saw it onstage earlier." I was pleased with myself for remembering, more for the fact that I *could* remember after that blow to the head than for the memory's potential relevance as a clue. After all, anyone might have picked it up and followed me backstage.

"We'll have it checked for fingerprints, though I suppose countless people will have touched it," Inspector Jones said, before turning back to me. "Did you see anyone?"

"No. Just the shadow or a flicker of movement from the corner of my vision and then the pain in my head."

He looked up at Milo. "And you found her?"

"No, Frederick Bell did. I had just arrived when he came hurrying in my direction and told me he'd found Amory unconscious."

"Indeed? What was he doing here?"

"He said he'd come to get a box of his sister's things that Miss Dearborn had collected."

I looked for the box I had noticed when I had visited here with Miss Dearborn. It was still on the floor by the settee.

"And where is Mr. Bell now?" Inspector Jones asked.

"Didn't he show you and the doctor in?"

"No," the doctor said. "We didn't see anyone. I've tended actors here before, however. I knew where the dressing rooms were located."

So Frederick Bell had evaded the police once again.

"What were you looking for in the dressing table drawer, Mrs. Ames?" Inspector Jones asked.

I hesitated. "Well, I'm not entirely sure. It

was locked, you see. It was just as I opened it that I was hit. But I think it may have contained some compromising letters between Mr. Holloway and Miss Bell. I wanted to retrieve them for Mr. Holloway before they could get out and do any more harm."

"You oughtn't to have put yourself in danger like that," Inspector Jones said, not unkindly. "You see, we already opened that drawer."

"What?" I asked, half hoping that I had heard him wrong.

"I'm afraid so," he said. "We located a key in one of the other drawers and removed the contents, mostly jewelry, some money, and banking receipts. A few strongly worded letters from her brother's creditors. We locked the drawer back as we had found it and gave the key to Mr. Holloway. You must have a duplicate."

They had already been in the drawer. I had been hit on the head for nothing. Somehow this seemed to make the pain worse.

"There were no letters in it?" I asked, unable to let go of the idea.

"Not that we found, though that doesn't mean there aren't letters elsewhere. Or that the killer didn't believe them to be in the drawer. You see, we told no one but Mr.

Holloway that we had opened it. If it was well known that Miss Bell kept things locked there, someone might have had reason to think you would discover something. Who do you suppose might have wanted the letters enough to harm you to get to them?"

"I don't know . . . Someone who wants to hurt Mr. Holloway's or Miss Bell's reputations, I suppose." There was something else, some memory that wanted to come to the surface, but I couldn't remember what it was. I rubbed a hand across my eyes, but it seemed that the harder I focused, the more my head began to ache. Milo realized I was struggling.

"I think that's enough for now," he said. "I'm going to take you home, and you can get some rest."

"Yes, I think that would be a good idea," Inspector Jones said.

"Make sure you don't do anything strenuous for a few days," the doctor said. "And if any of your symptoms get worse, be sure to notify me."

"Thank you, Doctor," I said.

Milo helped me to my feet, and slid a supporting arm around my waist.

"Do you want me to carry you?"

"No, no. I can walk."

We began to make our way toward the door. I glanced at Inspector Jones, who seemed to be deep in thought, and he looked up.

"One more thing, Mrs. Ames," he said. "Who all knew you were here today?"

"I don't know. Mr. Lebeau was the only one I saw, but he left before I came toward the dressing rooms."

"You're sure?"

"I saw him leave," I said. "I can't be certain, but I don't think he would have had time to follow me back."

"And you saw no one else?"

"No."

He turned his gaze to Milo. "What about you, Mr. Ames?"

"I saw only Mr. Bell."

"You said he was coming, as if to get help, when you entered the theatre?"

Milo nodded. "Mrs. Ames left a message at the flat saying she was coming to the theatre, so I came to meet her. I found the building unlocked and just as I was coming in, Mr. Bell was coming from backstage."

"Did he have anything in his hand?"

I realized suddenly that Inspector Jones was wondering if Mr. Bell had struck me and taken whatever was in the drawer.

"No," Milo said. "His hands were empty."

"Very well. I won't trouble you anymore. Get some rest, Mrs. Ames." He paused and then added, "And be careful."

24

I awoke the next morning with a splitting headache. Milo had taken me home from the theatre and put me straight to bed, refusing to discuss any aspect of the case. I had fallen promptly asleep and awakened only briefly to eat a bit of supper with Winnelda fussing over me and to take some pills the doctor had sent over.

My head had really not stopped hurting all night, and the dull ache had woven itself into an assortment of unpleasant dreams, the facts of the case twisting themselves into outlandish improbabilities that plagued me as I drifted fitfully in and out of sleep.

It was a relief when morning finally came. The sun was streaming through the window, and I closed my eyes at the brightness of it. I felt vaguely ill, but the feeling passed after a moment. I didn't dare try to move, however. I was certain that if I did, the pain in my head would become worse. I fought the urge to feel the bump on my temple to see how big it was.

I heard the door open and then Milo's voice.

"How are you feeling this morning, my love?"

"Awful," I replied, not opening my eyes.

"Yes, I was afraid of that. It's time to take some more of these pills. I've brought you some water."

"Thank you," I said, still not looking at him.

I heard him cross the room and close the curtains. Even with my eyes closed, I could tell the room had dimmed. The bed shifted slightly as he sat down on the edge of it. "You're going to have to sit up to take them, darling."

That's what I had been afraid of. I opened my eyes to look up at him, squinting even with the curtains drawn. He was looking down at me with a sympathetic expression I could not recall ever having seen before.

"You look terrible," he said, erasing the affection I was feeling.

"Thank you," I replied crossly. Very gingerly, I shifted my head on the pillow. The pain was steady, but did not seem to increase significantly. I moved to sit up, and Milo assisted me.

My head throbbed for a moment at the change in position and a wave of nausea passed over me, but I leaned back against the headboard and the throbbing subsided to the familiar dull ache and the nausea dissipated.

"Here you are," Milo said, handing me the pills and a glass of water. I took the tablets, hoping they would quickly do the trick.

Milo was watching me carefully, his blue eyes flickering over my face. "You're very pale."

"I'll be quite all right," I said.

"You're not to get up today."

"Did the doctor say that?"

"No. I did. You've been injured, and I will not have you traipsing about, doing yourself further harm."

It was sweet, if vaguely irritating. "I'll be perfectly all right after I take this medicine and have some coffee," I protested, though I was not at all sure that was the case. The way I felt right now, I was not even certain I would be able to make it across the room.

"You were lucky you weren't killed," he said, and there was no hint of exaggeration in his tone.

It was so seldom that he seemed really serious about anything that I couldn't help but feel a bit touched at his concern.

"I don't think it was as severe as all that," I said.

"I thought we agreed we were going to do this together," he said. "And yet you put yourself in harm's way alone. Again."

"I didn't know it was dangerous," I protested, though this was not, perhaps, entirely true. I was also still irked that it had all been for naught. Though I would never admit as much, this would teach me not to run off and do things rashly without first consulting Inspector Jones.

"Well, I've spoken to Inspector Jones and told him he's not to come and question you any more until tomorrow at the earliest," Milo said, bringing up the inspector even as my thoughts turned in his direction.

I couldn't help but smile at the sternness of his tone. "How did he feel about that?"

"I don't much care how he felt about it, but he didn't protest."

"Milo, I'm not an invalid. It's just a bump on the head."

He ignored me. "From now on, I don't want you going anywhere alone. If you're not with me or Inspector Jones, make sure you're with at least two people. I don't trust any of them at the theatre, not even Holloway, and I . . . What are you smiling at?"

"You're turning into a mother hen."

"Yes, well, you may as well get used to it. You know perfectly well how it annoys me when you put yourself in danger, and yet you're always . . ."

There was a tap on the door.

"Yes?" I called, glad to be interrupted.

The door opened and Winnelda peeked inside. "I've brought some breakfast, madam."

"Thank you, Winnelda," I said.

She pushed the door the rest of the way and came into the room, a tray in her hands. While the thought of food was not at all appealing, I was glad to see that she had brought a coffeepot.

"Winnelda, I want you to take care of Mrs. Ames today," Milo told her as she poured me a cup of coffee.

"Yes, sir," she said.

"I don't want her to leave this room. If she tries, you are to come and find me."

"Yes, sir," she said, looking hesitantly at me. Though she was a bit in awe of Milo, I had no doubt that I could countermand his orders, if necessary.

"And don't let her convince you otherwise," he added.

"Yes, sir," she said again before beating a hasty retreat.

I took a sip of the coffee, scalding my tongue. It was delicious, and it seemed that I felt a bit better already.

"Where do you intend to be all day, while I'm bedridden?" I asked.

"I'm going to look for Freddy Bell. I want to have a few words with him."

"Do you think he's the one who hit me?" I asked.

"I don't know, but I intend to find out."

I took another sip of coffee. In combination with the pills I had just taken, it was already helping my headache considerably.

For some reason, I didn't think it had been Freddy Bell who had delivered the blow to my head. After all, why would he want his sister's letters, if that was what he had believed to be in the drawer? The only reason I could think of was that he wanted to protect her reputation, and he needn't have hit me on the head to accomplish that. The same was true of his sister's valuables. They would come to him eventually, and he would have had no need to prevent me from finding them.

I remembered that Inspector Jones had also mentioned the drawer contained letters from Freddy's creditors. I thought of his furtive manner when I had mentioned letters to him at the café. Had it been the written demands for money that brought him concern, or something else? Furthermore, were these the letters Dahlia Dearborn had seen Flora tuck away and had assumed to be from a secret lover, or had there been other notes that Flora was hiding? There was so much we didn't know.

My thoughts returned to Mr. Lebeau.

"I learned something else," I told Milo. "When I went to Miss Bell's boardinghouse, the landlady told me that a gentleman had been coming to visit her, and do you know who it was? Mr. Lebeau."

"And so you went to the theatre and put yourself directly in the path of danger," Milo said, missing the point entirely.

"But why would Mr. Lebeau be visiting Miss Bell in her boardinghouse?" I asked.

"I'm sure I could hazard a guess," Milo said.

"I don't think it was like that," I said. "After all, the landlady said they always stayed in the sitting room and weren't alone for long."

"You'd be surprised what can be accomplished when two people are alone for a short amount of time," Milo said.

I frowned at him. "I do wish you wouldn't always think of things in a sordid way."

"I'm sorry to disillusion you, darling, but

most things are sordid."

I didn't agree with him, but now was not the time to have an argument about the state of British morality. Whatever Milo's insinuations, I didn't believe that Flora Bell and Balthazar Lebeau had been having an affair. But if it hadn't been a secret relationship, what had it been? Why would he visit her at her home in disguise? It was all so very strange.

"I might have pressed him on the matter, but I'm afraid he distracted me."

"Oh?"

"He is going to try to get the part of Armand if Christopher Landon leaves the play."

"*The Price of Victory* starring Dahlia Dearborn and Balthazar Lebeau," Milo intoned. "If that doesn't work out for them, perhaps they may find success in forming The Society for Preposterous Pseudonyms."

I laughed. "It's Mr. Lebeau's real name. He told me so."

"And what else did he tell you?"

"He had me read the lines with him, the scene right before Armand goes off to battle and must bid Victoire farewell."

Milo's brows rose. "That's the scene that ends in a passionate kiss, I believe."

"He's a wonderful actor," I said, ignoring

the implied question. "I've heard for years about him, you know, but I didn't realize . . ."

"Until he held you in his arms," Milo said dryly. "I'm sure it was a very touching scene."

"You aren't the only man capable of dazzling women with good looks and charm."

I thought again about my encounter with Balthazar Lebeau. On a practical level, I could admit that I had been awed by him. I supposed it was natural to find oneself impressed by a celebrity. But, on a deeper level, I had been impressed by the depth I had seen in him, the way in which he could draw from some well of emotion to become an entirely different person before my eyes.

He was capable of great deception. Perhaps all good actors were. What I wondered, however, was if he was also capable of violence.

I remembered the way that his fingers had trailed across my throat. Had he done the same thing to Flora Bell when he strangled her? A chill ran through me.

"Daydreaming about him even now?" Milo asked.

I made a face. "I certainly was not. I was thinking about him as a suspect."

"You mean to say you weren't sufficiently

wooed to remove him from your list of potential killers?"

"There's more to him than meets the eye."

"The same can be said of most people," he pointed out.

"Yes, every last one of our suspects, in fact," I said glumly.

Milo reached out and patted my hand. "Don't fret about it, darling. Things will work out."

I realized he was preparing to leave, and I found myself a bit disappointed. We had not, perhaps, quite resolved our argument about marriage, but I relished the easy closeness between us this morning.

It seemed his thoughts had gone the same way as mine, for suddenly he paused, the hand that was on mine taking hold of it. "I'm very glad you're all right, Amory. When I found you bleeding on the floor, I had the rather unpleasant urge to commit murder myself. If anything had happened to you . . ."

"It will take more than a crack on the head to rid you of me, I'm afraid."

"I don't ever want to be rid of you," he said. His free hand reached up to cup my face. "I care about you more than anything else in this world. I hope you know that."

I looked into his eyes even as I fought the

tears that threatened to spring to my own at this unexpected sentimentality. "I know," I said softly.

He leaned to kiss me gently then and rose from the bed. "I'll be back as soon as I can. You will behave yourself?"

"I'll try," I said with a smile.

He left and I had no time to process this latest development in our relationship before Winnelda came back into the room.

"I was terribly worried about you, madam," Winnelda said. "When you were coshed on the head, I thought how dreadful it would be if you woke up and didn't remember anything. I've heard of that. People get an injury to the head and sometimes they don't remember their own name or where they came from. And you wouldn't remember Mr. Ames. That would be an awful pity. Of course, I'm quite sure he could make you fall in love with him all over again, but I just think it would be so tragic if —"

"Well," I said, cutting her off, "let us be thankful I have not lost my memory or my love for Mr. Ames. I think perhaps you both worried more than the situation warranted."

"I think Mr. Ames is right, though, madam. You oughtn't be wandering around the house."

"I'm not going to remain in bed all day, Winnelda," I said firmly. "I won't do anything ill-advised, I promise you."

She looked uneasy, as though she were afraid I might dart past her toward the door if she let her guard down for a moment. There was no chance of that. Though I didn't intend to admit it, I felt as though I would much rather sit very still than do any moving about.

"Perhaps you might draw me a bath," I suggested.

"I'll draw one now," she said, glad, I supposed, that there was no means of escape from the bathroom.

I rose slowly and found that, thankfully, I was no longer dizzy. I went to the dressing table mirror to assess the damage. I did indeed have an ugly purple bruise. It ran from my temple almost to my hairline. Gingerly, I reached up to touch it and winced. Milo and Winnelda needn't have worried I would be going out today; it would hurt too much to apply makeup to cover my injury.

The bath did wonders, and by the time I had dressed and gone to the sitting room, I felt much more like my old self. I put on the radio and sat on the sofa, hoping the quiet music would soothe my thoughts and help me to make sense of everything that had happened. I did not have time for it to work, however, before there was a buzz at the door. A moment later Winnelda came into the sitting room.

"Mrs. Holloway is here to see you, madam," Winnelda said. "Shall I tell her you're ill?"

"No, no. Show her in, Winnelda," I said, surprised. I had not expected Georgina to call.

She came into the room and stopped when she saw my face.

"Oh, Amory! What's happened to you?" she asked.

"I'm afraid I had something of an accident," I said. Though this was not exactly true, I didn't want to cloud our conversation with the particulars.

"Are you sure you're all right?" she asked.

"Yes, I'm quite well now." In truth, my head still ached and even hard blinking caused a pain in my temple, but I did not intend to let that get in the way.

"Sit down, will you? What brings you here, Georgina?"

"I'm sorry to drop in on you unannounced like this," she said, taking her seat. "But Gerard came home yesterday."

"Oh . . . I see," I said. He must have gone

there after he left our flat. I wondered if he had confessed to Georgina his worries about her guilt. It made me even more curious to know why Georgina had come to see me.

"He told me that he had spent the night here." I wondered if she doubted his word and had come to verify his story. Well, at least I could put her mind at ease on that score.

"Yes," I said. "He slept on this sofa. I'm afraid he wasn't feeling well."

"Yes, I could see that," she said dryly.

There was a moment of somewhat awkward silence, and then Georgina charged forward.

"I've come to you for advice," she said.

"Oh?" I said carefully. I wondered if she was about to ask for advice on their relationship, or if it could possibly have something to do with the murder.

"Gerard has asked me to take him back. He wants to start again, but I don't know if I can."

I hesitated. I was not exactly comfortable giving advice of this sort. After all, I was still learning to find my way in my own marriage, even after six years. Up until this week, I would have thought that the Holloways could have given us marital advice.

"I'm sure you'll make the right decision,"

I said carefully.

"Do you remember the moment you knew you were in love?" she asked suddenly.

I was a bit surprised by the question, but I considered it. I had felt an attraction to Milo from the start. Most women did, of course. But there had been something between us that went deeper than that. Though I knew his reputation even then, I had felt that I understood him, that we complemented each other.

His proposal had been sudden and unexpected, and it was the moment he had asked me to marry him that I had realized that I loved him deeply.

"Yes," I said at last. "I remember."

"I don't," she said softly. "I've loved Gerard for as long as I can remember."

I believed her. For as long as I had known Georgina, she and Gerard Holloway had always been a pair, their names spoken together as often as they were separately. Perhaps that was why it was so hard for me to see their marriage in this state. Their love had always seemed to be a fact, something that one knew so well to be true that it was never questioned.

"We were children when we met," she said. "I was perhaps five or six, he a bit older. We took to each other instantly. Our parents laughingly joked that we would marry one day, but to me it wasn't a joke. I always knew that Gerard and I would be together forever."

It was a romantic story, and I felt again that sadness at the way such a strong bond had begun to crumble.

"That's why I knew this business with Flora Bell wouldn't last," she said. "He had a lapse in judgment, but it was only temporary. He loved me and I loved him. Flora Bell already had her eye on another prize."

I looked up. "What do you mean?"

"There was someone else she was interested in."

"Do you mean Mr. Landon?"

"I suppose so. I heard, just through gossip, mind you, that there was an actor she was very fond of. I always thought she was using Gerard for his connections, though I never would have said so to him."

"I see," I said, considering this information. Had Miss Bell and Mr. Landon continued their liaison after she had become involved with Mr. Holloway?

"So I was sure everything was going to be all right." She paused. "But now that she is dead, things are different."

"How so?"

She looked at me, the pain and worry

evident in her eyes, though she was clearly trying to hide it. "I will never know what he really felt for her. He said he was going to break things off with her, but I will never know the truth. How do I know that he loves me and that he is not merely turning to me now that she is gone?"

I hadn't considered this and felt a fresh wave of pity for Georgina.

"What would you advise me to do?" she asked. Her tone was so cool and composed. She might have been asking her solicitor for advice on a trivial matter. But I felt the weight of the question.

I thought of my conversation with Milo this morning, of the doubts and insecurities that had sometimes plagued me. When taken in total, marriage had not been easy for me. The ups and downs of my life with Milo were not the stuff that fairy tales were made of. But when we had spoken this morning I had realized that what he said was true. A storm doesn't necessarily mean shipwreck if the anchor goes deep enough. And then I realized the answer I would give.

"Some things are worth fighting for," I said simply. "You just have to decide if this is one of them."

She seemed to consider this. "Yes, perhaps you're right," she answered at last. "I shall have to think about it."

"You're certainly entitled to do that," I said. "And please know that, whatever your decision, you have a friend who is happy to support you."

She smiled at me, and I could see that some of the tension had left her posture. "Thank you, Amory. I appreciate that more than you know."

She rose then, brushing away any traces of sentiment. "I'm afraid I've kept you long enough. No, don't get up. Your head is troubling you, isn't it?"

"A bit," I admitted.

"I can show myself out. I do hope you feel better. Perhaps we may have tea when . . . when things are more settled."

"I shall look forward to it."

She left then and I sat for a long while thinking over our conversation. There were still a great many impediments to the Holloways' happiness, but perhaps it was not impossible after all.

After Georgina left, I found my headache had returned, and, though I had been inclined to fight it, I had followed the doctor's advice and stayed in bed for most of the day.

When I awoke from a nap, I felt much better. Winnelda brought me tea and another dose of medicine.

"Mr. Ames called while you were asleep, madam," she said as I took the tablets. "He told me not to disturb you and said he'd be home a bit later."

"Did he say where he was going?"

"No, only that he shouldn't be too late."

This meant, of course, that he hadn't wanted to account for his whereabouts. I did hope he wasn't putting himself in any danger.

I wished there was something I could do to pass the time. I was starting to feel restless after a day spent doing nothing. If only there was a way to get more information without leaving the flat. A thought occurred to me suddenly.

"Winnelda, did you have a chance to look through your scrapbooks?"

Excitement flashed across her face before she did a poor job of suppressing it. "Yes, madam," she said mildly. "But I don't suppose we had better look at them now."

"Why not?"

"It might not be good for your head."

"For heaven's sake, Winnelda, go and get them," I said. "They may be of use."

Needing no further urging, she hurried to fetch them. A moment later she returned with an armful of large, square books in a variety of colors.

"Set them here," I said, patting the bed beside me. "You can help me go through them."

She deposited the books beside me and then perched on the edge of the bed. "I've brought all my books, but I've marked the pages related to the people you mentioned."

"How very clever of you, Winnelda," I said.

She beamed. "I did want to be helpful, madam. As I said, my mum was sweet on Balthazar Lebeau, so I made a few pages about a play he was in." She flipped through one of the books and then pushed it toward me. "There."

I looked down at the neatly cut clippings that she had pasted to the page. There was an article about a play that Mr. Lebeau was set to star in.

" 'Balthazar Lebeau may soon be seen in the comedy *Too Many Husbands,*' " I read aloud. " 'This will be a departure from the more serious dramatic roles in which Mr. Lebeau has previously starred.' "

"And here are the pages I did on Christopher Landon," Winnelda said, handing me another book.

I looked down at the page, a clipping with

a photograph catching my eye, and for a moment I was very confused.

I looked at the headline. "Christopher Landon and Helen Whitney Are Pleased to Announce Their Engagement."

Helen Whitney. That was apparently the name of the woman Mrs. Roland and Inspector Jones had mentioned, the woman who had drowned in the Thames after a troubled relationship with Christopher Landon.

The article had obviously been written before they had parted for the last time, but it was not the contents of the article that interested me. It was that photograph. I looked at it again, marveling.

Helen Whitney had looked startlingly like Flora Bell.

25

By that evening my headache was gone and there was only the tender, bruised lump on my temple to remind me of the ordeal and the mystery that plagued my mind. We were close. I could feel it, as though the solution was waiting for the curtains to be pulled back so it could make itself known.

I felt, somehow, that I knew who the killer was and yet I could not make myself realize it.

It seemed that the more I considered it, the harder it was to determine who might be lying and who was telling the truth. There were so many conflicting accounts and tangled stories.

Perhaps the greatest difficulty arose from the fact that each of these people was accustomed to playing roles, to hiding the truth of their lives behind the characters they played. It was something they did on a daily basis. How much easier would it be for them to do it when their lives were on the line?

It was a depressing thought. I reminded myself, however, that there had been other cases that had seemed hopeless, and they had always worked out in the end.

As I always did when faced with a complicated problem, I began to make a list. As Winnelda protested about my sitting at the desk, I brought paper and pencil to bed and began working my way through the suspects.

The most obvious, perhaps, was Gerard Holloway. After all, the lover was always the first to be considered. He and Flora had quarreled that night, and the crime had apparently been a crime of passion. The fight might have become violent. Such things were more common than one would like to think.

Or had he been trying to break off their affair after Georgina had given him the ultimatum? I still had my doubts that he had meant to do so, whatever Georgina claimed. But, if he had, Flora might have refused to accept it. Perhaps she had threatened to create a scandal. Granted, most of London already knew about their dalliance, but she could draw things out, of course, sell her story to the gossip rags and drag his name through the mud. Mr. Holloway was a proud man from a good family. An affair was one thing, but a scandal was another. But was it enough to make him kill her?

I also considered the possibility that it might have been Georgina Holloway who had followed her to the theatre. After confronting her husband, she might have felt that she should speak with Flora Bell. If so, it would not have been a nice conversation. I could imagine such an exchange must be tense and unpleasant. Was it possible it had escalated into something violent?

Georgina was so cool and elegant; I found it hard to believe that she would have the brutality to strangle Miss Bell to death with a curtain rope, but there was also a strength in her, a deep resolve in her character that would not let me rule her out entirely. Besides, drunk or not, Mr. Holloway had thought her capable of it. I knew from my own experience how damaging it could be to suspect one's spouse of murder.

The doctor had said that it would be possible for a woman to do it, under the right circumstances. That meant that it could also be Dahlia Dearborn. She had wanted the role, had even jested that she would not likely get to take the stage unless something happened to Miss Bell. I had seen a ruthless ambition in Miss Dearborn, and it was not outside the realm of possibility that she had been willing to kill to get what she wanted.

I moved next to Freddy Bell. He had been seen skulking around the party that night, clearly in an unpleasant frame of mind. It was more than possible that he had asked her for more money. She might have said no, and he, in anger, might have strangled her, knowing that he was due to inherit what money she had.

Freddy Bell had also been there when I had been hit on the head. He might have done it and then, when he encountered Milo, feigned that he was seeking help. But what was to be gained by hitting me and stealing the letters in Flora Bell's dressing table drawer? Or had there been something else in the drawer that he was after?

For that matter, who might have benefitted from the love letters Mr. Holloway had written to Flora Bell? Gerard and Georgina Holloway might have wanted them kept quiet, but I thought they would both be much more inclined to ask me for the letters than to hit me on the head. One of the others might have wanted them for the purpose of blackmail, but how would they have known what was in the drawer? Had someone suspected I might find something in the drawer and hit me as a precaution? It was so difficult to know.

I moved next to Christopher Landon. What I had discovered about him today was too strange to be a coincidence. Flora Bell had looked almost exactly like the first woman in his life who had died a mysterious death. The resemblance had been so strong, I had even considered, for an instant, the possibility that the women might be one and the same. However, it was clear from the dates of the newspaper clippings that Helen Whitney was dead and buried long before Flora Bell had met Christopher Landon, and a closer inspection of the photograph showed subtle differences in appearance. What, then, was the relationship between the two women who looked so alike? Was Mr. Landon some sort of maniac who enjoyed seducing then killing women of similar appearance? That seemed farfetched.

Whatever his reason for wooing Flora Bell, I thought it possible that he had been going to see her in order to try to rekindle their romance. She might have agreed to meet with him and, when she refused his advances, he might have killed her.

The other possible option was Balthazar Lebeau. It wasn't just my growing fondness for the man that made me believe he was innocent of this crime. It was also that I found it difficult to believe he would become so deeply emotional that he would commit a murder in a fit of rage. He was too unaffected by everything around him. It was possible, of course, that this seeming indifference had finally reached its limit. Mrs. Roland had said that he had always felt things deeply and attempted to hide it. Sometimes a trickle of long-suppressed feeling can become a geyser.

I looked down at my list in disgust. I had effectively accomplished nothing. Despite my best efforts, I was having no success in making any sense of the clues. I lay back against the pillows with a sigh. I reminded myself of poor Victoire, trying so hard to make sense of everything falling apart around her.

If only life could have a neat resolution like a play.

Like a play. I thought suddenly of what Freddy Bell had told me Flora had said. "It's just like the play." I had assumed that she meant the tragic love story, the lover choosing nobility over the desires of the heart. That's what she would have thought if Mr. Holloway had decided to return to Georgina.

But what if she had meant something else?

I sat up in bed, my mind awhirl. It was just possible that there was something I had overlooked, something that would help to make sense of it all.

Grabbing my list of suspects and throwing back the covers, I left the bedroom and went to the sitting room. The copy of the script I had used when helping Mr. Lebeau practice the scene was still in my handbag.

I went to the desk and picked up a letter opener. Slipping it onto the binding, I carefully cut the pages free. Moving to the center of the sitting room, I set the stack of pages on the floor and began to push back the furniture. Luckily, there weren't any heavy pieces in this room, and it was the work of a few minutes to move the ivory-colored leather chairs and push the sofa off of the rug toward the wall.

Then, facing the fireplace, I began to set the pages out on the rug in chronological order. One by one, I laid the crisp white sheets of paper on the floor with a small space between each row for me to move as I went over everything.

I went back to the desk to collect a pencil, and then I sat on the floor before the first row, ready to see if I could learn anything of use.

Though I had seen the play more than once, I had not paid attention for anything that might hold special significance. Now I started at the beginning and underlined words and phrases I thought might mean something to Flora Bell, sometimes scribbling notes in the margins.

"Madam!" Winnelda cried from the doorway, clearly horrified that I was up and exerting energy.

"It's all right," I said. "My head doesn't even hurt."

"But . . ."

"Would you be so kind as to bring me some coffee?" I asked.

She let out a sigh, clearly knowing when she had been defeated. "Very well, madam."

I continued moving pages around, lost in thought, and was surprised at how quickly she returned with the coffee things on a little tray.

She stood for a moment, glancing around the room at the unfamiliar configuration of furniture. "Where shall I . . . ?"

"Just put it on the floor, there, Winnelda," I said, nodding to the space just off the rug, close enough to reach but not near enough to be in the way.

She leaned to set it on the floor. "Shall I pour it for you, madam?" she asked.

"No, I'll fix a cup in a few moments. Thank you, Winnelda."

"Are you sure . . ."

"Quite sure. It's getting late. You may go to bed if you like. I shan't be needing anything else."

"Very good, madam."

Winnelda went off to bed then, a bit miffed, I thought. She didn't like having been sent away when I was working, but there was no way she could be of help in this venture. In all honesty, it was likely she would only have been a distraction.

I leaned to pull off my satin bed slippers, tossing them aside. Then I returned to my work.

There was more to all of this than I had previously considered. Now that I looked at the lines, it seemed that any of them might contain a hidden meaning. It was possible, of course, that Flora's comment to her brother was unconnected to her murder, but something told me that I could not overlook the possibility that they were related. I had had the impression that day in her dressing room that she knew more than she was saying. Perhaps she had realized that someone meant her harm, but had been protecting that person for unknown reasons.

Whatever the case, I was going to work my way through the entire play so that I could have a full idea of what she might have meant. I sorted the papers into stacks of those which might prove useful and those which would not.

I worked in silence for some time, the only sound the ticking of the clock on the mantel.

"What have we here?"

I looked over my shoulder to see Milo leaning against the doorframe, his eyes taking in the tableau before him with an expression of vague interest. I had been so engrossed in my task that I had not even heard him come in the front door.

Out of habit, I glanced at the clock and saw it was not yet ten o'clock. He was home early.

"Hello, Milo," I said, turning my attention back to the page before me. There was a line on it about a romantic rival and the danger of passion. Could it be a reference to Dahlia Dearborn? Had Flora sensed that she might be dangerous? I made a note and put the paper in the "possibly useful" stack.

"Did you find Freddy Bell?" I asked, my eyes moving to the next page.

"No, but I left a message at the gambling club. Said I want to give him a reward for helping you. I expect he'll show up soon enough. I have a bit of other information that, while likely insignificant, is a bit interesting."

"I shall be delighted to hear it when I've finished with this," I said, trying not to lose my train of thought.

"Certainly. Might I ask what you're doing?" he asked, coming into the room.

"I'm working."

"I can see that. Working on what?"

I spared him another glance. "I'm reading over the play and making some notes."

He came further into the room, loosening his necktie. "What sort of notes?"

"Don't step on anything," I said, waving a hand in a preemptive attempt to keep him from stepping on the rug and upsetting any of the neat stacks of paper I had made. "Flora told Freddy Bell that something was 'just like in the play.' I think she knew she was in danger. If so, there might be a clue somewhere in the script. I'm going through the play looking at lines that might hold a special significance."

"An interesting theory." He stepped carefully around the rug and looked down at me. "How are you feeling?"

"Much better, thank you."

"I'm glad to hear it. You certainly make a pretty picture in your bare feet, with your hair mussed and a pencil behind your ear."

"Yes, well, I hope you won't mind if I continue."

"By all means," he said, with a courteous wave of his hand.

I looked back down at the paper before me and tried to read, but I was very aware of Milo standing over me.

I looked up. "Do you intend to stand there for the remainder of the evening?"

"Certainly not. I can make myself comfortable as well," he said. He removed his jacket, tossing it across the back of a chair, and then lowered himself to the floor beside me.

I glanced at him warily over my shoulder. I had the distinct feeling he was going to be much more of a hindrance than a help. Probably even more so than Winnelda would have been.

"What's this coffee doing here?" he asked, indicating the tray Winnelda had left on the floor at the edge of the rug.

"Winnelda brought it for me, but I forgot to drink it."

He reached out and poured some into the cup. Though I had neglected it for some time, steam rose up as he poured and the aroma drifted over to me.

He stirred in the milk and sugar and

handed the cup to me. I took a sip of the coffee, the warmth trailing its way down my throat.

I handed the cup back to him, and he took a sip, glancing down at the papers beside him. I was gratified that he didn't touch anything.

"Now, what have you discovered?" Milo asked.

"I don't know, exactly," I said, leaning down to mark another line, one about the dangers of the past — a reference to Christopher Landon? — a piece of hair falling across my forehead.

"Did I mention how beautiful you look tonight?"

I turned to look at him skeptically. "Pale as parchment, with this unsightly bruise covering half my face?"

"Yes," he said with a credibly straight expression. "The purple gives a violet cast to your gray eyes."

"Milo . . ."

"In fact, you're so lovely that I think I must kiss you." He deposited the cup back on the tray and leaned toward me.

I shifted away and my hand hit a pile of papers, knocking them askew. I straightened, shoving him back. "Stop this at once," I laughed. "I'm trying to concentrate."

He smiled, but he sat back and didn't try to kiss me again.

"Very well. Tell me how I can help." I resisted the urge to tell him that he could be the most helpful by going to bed and leaving me to work through this on my own. I knew, however, that he wasn't likely to oblige me.

"I'm not sure," I said. "Perhaps you may look over some of these pages I've marked and see if anything jumps out at you."

He took the stack I handed him, glancing over it. "You've marked half the script."

"Everything seems to hold significance when you look for it," I said with a sigh.

"Perhaps we ought to make a list," Milo suggested.

"I've already made one." I rose and, moving carefully to avoid stepping on any of the play pages on the floor, went to the desk where I had deposited my list when I had come into the sitting room. Then I moved back to my place on the rug and handed it to him.

He scanned it. "You haven't addressed the threatening letters."

"No," I said. "You're right. There is just so much to consider."

"One does wonder why the killer sent them in the first place," Milo said.

"Yes," I agreed. "It just doesn't make sense."

So engrossed were we in our conversation that the sound of an unexpected voice from the doorway was startling.

"Well, isn't this a pretty picture."

I looked up to see my mother standing there, her eyes taking in the scene before her.

Milo glanced at me as he rose to his feet. "Good evening, Mrs. Ames."

"Good evening," she said coolly.

"Hello, Mother," I said. "I didn't hear you knock."

"That's because I didn't. The door was ajar, and I heard voices. I must say, if this is the way you spend your evenings alone, it's no wonder I haven't any grandchildren."

I shot Milo a glance, knowing very well that he would make some sort of embarrassing remark if I didn't stop him. It seemed I had judged correctly, for he was just about to speak when my gaze stopped him.

"What brings you here at this time of night?" I asked.

"Your father and I are going out of town in the morning, and I thought that I would stop in and see you."

It was a poor excuse, and I knew then that

there was some ulterior motive for her visit.

She looked at me closely, a frown creasing her brow. "Whatever has happened to your face?"

Something in the way she said it made me think she had already known about my injury. Who had told her? My mother had a great many friends. I could only assume that one of them had seen Milo helping me from the theatre after I had been hit.

I hesitated, not wanting to tell her the truth but not knowing exactly how to avoid it.

She seemed to misinterpret my reluctance and leveled her gaze on Milo. "Young man, I hope you had nothing to do with this. Carousing is one thing, but . . ."

"Certainly not, Mother!" I said. "Milo had nothing to do with it. In fact, he came to my rescue."

I glanced at Milo to see if he was angry, but he appeared more amused than anything.

"I suppose it has something to do with this investigation you've become involved in," she said. She fixed me with her piercing gaze, and it seemed there was no use in denying it.

"Yes, I'm afraid I was hit on the head by a killer." If I was going to tell her the truth, I might at least have the satisfaction of shocking her.

She blinked, and I was gratified that I seemed to have rendered her speechless.

Alas, her next words took some of the wind from my sails. "You've caught the killer then?"

"Not exactly," I said with a sigh.

"Hmm."

"That's what we're doing now," I said, waving a hand at the papers scattered about the room. "We're going over the evidence."

She looked around, clearly not impressed. "If the police are incapable of solving crimes on their own, perhaps it is something that ought to be addressed in Parliament."

"Well, we all know that government needs a bit of assistance here and there," Milo said with a smile.

"That's true," she said grudgingly. "But I don't see why my daughter must be the one to do it. If anyone need go about getting hit on the head, send your husband to do it."

I bit back a laugh. "Remember that, Milo," I instructed.

"I shall," he replied.

"Well, I clearly can't stop from you behaving recklessly, but I do hope you'll be careful. Perhaps your father and I ought to stay in town a few more days. You clearly need looking after."

It was touching, in a way, that she had been concerned enough about my safety to pay me this unexpected visit, but I had no desire for her to make good on her threat to look after me. She had never been the sort of mother to fuss over my well-being, and it would be disconcerting if she were to start now.

"That won't be necessary," I assured her quickly. "We're very close to a solution. I'm sure of it."

"I'm very distressed that you've put yourself in danger, and over an amateur production, no less. I've just been to dinner with the Carvers, and they tell me that *The Price of Victory,* while amusing, is not up to the standard of a good many plays this season."

I knew now who my mother's informant was. Mrs. Carver had an eagle eye and a serpent's tongue. She was especially fond of gossiping about the goings-on in the theatre district. No doubt she had heard about my incident from one of her sources. My only surprise was that it had taken the news a full day to get back to my mother.

"Oh, I know that Gerard Holloway has always had delusions of grandeur and a desire for accolades, but he hasn't the true spark for theatre. I believe acting must be in one's blood, not something that can be learned. Of course, I know that so many people enjoy the theatre because it allows them the opportunity to pretend. People do like earning reputations for themselves and going about trying to live up to them. But, on the whole, I dislike amateur productions. The acting is never very good, and everything is so obviously an illusion. Even the stage props look excessively unrealistic. It takes away from the experience, really, and I, for one . . ."

An unfortunate side effect of my somewhat strained relationship with my mother is that it often takes some time for her words to work their way through the filters I have built up over the years. My mind was slowly turning as she spoke, only half listening, but suddenly I started, a chill sweeping through me. In an instant, everything seemed to fall into place, as clearly as if I were watching it play out on a stage before me.

I didn't even notice that my mother had stopped speaking.

"Whatever's the matter, Amory?" she said. "You've gone all white."

"I . . . you've made me think of something." I looked up at her. "You may have just helped me solve the murder."

"What?" Though I think the word was

meant to sound aghast, she could not hide the note of excitement that was there.

"I think I know what happened," I said. "Something you've just said . . ."

"Well, what is it?" she demanded.

I looked over at Milo. My mind was still whirling. The solution seemed impossible, and yet, somehow, I knew that it was not.

"I'll explain in a moment," I said, getting quickly to my feet. "I just need to think . . ."

"Take your time, darling," Milo said.

I looked again at my mother and was surprised to see a glimmer of admiration in her eyes. Despite her disapproval at my involvement in the matter, she was clearly impressed that I had come to the truth. Yet some part of me wished that I were wrong.

Slowly I worked through the pieces of the puzzle in my mind, hoping that one would prove an ill fit, hoping that the solution was not correct. But piece by piece it all fit into place.

"I . . . I'll explain," I said again. "But I need to speak to Inspector Jones."

My mother moved to the sofa and perched on the edge, clasping her hands in her lap. "I shall wait. I don't mean to leave before I learn the truth."

"It's a good thing you dropped in, Mrs. Ames," Milo said, turning to her. "It was very kind of you to sweep through and solve our mystery for us."

"I suppose now I can see why you get a certain thrill from such things," she said. "Vulgar though it may be."

"Vulgarity can be very amusing on occasion," Milo said, a wicked glint in his eyes.

My mother gave him a disapproving glance before turning back to me. "What will you do once you've telephoned the police? Will they arrest the suspect directly?"

"I don't know," I said. "The trouble is, it's going to be difficult to prove. We must find a way to bring the truth to light."

"How do you mean to do that?" my mother asked. She was clearly becoming invested in the matter, and I wondered for the first time if my mother had a bit of a taste for adventure herself. Perhaps it was a trait I had inherited without realizing it.

"These are theatrical people," I said. "They won't respond to the usual methods. We're going to have to create some sort of drama to get a confession."

My mother's brows rose expectantly. "Well, then, I suppose you shall have to put on a show."

26

We gathered at the Penworth Theatre the next morning. I had telephoned Inspector Jones very late, but, once I told him what I had in mind, he had gone immediately into action. Even with that very short notice and the fact that it was a Sunday morning, he had managed to have each of the players present for the drama that was about to play out.

The stage was still set for the first scene, in Victoire's drawing room, but several additional chairs had been set up there, and there was a seat for everyone. As each of the suspects took their seats, I felt a flurry of nervousness in my stomach. Stage fright, I supposed one might call it.

I glanced at Inspector Jones, and he met my gaze and gave me the slightest nod. It was an immeasurable boost to my confidence. So, too, was Milo's presence behind me. I couldn't see him from where I stood, but I knew that he was there and that he was my partner in this. Whatever happened today, he would be behind me.

I had expected there would be grumblings and protests as everyone gathered at this rather unorthodox location, but there was nothing until everyone was seated. It was no great surprise to me that it was Dahlia Dearborn who first voiced her disapproval.

"I don't understand why we've all been called here," she said.

"Yes, what the devil is this all about?" demanded Christopher Landon.

"This will only take a few minutes, Miss Dearborn, Mr. Landon," Inspector Jones said. And that was all he said. He didn't elaborate further, and yet silence descended over the actors.

It never ceased to amaze me how Inspector Jones's calm, matter-of-fact manner set everything to rights. When he spoke, people accepted his authority and proceeded from a place of respect. It was really a remarkable quality.

I expected that he would begin then, but he waited for a moment, as though to further emphasize that those present were here at his request and would remain so until he had dismissed them. I knew he was not the sort of person who reveled in his authority, but he was also clever enough to know when it could be wielded to its best advantage. This room was full of people who appreciated a display.

I looked at Gerard and Georgina Holloway. Though they sat next to each other, they didn't speak. Mr. Holloway looked perfectly miserable, his face drawn and grim. Georgina had her arms crossed, as though protecting herself from something. It appeared the rift between them was not yet mended.

Balthazar Lebeau sat back easily in his chair, one leg crossed over the other. As ever, he looked as though the world was his to command. If he was at all concerned about the proceedings, he gave no sign of it. After all, there was no place where he was more at home than on the stage. Nevertheless, I noted that, despite his perpetual expression of mild amusement, his eyes were moving from person to person, as though he, too, was observing them.

Dahlia Dearborn was trying very hard to act as though the entire thing was nothing but a nuisance, but I could tell that she was nervous. She was tapping her long red fingernails against her leg and biting her lip.

Christopher Landon was seated beside her, his handsome face set in hard lines.

Freddy Bell sat a bit apart from the others. He had a look of almost defiant indifference on his face, but his eyes betrayed him. That blue gaze, so like Flora's, was darting around the room, fear evident.

"I suppose we can begin," Inspector Jones said at last, and all conversation ceased as he stepped forward. "Mrs. Ames has graciously agreed to help me, and I would like all of you to afford her every courtesy."

That was my cue.

I felt the weight of every pair of eyes turn toward me, and I knew what it must be like to step out onto the stage in one's premier performance, exposed and ready to be judged. Only, this time so much more lay in the balance than applause and acclaim, and the thought made me more nervous than ever. What if this didn't work?

"I was drawn into this matter when I learned that Flora Bell had been receiving threatening letters," I began, my voice echoing out onto the stage and into the darkness beyond. I was pleased that I sounded much more confident than I felt. "It seemed, at first, that they might have been designed to simply frighten her, a mean-spirited joke by someone who envied her and wanted her to fail. But when she was killed, it became clear that there must be more to the letters than that."

I paused. There was no reaction. Everyone was silent, watchful.

I went on. "What was puzzling was the nature of the letters. They gave no instructions, nor did they make demands. They only warned of impending danger. Therefore, it seemed their purpose was merely to make her aware that harm was coming, to cause her suffering before she died. In order to determine who might want to do this, I began to examine the motives each of you had for wanting to kill her."

"This is preposterous," Freddy Bell said. "I had no reason to kill my sister, and I resent your saying that I did."

For some reason, this protest did not deter me. Instead, it only made me more determined. It was time that we came to the truth.

"That isn't quite true, Mr. Bell," I said. "You were — and still are — in rather dire financial straits. Your sister, who had always been a steady source of income, had refused to give you any more money. You are, however, her heir. Her death has benefited you."

His face turned crimson, some combination of embarrassment and fury. "You haven't any right to say things like that." He shot to his feet. "I won't stay here and listen to this."

"Sit down, Mr. Bell," Inspector Jones commanded softly.

Freddy Bell hesitated ever so slightly, almost wobbled on his feet, and then he dropped back into his seat, his face still a bright shade of red. He looked almost as though he was about to cry, and I felt a sudden pang of pity for him. It would not do to lose focus, however.

"Not only that, it came to my attention that you had been stealing from her."

"I never . . ."

"Flora told her landlady you had taken money from her room, and she was forced to hide valuables in her dressing room. It was possible that she had noticed something else was missing that night and took you to the theatre to confront you about it. You might have argued with her and, when things got heated, killed her."

"I didn't do it," he said weakly. "She was my sister, my only family. I loved her . . ."

"Mr. Bell was not the only one, of course," I said. "As I got to know each of you, I realized you all harbored ill feelings toward Miss Bell in your own ways. There was, first of all, the . . . relationship between Mr. Holloway and Miss Bell."

I looked directly at Mr. Holloway as I said this, but his eyes were on the floor. Georgina's gaze met mine briefly, something unreadable in it, and then she, too, looked away.

"Their relationship was an intense one, and more than one person heard them arguing on several occasions."

I waited for Gerard Holloway to contest this, but he did not. I wondered if he was simply too embarrassed to discuss it in front of his wife.

"There was, in fact, the matter of a rather intense row that Mr. Landon heard after the opening performance."

"Would you like to tell us about that, Mr. Holloway?" Inspector Jones asked.

"That was nothing," Mr. Holloway said calmly. "We were both a bit excitable after the performance. It has no bearing on anything. I didn't kill Flora."

"Mr. Landon said you asked her about Mr. Lebeau."

"I don't remember," he said. "It was insignificant."

I let this pass for a moment, moving on. "It was also possible, of course, that Georgina might have done it."

Her eyes came up to mine again, cool and unconcerned. Mr. Holloway, however, did

431

not take these words with such equanimity.

"You know it wasn't Georgina, Mrs. Ames," he said, his voice tight. "She would never do such a thing."

"There is very little one will not do when pressed to the limits of desperation, Mr. Holloway," I replied softly.

He looked as though he was about to say something, but then he stopped, sinking back further into his chair.

"Of course, there was no love between Flora Bell and me," Georgina said calmly, her cool, smooth voice washing over the stage, as lovely as any actress's. "She ruined my marriage, took my children's father from me —"

"Georgina . . ." Holloway broke in, his voice ragged.

She ignored him, didn't even look at him. "I didn't like her, and I didn't mourn her death, but I also didn't kill her. I am not a woman to make grand gestures for the sake of love. If Gerard wanted her that much, he could have her."

"Georgina, darling . . ." Holloway said, but then he stopped, as though remembering suddenly where they were.

I felt the knot in the pit of my stomach growing. No matter what happened here, the outcome was not going to be what I had hoped. There was too much damage done.

Almost without realizing it, I glanced over my shoulder at Milo. It was as though he had been expecting it, for he was already looking in my direction, waiting for my gaze to meet his.

I turned back to the group. "The Holloways were not the only ones who wished Miss Bell ill. Miss Dearborn, too, had a reason to resent her."

"I?" she asked, her hand moving to her chest in a very poor imitation of surprised indignation. "I didn't want anything to happen to Flora."

"Perhaps not," I said. "But she did stand between you and a starring role in *The Price of Victory.*"

She shrugged. "There are a lot of roles, Mrs. Ames," she said coolly. "This is a good play, yes, but it's not good enough to kill for." She gave a little laugh. "It's preposterous to think such a thing. If I wanted a part, I could get one in easier ways than committing murder."

She was right about that, of course, but there was more.

"But it wasn't only the role," I went on. "You hated Flora Bell because the role was nearly yours and she took it. As well as Mr. Holloway's attentions."

"That's not true!"

"There was another incident in the past that also seemed to point to you," I said. "A case that involved unsavory letters."

"That has nothing to do with this!" She was growing angry now, her face very red. "I was a silly schoolgirl. It means nothing."

"It was interesting all the same," I said.

She glared at me, but didn't respond. For the moment I would press her no further.

"You'll read my fortune next, I suppose," Mr. Landon said, an unpleasant smile playing on his lips. I had never taken him for a nice young man, but there was something even less agreeable about him now. His eyes were very hard, cold, and he was watching the rest of us as though he held us in the greatest contempt. I would not have been at all surprised if he got up and attempted to leave the theatre. I knew, however, that Inspector Jones had men stationed at the exits.

"Yes, Mr. Landon. You, too, had your reasons for resenting Miss Bell."

He shrugged. "It seems we all did. That doesn't prove that any of us killed her."

"No, it doesn't," I agreed. "But there were other clues that pointed to the fact that you might have been the one to kill her."

He smirked, putting a cigarette to his

mouth. The rasping scrape of the match seemed very loud on the quiet stage. "By all means, do enlighten us, Mrs. Ames," he said.

I refused to be intimidated by his evident disdain.

"You and Miss Bell had formed a relationship at one point."

"What of it? I've had a lot of *relationships.*" Despite his arrogance, he was growing uneasy. I could sense it. He had, for that moment we sat on the edge of this stage together, let his guard down, and I knew that he was regretting it now.

"You cared for her, but she cast you aside in favor of Mr. Holloway."

"He has money, and I am but a lowly player. It was not so great a shock." I saw Mr. Holloway shift a bit uneasily from the corner of my eye. Georgina still sat stonefaced.

"That doesn't mean you took it well."

He looked up at me. "I took it just fine. I cared for Flora, yes. But if she was happy with Holloway, I wasn't going to quibble. Things have always ended well with my lovers."

I supposed he meant to shock me with this referral to numerous love affairs, but it was I who shocked him in the end.

"That's not exactly true, is it?" I asked softly.

"What are you getting at?" he demanded. I could tell from the way he was looking at me that he knew precisely what I meant.

"There was, unfortunately, another woman in your past who met a tragic end."

"Don't you drag her into this," he said in a low voice.

I knew it must be unpleasant, perhaps even painful, for him to have the past dredged up, but I had no choice.

"You had a falling-out, and her body was later found in the Thames."

"You shut up," he said, his eyes suddenly blazing.

Undeterred, I went on. "It was ruled a suicide, but there were people who doubted it."

"Don't you say another word, you lying little —"

"Careful, Landon," Milo said from behind me.

Mr. Landon paid Milo no heed. His eyes were still on me, pure hatred emanating from them. "You filthy liar. If you weren't a woman, I'd bash your head in."

This unexpected threat of violence caught me by surprise, and I heard a murmur of dismay from Miss Dearborn as well as protests from the other gentlemen.

"Another remark such as that, and I expect Mr. Ames may return the favor," Inspector Jones said, his normally steady tone surprisingly tight. "And I'd be obliged to turn away while he did it."

Mr. Landon's face looked thunderous. "You can't threaten me," he said.

"No," Inspector Jones replied. "But Mr. Ames can."

"Consider yourself threatened," Milo said in a deceptively pleasant tone.

With the greatest of efforts, Landon seemed to master his emotions. At last he spoke, his voice almost returned to normal. "That woman's death had nothing to do with Flora. Don't bring her into this."

"I'm sorry, Mr. Landon," I said sincerely. "I don't mean to cause you pain. But we must look at things from every angle."

"I loved Helen," he said. "We had a row and I broke things off, but I didn't mean it. I thought we would reconcile. But Helen was distraught . . . I didn't realize . . ."

"The death of Helen Whitney was tragic, but it became even more curious when I saw a photograph of her. You will admit that she bore a striking resemblance to Flora Bell. It was almost as though Miss Bell served as a replica of the woman you lost."

His face grew tight, and I thought for a moment that he might hurl further abuse at me, but then his shoulders slumped. "Flora reminded me of Helen," he said at last. "She looked so much like her that it took my breath away. But then I got to know Flora, and I found myself falling in love with her. I thought we could be happy together. It had nothing to do with Helen, not anymore."

"Mr. Bell said that Flora told him one couldn't live in the past, that it wasn't healthy. She found out about Miss Whitney, didn't she?"

His jaw clenched. "One day she found a photograph of Helen in my flat. I had kept it hidden, but she came across it somehow. And that was the end of it, just like that. She was convinced that I only loved her as a substitute for Helen, and nothing I could say would convince her otherwise. She broke it off and took up with Holloway shortly afterward."

"That was what you meant when you told me you were doomed to love a dead woman," I said softly. "You loved Helen Whitney and then Flora."

He nodded. "Now there are two of them. Two beautiful blond dead women who will haunt me as long as I live."

With this pronouncement, his head

dropped into his hands, and I could no longer bear to go on pestering him.

That left only one more person.

I turned to Balthazar Lebeau.

He had been watching the proceedings with that same expression of aloof amusement, as though all of this were an inferior play he had deigned to watch. Now that I turned my gaze to him, he met it with a slight, almost expectant, raising of his dark brows.

"Mr. Lebeau, I'm afraid you're next," I said.

"Ah, yes. I'm interested to see what you've discovered about me," he said.

Looking at his calm, confident expression, I felt a twinge of nervousness, but I pressed forward.

"From the beginning, I noticed that you and Miss Bell didn't seem to get along."

"I don't think that was a secret."

"But the reason why was rather a secret, wasn't it?" His expression didn't change, but I saw the flicker of something in his eyes.

"I'm sure I don't know what you mean, Mrs. Ames. I didn't care for Flora Bell because she thought she knew everything there was to know about acting. I don't think there's any secret about that."

"No. The secret was that you did not dislike Miss Bell as much as you pretended to."

He smiled. "I don't know what you're getting at."

"I first began to realize it when I learned that you had visited her boardinghouse."

"What?" Mr. Holloway exclaimed.

"I've already explained that to you, my dear," Mr. Lebeau said calmly. "I was helping her rehearse her part."

"Yes, you explained that," I said. "Unfortunately, it doesn't make sense. For one thing, Flora was confident in her abilities and didn't like being instructed on what to do. For another, she had professed to dislike you."

He said nothing.

"So why, then, would you have visited her there? I began to wonder if Flora had really disliked you as much as she claimed. She told her brother that she should not have fallen in love with an actor, that they're too good at pretending. I thought it was likely this referred to Mr. Landon, but as the details fell into place, it began to make sense."

"There was nothing between Flora Bell and me," he said. He still appeared perfectly relaxed, but I could sense an alertness in him now, a sharpness in his gaze.

"I'm afraid that isn't true."

The corner of his mouth tipped up. "Flora Bell wasn't much my type of woman."

"Perhaps not," I said. "But you weren't trying to win her over for the usual reasons."

"What is this all about?" Holloway asked. I looked over at him and saw the flash of annoyance in Georgina's eyes.

"It didn't start with Miss Bell," I said. "It started with you, Mr. Holloway."

"What do you mean?" Mr. Holloway asked.

I turned back to Mr. Lebeau. "Several years ago, you lost a role to Mr. Holloway. It was, unfortunately, the beginning of a decline in your career."

Though he smiled, his eyes narrowed ever so slightly, giving him a wolfish look. "You're mistaken," he said. "My career has not declined."

I would not argue this point with him, but nor was I about to back down.

"You hated Mr. Holloway ever since that moment, resented what you thought was his negative impact on your career. It was an insult to you when he offered you a supporting role in his play, but you agreed to do it because you wanted to find a way to pay him back for what he had done to you. When you met Flora Bell, you had the idea.

441

You told me once that the best way to hurt a man was to win over the woman he loves, and that was what you set out to do. You wooed Flora Bell and won her over."

Gerard Holloway drew in a startled breath.

"She was likely still hurting from her break with Mr. Landon and vulnerable to your charms. Unfortunately, she realized the truth sooner than you hoped. She discovered that you didn't love her as you claimed. That you had seduced her for another reason, as revenge on Mr. Holloway. " 'One can't go on living in the past; it isn't healthy.' " That's what she told Mr. Bell. That statement might also have applied to you. She broke off the affair with you, and that was when you began sending the letters."

"Why would I do something like that?" he asked.

"That was a question I asked myself," I admitted. "Then I realized they were meant to be a taunt that you were planning to reveal the affair to Holloway, to ruin Flora Bell's career. That final note read 'Let your opening performance be your best. It will be your last.' Because you knew once Holloway found out about the two of you, he would dismiss her from the play."

"A pretty theory, Mrs. Ames. But you have no proof of any of this."

"I'm getting to that," I said. "I wondered why it was that someone had hit me on the head that day after we did our scene together. I assumed the culprit believed the letters from Mr. Holloway to Miss Bell were in that drawer, and I wondered why should anyone want them. But then I realized that perhaps you thought there were other letters there. Letters from you to Miss Bell. Letters that would prove you were trying to win her over. Perhaps even a letter asking her to meet you in the theatre alone during the gala."

"I left the gala before she was killed. You saw me."

"I saw you preparing to leave. You told me you had an appointment, a meeting with a producer arranged by a telegraph that mysteriously disappeared. But in reality you met with her in the theatre, here on the stage."

He said nothing, only watched me.

"She agreed to meet with you that night in order to discuss things. Perhaps she thought she could plead with you not to reveal the affair. Perhaps it was never your intention to kill her."

"I didn't kill her," he said.

"I'm afraid you did," I said softly. "I imagine she grew angry with you. Flora was a woman who spoke her mind. She must have told you what she thought of you, an aging actor whose career had sunk so far he could only live on memories of the past. Whatever the reason, you lost your temper. You've lost it in the past, after all. You were already on the stage. The curtain was there, right at hand. You had only to reach out and grab the rope, wrap it around her neck."

I heard Georgina Holloway gasp and then Mr. Holloway was on his feet. "It was you, Lebeau," he said.

He moved toward him, but a policeman stepped forward and stopped him.

"As an actor, you might have thought it was a fitting way for her to be found, hanging there onstage in one final performance. So you left her there. You see, Mr. Lebeau: it all fits."

He looked at me, the pleasant expression on his face suddenly masking something much darker. "You're very charming, Mrs. Ames. But I'm afraid you're mistaken."

"I'm afraid I'm not," I said softly. "I wanted very much to believe it wasn't you, Mr. Lebeau, but it was. Flora told her brother, 'It's just like in the play.' She recognized you for the villain you played onstage."

His jaw had grown tight, his face very hard. Despite myself, I felt a little chill at the look he leveled at me.

"You can't prove it," he said. "You'll never prove I did."

"Oh, but I'm afraid we already have," Inspector Jones said. "You see, we searched your dressing room this afternoon and discovered paper and ink that appear to be a match for the threatening letters sent to Miss Bell."

"That proves nothing," he said, though he was beginning to sound less confident than he had a moment ago. Though it was ridiculous, I almost pitied him.

"But there were also letters there from Miss Bell, apparently from early in your relationship."

"There are no letters!" he said. "Flora never wrote to me."

"I'm afraid that's a lie," Inspector Jones said.

"I didn't kill her," he said, great dignity in his voice despite the proof piled against him.

"You'll have a chance to protest your innocence at your trial, Mr. Lebeau," Inspector Jones replied.

Mr. Lebeau seemed about to argue further, but then a look of resignation crossed his features and he drew himself up. "Then it seems there is nothing left for me to say. I shall save my best lines for the dock."

Two officers came and escorted him off the stage, but not before he turned to me and offered one final bow.

27

It was Inspector Jones who broke into the stunned silence. "I'm sorry for the inconvenience this caused all of you, but I thank you for coming."

"That's it, then?" Christopher Landon asked, looking up, his expression clouded. "We're free to go?"

"You're free to go," Inspector Jones said.

He rose quickly to his feet, as though he couldn't wait to be gone. He glanced my way before he left, and I gave him a sympathetic smile, despite his ill-tempered remarks. "I'm sorry, Mr. Landon."

He nodded, then walked quickly off the stage.

"I shall never forget this for as long as I live," Dahlia Dearborn declared, standing and elaborately wrapping her furs around herself. "I always knew that there was something off about Balthazar Lebeau. For one thing, he never looked my way twice.

To think that he was a murderer. What a tale I have to tell!" With that, she swept off the stage, following Mr. Landon out of the building.

Freddy Bell still sat, as though in a daze. At last he looked up and rose slowly to his feet.

"Thank you for what you've done, Mrs. Ames," he said. "I . . . I don't know how I'll get on without Flora, but I'm glad to know her killer has been brought to justice."

"I'm happy I could help," I said. "Your sister believed in you, Mr. Bell. I have every confidence that you will make her proud."

He nodded solemnly and left then, and I turned to face the Holloways. They still sat near each other, though they had not spoken. At last, Mr. Holloway turned to face her. "Georgina, darling. Can you forgive me?"

"I don't want to discuss it now," she said softly.

"But we can discuss it eventually?" he pleaded.

She looked at him, a sudden softness flickering across her expression. "Yes," she said. "We'll discuss it."

He rose and offered her his hand. After the slightest hesitation, she took it. If this had been a play, it would have been a beautiful ending.

"I can't thank you enough, Mrs. Ames," he said, turning to me. "I don't know what we would have done without you."

"I'm glad everything has worked out," I said. "I . . . I hope things will continue to do so." I glanced between them, and he smiled.

"I think they will," he said.

Then he and Georgina exited the stage.

"Well, I suppose I'll be off too," Inspector Jones said. "I've a great deal of paperwork to tend to. Thank you again for your help, Mrs. Ames. I don't like to say so, but it would have been difficult for us to manage this without your keen perception. I'll be in touch."

He followed the others backstage, and Milo and I were left alone.

"Are you ready, darling?" Milo asked. I looked out at the empty theatre. It was dark, most of the seats hidden in shadow, and I thought how sad and lonely the place seemed.

"In just a moment. I . . . I think I'd like a few moments here to think about everything."

"Very well. I'll just bring the car around."

Milo took his leave, and I was left alone on the stage, a thousand thoughts whirling in my head. A moment later, there was movement behind me.

"Oh, Mrs. Ames. You're still here?" It was Gerard Holloway. He walked out to where I still stood. He seemed much more relaxed now that Mr. Lebeau had been arrested and he had hope of making amends with Georgina, the tension and worry that had clouded his countenance the past week evaporating from his features.

"Oh, yes," I said with a self-conscious laugh. "I'm afraid I was lost in thought."

He smiled. "There's a lot to think about."

"Yes," I agreed. "This has all been such a shock. I never would have thought Mr. Lebeau capable of such a thing."

"Perhaps you're not quite as perceptive as you thought," he said lightly.

I glanced at him. "Perhaps not."

"Of course, you did do an excellent job of picking up on the clues. They led rather neatly to Mr. Lebeau, don't you think?"

"Yes, I suppose so."

"The perfect final scene to a most excellent tragedy."

"What do you mean?" I asked slowly.

He smiled, and suddenly the amiable countenance I had always known seemed to alter before my eyes. "I mean I am in your debt, Mrs. Ames. Balthazar Lebeau got what was coming to him after a very long time, and I have you to thank for it."

"I told you she was clever, Gerard." The voice came from behind him, and Georgina Holloway stepped out onto the stage to join us.

"Yes, I've always known she was clever," Gerard Holloway said pleasantly. "Not too clever, of course. But clever enough."

"What are you talking about?" I asked uneasily. My heart had begun to pick up the pace.

"We knew, of course, that it would be no good to hand him to you on a silver platter; that would be too obvious. And so we dropped the breadcrumbs in a more circuitous route. I congratulate you on following them, undeterred, to Mr. Lebeau."

"You did it," I whispered, my voice filled with horror.

"Brava, Mrs. Ames," Mr. Holloway said. "You come to the truth at last."

"Gerard," Georgina said sharply. "You shouldn't say such things."

"Oh, but I must," he said, his eyes still on me. "Mrs. Ames believed herself so smart. I want her to know what really happened."

"Always the braggart, Gerard," Georgina said. Her voice had taken an amused tone that somehow chilled me more than malice might have done. "But Amory has a finely tuned sense of morality. She's going to tell the police."

He shook his head, that once-familiar smile now sinister. "I don't think you'll spread rumors, will you, Mrs. Ames? After all, I should hate for another blow to the head — a fatal one, this time — to befall you."

"It was you who hit me that day," I said.

He nodded. "Another black mark leveled against Mr. Lebeau, I'm afraid."

"You might have killed me," I said, my head throbbing at the memory of that ringing blow.

"I would have, if I'd have had the time," he said in a tone that made my blood run cold. "That idiot Freddy Bell wandered into the theatre. I heard him coming and was able to hide, and when he went for help, I slipped out."

"Georgina, why are you shielding him from the police?" I asked, turning to my friend. "Your husband is a killer. Doesn't that matter to you?"

She smiled. "Dear, sweet Amory. I'm afraid Gerard is right; you're not quite as smart as I believed."

"No," Mr. Holloway said. "You see, Mrs. Ames, we killed Flora Bell together."

I gasped. "No!"

"Yes, I'm afraid so."

My eyes darted between them. "But . . . but why?"

Mr. Holloway looked over at Georgina. "We learned long ago that there is nothing like danger to heat the blood. It builds passion, a connection like nothing else."

"You . . . you mean you did it for . . . sport?"

"It's much more amusing than killing lions and elephants," he said dryly.

I blinked. I had a surreal feeling, as though I were in a dream. Or perhaps some very bad play.

I licked my lips, but my mouth was dry. "Why Flora Bell?"

He shrugged. "Why not."

I felt ill at the implication. "You selected her randomly."

"Not exactly."

"Gerard, don't do this," Georgina said. "You needn't give her the details."

"There's no harm done," he said. "She's worked very hard on the case, after all. She deserves to know."

"What do you mean 'not exactly'?" I pressed.

"I mean that I actually selected Dahlia Dearborn. A young, pretty girl who would look very nice dead onstage. It was only when I realized that she had an uncle in government that I knew it would be risky to use her. Flora was a much better choice. She was, after all, nearly alone in the world. We decided to kill Flora and then, for added amusement, to implicate Mr. Lebeau in her murder."

"But why?"

"When I was first starting out in the theatre world, I was able to get a role he wanted, a role that would have suited him. But the critics compared me unfavorably to him, wrote that it would have been a better play had he been in it. It ruined my chances at making a name for myself."

I frowned at this illogic. "You've been producing plays for years. You might have given yourself a role in any of them."

"The critics were already biased against me. And it was Lebeau's fault."

This was so astoundingly irrational that I could not make sense of it, but then nothing I was hearing made the least amount of sense, not to a sane person.

"And where did Milo and I come into this?" I asked.

"I wrote the threatening letters to bring the police into the matter," he said. "All the better to prove that I wasn't involved. But

Flora was adamantly opposed. Her brother has been in some trouble with the law, and she was very protective of him. She was always trying to shield him, even when he stole money from her. She threatened to leave the play if I called them, and we didn't want that. Not after all our planning. And then I happened across you and Mr. Ames outside the theatre that night, and it gave me an idea."

"We became your unknowing adversaries," I whispered.

He smiled. "I realized it would be even more amusing than the police. After all, you and your husband have something of a reputation. It was nice to have a foil of our own class."

"And so the night of the gala, you put your plan into operation," I said.

"It was all arranged ahead of time," he said. "I had quarreled with Flora earlier in the evening. I knew people are always listening and mentioned Lebeau loudly, for she had done her scene differently than we had rehearsed. Later, I told her I wanted to speak to her alone, to make up, she thought. We arranged to meet in the theatre. Then it was time for the real performance to begin. Georgina took care to wave at you across the ballroom. She knew you would come looking for us, and we let you overhear our argument. I thought that was rather a nice touch. Naturally, it was important everyone believe we were still at odds."

My head was pounding and was beginning to feel dizzy, as though what they were telling me was too much for me to take in.

"When we knew you had gone, we slipped across the alleyway through the stage entrance. Georgina went up to one of the boxes to watch, and I met Flora onstage. Then I killed her."

He said this so calmly that I felt a wave of nausea pass over me.

"It was a shame, really, with that sort of talent. But I'm afraid Georgina wouldn't let me change our plans."

I glanced at Georgina and found that her eyes were hard. "He romanced Dahlia and then Flora. Two women were quite enough. I didn't want another one involved."

He shrugged. "And so Flora it was. When it was finished, I came back through the alleyway entrance to the gala and came out to send you in search of Georgina. She was, of course, waiting in the theatre to watch you discover the body."

The ill feeling in my stomach increased. I had felt eyes on me. It had been Georgina, watching from the box.

"You took it rather well, all things considered," Georgina said. "Not even a scream. I was a bit disappointed."

"When you hurried out, Georgina slipped out of the theatre and back to the gala through the alleyway before the police arrived. From there on, it was just a matter of leading you in the right direction. There was a fine balance between giving you too much direction and not enough. I must say, you took your cues very nicely."

I thought of how Mr. Holloway had arranged for me and Milo to be a part of everything, of their visits to our flat, of the subtle ways in which both of them had given me information that would lead me to suspect Balthazar Lebeau.

"You sent that telegram to him, the one from a mysterious producer. You wanted him to leave the gala so he would be without an alibi."

"Yes. And like the fool he is, he fell for it."

One thing didn't make sense. "Why did you send me to Flora's boardinghouse?" I asked.

"That was a gamble, but it paid off. I had discovered recently that Mr. Lebeau had been paying visits to her boardinghouse. I knew if you went, you wouldn't be able to resist asking questions and that gossip of a landlady would be only too happy to tell you."

"Why was he going to see her?" I asked.

"That I don't know. Even sweet little Flora kept her secrets. She never breathed a word to me, though it suited my purposes well enough. I assume he was trying to woo her. Flora was, after all, easily wooed."

"And, of course, you weren't really drunk that night you came to our flat," I said.

"No, though I wasted a good bottle of whiskey spilling it over my clothes. The critics were wrong, you see. I'm an excellent actor."

"If we're taking credit for our achievements, I applied makeup to give him an ill appearance," Georgina put in. "He looked very grim indeed by the time I was done with him."

I remembered his ashen face and couldn't help but agree she had done a good job of it.

"But why come to our flat at all?" I asked.

"I wanted to make you worry, if only slightly, that Georgina might be guilty. I knew it would make you try even harder to prove that someone else had done it."

"Why are you telling me this?" I asked, though he had already given me the answer. He wanted his accolades. He had given a masterful performance and felt he had earned the applause. His next words confirmed it.

"Because it was so very much work," he said. "One doesn't paint a great work of art without signing one's signature."

"You haven't thought of everything," I said. "You may threaten me all you like, but you can't expect me to stand idly by while an innocent man hangs."

"That's precisely what you're going to do," he said calmly. "You have no proof, and no one will believe you."

"They might, if I lay out the evidence."

"Perhaps." He stepped closer. "But if you say anything, your husband might just encounter a thief with a knife one night on the way home from one of his gambling clubs. They're dangerous places, after all. One never knows what might happen."

I felt sick, and my hands were shaking. "You can't be serious."

"I'm afraid I am," he said. "We've killed and gotten away with it. Aside from you, no one will ever be the wiser. You may as well accept it. Do you remember what I told you the night you asked me about Victoire's final choice?"

I did, but I would not give him the satisfaction of repeating it.

He smiled. "Sometimes the villain wins, Mrs. Ames."

"And sometimes he doesn't," a voice called.

The houselights turned on suddenly, throwing the entire theatre into a blaze of light. Gerard Holloway froze and an expression of incredulity passed across Georgina's normally composed features.

Then I heard the sound of someone clapping from the back of the theatre.

28

"Brava, Mrs. Ames," Inspector Jones called in a pleasant tone. "That was an excellent performance, and it served its aim."

It was only then, I think, that Mr. Holloway realized what had happened.

"Why you . . ." He stepped toward me again, but this time a burly policeman had made his entrance while a second came and took hold of Georgina. The expressions of absolute astonishment on their faces might have been comical if it wasn't all so horrible.

Then Milo took the stage, his expression as dark as I had ever seen it. He had been standing hidden in the wings for the duration of our little encore performance, and I imagined it had been very difficult for him not to charge onto the stage earlier than this.

I wanted nothing more than to leave this stage and never set foot here again, but I felt that first I must show Flora Bell's killers that they were not as smart as they had believed. And so I turned to face the Holloways.

"I had wondered what would have happened if one of you was the killer," I said. "But it took me a long time to realize that you had done it together."

They remained silent, both of them watching me in an expressionless way that chilled me more than outright fury would have done.

"When the thought first occurred to me, I was sure it was madness," I continued. I was glad that my voice sounded calm, though my heart had begun to beat a bit more rapidly. "I could think of no reason why the two of you should have done something like this. After all, you were at odds. Flora Bell meant something different to each of you. Not only that, the amount of time in which either of you could have done it after the argument I overheard was very limited, and it could not have been you that I heard in the theatre, Mr. Holloway, as I had just left you at the gala."

Georgina watched me, the barest hint of a smile on her face. She looked as though she were watching a performance she enjoyed, not as though she was being confronted with the evidence of a murder she had committed.

"It would probably never have occurred to me," I said. "After all, one doesn't normally escalate from safaris and mountain climbing to murder. But when going over the evidence I remembered something Inspector Jones said. It was strangely theatrical to kill Flora Bell in such a way. It might have been a crime of passion as we originally assumed, but why send her threatening notes? Why kill her with the curtain rope when there were other weapons available? Why leave her positioned in that ghastly final bow? It seemed it must have been done to set a scene."

"It was another thing that pointed to Mr. Lebeau initially," Inspector Jones said. "After all, he is known for his flair for the dramatic."

"But then my mother said something last night," I went on. "Something about people enjoying the theatre because it allows them the opportunity to pretend, to build a reputation for themselves, and, for some reason, it began to turn the wheels in my brain. Then she said something about stage props looking excessively unrealistic. And I thought suddenly of the gun."

Mr. Holloway said nothing, but I saw the

flash of anger in his eyes.

"I believed someone had hit me in the head to prevent my finding your letters, which they believed to be in that drawer. It didn't cross my mind that it might have been you, for Inspector Jones told me you were the only one who knew the police had already removed the drawer's contents. But then I thought that, perhaps, it wasn't that drawer that you wanted to keep me from opening. You see, I remembered that you had put the gun in a drawer the day we came to see about Miss Bell's letters. I thought it looked strange in your hand, and then I realized why. It was a prop gun, wasn't it? Meant to impress Flora Bell and us with your sincerity, your concern for her well-being. But you forgot about it. The police had already seen it, but, as a prop, it was not unusual to them. However, you knew if I came across that gun there, if I realized that it wasn't genuine, that I might also guess your concern had been artificial."

"That doesn't prove anything," Holloway said. "There was no gun in the drawer."

"No," I agreed. "You removed it after you hit me. But when Inspector Jones found the love letters from Flora Bell in Balthazar Lebeau's dressing room today, it was further proof."

"Proof against us? I don't see how," Holloway retorted.

"After speaking with Mr. Lebeau, we knew they had been planted there. You see, you misjudged in your attempts to make everyone believe that Balthazar Lebeau had been trying to seduce Flora Bell. For one thing, she was in love with Mr. Landon."

"Flora was in love with everyone," Mr. Holloway said in a tone that made me want to hit him.

"She truly loved Mr. Landon," I replied. "And I think she would have returned to him eventually. She was beginning to realize that you were not what you seemed. 'Actors are too good at pretending,' she told her brother. When she said that things were just like in the play, I think she recognized that she would have to choose between darkness and light. And she was beginning to understand that you were the darkness, Mr. Holloway."

"Nonsense," he said scathingly.

"But that wasn't the only reason she wouldn't have been wooed by Mr. Lebeau. You see, he's her uncle."

Mr. Holloway had not wanted to show surprise, but this was too big of a revelation for him to conceal it.

"I didn't put all the pieces together until

this morning when we spoke to him about the role he was to play in our little performance. That's when Mr. Lebeau told us why he had agreed to take a bit part in your play to begin with. He had only just realized that Freddy and Flora Bell were his sister's children. Their mother split with the family long ago after a falling-out. She even changed her name. From Lebeau to Bell. The French for 'handsome' to an anglicized version of the French for 'beautiful.' She never wanted Flora to pursue this life, but, as Mr. Lebeau once said, acting is in the blood.

"Flora's landlady overheard one of their conversations, and she remembered Mr. Lebeau uttering the phrase 'love doesn't end with time, and not all bonds can be easily broken.' Mr. Lebeau had cared for his sister, had spent years searching for her, and he wanted to do right by his niece and nephew. However, Flora was used to being independent and refused to acknowledge the connection. She hadn't even told her brother about it. She was determined to win fame on her own merits and did not want Mr. Lebeau's interference either in her life or onstage. I saw for myself how his critique of her performance annoyed her. Mr. Lebeau respected her wishes and told no one, for he appreciated that she wanted to make a name for herself. And she would have. If the two of you hadn't killed her."

The frown on Georgina's perfect brows gave way suddenly and she smiled. It was that perfect hostess smile that I had seen so many times. "It all fits together very nicely," she said. "But I'm afraid you're mistaken. Gerard was playing a joke on you, Amory. Not a nice one, but there you have it. You'll never be able to prove anything."

"No, we wouldn't," I agreed. "Which is why we set up this elaborate performance. I knew that, even cleared of the crime, you would not be able to resist the urge to boast about it. You have presented a perfect front all these years, but, as someone once told me, even the best masks slip eventually."

"There is a bit of further proof," Inspector Jones said. "Not that we require it after a confession. The knot in the curtain rope tied around Miss Bell's neck was unusual, and no one could place it. That is, not until we asked the right people. It was a butterfly loop. Used in mountaineering."

"You have always liked to oversee every detail, Mr. Holloway," I said. "But I'm afraid this time you overlooked a few things."

His face turned so red with fury then that

it was almost purple. "We should have killed you when we had the chance," Mr. Holloway said through gritted teeth.

There was a flash of movement so fast I barely had time to register it. And then Holloway was slumping in the policeman's grasp, Milo having delivered a crushing blow to his jaw. I had never seen Milo so openly lose his temper, and I think I was as startled as Mr. Holloway.

"Gerard!" Georgina moved toward her husband, but the policeman caught her arm.

"He's all right, madam. Come along."

Georgina's gaze came up to mine, her eyes hard and bright. "You can't understand what Gerard and I have because you don't know what real love is."

"That's the sort of love I can do without, Georgina," I said.

"Take them away," Inspector Jones said. And with that they were led offstage.

I turned to Milo and he stepped toward me, catching my hand in his. "Are you all right, darling?"

"I still can't believe it," I said. "Even as I took the stage to speak with them, I hoped that I would be proven wrong. It's just so horrible. To think that they were our friends . . ."

"The world is full of wicked people; we're

bound to know some of them," Milo said, with a typical lack of astonishment in the face of evil. When the whole thing had become clear, he had displayed only a modicum of surprise. It made me wonder if perhaps he had suspected something all along.

"You knew there was something amiss with Holloway, didn't you?" I asked.

"I knew that he was not all he seemed," he admitted. "There have been indications for several years that he might not be quite the gentleman everyone believes he is. He has always seemed to me to be an actor playing a part. I had just not imagined the extent of the true self he was hiding."

"But you didn't suspect something like this?"

"Not at first. After all, a murder for the thrill of it is not something one likes to suspect people of offhand."

He was right. I couldn't imagine the scandal that would come of this. I wondered if people would even believe that such a thing was possible. The Holloways had always been the epitome of a perfect society couple. This revelation was going to prove a scandal of enormous proportions.

What I was thinking about, however, was their children. How dreadful it would be to grow up under such a stigma. I prayed they were young enough to recover from this blow, but I did not imagine they would ever completely surmount it. Presented in this light, my mother's obsession with avoiding familial disgrace seemed a blessing rather than a perpetual nuisance. Perhaps, in her own way, she had been doing her best to protect me.

"However, yesterday I talked to some people who knew the Holloways — the news I was going to relate to you last night — and began to suspect this may not be the first time they have done such a thing," Milo said. "They hinted that one of their safari guides died rather mysteriously. And the avalanche that killed a large portion of their mountain expedition was started by a gunshot. No one was ever able to identify who had shot it off, but Mr. and Mrs. Holloway were both absent from the camp at the time."

I shuddered. "So they've been killing people for years."

Inspector Jones gave a curt nod. "I had heard rumblings along the same lines. There's no proof, of course. But it does seem as though they have been seeking thrills of this nature for quite some time."

My stomach churned at the thought of

the innocent lives that had been lost to their bloodlust. Poor Flora Bell. Her future had held so much promise.

"I must thank you again for your help, Mr. and Mrs. Ames," Inspector Jones said. "Without you, it would have been terribly difficult to prove."

"As it is, I imagine the earl will have a few things to say in his son's defense," Milo said.

"Perhaps," Inspector Jones replied. "Or perhaps the earl already knows what his son is capable of."

"Their confession should certainly help," Milo said. "Though, when Amory told me her idea, I wasn't sure you'd go along with it. I didn't take you for much of a theatre aficionado."

"We all have our little secrets, Mr. Ames," Inspector Jones said. And with that he gave a little bow and exited stage left.

"Shall we go, darling?" Milo asked.

"Yes. Please," I said. I couldn't wait to be out of the theatre. There was something so very surreal about standing on this stage having witnessed what we just had.

We made our way out of the theatre and I took a relieved breath of the fresh morning air. The sunshine felt good on my face after the artificial glow of the stage lights.

"I hope this sets your mind at ease, darling," Milo said.

"At ease?" I asked incredulously. "Hardly."

"About marriage, I mean."

I turned to look at him. "What on earth are you talking about?"

"You've been fretting about marriage as an institution, worrying that if a couple like Gerard and Georgina Holloway couldn't make a marriage work, what hope had the rest of us mere mortals?"

He was right, of course. I had always thought their marriage the highest standard. What a horrible disillusionment this had been.

"Their love always seemed so perfect," I said.

"I daresay no marriage is built on perfect love," Milo replied. "But an imperfect love with the perfect person is the sort of thing that makes life worthwhile."

I looked up at him. "Yes," I said softly. "I think you're right."

He leaned to brush a kiss across my lips, and then his arm slipped around me as we walked toward our car.

29

I met Balthazar Lebeau the next day for tea. It had been, he said, the only payment he asked in exchange for delivering the performance of his career. Inspector Jones had not allowed him to stay for the denouement, and so he was very anxious for the details.

As I sat at the table waiting for him, I marveled at how everything had turned out. It was all so horrible that I sometimes found myself wondering if it was real. The newspapers had been full of the story, and, of course, Milo and I had featured prominently, word of our involvement having somehow made its way to the press.

My mother had telephoned to inform me that, though she approved of none of it, she was glad the Holloways had been apprehended. Her final words had given me hope that she might reconcile herself to my "vulgar hobbies," as she had once called them. "I know we have likely not seen the last of this, and I am becoming resigned to it. But do be careful. And if you find yourself stuck again, dear, remember that mothers are good for advice."

My attention was called back to the present as Balthazar Lebeau made his appearance. He stopped in the doorway of the tearoom, his broad shoulders filling up most of the frame. I had the impression that he was a man who always liked to make an entrance wherever he went. Indeed, I noticed that there were several admiring glances in his direction, and the ladies at more than one table leaned to whisper to one another about the actor's arrival.

I thought he looked a bit younger today, somehow, a bit more carefree.

He caught sight of me at my table and made his way to me, bowing over my hand as I extended it to him. "You're looking lovely this afternoon, Mrs. Ames. Of course, you always look lovely."

"Thank you."

"I am delighted to have the opportunity to see more of you," he said, settling into the seat across from me. "I am not much of a tea drinker, mind you. I prefer my libations a bit stronger. But for the pleasure of your company, I shall drink the juice from as many leaves as you see fit to command me."

I laughed. "I shall not command you to drink anything," I said. "But I hear the cakes here are rather excellent."

"Then cake it shall be."

"I just wanted to thank you for taking part in our little performance yesterday," I said, serving him a slice of Madeira cake. "If you had not been willing to act the part, I don't think they would have felt the need to confess."

"It was my pleasure."

I related to him the details of what occurred when he left, and he shook his head. "I have always disliked Holloway. It is gratifying to see that my feelings were justified."

There were a great many people I had not particularly cared for that I would not care to learn were murderers, but I would not argue the point.

"Of course, the most important thing is justice for my poor niece."

"I'm so sorry for your loss, Mr. Lebeau."

"I cared a great deal for my sister," he said, allowing his real feelings to show on his face for just a moment. "When I found Flora and Freddy, it was as though I had been given a chance to make things right.

Flora was a headstrong girl, wanted nothing to do with me or my help at first, but I admired her for it. The Lebeaus have always been headstrong. Headstrong and talented."

"She was a wonderful actress," I said. "She would have done your family proud."

He nodded. "I only wish we might have set things right before she died."

"Freddy Bell told me that she had recently told him that family is the most important thing. Perhaps she was coming around."

"I hope so." He paused, seeming to remember something. "That night during the performance, there was a moment where Durant attempts to embrace her and she pushes away. But Flora didn't do it the way we had rehearsed. Instead of shoving me back, she held on to me for just a moment. Perhaps it was her way of saying that she did not resent me as much as she once did."

That must have been the moment Mr. Holloway had argued with her about, the part of the scene that she had done differently from how she had at the rehearsals. Had that impulsive deviation from the script been Flora's way of breaking through the barrier that existed between herself and her uncle? I liked to think so. Flora Bell had been strong-willed, but I believed that eventually she would have accepted Baltha-

476

zar Lebeau as a member of her family and perhaps even a theatrical mentor. It was tragic they would never have the chance to really get to know each other, but that did not mean all was lost.

"There's still a chance for you to do right by your sister, you know," I said. "Freddy Bell needs someone to look after him."

Mr. Lebeau smiled. "Yes, that same thought occurred to me. I always meant to reveal myself to him when the time was right."

"The time may be right now," I suggested. "He's grieving and in need of guidance."

"I have never been what one might call a role model, Mrs. Ames. But I intend to set the young man to rights if at all possible. He won't go by the wayside."

"I'm glad to hear it," I said, immeasurably relieved that Freddy Bell would no longer be alone in the world.

Mr. Lebeau lifted his cup of tea. "To Flora."

"To Flora," I said.

He took a sip. "Do you know, this is not half bad."

I laughed.

"I'm glad you asked me to tea." His eyes met mine and he reached out on the table to clasp my hand, dismissing the sentimental feelings of a moment ago. "Just the two of us."

"I'm afraid I forgot to mention that there will be one more person joining us," I said, gently pulling my hand from his grasp.

An expression of resignation crossed his features. "Your husband?"

I suppressed a laugh. "No, a lady. One you know."

I did not think it was my imagination that a sudden wariness crossed his features.

"And what lady might that be?"

I nodded in the direction of the doorway. "See for yourself."

He turned as Yvonne Roland entered the room, resplendent in a gown of crimson velvet with flowing sleeves and a train. She caught sight of us, and I couldn't help but feel the scene I was about to witness would be greater than anything I would see on the stage.

Balthazar Lebeau rose from his seat as she swept toward him, the long train of her gown flowing behind her.

"Balty," she said, moving, her jewel-bedecked hands outstretched.

I was watching his face carefully, wondering what his reaction would be to seeing her after all this time. To my relief, he appeared delighted.

"Yvonne," he said, moving forward to clutch her hands in his. He leaned forward, brushing kisses across both of her cheeks. "My darling, you haven't aged a day."

She gave a delighted laugh, still clutching his hands. "What a rogue you are, Balty. I have certainly aged a good deal since we've seen each other last."

"To me, you will always be as fresh and lovely as a rose."

"What a wretched man you are, going all these years without so much as a word. You know perfectly well I should have liked to be your friend, if nothing else."

The corner of his mouth tipped up. "I have always hoped to catch you between husbands, but you don't give a man much time to act."

She laughed. "Naughty man. You must tell me what you have been doing all these years. I'm sure I shall be scandalized."

He pulled out a chair for her, and she sat.

I realized that perhaps I should not linger, as this was a private exchange, but I found it difficult to pull myself away. I had to admit, they made a handsome pair. Mrs. Roland, despite her ostentatious — and occasionally garish — ensembles, was a rather pretty woman. Somehow her colorful flashiness was balanced by Mr. Lebeau's rugged dark good looks. Against all odds, it almost seemed as though their mutual flamboyance cancelled each other's out.

The romantic in me felt as though it would be lovely if their love could be rekindled. If not, at least they could enjoy the memories of old times.

From the way they were talking, it seemed they would not need my help in carrying on a conversation.

"Well, if you will excuse me, I have another appointment," I said.

Balthazar Lebeau took my hand. "Thank you for this lovely surprise, Mrs. Ames. I shall consider myself in your debt."

"Yes, Amory dear. It was ever so kind of you to arrange it," Mrs. Roland said. Her color was high, and she looked younger than I had ever seen her look. "You'll come to tea at my home again soon, I hope."

"I should like that very much, Mrs. Roland." I suspected that this time the gossip she would have to share would be her own.

They turned back to each other then, and I slipped quietly away.

Milo was waiting for me outside.

"Well?" he asked.

"They barely noticed I left," I said with a laugh.

"I can't imagine the sort of conversation

those two might have," Milo said, opening the car door for me. I got in, and Milo went around to the other side.

"There's something special about Mr. Lebeau," I said thoughtfully as he slid in beside me and Markham pulled away from the curb. "I do hope his career makes a resurgence. I think he has a lot more to offer."

"Amory, I believe you're half in love with that man," Milo said.

I looked up, flushing. "I don't know what you mean."

"Then why are you blushing?"

"I'm not."

"You most certainly are. I may as well tell you now, darling, that I don't intend to lose you to an old roué like Balthazar Lebeau."

"Well, after all, half the women in London have been in love with him at one time or another," I teased.

"What qualities, might I ask, does he have that I haven't?"

I considered. "You both have dark good looks and very blue eyes. You both know the right things to say at the right time. You both know just the right way to hold a woman in your arms . . ."

"I see I shall have to keep you away from him in the future. Or perhaps the more dramatic solution would be best. We'll go about things the way Armand and Durant might have: pistols at dawn."

"Nonsense," I said, recovering my equilibrium. "You'd never get up so early in the morning."

"To fight for you, I would," he replied.

I looked up at him, touched by the sentiment despite the fact that he was jesting.

"Pistols won't be necessary," I said with a smile. "I haven't time for Mr. Lebeau. I already have my hands quite full managing you."

"I don't deserve you, darling."

"No," I agreed. "You don't."

He laughed. "Well, what now? Shall we go out this evening?"

Something in his tone gave me pause. "What do you have in mind?" I asked warily.

Mischief glinted in his eyes, confirming my suspicions. "I've heard there's an excellent new mystery play premiering tonight."

ACKNOWLEDGMENTS

Mere words seem inadequate to express my sincere appreciation to everyone who played a part in this book's creation. Many thanks to my wonderful editor, Catherine Richards, whose insight, skill, and keen eye for detail helped shape this story into a better version of itself; to Nettie Finn and all the great people at Minotaur for their efforts on my behalf; to my agent, Ann Collette, who is always available to answer questions or just to have a friendly chat; and, as always, to my family and friends for their continued support, feedback, and words of encouragement.

ABOUT THE AUTHOR

Ashley Weaver is the technical services coordinator at the Allen Parish Libraries in Oberlin, Louisiana. Weaver has worked in libraries since she was fourteen; she was a page and then a clerk before obtaining her MLIS from Louisiana State University. She is the author of four previous Amory Ames mysteries: *Murder at the Brightwell, Death Wears a Mask, A Most Novel Revenge,* and *The Essence of Malice.*